Praise for [...]

"Faith is like a breath of fresh air, particularly in her fearless nature, earnestness in pursuing her dreams and her ability to see beyond physical scars (just as God sees us). There is also strong characterization."
—*RT Book Reviews* on *The Cowboy's Twins*

"Deb Kastner creates two very likeable characters with her seemingly effortless writing style."
—*RT Book Reviews* on *Black Hills Bride*

"*Daddy's Home* by Deb Kastner sparkles with passion, emotion and stunning secrets."
—*RT Book Reviews* on *Daddy's Home*

Praise for Lois Richer and her novels

"The warm characters struggle with common issues, such as trusting God to see us through the dark situations. Cade's father is a prime example of the adage, 'hurting people hurt people.'"
—*RT Book Reviews* on *A Dad for Her Twins*

"Richer delivers a touching, evocative, wonderful story of selfless love."
—*RT Book Reviews* on *A Cowboy's Honor*

"[An] emotionally heartwarming story."
—*RT Book Reviews* on *Twice Upon a Time*

A *Publishers Weekly* bestselling and award-winning author with over 1.5 million books in print, **Deb Kastner** writes stories of faith, family and community in a small-town Western setting. She lives in Colorado with her husband and a pack of miscreant mutts, and is blessed with three daughters and two grandchildren. She enjoys spoiling her grandkids, movies, music (The Texas Tenors!), singing in the church choir and exploring Colorado on horseback.

Lois Richer loves traveling, swimming and quilting, but mostly she loves writing stories that show God's boundless love for His precious children. As she says, "His love never changes or gives up. It's always waiting for me. My stories feature imperfect characters learning that love doesn't mean attaining perfection. Love is about keeping on keeping on." You can contact Lois via email, loisricher@gmail.com, or visit her on Facebook at "Lois Richer Author."

The Cowboy's Twin Blessings

Deb Kastner

&

Lois Richer

Previously published as
The Cowboy's Twins and *A Dad for Her Twins*

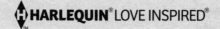

H HARLEQUIN® LOVE INSPIRED®

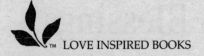 LOVE INSPIRED BOOKS

Recycling programs for this product may not exist in your area.

ISBN-13: 978-1-335-46853-6

The Cowboy's Twin Blessings

Copyright © 2019 by Harlequin Books S.A.

First published as The Cowboy's Twins by Harlequin Books in 2016 and A Dad for Her Twins by Harlequin Books in 2015.

The publisher acknowledges the copyright holders of the individual works as follows:

The Cowboy's Twins
Copyright © 2016 by Debra Kastner

A Dad for Her Twins
Copyright © 2015 by Lois M. Richer

www.Harlequin.com

Printed in U.S.A.

CONTENTS

THE COWBOY'S TWINS

Deb Kastner

To my husband, Joe, who demonstrates every day
what it means to be a loving, God-fearing man.
You are an excellent male role model and
I join with your children and grandchildren in
proclaiming you the best Daddy and Grampy ever.
I couldn't write these stories about men of faith
without you to inspire me.

And to my sister at Happy Haven Farm and
Sanctuary, for the work you do rescuing horses
(and dogs, and cats, and goats, and everything else
with fur). Thank you for all your help with
my research into the plight of wild horses.
Any mistakes are entirely my own.

Now may our Lord Jesus Christ Himself,
and our God and Father, who has loved us and given
us everlasting consolation and good hope by grace,
comfort your hearts and establish you
in every good word and work.
—*2 Thessalonians* 2:16–17

Chapter One

There was only one conceivable reason why Jax McKenna would ever consider putting himself at Serendipity, Texas's Bachelors and Baskets auction like a mule among thoroughbreds—and it *wasn't* because his loudmouthed brothers, Slade and Nick, were forcing him into it.

Nor was it the sweet talking of Jo Spencer, the spry, seventy-something redhead who owned the town's only public eatery, Cup O' Jo's Café. She was the one who'd organized the event in the first place and she was pretty much capable of talking anyone into anything—but it hadn't been necessary this time. Not with Jax.

They all might think they were strong-arming him, but if he hadn't ultimately made the final decision to do this, he wouldn't be here, and no amount of coercing or cajoling on their part would have seen him do otherwise.

He'd made the choice to be here because the fundraiser was important to him. He'd do his bit to help it succeed, even if it meant humiliating himself in front of the town. But that didn't mean he had to be happy about it.

He scoffed quietly and glared at Slade, whose lips twitched to keep back a grin. Jax's scowl deepened.

"Settle down, people. Settle down." Jo spoke directly

into the microphone, cringed at the earsplitting feedback and flipped it off. It wasn't as if she needed the thing. Her voice easily carried across the distance of Serendipity, Texas's community green, where practically everyone in town had gathered for this *event*. "Time to get this party started."

Jax crossed his arms over his chest and grunted. Since when was pure torture considered a festive occasion?

Today, apparently.

When the ruckus didn't immediately subside, old Frank Spencer—Jo's crotchety husband—put his fingers to his lips and whistled shrilly. "Listen up, folks. The First Annual Bachelors and Baskets Auction is about to begin. Gather 'round, y'all."

Jax crushed the toe of his tan cowboy boot into the soft grass, wishing he was anywhere else. Where did Jo come up with this silly idea, anyway? It wasn't like any auction he had ever heard of, although he didn't know why he was so surprised by the fact. Serendipity wasn't exactly known for being *normal* with anything, especially with Jo Spencer at the helm.

What had started out as Jo's simple if archaic idea to pawn off the single men for money had grown into something much larger and more complex. She might have originally set out to nab the town bachelors, but her idea had spun so far out of control that now nearly every man in town was lined up to strut his stuff, single and married alike. Now, the idea was that the women could bid on men for *tasks* instead of dates—with the tasks to be determined by the winning bidder.

Want someone to do the cooking for your barbecue party next weekend? Bid on the man with the secret-family-recipe barbecue sauce that he refused to share with a soul. Want someone to fix up that rusting old truck in your barn? Bid on the town mechanic, and he'll get it running like new. Or go ahead and bid on your husband or sweet-heart…and then put him to work. Jax had overheard one woman saying that when she won her husband, she was going to make him clean out the garage, the way he'd been promising to do for the past five years.

The new twist meant that anyone could participate, even if he was already married or dating. Apparently, Jo figured the more men, the more money would be raised, and Jax supposed there was some truth to that. He just wished he wasn't wrapped up in it. With this many men, did they really need him?

He scoffed under his breath. Tell folks they were meeting for a good cause and they showed up in spades. Actually, just tell people there was a party. *Any* reason to celebrate was reason enough for Serendipity, and the fact that the auction was to benefit the building fund for the new town council–approved senior center and hospice was icing on the cake. It *was* a good cause—one close to his heart, which was the only reason Jax had come out this morning.

Not to be outdone, the ladies in town had started offering to bring picnic baskets to share with the men they won in the auction. Then the event had morphed into bachelors and baskets—which was catchy, even if it was far from accurate, since a good half of the men being auctioned off were married or in serious relationships. If nothing else, Jax was looking forward to the food. He never turned down a good meal. Delicious, down-home country cooking. Too bad he had to put himself through such a ridiculous spectacle just to be able to fill his belly.

Slade nudged Jax with his elbow. "Who do you think is gonna bid on you?"

"How should I know?" Jax snapped derisively. He didn't expect much. He didn't expect anything at all. Most likely he was going to stand up on the stage and make a fool of himself for nothing. No woman in her right mind would bid on his ugly mug, no matter how worthy the cause.

"I can't wait to eat Laney's picnic lunch. She packed fried chicken." Slade licked his lips in an overstated motion that made Jax want to snort in exasperation. For a moment he wished he were Slade, who knew exactly whom he'd be spending the day with—his wife. Slade and Laney were expecting a child in the fall, a baby sister for two-year-old Brody, but they still acted like a couple of goofy newlyweds.

"You sure she's gonna bid on you, baby brother?" Nick goaded, bumping Slade's shoulder with his. "Maybe she'll take your money and bid on a handsome man—like me, for example." He chuckled.

Nick was a big bear of a man with a grouchy personality to match, but he knew how to turn on the charm when he wanted to and he was no slouch with the ladies. Laney might favor her own husband over Nick, but there was no doubt Nick would get his fair share of interest at the auction. He'd get bid on, or bought or whatever crazy word they were using for it.

Slade winked and flashed his wedding ring at his brothers. "I have it on good authority that it's a done deal."

Jax wanted to slug the self-satisfied look right off Slade's face. Just because he was happy with his married life didn't mean the rest of the world had to suffer his gloating. Especially when Slade knew that the topic of marriage was still a tender wound for Jax right now.

Jo pounded a gavel—probably the same one her town-council president husband, Frank, used—on the podium in front of her.

"First up, I'd like to offer Slade McKenna to our viewing public."

Slade flashed his brothers a confident grin and stepped onto the platform. He tipped his hat to the roaring crowd and then flexed his biceps for good measure.

Seriously? If anyone—*anyone*—thought Jax was going to get up on that stage and make a raging fool out of himself like his brother was doing…yeah, that was so not happening.

The crowd roared with delight, hooting and hollering. Actually encouraging Slade, as if he needed a bigger ego than he already had.

"Look at the strength in those shoulders," Jo said, punctuating her statement with a hoot of her own. "Former bull rider and current member of our esteemed police force, Slade will pitch in and use that brawn and brute strength for any project of your choosing. Laney, dear, would you like to open up the bidding?" Jo suggested with a chuckle. "Surely you must want this handsome hunk all to yourself."

Jax thought it was silly for Laney to bid on her own husband. Slade was pretty much at her beck and call anyway, and all she had to do was smile at him—it didn't cost her a dime.

"Oh, I have the perfect project for him." Laney jumped in without a moment's hesitation. "Dishes and laundry for a month."

Slade groaned. "Really?"

Jax chuckled. Served his brother right for being so cocky.

"Three hundred dollars," Laney offered, already halfway up to the podium. There was no question that she was the clear winner of *this* particular item.

Alexis Haddon, a local rancher and part of the fundraising committee, stood at the foot of the stairs, waiting to pass a lariat to Laney.

"Make it a good one, darlin'," Slade coaxed his wife with a sideways grin.

She whooped and swung the lariat toward Slade. Jax scoffed under his breath. Laney wouldn't be able to rope the broad side of a barn with technique like that—or rather, total lack of technique.

She gave her best effort but the lariat soared a good couple of feet past Slade's head. She yanked on the end of the rope in a vain attempt to correct her overthrow but to no avail. She would have come up empty-handed were it not for Slade's quick thinking. He dived for the loop and slipped it over his head, then rolled toward her until he was completely wound up in the line.

"Guess you caught me," Slade said, laughing with the crowd.

Jax shook his head. He had to give his little brother props for putting on a good show. Even when he was little he had loved to be in the limelight, the center of attention. Probably because he was the baby of the family.

Over the din, Frank stepped up to the podium and grabbed the gavel from Jo's hand, pounding it against the podium. "Now, see here. Jo never even got to say he was sold yet, and y'all are already draggin' him off the stage? Let's have some order to these here proceedings."

Jo snorted and grabbed the gavel back from him. "Go sit down, old man," she demanded, giving his grizzled cheek an affectionate buss. "Everyone knew from the get-go that Slade's wife was going to win him. Now you just be good and wait your turn, or *your* wife might just leave you a-hanging."

Honestly, Jax didn't know how Frank and Jo managed to live together without killing one another, but at the heart of it, their unconventional love for each other worked for them.

If Jax had had half the wisdom and foresight that this old couple shared, maybe his own marriage would have—

"Jax McKenna."

The sound of his name pierced into his thoughts like a dart popping a balloon.

Nick gave him a none-too-gentle shove. "You're up, bro. Go get 'em."

"No, I—" Jax protested. He wasn't ready to be paraded around like a piece of prime horseflesh. Not that he would ever be ready to face this moment, but he'd at least hoped to have a little more time to get used to the idea, to see how it went with some of the other guys before it was his turn to go.

With reluctant steps he dragged himself onto the platform, his jaw, his fists and his stomach clenched so tight he thought he might be sick. Folks were staring at him, and though the rational part of him knew that he was imagining it, he felt as if everyone's gaze was glued to the ragged scar that ran from the corner of his mouth to his left temple.

He'd never been overly concerned about his appearance—at least not until after his face had been scarred in an accident and his wife, Susie, had left him for another man. The pain of his divorce was still too fresh for him to ignore, on top of the pain of the scars that marked him both inside and out, marring his features, badly damaging his hearing and shattering his confidence in himself. Everything combined to make participating in this auction all the more excruciating, no matter how good the cause.

He turned and started back the way he came. They had plenty of guys willing and able to compete in the auction. They would do just fine without him. He wouldn't fetch much of a price, anyway.

"Jackson Daniel McKenna, you freeze right where you are." Jax might be deaf in one ear, but that was no obstacle to Jo Spencer. Jax firmly believed her voice was loud enough and powerful enough to pierce through a stone wall, if she set her mind to it. And in this instance, it stopped him dead in his tracks. She was like a second mother to most of the town, Jax included, and her tone brooked no nonsense, making him feel as if he was a troublemaking five-year-old all over again.

"Turn your cute little fanny around and get on back over here, son. We need all the genuine bachelors we can get in this here auction. There might be a lady out there who's just been waiting for an opportunity like this to get to know you, handsome fellow that you are."

Jax flinched inwardly. He was one *bachelor* Serendipity could do without.

But denying Jo what she wanted? He couldn't do that, especially in front of a crowd. He was painfully aware he was making an even bigger spectacle of himself by balking on the stage.

"Yes, ma'am," he muttered, heading toward the front of the stage, dragging his feet with every step. When he got there, he stood stock-still, as if he was facing a firing squad. It kind of felt that way. There was no laughter or cheers this time, as there had been with his brother. That was fine by Jax. He might have to give in to Jo's prodding, but he would not—*not*—flex his muscles the way Slade had done. He pulled the brim of his tan cowboy hat down lower over his eyes and jammed his hands in the front pockets of his blue jeans for good measure.

"Who is going to start the bidding for us today on this fine specimen of a man?" She gestured for him to pose like Slade had done but Jax ignored her. "Just look at the size of him. Which lovely young lady out there has some heavy lifting they need Jax here to do for them?"

The assembly was deathly silent—exactly as Jax had

expected. No surprise there. He could hear his own breath, loud and ragged, scratching through the hush of the crowd.

He wanted to curl in on himself, but instead he straightened his shoulders. He wouldn't cower, nor would he let anyone know how difficult this was for him. If he stood still long enough, the charade would play itself out and be over in a minute.

No one would bid on him. He'd swallow his pride and humiliation and go back to his ranch where he belonged. At least there he could find a semblance of peace among his award-winning herd of quarter horses, bred and trained for the rodeo circuit.

"Don't tell me there's not a-one of you ladies out there who needs a few chores done around your houses or ranches—something that requires a big, strapping man? Moving boxes, maybe? Bales of hay?"

Still nothing. Just the rustling sound of a few awkwardly shifting feet. A cough or two.

Jax caught Jo's gaze, silently begging her to shoot him now and put him out of his misery. Honestly, he'd be willing to cough up a couple of hundred bucks out of his own pocket if it meant he could just walk away.

Jo frowned, lifted her chin and shook her head.

Stubborn old woman.

"I know most of y'all already know this about him, but he's a wonder with horses. Top-notch. Anyone have a horse that needs training?"

This was ridiculous. Jax had had enough, and no doubt the crowd had, too. They were a nice enough bunch and they were probably feeling a whole lot of sorry for him right now.

Well, he didn't want their pity.

"Five," came a sweet, soft soprano located somewhere near the back of the crowd. Jax didn't believe he recognized the woman's voice, which was odd, since he knew most everyone in the small town.

"I'm sorry, dear," Jo said, cupping a hand to her ear. "You'll have to speak up. I couldn't quite make out what you said."

"Five," the voice repeated, stronger and nearer to the platform now. "Hundred. Dollars. Five hundred dollars for the cowboy."

Half a grand? For him?

Jax scanned the crowd until his gaze locked on the clearest, most sparkling hazel eyes he'd ever seen. The gaze belonged to a tall, lithe, blond-haired young lady who'd finally managed to work her way to the front of the crowd.

He'd definitely never seen her before. No way would he forget the kind of beauty she possessed. She looked as if she'd just walked off the cover of one of those fancy New York fashion magazines. Dressed that way, too, with a poofy purple scarf wound multiple times around her supple neck, a silky emerald shirt and designer jeans that emphasized her long legs but had definitely never seen the back of a horse. Most telling were her three-inch spiked heels that sunk into the soft grass with every step.

The woman actually had cash in her hand—five crisp Benjamin Franklins, which she waved in the air like a flag.

"Five hundred dollars," she repeated for the third time. "But please, don't make me lasso the poor man."

The woman operating the cash box flashed Faith Dugan a welcome smile as Faith pressed five hundred-dollar bills into her palm. She hadn't had time to visit the local branch of Serendipity's bank to establish a checking account, and she felt awkward waving around that kind of cash. Apparently, she looked awkward, too—which she imagined was the reason all eyes were now upon her.

That and the fact that she was a newcomer in a crowd of people who had no doubt been born and raised in this town. Serendipity, Texas, wasn't the kind of place folks moved in and out of. She was the exception. And she seemed to have shocked everyone by shelling out five hundred dollars for the brooding cowboy.

Faith wasn't trying to impress anyone. She just needed help rebuilding her newly purchased ranch property, which she hoped soon would be a bona fide mustang rescue.

"You're new in town?" the woman asked. "Jo mentioned we had a new resident. I'm glad to meet you. I'm Alexis Haddon. You're going to love living in Serendipity." To Faith's surprise, Alexis pulled her into an exuberant hug, as if they were old friends. She'd had plenty of smiles and welcomes in the few days she'd been in town. Folks around here sure were outgoing and friendly. It was nothing like large, busy and somewhat impersonal Hartford, Connecticut, where she'd been born and raised.

"Thank you." Faith hoped her response to Alexis's hug didn't appear as awkward as she felt. "I'm Faith Dugan. I just bought the Dennys' old property."

Excitement bubbled up inside her every time she thought about her plans for the place, but she bit her tongue to keep from bursting out her intentions. Now was hardly the time to get into her reasons for settling in town.

Alexis blew out a low whistle. "I'd heard that someone had picked up the place. You sure chose a fixer-upper. I hope you enjoy a challenge. Old man Denny was an eighty-five-year-old widower, and his health got so poor that he couldn't work the place himself for the last ten years of his life. He didn't have any family, and he was in a senior center in San Antonio for the last couple of years. His ranch just sat there vacant. Such a shame."

Despite her eagerness for the project, Faith cringed inwardly at the reminder of the size of the task ahead of her. She'd been evaluating the ranch for repairs, but she'd hoped it wasn't in quite as bad of shape as it seemed. Apparently, her assessment had been fairly accurate. There was a reason the asking price for the property had been well under market value. It was going to take a lot of work to get her new ranch into running condition so she could host the herd of wild mustangs she intended to save.

But that was fine—she was up for the challenge. She wasn't going to let a little hard work put her off her dreams.

"People like Mr. Denny are the reason we're holding the auction today," Alexis went on. "So we can build a senior center and hospice here in town. Poor Mr. Denny wouldn't have had to have spent his last years so far away from the town he was born and raised in if we'd had a facility available. It wouldn't have made any difference to the state of his ranch, of course, but he could have come to church, spent time with some familiar faces. Serendipity folk like to take care of their own."

"It's a good cause," Faith agreed, offering up a silent prayer for Mr. Denny, the poor man who'd died alone, far from his home. She knew what it felt like to be lonely.

"We appreciate your generosity, bidding in our auction," Alexis continued with her vibrant, upbeat chatter, "especially since you're a newcomer. I'm sure your neighbors will be around to introduce themselves to you if they haven't already. Everyone is a friend here. As an added bonus, you've won Jax. You've made a good choice. He's a big ol' brute, but don't let that scare you off. He has a heart of gold and those muscles of his were earned through hard labor. He knows ranching backward and forward. I'm sure you'll find plenty of uses for him at the ranch."

Faith wasn't certain how Jax would feel about Alexis's summation of his capabilities and value. Faith had a hard time picturing Jax with a heart of *gold* given the sheen of ice obscuring his dark brown eyes.

She didn't require his heart for this job, nor did she have any interest in what color it was. What she needed was a pair of strong arms and maybe some good advice from someone who knew his way around a ranch. Jo had mentioned Jax was good with horses. If he could also pound nails and mend fences, so much the better.

She would have had to hire someone to do the work, anyway. How awesome was it that her money would be doing double duty? She'd get the help she needed—for a little while, anyway—and the town would get its senior center built.

Win, win.

Though poor Jax sure didn't seem to think he'd won anything.

He definitely hadn't looked as if he'd wanted to be standing on a platform hawking himself, but she was sure he hadn't been able to say no to gregarious, winsome Jo any more than Faith had. It was Jo who had convinced her it would be worthwhile to attend the auction today, to bid for one of the local men to help her clean up her run-down property. It had seemed like a good idea at the time, but in hindsight, she now decided she must have been clean out of her mind to have bid on a perfect stranger—one who had looked large and intimidating even from a distance.

Jax exited the stage, taking the stairs one slow step at a time, his gaze narrowed onto her and he frowned. The reluctance with which he moved to her side was palpable.

Now, as he approached her, *intimidated* didn't even begin to cover what she was feeling. At five feet ten inches in her bare feet—and three inches taller than that at the moment, thanks to her heels—Faith wasn't in any way diminutive. She was taller than most women and many men, but Jax towered over her.

Faith found it hard to believe that Jo had had the audacity to call him out by his given and middle names together, reminding her of the way a mother would scold an errant youngster climbing a tree. And right in front of the whole town, to boot. Jo and Jax must have a special relationship, because Faith had been shocked down to her shoes when Jax *had* turned around and returned to the platform just as Jo had asked.

Yet he was no wayward child. Far from it. If she had to guess, she'd put him a few years older than her own twenty-seven years. Thirty-ish. She judged him to be over two hundred pounds of raw muscle and a good six feet four inches tall, cartoonishly huge next to Jo's five-feet-nothing. He dwarfed the friendly redhead.

Unlike the guy who'd come before him, he hadn't even needed to flex for her—er—for the *crowd* to appreciate the strength of his broad shoulders and powerful biceps. Now in closer proximity, she inhaled the smell of him— all leather and raw man. Just the way he looked. The crazy thing was, that heady scent wasn't unpleasant. Quite the opposite, in fact.

If it weren't for the scar on his face, she'd have thought he'd walked right out of an advertisement for aftershave or something else meant to be rugged and manly. Though honestly, the ragged, puckered scar that slashed across the man's temple didn't bother her as much as the fact that he appeared to be glowering. Not at her, thankfully, but at a couple of sturdy cowboys standing together near the other side of the stage. The guy who'd been bid on first was there, his arm curved familiarly around his wife's waist. The other fellow, a big bear of a man whom Faith immediately dubbed *Grizzly Adams*, was grinning as if he'd triumphed in a race.

Jax's brothers, were Faith to guess. The family resemblance was striking in their similar strong features—the dark wavy hair and chiseled jaws.

Alexis gave Faith's shoulder an encouraging pat and turned back to the auction, where the next bachelor had broken into an impromptu round of "Home on the Range," presumably to impress the ladies with his vocal capabilities. Faith thought perhaps the guy should have chosen another talent to display. Singing in tune didn't appear to be part of his skill set. To Faith's ears, he sounded a bit like a crowing rooster, but she supposed it was the thought that counted. For some inexplicable reason the crowd was encouraging the poor bachelor, which only made him bellow all the louder.

She turned her attention to Jax. He was watching the guy on stage, but he didn't appear to care one way or another about the assault on his ears. She observed him quietly, hoping to discern what he might be thinking by the look on his face. She could read nothing in his expression. It wasn't empty so much as—*hard*. Frozen solid, like the frost in his eyes. His body language was equally as closed off, with his arms crossed over the bulk of his chest.

"So," she said, not at all certain how to start a conversation with him. "I brought a picnic basket full of goodies so we can share lunch together." She knew she was rambling but didn't seem to know how to stop. "I thought Jo's idea was a clever twist to the event, allowing everyone to participate in one way or another. Men, women, singles and married alike. Don't you think?"

He didn't respond, not even to acknowledge that she'd spoken to him. He hadn't even bothered to turn his head in her direction.

"Jax?" She touched his elbow to get his attention.

He turned, his piercing, chocolate-brown eyes shifting to hers and widening in surprise, as if he'd forgotten she was there.

Maybe he had.

"I—er—" she stammered. "Did you want to stay and watch the rest of the auction?"

Jax snorted. "Thank you, no. I am *so* done with this stupid event."

Faith smiled. "I thought you might be. I certainly wouldn't want to have to put myself up for display on the auction block, but I appreciate your sacrifice for the sake of the senior center building fund."

"Oh, believe me, I *felt* like a sacrifice. The lamb-to-the-slaughter kind." Jax grinned, his smile made slightly crooked by the tension created by his scar, which pulled the left side of his mouth higher than the right. It would have looked a bit like a grimace, except that his eyes were gleaming with amusement. "Thanks for rescuing me."

"My pleasure." Her cheeks warmed. She couldn't imagine why his words would make her blush. She swallowed and quickly recovered her composure. She pointed down the lawn. "I set my picnic basket under that oak tree over there. Are you hungry?"

A laugh that sounded a little bit like a growl emerged from deep in his chest. "I'm always hungry."

Well, duh. She should have guessed that. Put fur on the guy and he could probably pass for Bigfoot. Of course he was hungry.

"I hope I packed enough."

His right brow arched and the strained half grin returned.

She was already blushing, but now heat rushed to her

face and spread to her cheeks like a wildfire. Had she just said those words out loud?

Open mouth, insert foot. Way to go, Faith. Insult the man ten seconds after meeting him.

She quickly tried to recover, feeling as if she were scrambling backward as she stammered her way through her sentence. "Oh, n-no. That's not what I intended to say. My words didn't come out right at *all*. I—I only meant—"

He held up one large work-calloused hand to stem the flow of her sputtering words. "It's okay, ma'am. Whatever you've brought will be just fine, I'm sure. I'm not a difficult man to please."

"Please call me Faith," she urged, brushing her suddenly sweaty palms against the denim of her designer skinny jeans.

Acquiring new, more practical boot-cut jeans was on her priority list of things to do now that she was finally here in Serendipity. And as much as she loved her Jimmy Choos, her good pair of cowboy boots would have been much more sensible for the occasion. She was practically aerating the park grass with her three-inch spikes.

"Faith," he repeated, his rich, lyrical voice making her name sound like a musical note. "I'm Jax McKenna, and apparently I am at your service."

"It's nice to officially meet you, Jax." She held out her hand and he dwarfed it in his own. Again she had the impression of hard work and calluses, a complete contrast to her own lotion-softened, office-cubicle working hands.

That will change. Soon.

She'd spent the last few years working in accounting for a non-profit organization to save up the money for her horse sanctuary. Mere months from now she hoped and prayed that her palms would likewise carry the blisters of hard country labor. She could barely wait for that day, anticipating it like a child would Christmas morning. She was a city girl with a country heart.

"Here we are," she said, gesturing to a rather plain-looking brown wicker basket lingering next to the trunk of an oak, shaded from the glare of the sun by the old tree's branches. As she looked around at the other baskets dotting the lawn, she couldn't help but feel a little bit embarrassed. Her own meager offering looked so bare and ordinary next to the others. Many of the women had decorated their baskets with colorful plumes and ribbons. She wished she'd thought of that—especially because the man she'd be sharing a meal with looked as if he could use a few kindhearted gestures. But on the other hand, he didn't seem like the sort of man who'd really be comfortable with something dolled up and fancy. Maybe plain was best, after all.

Without speaking, Jax crouched over the basket, withdrawing a blue-checked plastic tablecloth that had been the best Faith could do under the circumstances. She'd arrived in Serendipity only two days ago and hadn't learned of the auction until the day prior.

How she'd come to bet on *this* particular tall, sturdy cowboy was a mystery even to her. It was nothing more than a gut feeling, but she'd learned over the years to follow those silent promptings.

Thankfully, the man with the rooster voice had stopped singing, but the crowd was still hooting and hollering in the background. Jax didn't seem to notice, nor, apparently, did he want to wait for the rest of the town to finish with the auction before he and Faith started on their picnic.

He spread the tablecloth across the grass and gestured for her to sit. Then he pulled out plates and silverware and popped the top of a cola can before offering it to her.

"Thanks," she said, dropping onto the far corner of the

plastic and folding her legs under her. "Although I feel like I ought to be doing the serving," she said as he inspected the club sandwiches she'd made for the occasion. At least she'd used foot-long sub buns and loaded the sandwiches with meat, cheese and veggies. Dagwood would be proud of her creation.

Jax glanced up at her, and the unscarred side of his lips curled upward. Close to a smile, at any rate. Faith would take it.

"You paid for my time," he reminded her. "I figured now is as good a time as any to start working off my—" He paused and bent his head as he considered how best to finish the sentence.

"Community service?" she suggested, chuckling at the double meaning.

"Yeah. That." He wasn't laughing.

"I—uh—okay, right," she stammered. She didn't usually stutter like a schoolgirl with her first crush. If she didn't get a hold of her tongue soon, he would think he was working for an idiot.

His gaze had returned to the basket, giving Faith a modicum of reprieve. She took a deep, calming breath. There was no reason spending time with this man should visibly shake her, and the sooner she got comfortable around him, the better. After all, if he was as good with horses as Jo claimed, she hoped she might be able to convince him to stretch out his community service and continue working with her until her project was—if not finished, then a great deal closer than it was right now.

Then again, maybe he was expecting nothing more than to provide one day's labor. No one had really set the guidelines for what happened after the auction, or at least nothing that Faith had heard.

"There are canisters of potato salad and barbecue baked

beans, as well," she added, relieved when her voice came out sounding normal. "I'm not much of a cook, but I made them myself. The beans are an old family recipe. Back home we called them Cowboy Beans." The thought struck her as funny and she chuckled.

"Well, that's fittin'." He pulled out the plastic container of beans and scooped a heaping portion onto each of their plates. "Where's home?"

He sounded genuinely interested, putting her more at ease. She leaned back on her hands. "I was born out east. Connecticut. I attended college in Wyoming. That's where I got interested in horses." It was also where she'd met...

She cut the thought off firmly, refusing to let her mind wander in that direction again. It still hurt to think about Keith and his son. She coughed, realizing Jax was speaking and she'd missed what he'd just said. "I'm sorry. My mind wandered for a second there. What did you say?"

His dark eyebrows lowered over stormy brown eyes. He assessed her, the working side of his lip curving into a frown. "Nothing important. Just that there's good horse country out in Wyoming. Potato salad?"

"Yes, please." She was relieved that he didn't push her on what had caused her distraction. She wasn't ready to talk about Keith, or about his precious son.

They ate in silence for a while, each lost in thought. As the auction continued, more people moved to the green, milling around them, talking and laughing. Some even stopped to introduce themselves. Faith should have been happy to be so welcomed by her new community, but her empty chest echoed with the sounds.

Before she knew it, Jax had cleaned his plate—not once, but twice, leaving her glad she'd thought to pack extra. Jo Spencer had advised her on the eating habits of the Texas male, and Jax was no slouch in that department.

"If you don't mind me asking—why?" Jax's voice had a hard edge to it, and he didn't quite meet her gaze.

"Why?" she repeated, bracing herself. She wasn't ready for him to elaborate on his question, to have to explain why a city woman wanted to open up a mustang sanctuary in the country, but sometimes there was no way out but through.

"Yeah. Why?" He lifted his tan cowboy hat and brushed his forearm across his brow. "Why did you bid on me?"

Her heart skipped a beat. Why *had* she bid on him?

"You mean why did I bid in the auction in general, or why bid for you, specifically?"

He shrugged. "Both, I guess."

The truth was, he'd looked miserable up on the auction block, especially when there was hesitation from the crowd on bidding for him. She couldn't imagine why that was. Despite his scar, he was quite handsome, if a woman liked her men strong and rugged. Faith would have expected the town's single ladies to be shouting over each other in order to get a chance to spend time with this guy.

And yet there had been silence. The drop-of-a-pin kind.

Maybe it was too early in the game. Jax was only the second man to be auctioned, and the first bachelor. Perhaps the ladies were waiting to see who else was offering their services. Or maybe there was something about Jax that Faith didn't yet know about, such as that he was conceited or had a bad temper.

She hoped not, but she was about to find out—because Jax was frowning again.

"Look—I don't want your pity," he said, his voice husky.

"What? No."

"Are you seriously going to sit there and tell me you didn't feel sorry for this scarred old monster? Because I won't believe you."

"I was standing at the back of the crowd. I couldn't even see your scar."

He shook his head. "That's even worse."

Now she was the one feeling insulted. "Why? You think I'm so shallow that I would want to bow out of our agreement just because of a gash on your face?"

He scoffed. "Wouldn't be the first time."

She heard the bitterness behind his words. Someone in his past had injured him deeply. The wound in his heart was deeper than the one on his face.

"Well, that's not me. I came here today looking for someone to help me with my ranch. I bought the Dennys' old place, and it will take a lot of labor to get it in working order. If you're going to pitch in, then I couldn't care less what you look like. Wear a paper bag over your face, if you like. It won't matter to me. I'll take all the help I can get."

His jaw lost its tightness at the welcome change of subject. He whistled softly.

"That place is pretty run-down. What do you plan to do with it?"

"I'm going to save wild mustangs." Her voice rose in pitch as enthusiasm for her life's dream engulfed her.

His gaze turned skeptical and his lips quirked. "Are you serious?"

Of course she was serious. Ever since she'd heard of the plight of wild mustangs as a child, she'd had it in her heart to take action, to make a difference. That's why she'd left the East Coast and picked a college in Wyoming. For a while, life had gotten in the way and she'd set aside her dreams. But after what happened with Keith—she refused to dwell on that part of her life—she'd started making legitimate plans to fulfill her goals, and now here she was, in Serendipity, a brand-new owner of a ranch, however derelict it was.

Baby steps.

"You doubt me?"

He leaned his back against the solid trunk of the oak and stretched out his legs, crossing them at the ankles, and giving her a once-over that sent chills down her spine.

His gaze lingered on her shoes.

"Forgive me if I'm a little bit skeptical. You're clearly a city girl. What do you know about ranching?"

The only reason she didn't punch him in the arm for his sarcasm—apart from not really knowing the man and how he'd react to that kind of attack—was that his words were lined with amusement. Hopefully not at her expense.

"All right. I'll admit I was born and raised in a metropolitan area and have never lived on a ranch. However, I have spent several years volunteering at a wild-horse sanctuary. I realize I'm on a learning curve here, but I have read a lot and my bachelor's degree is in business management with a minor in conservation and environmental science. I've done a lot of studying on the subject. Wyoming isn't tolerant of wild horses."

He snorted. "You've *read* about it? Like in a library? And you think a little piece of paper somehow makes you qualified to manage a horse farm? With wild mustangs, no less. Exactly how many wranglers do you intend to hire?"

She shook her head. She was afraid this subject might come up. "None. At least at first. I'm working to find like-minded donors to help me reach my vision, but until more funds come in, I can't afford to hire any help."

"You're doing this alone?"

"Well, not *all* alone, obviously. I have you, don't I? At least for a little while? I don't think we've talked about the length of your—*indenture*."

"I think most guys are going a month of weekends."

"That'll do. You can show me how to get the ranch up to scratch. I'm a fast learner."

"You're going to have to be, because fixing up the ranch won't be your only obstacle. Just how much experience do you have with mustangs? I've spent my whole life working with horses, and they still surprise me from time to time. Wild mustangs? That's a whole other thing."

"Yes, but they need my help." Her pulse quickened as adrenaline blasted through her and her spirit lifted. For a moment Jax's words and attitude had discouraged her, but then she remembered how many ways the Lord had come through for her. He'd guided her to Jax. She didn't believe in coincidences.

"You train horses, then?" She wanted specifics.

"Quarter horses for ranching and rodeo." His eyes gleamed with pride. It appeared they shared a love of horses. She just had to convince him she was serious in her intentions.

"I'd love to see your herd."

His gaze widened epically and Faith choked on her breath. Had she just invited herself over to his property? Heat flared to her cheeks.

To her surprise, he nodded. "Sure. Why not? If you don't have any other plans this afternoon, we can head on over there after we've finished eating. Give you the opportunity to see a working ranch in action and get up close and personal with a real, live horse."

"Excuse me?" she huffed. "I've been around horses, thank you very much—and ranches, too. I worked at a ranch every summer while I was in college, and since I graduated, I've been volunteering weekends at Mustang Mission. I'm not the greenhorn you seem to think I am."

"Your shoes would suggest otherwise."

She chuckled. "Hey. I wasn't planning to go riding

today. I'm new in town. I had to guess at the dress code. For all I knew this auction would be a black-tie event. Were we in a larger metropolitan area it probably would have been tuxes and cocktail dresses."

A rich, deep laugh rumbled through his chest. "In Serendipity, honey, we have exactly two dress codes. Go-to-church clothes and everything else. If you ever have a doubt, dress casual."

He tipped his hat and her heart purred. This was where she wanted to be. In the country, with real horses, real cowboys and a real chance to make a difference. Not back home where no one—except her friends at Mustang Mission—seemed to understand what she wanted to achieve.

This was *home*. She felt it in every fiber of her being.

Now she just had to convince her new neighbors—and the possibly hostile cattle community—that she and her mustangs belonged there.

Chapter Two

Jax's phone trilled. He slipped it out of the plain black leather case he wore on his belt, glanced at the number and scowled.

Susie.

"Now why would she...?" The rest of his sentence trailed off into puzzled silence. He grimaced. His ex-wife was the last person he wanted to talk to, especially today. Faith had somehow, although he had no idea how, gotten him out of his own head for a while. He'd actually been enjoying himself for a change, and that had happened far too little in his life in the nine months since Susie left him.

Count on Susie to dump ice water on his good mood. Without even answering the phone, he sensed she was about to completely ruin what up until now had been a perfectly good day.

It just figured.

He cupped his hand over the receiver and flashed Faith an apologetic shrug.

"Excuse me just a moment, will you, Faith? I'd better take this. It's my ex-wife on the line."

"Of course," she said with an encouraging smile. "Take all the time you need."

He strode a few steps away from Faith and held the phone to his ear, trying not to grit his teeth when he spoke.

"Did you need something?" Jax didn't bother with pleasantries. He couldn't imagine what she wanted. He'd already done what he could for her. He hadn't contested the divorce, hadn't protested the way she'd taken almost everything of value from the house when she left, hadn't even argued over the amount of money she'd taken from their shared accounts—though he remained deeply grateful that the ranch's accounts were separate and that she hadn't been able to access them. She'd drained away everything she could from him, including his confidence and pride, until the love he'd once felt for her had withered into dust. He had nothing left to give her.

So why was she contacting him now?

"Are you at the house?"

"No, I'm not." He started to tell her he was at the auction but then cut his words short. His shoulders tightened with strain and his gut squeezed so forcefully he could barely breathe. He didn't have to answer to her, not about his whereabouts or any other part of his life.

Besides, Susie didn't even live in Serendipity anymore. She despised the small town in which she'd been born and raised. She probably didn't even know about the auction, seeing as it was the first—and Jax hoped *only*—one ever.

"Why are you asking? Are you in town? Do you need to see me for something?" Had there been some kind of legal hang-up? He hoped not. He'd thought the divorce was a done deal.

"Go home. Now."

"What?" Jax asked, his voice a low rumble. He didn't care for the way she was ordering him around.

"Just go." She sounded a little desperate.

"Wait—" Heat flared through him in a flash of foreboding and he muttered something unintelligible under his breath. "Susie? Susie?"

Dead air met his ear and he glanced at the face of his phone. She'd hung up on him. Tried to boss him around and then hung up on him. He growled and pressed the re-dial button but the call went straight to voice mail.

"Are you okay?" Faith asked when he returned to the picnic blanket and slumped to his knees, bracing his hands on his thighs and breathing raggedly. Her gaze looked troubled, though why she should care was beyond him.

He lifted his hat by the crown and shoved his fingers through his thick, unmanageable hair, then replaced it and pulled the brim low over his eyes to shadow his scar.

"Yeah," he answered with a clipped nod. His pulse was still thundering and the notion that something was amiss continued to hover over him like a storm cloud. "Well, no. Not really. To tell you the truth, I'm not sure."

She remained silent while Jax worked through his thoughts, her gaze more compassionate than curious. He appreciated that she didn't try to push him to speak be-fore he was ready.

Go home. Now.

He thought about just ignoring Susie's words and going back to his very pleasant picnic, but there was something off in her tone. Desperate. A sharp edge in his gut nagged at him, obliging him to change his plans.

"I hate to rush you, but would you mind if we pack up our picnic and take off now?"

"Sure thing," she said, reaching for the plastic lids to cover the leftover potato salad and baked beans. "Not a problem. I hope everything is okay."

"Thanks." He was already haphazardly folding the checked tablecloth and stuffing it into the picnic basket along with the plates and napkins Faith handed to him. His ex-wife's words echoed through him, rattling his cage.

He frowned. He wouldn't give her the gratification of knowing how rough these months had been. He wasn't certain he could face her now, but that's what she must have meant—that she was waiting for him at the house. But if she had something to tell him, why couldn't she have just said it over the phone?

Faith touched his forearm. When he turned and met her gaze, she was looking at him expectantly. Clearly, she'd asked him a question and he hadn't responded.

It wasn't the first time he'd found himself in this position. He floundered through the options but came up with too many possibilities for him to narrow down. What had she asked him about?

The auction? The picnic? His ex?

He generally tried to stay on the offensive when it came to his hearing deficiency. After his accident he'd lost nearly 100 percent of his hearing in his left ear. He'd become proficient at lipreading and responding to subtle body-language cues. Most of the time it was enough to get by, although he hated that he occasionally gave the wrong answer or said something that didn't fit in the conversation.

It was an embarrassing disability and one he didn't like to talk about. Few in town even knew about it.

His family—his mom and his two brothers, Nick and Slade—were patient with him, understanding his dilemma. He'd become kind of a recluse after the accident—after Susie left. He emerged only for Sunday services at church and the occasional necessary trip to town for supplies. He was quick to leave church right afterward, not staying around to socialize, and he'd quit stopping in at Cup O' Jo's Café to catch up on the news.

"I'm sorry, what?" he asked Faith after an extended

pause, smiling apologetically and hoping she wouldn't catch on to his disability. It was bad enough having hearing loss without having to talk about it. Though he'd kept his condition mostly secret, he knew that deafness—even only partial deafness—made many folks uneasy.

"I asked if you'd rather that I make my visit to your ranch another day. It sounds like you've got your hands full right now."

He immediately shook his head. "No. Please. I'm anxious to show you my herd."

He did want to show her his prize-winning horses, but at the moment he just felt the overwhelming need for backup in case Susie was there. Better not to be alone in that case. Having someone else around might keep her from making a scene. He could ask one of his brothers, but there was no sense interrupting their day when Jax and Faith had already made plans together.

Besides, it was probably nothing.

"Okay, then. I'll come with you," she said, her voice just a hair too high and bright. "If you don't mind my asking, though—why the sudden hurry?"

"My ex-wife just called. Said I needed to hurry home. Honestly, I don't know what she's up to, but I figured I'd better find out."

"I see." Faith nodded, but thankfully didn't ask any more probing questions to which he didn't have any answers.

They loaded the picnic basket in the bed of Jax's truck and drove back toward his ranch. He clenched his fists on the steering wheel and forced himself to breathe evenly, concentrating on tamping back the fury burning in his chest. He thought he was over feeling *anything* when it came to Susie. He'd been on his knees dozens of times praying he could forgive her for the hurt she'd caused him.

Apparently, he hadn't prayed hard enough.

He barely registered it when he turned into the long gravel driveway that housed the Circle M ranch. His mother, Alice, a recent widow, lived in the main ranch house, while Jax and Nick held separate residences on the land, smaller cabins that better fit their bachelor status. Slade had moved to the Beckett ranch next door when he'd married Laney.

He pulled up before his cabin, expecting to see Susie's red AWD parked in front, or worse yet, a courier with more unpleasant papers to sign. He scanned the area for an unfamiliar vehicle but didn't find one. He'd seen a truck kicking up dust on the road that led to the Circle M, but it hadn't occurred to him that it might be Susie. He'd seen only the back of the relatively new blue pickup, but now that he thought about it, it had appeared to be exceeding the speed limit on its way out of town.

Great. What was Susie up to, anyway? He was going to be good and angry if she'd pulled him away from the picnic and the nicest day he'd had in—well, he couldn't remember how long—for no good reason.

Oh, who was he kidding? He was *good and angry* now.

He hopped out of the cab and hurried around to open up the door for Faith. It wasn't just that his mama had taught him to be a gentleman. With those ridiculously high heels she was wearing, she was bound to take a digger if she tried to get down by herself. He was having a hard enough day without becoming responsible for the impractically dressed woman twisting her ankle.

She smiled up at him gratefully as he grasped her tiny waist and lifted her from the cab. She reached for his shoulders to maintain her balance, and his hands lingered on her waist.

Their eyes met and held, and her cheeks turned a pretty

shade of rose before she cleared her throat and stepped away from him, her gaze shifting from his face to the front of his cabin.

"What a lovely place," she complimented. "Your cabin looks like it belongs in a magazine."

He cringed inwardly. It only now occurred to him that he might not want to invite her inside. He couldn't remember if he'd picked up his laundry or not, and he had a bad habit of leaving his soiled socks where he shed them, not to mention a week's worth of dirty dishes he had piled in the sink. He didn't have a dishwasher and usually got to washing the dishes only when he didn't have anything left to eat on.

He was busy formulating a reasonable explanation for the mess inside when Faith's eyes widened and her mouth made a perfect O. And she hadn't even seen his dirty laundry yet.

"Jax?" She whispered his name like a question, her voice sounding like sandpaper, not at all the sweet, high, smooth timbre she'd used earlier in the day.

The warning in her tone sent a ripple of apprehension down his spine. Slowly he turned, afraid to see what had so obviously shaken her. He wouldn't put anything past Susie at this point.

Oh, dear Lord, no.

His gut clenched as he gasped for air and a proverbial sideswipe to his jaw sent him reeling.

No. It couldn't be. It could. Not. Be.

Jax blinked and scrubbed a hand down his face.

Were his eyes deceiving him?

Impossible.

Even if he was blind as a bat, and even though his hearing was half what it used to be, there was no mistaking the sound of distinctive, distraught mewling coming from two tiny swaddled infants, bundled into their car seats and blocking the front door of his cabin.

Babies?

He took the steps two at a time and crouched before the baby on his left, gently adjusting the pink blanket covering her and making what he hoped were calming shushing noises. His expertise was horses. He knew zero about babies.

She was incredibly tiny next to his large palm. So vulnerable. So defenseless. He swallowed hard.

How long had they been here, *alone*, where any number of ills could befall them?

The—*babies*.

Fury roared and blazed like a wildfire in his chest. Susie had left two helpless infants on his front porch? She was going to answer for this. She'd always been irresponsible and often acted with poor judgment, but this went far beyond the pale even for her.

"Jax?" Faith asked again, her voice faltering. She knelt before the other baby, presumably also a girl, given the identical pink blanket tucked around her, and gently rocked the seat to calm the infant. "Are these…?"

"I don't—I'm not—" Jax stammered, his head spinning. He considered himself calm and rational. His emotions rarely got the better of him. But right now he was fighting with every ounce of his courage against succumbing to the conflicting feelings pelting him—a lone unarmed man against an army of men with razor-sharp swords and blistering bows and arrows.

Shock. Surprise. Anger. Betrayal. Guilt. Pain.

Wonder.

Were these…? Could it be that these precious little pieces of humanity were…?

His heart welled and tears pricked at the corners of his eyes. He couldn't lose it now. He just couldn't.

He stood abruptly, and the baby at his feet protested with a wail. She had a nice, healthy pair of lungs on her, and Jax winced, then crouched back down and rocked the car seat as Faith was doing.

Where was Susie? How could she possibly have just *left* these babies behind without an explanation? He had a million questions to ask her, and he wanted to tell her exactly what he thought of her inconceivably selfish behavior. He'd never actually throttle a woman, even Susie, but the thought did cross his mind, to shake a little sense into her.

How could she?

How could she keep such an enormous secret from him? If these were, in fact, his daughters…

She'd kept his *children* from him, kept him from knowing they even existed. They were probably no more than a month old—not that he could guess with any accuracy. She should have told him she was pregnant as soon as she *knew* she was pregnant. He should have been there when the babies were born.

He was their father. He had rights. Responsibilities. Privileges.

How *dare* she?

He fished out his phone and punched Susie's number again, but not surprisingly, it went straight to voice mail. Again. She was avoiding him, as well she might, considering what she'd just done. Was she seriously just dumping a couple of babies on his doorstep and running away?

No. Not just a couple of babies.

His babies.

He didn't know how he knew they were his children. Given Susie's actions during the past year, their paternity might well be called into question, but his heart and his gut were telling him there was no doubt that he was the babies' father. And not just because Susie had dumped them on his doorstep.

Overcoming every other emotion he was feeling, even the most heated ones, amazement and wonder and love warmed his chest, swirling and curling around and filling his heart full to the brim.

He was astounded by how instantly those feelings appeared and how strong they were. He'd woken up this morning a man who had been living practically like a hermit, deliberately isolating himself, mucking through the mire of his own despair.

Alone.

And now—

Now he was a *father*.

"Should we take them inside, do you think?" Faith asked hesitantly.

"What? Yes." He'd nearly forgotten Faith was there, but he was grateful she was. He wasn't even remotely capable of dealing with this crisis on his own, and her question proved it. He didn't know what to do with one baby, never mind two.

Of course he needed to take the infants inside the cabin, and then...

What next?

He didn't know the first thing about infants. Not what they ate, though presumably it was milk of some kind. Not how to get them to sleep, or even where they should sleep. It wasn't as if he had a crib in his spare room. He didn't even know how to change a diaper.

Faith stood and touched his shoulder. "You look lost."

And frightened.

She didn't say it, but they both knew it.

He met her empathetic hazel eyes and groaned. "I feel

lost. Like on-another-planet lost. I don't have a clue what I should do next. This is so beyond my realm of experience—almost beyond reality, actually."

She nodded. "I can't even imagine what you're going through. It's not every day a man learns he's a father when his babies show up at his door. Let's get these two little darlings in out of the heat and tend to their immediate needs, and then we can make a plan."

She'd said *we* as if it were just a given that she'd be part of—whatever this was. Her voice teemed with compassion and confidence. He was grateful that she'd come to Serendipity and chosen it to be her home. He was glad he'd met her. It was no accident that she'd bid on him today.

He knew in his heart that as crazy as this whole thing was, the Lord was watching over him. Faith's presence proved it. Even though she hadn't known him for more than a few hours, she offered her support and was willing to stay with him—with *them*. He *needed* her here.

He unlocked the door to his cabin, and Faith held the screen door for him as he grabbed the handles of both of the car seats and carefully transferred the children—*his* children—indoors. He scanned the area for the best place to put the car seats and settled on the carpet between the front of the couch and the coffee table.

Faith followed with a diaper bag in her hand—which, in the shock and devastation of the moment, had escaped Jax's notice. He supposed he should be grateful Susie had left him a modicum of supplies, but he was too angry to give her even that. He hoped she'd left a note giving him some idea of her state of mind—and the children's names would be nice, at the very least.

He turned his attention to one of the babies while Faith took care of the other. It took him a moment to figure out the lock system on the car seat, and by the time he was ready to lift the infant out, Faith already had hers tucked safely in the crook of her arm and was smiling and making delightful cooing noises to the contented infant.

He'd finally managed to unhook the straps but hesitated in removing the tiny little human being from the seat. He didn't know what he was doing. What if he accidentally hurt her?

"Support her neck with one hand and slide the other one behind her back," Faith instructed, as if she knew what he'd been thinking.

"Right." He cleared his throat and rubbed a hand down his jaw. This wasn't going to get any easier by waiting, and unlike the infant Faith held, his baby girl was starting to fuss again.

He held his breath and slid his hand underneath her, trying to be gentle but feeling like a clumsy giant. His daughter was so tiny he could easily support her neck and back with one hand, but he didn't take any chances. He followed Faith's directions to the letter.

The baby was incredibly fragile, weighing next to nothing. He held her out in front of him and swallowed hard around the lump of emotion in his throat.

"She's crying and yours isn't," he said, his voice scratchy. "What am I doing wrong?"

Faith chuckled. "You're doing fine. Don't worry about the fussing. Babies do that. She's just communicating with you. Put her up against your shoulder and pat her back. She's likely hungry or wet or both. The first thing we should do is see about getting these sweethearts changed into dry diapers and then get them some bottles of formula to warm and fill their little bellies." She sat down on the sofa and kissed her baby's forehead. "Let's see what we've got here."

Jax adjusted the baby he was holding to his shoulder, and

to his surprise, she immediately calmed down. He watched Faith remove the contents of the stylish red diaper bag. She placed everything she found on the coffee table—a stack of diapers, a box of wet wipes, four plastic bottles and a couple of yellow cans bearing a brand name Jax didn't recognize. He couldn't even begin to guess what was inside. A couple of yellow T-shirts with snaps on the bottom.

"Diapers first, then formula." Faith spread a blanket on the floor and laid her baby down, gesturing for Jax to do the same.

"What's formula?" Jax asked, following Faith's lead. He carefully unwrapped the blankets swaddled around his infant and removed the wet diaper.

"It's like milk, only it's specifically made for babies' sensitive stomachs."

"I don't have any formula." Jax gently lifted the baby's legs and slid a diaper underneath her. He started to tape the tabs only to realize the diaper was backward.

Tabs in back, cartoon picture in front.

Good thing he was a fast learner.

"Yes, you do." Faith nodded toward the yellow cans. "But that stash won't last very long, especially with two little ones. You'll have to get to the store soon."

Like *today*. And not just for formula, but for all the other things two babies would need.

Most people had nine months to plan their baby's arrival. He hadn't had a single second. And with the whole town wrapped up for the weekend with the special event, he wouldn't be able to visit Sam's Grocery until Monday. He hoped he could make it that long. When he had the opportunity, he'd call Slade and Laney and see if they had anything he could use.

Satisfied that he had his daughter's diaper fastened—if not perfectly then at least adequately—he lifted her back into his arms. Faith likewise picked up her infant, but then also somehow managed to balance two bottles and a can of formula in her other arm. Talented woman.

"Kitchen?"

"Through the door on the left," he said, nodding toward the small space that served him as a kitchen.

"Can I help?" he asked her, not knowing how much assistance he could actually provide.

"No need." She chuckled.

She was obviously going to set up the bottles for the infants, though Jax had no clue what that entailed, much less how she was going to manage with only one free hand. He looked around, wondering what he ought to do next and wishing babies came with a written how-to manual.

Well, okay, maybe not a *manual*. He wasn't much on reading directions. But a bulleted list, at least.

He stared down at the tiny slip of humanity nestled in the crook of his arm, smacking noisily on her little fist that she'd caught in her mouth, and felt yet another overwhelming surge of joy and amazement. His throat closed around the emotion, clogging his breath.

His baby. Sweet...

His mind sluggishly wrapped around his biggest problem yet. He hadn't seen a note in the paraphernalia Faith had emptied from the diaper bag.

"What's your name, little darlin'?"

Her arms laden with the second twin and trying to balance two warm bottles, Faith froze in the doorway, her gaze checked on the large man with the tiny infant enfolded in his muscular arms.

He'd spoken aloud. And he was right.

How was he supposed to deal with *that* issue? He could hardly care for the twins without names. Susie wasn't answering her phone and there didn't appear to be a note anywhere.

She shook her head and scoffed softly. This whole thing was messed up on so many levels that she couldn't even begin to catalog them. It was surreal.

They couldn't continue to refer to the two babies as *your baby* and *my baby* based on which infant they were holding, first because they were both his children and second because Faith would be leaving soon, or at least as soon as they could find someone else to assist him. There was no question that he'd need round-the-clock help, at least for the first few days.

Jax pulled out his phone and from the expression on his face, she could tell that he'd dialed Susie once again, but of course the senseless woman wasn't answering. Not that Faith expected her to. What woman in her right mind would drop her babies on someone's front step, even if that someone was the unsuspecting father? She was clearly immature and running away from her responsibilities. It was highly unlikely she'd offer Jax any kind of assistance now.

Faith coughed to let Jax know she was standing there, but he didn't acknowledge her. He didn't even look up. He was entirely focused on the baby in his arms.

He seemed to notice her only when she entered the living room and sat down on the couch across from his easy chair. She handed him a bottle and smiled encouragingly. With more actions than words, she showed him how to hold and angle the bottle for the precious little one in his arms. The baby took right to it, although Jax appeared a little self-conscious.

She leaned back into the middle cushion of the plush chocolate-colored couch and encouraged her baby—or rather, not *her* baby, but the infant she was holding—to root for the bottle. She was as hungry as her sister, and in moments the room was silent except for the sound of contented gurgling.

"I've got so many problems I don't know where to start. For one thing, I can't tell them apart," Jax admitted, his lips tightening into a thin, straight line. "And even if I could, Susie didn't leave a note to tell me what to call them. She could have at least pinned a name on them or something."

Faith looked from one baby to the other. Jax was right. The children looked exactly the same, from their scrunched-up expressions as they held the bottles to their chocolate-brown eyes. They were even dressed alike.

"You're right," she agreed. "That's a complication, but we'll figure it out. We don't know if they are identical or fraternal twins, but at this point in the game they are unquestionably going to be hard to tell one from the other. We need to look for some kind of defining features, something that sets the two apart."

He frowned and studied the infant in his arms, who was noisily enjoying her late lunch. "Like what?"

"I don't know. Let's compare. They both have the same thick tufts of brown hair."

Just like their daddy.

"Your baby's hair seems slightly curlier, but that could change after they've had a bath."

Jax's face paled and he made a choking sound. "A bath?"

She chuckled at his insecurity. He seemed like a take-charge kind of man, and yet a baby—two babies—left him helpless. It would be kind of cute, were it not so serious.

"With water," she teased. "Don't worry, we'll get there. I'm sure somebody can show you how it's done. Your mom has probably given babies a bath or two in her time."

"No doubt," he said, the corner of his mouth stretching up. "And I imagine my brothers and I were more trouble than these little girls are going to be."

Faith chuckled, imagining three rough-and-tumble boys in the bathtub. Jax's mother must have had a stern hand to have kept them in line.

"Maybe one of them has a birthmark," he suggested, bringing Faith's mind back to the present.

"How about dimples?" She'd known identical twins in high school, and that was how she'd been able to tell them apart, especially at first.

"Great idea. My baby has them. Both cheeks and a big one on her little chin."

"There you go, then." She nodded toward the baby in her arms. "This little sweetheart doesn't."

"One problem solved." Jax groaned. "But being able to tell them apart isn't going to help me if I don't know their names. I can't believe Susie did this to them."

Faith's heart swelled into her throat, and she could barely breathe around it. He wasn't thinking of the inconvenience to himself as much as the well-being of his babies. As for Faith, she couldn't believe Jax's ex-wife could do that to *him*. Maybe it was a good thing this Susie character had decided to leave the sweet little babies with Jax. At least he was mature and responsible. He'd take care of them. A woman who'd just leave her helpless babies on a doorstep in the Texas heat didn't even deserve to be called a mother.

"Thing One and Thing Two?" She spoke blithely, hoping somehow to lighten his very heavy load.

The other corner of his lips rose like the first, but his expression still looked strained, especially around his scar. "That would be one solution."

"I'm sorry, I really shouldn't be making so light of it," Faith continued. "It's pretty heavy stuff. I'm still trying to wrap my mind around Susie's actions. I can't believe a mother would up and abandon the babies the way she did. You have so little to go on, and it's not just baby supplies that you're lacking. You don't have a clue about what names might be on their birth certificates."

Jax scowled. "I don't even know if *I'm* listed on the birth certificates."

Probably not.

Given the circumstances, Faith doubted the woman would have officially acknowledged Jax's paternity until it suited her purposes, but she didn't tell him so. "You'll have to investigate that. I'm sure there are legal ways you can establish your paternity, whether your name is listed on the birth certificate or not. But in the meantime, I suggest you come up with nicknames for your daughters. You have to call them something."

The crease between his eyes deepened. "Like what?"

She shrugged. "I don't know. You could use family names. Maybe your grandmothers'?"

His jaw worked as he thought it over. "I like the idea of naming them after Granny Jane and Grandma Victoria, and if I'd had any say in it—on what went on their birth certificates—I might have suggested just those names. But if I name them Jane and Victoria, don't you think that might confuse them later when they realize the names on their birth certificates don't match what I've always called them?"

That was true enough. She nodded.

"I can probably explain a nickname as just a pet name I came up with, though that's not a conversation I ever want to have to have. I can't believe this. It's imperative that I speak to Susie again, and the sooner, the better. I'm sure that's why she's not picking up her phone. She's going to avoid me for as long as possible."

He growled in frustration. The baby he was holding squeaked and flapped her arms in distress, and Jax softened his tone. "It's okay, sweetheart. Daddy's here."

Faith's heart welled again. Everything Jax did with the babies seemed to have that effect on her.

He cringed and sent her a pleading glance. "Help me out here, Faith. I want to think of something soft and feminine but I'm at a complete loss. Sweetheart and Little Darlin' just aren't going to cut it, and I'm just not good at stuff like this."

This was new territory for Faith as well, but she didn't say so.

"Flowers?" Faith suggested tentatively. "Or colors?"

"How do you mean?"

"Marigold and you could call her Mary?"

His brow creased. Given the angle of his scar, she couldn't tell if he was amused or cringing.

"Daffodil and we could call her Daffy?"

A chuckle rumbled through his chest.

It was amusement, then. He was a hard man to read. She'd have to remember what his smile looked like.

She admired someone who could laugh in the face of adversity, and Jax was taking this remarkably well. She suspected most people would have fallen completely apart.

Her, for example. She would have lost it and would have been useless to anyone. She knew she would have. Unlike Jax, who was working through the stress and holding himself together, Faith was more inclined toward outright panic.

Even though she hadn't known him for more than a handful of hours, she already perceived that the infants were blessed to have a father like Jax. It was clear he'd take good care of them. They were so sweet and delicate, and oh so vulnerable, but they had someone to protect them.

Jax.

And he was right. They did deserve graceful names

that befitted how precious and lovely they already were to him.

Suddenly an idea came to her. "Hey, I know. How about Rose and Violet?"

"Great idea. I like it." He sat back in the chair, and Faith could almost palpably feel relief rolling off his broad shoulders. "Flowers and colors. Really clever, Faith."

They shared a few minutes of silence, both attending to the needs of the twin in their arms. Faith's mind was spinning, organizing and prioritizing many of the details she was sure Jax had yet to consider. She didn't want to burden him further, but she couldn't even think about leaving until he'd made a few more decisions, and night was rapidly closing in.

"Do you have someone you can call to help you out tonight? A sister? Your mother?"

"No sisters, unfortunately. Only my two big-lug brothers. I do have a sister-in-law, Slade's wife, Laney, whom I could call in a pinch, I imagine. But I hate to burden her with this. She has a toddler of her own to care for, not to mention being about ready to pop with her next kid. Due in a couple of weeks, I think."

Faith chuckled. "Then you're right. Laney probably needs all the sleep she can get—though she might be able to stock you up on some baby supplies, if she's already got her nursery ready. And your mom?"

"Yes, maybe," he said, but he didn't sound too sure of himself. "She lives in the big ranch house we passed on our way in. She's all alone up there, and she definitely knows everything there is to know about baby care. It's just that—" He paused and shook his head.

Faith transferred her baby—little *Rose*—to her shoulder and gently patted the bubbles out while she waited for Jax to finish his sentence.

"My dad died about a year ago and she hasn't been the same since."

"Oh, that's too bad. I'm so sorry for your loss. How long were they together?"

"Forty-eight years."

Faith's breath escaped in a low gasp. "I can't imagine how difficult that must be for her."

Jax nodded. "She used to be bubbly and upbeat, the first in line at social events." Mimicking Faith's movements, he brought Violet to his shoulder and tapped lightly on her back. "But since Dad passed away, she's mostly just kept to herself. I hate to burden her with—"

"Her granddaughters?" Faith finished for him. Excitement welled in her chest as the idea expanded. "Jax, this might be a blessing in disguise. I—I mean, more than just that you've discovered you have two lovely infants," she stammered. "That's a blessing in itself, of course. But these precious babies might be just what your mother needs—a reason to hope and a way to feel like she matters again."

"She matters to my brothers and me."

"Yes, but you're grown men now with lives of your own. You don't need her the ways a baby would. Much less *two* babies."

"You know what? I see your point. She brightens up every time she holds her little grandson, Brody. I'll call her and see what she thinks."

Not having anywhere else to put her, Faith laid the now-sleeping Rose back into her car seat and took Violet from Jax's arms. "I'll rock Violet to sleep. You call your mom."

He flashed her a grateful half smile and reached for his phone. From what Faith gleaned from Jax's side of the conversation, his mother was in turn angry and then exhilarated. Pretty much the emotions they'd all experienced today.

"She's on her way," he said after he ended the call. "I haven't heard that kind of energy in her voice since—well, it's been a long time. I think you're right about this being a blessing for her. I'll tell you one thing, though. I sure wouldn't want to be Susie if my mom gets a hold of her. I've never heard her so angry."

"I imagine she'll have to stand in line where Susie is concerned."

"Isn't that the truth?"

Faith was glad for Jax that he had people who loved him enough to defend him, but it made her ache with loneliness. Mostly she was fine on her own, but there were moments where being alone segued into being *lonely*, and that was not the same thing at all.

This was one of those moments.

"I'm sorry I didn't have the chance to show you my horses today. That was the whole reason you came over, and then you got pulled into this drama. I really apologize for this. I was looking forward to showing off some of my training methods."

"It's not necessary to apologize. I'm glad I could be here for you. And I can see your horses and your training methods another time," she assured him. "You have far more important things to do right now than worry about my interests. That said, since your mom is on her way, I think I'll just skip out for now."

"But I drove you here."

"The community green isn't that far away, and I don't mind the walk."

"I'd really like to introduce you to my mother."

"I'd enjoy that, as well. But not today, I don't think.

Grandma is going to want to focus all her attention on loving up your babies. I'd just be in the way."

Jax started to protest but Faith held up her hand.

It was time for her to make her exit, to let the new family adjust to being together.

And Faith? She would go home to an empty house.

Chapter Three

Jax was still marveling at the way his mother's countenance had sparked upon seeing her grandbabies. Faith had been right on every count. His mom had burst on the scene in a flurry of motion and energy the likes of which he hadn't seen in the past year, and had promptly taken over, calling a family meeting to inform everyone about the afternoon's events.

Though Jax was close to his brothers, it wouldn't have occurred to him to bring his whole family up to speed on the situation on the very first night. He trusted that his mom knew exactly what she was doing, and she had.

Not only that, she knew everything that the babies needed, and the when and how and why. She'd mentioned something about a schedule but Jax didn't see any real pattern to the babies' activities. Jax was picturing spreadsheets, but he was fairly certain he was off on that point.

His mother had sent Slade to fetch a bassinet from her spare room—the same one she'd used with Jax and his brothers when they were infants. He was grateful beyond all measure that Mom was too sentimental to throw those old baby things away, or he might have been in real trouble trying to find the twins a place to sleep.

Not that they slept much. Jax spent the weekend at his mother's house so she could share in caring for the infants, but he still felt as if he spent most of his time pacing up and down the hallway trying to comfort one baby or the other.

Monday morning he and his mother visited Emerson's Hardware and Sam's Grocery for infant paraphernalia. Jax was quickly learning that babies required a *lot* of stuff.

Cribs, a stroller, a changing table and a little plastic tub that fit in the kitchen sink so he could give his children baths. Then there were the clothes—the part about which his mother was most excited. Pink, pink and more pink. Ruffles and bows galore.

And as if that weren't enough, there were the recurring needs—diapers, wipes and formula. Baby powder and baby shampoo. Jax's pocketbook was taking almost as much of a hit as his heart was.

But he'd been visited by several friends and neighbors who'd heard about his dilemma through Jo. He was grateful for their donations of baby items and even more for their emotional and spiritual support.

There was still no word from Susie, despite the fact that he'd left her countless messages. He was beginning to wonder if she was even more unstable than he'd originally believed her to be. Even before she'd abandoned her own children, her lifestyle had been less than stellar, which concerned Jax in regard to the health of his girls. One of his first stops on Monday had been to Dr. Delia. Thankfully, the twins appeared to be well and thriving.

If Susie *had* disappeared for good, Jax was legally at ground zero. He didn't even know where the babies had been born, never mind what hospital. It would take him some serious digging to find what he needed to lay claim to his children.

Even with the added hassle, he was beginning to believe it was just as well that Susie was gone. The fact that she had clearly abandoned the girls would help him in court, if it came to that. Now that he knew about his little darlin's, there was no way he would give up his custody of them, even if he had to fight Susie tooth and nail every step of the way. His daughters needed the kind of love and stability Susie clearly couldn't offer them right now. Even feeling as queasy-in-the-stomach overwhelmed as he did right now, he knew that with his family's help, he could provide everything his children needed.

Somehow, Lord help him, he would.

After setting up the cribs in his spare room that had been hastily converted into a nursery, his mom offered— no, *insisted*—that he take a break and go visit Faith. Jax and his mom had used caring for the babies together to mend some of the emotional stitching that had unraveled when his father had died and then when he'd had his accident.

They'd grown apart and Jax hadn't even realized it. It was only when they were speaking again that he realized how much he'd missed talking to his mom.

He'd told her how much he'd enjoyed the picnic with Faith, and a mischievous gleam immediately appeared in her eyes. And then she'd practically pushed him out the door, assuring him she had everything under control and he should get out and enjoy the sunshine.

Right. The sunshine.

Nothing would come of her overt attempt at matchmaking, but it was nice to see her smiling again. Besides, he owed Faith his time and labor. She had purchased him at the auction, after all, and for far more money than he was worth.

Jax knew the Dennys' spread hadn't been kept up over the past couple of years, but he never imagined the sorry state of the ranch he encountered as he drove up and parked in front of Faith's new home. Rotted shutters hung half off the hinges, and the screens covering the windows were torn through. It looked as though some animal or another had made use of the ranch house while the Dennys were elsewhere. The house needed a fresh coat of paint and new shingles on the roof. The wraparound deck was weather-worn and needed varnishing, and the flower beds in front were overgrown with weeds.

And that was to say nothing of the outbuildings and land around the house. He guessed the barn must have been red once, but now it was a muted orange color. The fences that were supposed to contain the corral and what he could see of the pasture land were in dire need of repair. The hay field was so overgrown it would take a season, maybe two, to set it right, and that was assuming Faith owned the appropriate farm equipment, which he highly doubted.

He wasn't even sure she had the right shoes.

It took him less than a minute of perusal before he knew that, on his own, his labor wouldn't be nearly enough for Faith to get this place into shape as quickly as she wanted. A community workday might be in order, and soon. She'd soon find her neighbors in Serendipity were generous with their time and talents.

One thing was certain—the property was in no way ready to host horses, especially wild ones.

He approached the front door, careful to avoid the rickety step, and rang the bell. When that yielded nothing, he knocked twice. When she still didn't answer, he decided to have a better look around the place. Faith's enormous, beat-up black SUV was parked in front of the house, so presumably she was around here somewhere. Searching for her was the perfect excuse—er—*opportunity* to take a closer look at the barn and surrounding countryside.

Get the lay of the land, so to speak.

Babies might not need spreadsheets, but it looked as if Faith's ranch was going to take a lot of them. This was a huge, huge project. He suspected she had no idea how big.

It didn't take him long to locate Faith. He called her name as he circled the barn, and she popped her head up from behind a wall of hay bales. She'd tied her platinum-blond hair into a loose bun held together with what looked like a pencil. Wisps had broken free to frame her exertion-reddened face. She wiped her elbow across her brow and smiled.

"What are you doing here?" Her question might have sounded abrupt but instead held a tone of pleasant surprise.

He saluted sloppily. "Jax McKenna, reporting for duty, ma'am."

She shook her head. "Oh. I wasn't expecting you. You don't have to do this, you know."

Having seen the state of her ranch, he had to disagree. "I think I do."

"There's no need to feel obligated. I'm sure you're up to your ears caring for your twins." She absently brushed hay strands from her jeans. "How are they, by the way?"

"Active," he answered. "Noisy. Up at all hours. Adorable. Perfect. And you were right about Mom—she's gone nuts over them. This is the happiest I've seen her since before Dad got sick."

"I'm glad," she replied, sincerity beaming out of her warm smile. "So why are you here, instead of home with them?"

"I owe you." Did she think he was the kind of man to renege on his debts?

Her gaze widened on him and Jax swallowed hard, struck by the sparkle gleaming in her hazel eyes. They were a beautiful, swirling mixture of green and gold that he found quite captivating.

"Oh, that." She waved him away with a sweep of her hand. "I hereby absolve you of all your obligations inherent in offering yourself up for auction. Go live your life. Enjoy your babies. Be free."

She wasn't making this easy.

Go live his life? What life?

Until Faith and the twins had suddenly entered his life two days ago, he hadn't even realized that he hadn't been living—just going through the motions. He couldn't do that anymore.

He didn't want to.

He *owed* her, and not just because she had bought him at that silly auction.

Besides, she needed him, whether she was willing to admit it or not. And probably far more than she realized, if the state of her property was anything to go by.

"What are you doing?" he asked, ignoring the absolution of his commitment.

"Moving hay bales around. The guy who delivered them this morning dumped them right in the middle of my driveway and took off without a word. I've been hauling them one by one to the side of the barn. Hay bales are heavier than they look, by the way."

Jax chuckled. Toting hay bales wasn't much of a challenge for him. He could tote them two at a time and not even break a sweat, but then he was twice her size and had been doing it all of his life.

And why was she worrying about hay, anyway? Horses were a long time off, weren't they? First things first. Her house was falling down around her, and she was out here performing unnecessary manual labor?

"You could have called me."

She shook her head. "No. I can do this myself."

He lifted a brow. She was nothing if not stubborn. But he couldn't fault her for that. It took a tough person to handle life on a ranch. He wasn't convinced she was that person, but she certainly showed gumption.

"Can you give me a hand with the tarp?" She pressed one side of an olivegreen tarp into his hands, and he helped her unfold it. Together they parachuted it over the top of the stack of hay.

"What are you pegging it down with?" he asked, scanning the ground for tent pegs and a mallet.

"Pegs?" Her brows lowered, crinkling over her nose. "Right. To keep the tarp from blowing away. I should have thought of that. I—" She stalled, dropping her gaze. "I don't know what I'll be using."

Of course she didn't. Now why wasn't Jax surprised? If ever he'd known someone completely unprepared for the challenges facing her, it was Faith Dugan. Initiative and good intentions could take a person only so far.

"I found the old tarp in a corner of the barn," she explained. "Maybe there are some pegs there, as well."

"Hold on a sec. I'll go look." Jax jogged into the barn, figuring he'd have a better chance of finding something that would work for the tarp, especially if they had to improvise.

He couldn't find any tent pegs, but he did locate some large nails that were long enough and thick enough to do the task. He grabbed a handful of them, along with a rusty old hammer that was hanging on the tool wall.

When he returned to Faith, she was standing with her back against the wall of hay, a distant gleam in her gaze. She looked tired, and for the first time he noticed the dark circles under her eyes.

She brightened when she saw what Jax was carrying.

"I know I must seem woefully ill-equipped to you," she admitted as Jax went to work nailing down the tarp. "It's a slow process, but I've been making a list of everything I'll be needing to keep the ranch running. I'll add pegs to the list, and maybe even an extra tarp or two."

That must be some list.

Jax fought against the smile that crept up the right side of his lips.

"So if you see anything you think I ought to add," she continued, obviously not seeing Jax's expression, "please speak up."

If it were anyone but Faith, he *would* have spoken. He would have told her how crazy her whole scheme was and how she should turn around and go back to wherever home was. He would have told her flat out how he doubted her ability to turn the falling-down-around-her house and equally scrappy outbuildings and land into a working ranch. Unless she was independently wealthy, she'd have money issues to add to what must already be multiple quandaries. Running a rescue operation on her own would be a challenge even on a tip-top ranch. Setting up her sanctuary while keeping the place from falling apart was a heavier load than any one person should be able to manage.

But Faith?

She was so—*so* earnest. She was obviously trying hard to make it work, and she wasn't about to take no for an answer. He didn't think she'd listen to him even if he did list all the reasons her plans would not work. She appeared dauntless, despite the mountains she was looking to scale. She didn't see the process as much as the end product.

Her dreams were real to her.

Vibrant.

And completely outrageous.

In some ways he envied her that outlook. He saw things in black-and-white. Mostly black. Definitely no pink—at least until his daughters had shown up in his life.

Either Faith didn't see the problems she was facing or she was making a conscious choice to ignore them. Of course, a rainbows-and-unicorns attitude would take her only so far. Eventually, she'd figure out that her operation was far too grand a scale for one woman. But he decided he wasn't going to be the one to bust her bubble. Not today.

"My first two horses are arriving right away," she informed him brightly as she tugged one of the ends of the tarp so he could nail it down.

Jax's hand slipped, and he slammed the hammer into his thumb. He yelped in pain and shook his hand in the air, then stuck it in his mouth to nurse it.

In an instant, Faith was crouched by his side, pulling her hand into hers. She examined him closely and murmured sweet nothings.

Jax was muttering, too. Something else.

"I'm fine," he insisted, snatching his hand out of her grip. His thumb was throbbing, and all he could think about was how soft and supple her palms and fingers were and how it was a shame ranch work would ruin them. Something was really messed up about that.

"At least let me get a bandage for you."

He uttered a sound that was half a laugh, half a scoff. "I don't need a bandage, Faith. Nothing's broken. The hammer didn't even pierce the skin."

Her expression fell, and only then did he realize she was offering a bandage because she wanted to do something for him. Because she felt sorry for him.

He hated it when that happened. Pity was the worst, even if it was over something as stupid as him being careless with a hammer and slamming it on his lousy thumb. He barely restrained himself from growling in frustration.

"I'm *fine*," he said again and then figured he'd better distract her before she ended up threatening to put his whole arm in a sling. "What's next after the hay?"

If she said *horses*, he was going to burst something.

"First things first. I need to fill the troughs with water from the pump."

He gaped at her but she didn't notice.

Did she realize how many trips it would take to fill a large trough with buckets of water from the pump? And that was to say nothing about the strain of doing all that pumping or hauling heavy buckets of water.

He sighed. This was going to be a long afternoon.

But apparently she was just getting warmed up.

"I figure I'll put hay down and hang an oat mixture in a bucket in the corral and then leave the gate to the front pasture open for easy access. I know the horses will need plenty of room to run, especially since they'll have been cooped up in a trailer for so long by the time they arrive here."

She pointed to the gate that led to a small meadow. Her plan would work in theory, if it wasn't for the terrible condition of the fences. The fence next to the road was in the worst shape. Wooden beams had been knocked about and some of the poles were completely unearthed.

Repairing that part alone would be a lot of work, but she could take her time with that—if she'd given herself time. The land wasn't going anywhere and neither were the fences. The problem was, there wasn't any time and there were a lot of fences. If the ones closest to the house were in this bad of condition, he dreaded to see what the rest of the thousand acres looked like.

Faith was a smart woman—she'd just never had to work

on a ranch in such poor condition before. She still didn't understand just how much effort it would take to fix up this dump. She'd no doubt soon realize that his help alone would be nowhere near enough, even if he continued to help her, and at this point, he couldn't see how he could *not*. It wasn't in him to walk away from a lady in distress, even if the woman in question had bitten off far more than she could ever chew.

She'd said that she didn't have the money to hire any help, but he'd say she needed two wranglers at least. Worse, even if she had the funds, she might discover it was difficult to find a wrangler willing to work a horse farm—especially a sanctuary with wild horses. Serendipity was cattle country. Jax was one of the few who raised horses, and he trained his herd for cattle ranching.

Unlike many areas, the ranchers around Serendipity didn't necessarily object to horse farms. They just knew cattle. A wild-horse refuge? Some would believe it was a sad waste of good grazing land. There might be some resentment, although Jax hoped her neighbors would be better people than that.

Maybe she could find a teenager willing to do some work for her after school and on weekends. A youth working part-time wouldn't charge as much as a full-time professional wrangler. He had a couple of girls in mind who were especially good with horses. Before he brought his idea up to Faith, he decided he'd speak to the girls and their families to see if they were interested.

It would have to be soon, if Faith had horses coming in immediately.

"You're planning to fix the house up before you get too busy bringing in too many horses, right?"

He hadn't even seen the inside of the place, but based on everything else he'd viewed so far, he imagined it would be far from livable. "Are you staying at the Howells' Bed-and-Breakfast until you're ready to move in?"

It was a reasonable guess, seeing as there was no hotel in Serendipity. The Howells' B and B was the one and only place for guests in town to stay.

"Oh, I'm already moved into the house." She waved a hand as if to dismiss the thought. "I brought everything I needed to live on in my SUV."

He'd been thinking about the condition of the house itself, but moving her belongings was yet another hurdle to jump. She couldn't possibly have fit everything she owned into her SUV, even if it was one of the bigger models. What about her furniture? Dishes? Sheets and towels?

A toothbrush?

There might be a functional appliance or two inside the house, but Jax doubted Faith had found much in working condition. He imagined it would take weeks to put together anything remotely livable.

If she hadn't hired a moving company yet, he'd probably have to help her with that, as well. There was no way she would be able to move big furniture on her own, and even if she could, he wouldn't let her. He supposed he could always get his brothers to help with that. Their thick muscles were good for something, even if their thick heads were not.

"So you have the rest of your stuff left in storage somewhere?"

"Oh, no. I sold or gave away everything I wasn't bringing with me. I've got everything I need. I towed a horse trailer in with me. It's old and not pretty to look at, but it's reliable."

That was better. Not ideal, but better. He wouldn't have thought of moving his belongings in a horse trailer, but whatever worked for her. "I see. So you brought your furniture in your horse trailer, then. How bad is the interior of the house?"

She gazed at him as if he'd just grown a horn in the middle of his forehead. It wasn't as if he'd asked her to explain the theory of relativity—just how she planned to live in a house that raccoons and field mice probably rejected.

"Of course not. Why would I bring furniture in a horse trailer? That was for all my horsey stuff."

Horsey stuff?

It was all Jax could do not to burst out laughing, or smack his palm against his forehead or both. This woman had clearly tied her good sense to the top of her SUV on her way down to Texas and it had come loose from its binding and bounced off to the side of the road. On second thought, since no sane person would have bought this run-down ranch in the first place, maybe her good sense was something she'd lost a long time ago.

And didn't it just figure that *he'd* be the one to get caught up in this totally implausible and thoroughly ridiculous project?

As if he didn't have enough *totally implausible* drama brewing in his own house.

Had he stepped into some nutty alternate universe where everyday life was upside down and backward?

She hadn't really answered his question about the condition of the interior of her house. He was afraid to ask again, but he did it anyway.

"So you're—what? Camping out in your living room?"

Her smile was so fast and genuine that he found himself almost completely drawn into it.

"Pretty much. The Dennys left some furniture. It's not anywhere close to new condition, but I don't need much. I brought my sleeping bag, and the old couch is comfortable enough for now. There's no air conditioner, so it gets pretty hot in the daytime, but I'm outside most of the time anyway, so that won't matter. I open windows at night. I have plenty of food in the pantry. God is good. I have no complaints."

Maybe *she* didn't, but he did.

"Nevertheless, don't you think we ought to start by repairing the house?" It wasn't a suggestion, it was a rhetorical question, but Faith apparently interpreted it as if he were asking.

"Oh, my. No," she exclaimed, waving her hands in a dismissive motion. "I don't have time to worry about myself. My living conditions are just fine. I need your help to fix the front pasture." Her teeth nipped out and grabbed her bottom lip again as she thoughtfully surveyed the meadow in question. "I think we can lodge the horses in that field until I have enough time and resources to repair the other fences. I know the hay field is a disaster and I'll need to rotate the herd so they can graze, but one step at a time, right?"

Horses? Herd?

Jax felt as if he was tripping over those *steps* she mentioned.

"I can help mend fences," he offered cautiously. "But you're right. The perimeter is going to take a while to fully secure, not to mention the fences between pastures. The Dennys didn't happen to leave you a swather for the hay field, did they? It's severely overgrown. You should take care of that soon—you know, in all that free time you'll have because this place will be so easy to fix up."

He was teasing.

Kind of.

Her gaze widened in alarm, but when he curved his mouth up, she chuckled. "I thought you meant it needed to happen right now. Today."

"I'm sure we can borrow a swather from one of your neighbors when the time comes. Not today."

She nodded. "And the fence? How fast do you think you can help me fix the loose beams in the front meadow? I know I'm asking a lot out of you, but is there any possible way you can take care of it today?"

"Today?" he repeated, his voice tightening. He'd come over to see how she was settling in. She hadn't even been expecting him. And now she thought he was somehow going to be able to mend her impossibly unfixable property in a single afternoon? Did she realize how labor intensive fence-mending was? And what would she have done if he hadn't shown up? Tried to handle it all herself? "Faith, you can't just—"

"But it's important," she interrupted. Red splashed across her cheeks. "You see, I've got a mare and her foal coming in this afternoon."

"This afternoon?" he roared, caught completely by surprise. When she'd said she was expecting horses to arrive right away, he thought she meant this month, or this week.

Not *today.*

Her eyes widened epically, and he realized he'd hurt her feelings, maybe even scared her. He took a mental step backward, lifted his hat by the crown and ran a hand through his hair.

"Look," he said, carefully modulating both the tenor and the tone of his voice. "I understand how important this is to you."

"Do you?" She folded her arms in a defensive gesture and narrowed her gaze on him. "Do you really? Because honestly, that's not what I'm getting from you."

He frowned and settled his hat back on his head. "Is that right?"

"Yes. I'm getting more of a grizzly-with-a-thorn-stuck-in-his-paw vibe. So if that's all you have to offer, then thank you, but I'd rather figure this out on my own." She was looking toward him but yet not really looking *at* him, her gaze just slightly averted.

Jax cringed. For a moment he'd thought Faith might be different. That she might be able to look beyond his scarred face to the man within. There had been a few minutes at the picnic when he'd thought they'd shared something, if not special, then at least normal.

But at the end of the day, she called it as she saw it— saw *him*.

A grizzly.

"If that's what you want," he muttered.

Even as he said the words, he knew he couldn't just walk away from Faith and leave her to do it all on her own. At the very least, there were plenty of fences to be mended, over many acres of land. He could do the work somewhere far away from the house and she wouldn't even have to know he'd been there.

If she didn't want him on her property, he wouldn't be able to fix up her house for her, at least not directly. But he would find others who could, people he trusted to do their best work and give her a good deal for it.

"Go." She choked out the word and pointed at his truck. "Just go."

"Yeah. Okay." He nodded and tipped his hat, conceding as graciously as he knew how. His gut tightened painfully but he ignored it. "Best wishes to you with your hobby horses."

Hobby horses.

Hobby horses? Had he just referred to her future mustang rescue as a *hobby*?

"Jax."

He was halfway to his truck and didn't even bother to acknowledge her.

"Jax," she said again, her tone urgent as she hurried to catch up with him.

How rude of him to outright ignore her. Hadn't his mother taught him manners? She grabbed his elbow and yanked him around to face her.

"How dare you make fun of my work!"

He blew out a breath, ran a hand across his jaw and then lifted his hat and threaded his fingers through his thick dark brown curls.

"Look. That probably came out all wrong."

"Ya think?"

He held up a hand in surrender. "I didn't mean to insult you."

"Well, you—you—" she stammered. Tears welled in her eyes, and she dashed them away with the back of her hand.

Why, oh why did she have to cry when she got angry? The wetness gleaming in her eyes probably just reinforced everything Jax was already thinking about her—that she was a fragile, foolish woman who bawled at the drop of a hat and couldn't possibly be successful running any kind of ranch, much less a wild-horse refuge.

When she finally dared to glance up at him, she didn't find judgment or censure in the chocolate depths of his eyes.

He looked as uncomfortable as all get-out and downright flustered.

Now, what did he have to be anxious about? She was the one who'd apparently planned herself into a corner—or rather, failed to plan enough for these early stages when there was so much that needed to be done.

Whatever it was, Jax wasn't taking her seriously. And that was a problem.

Fences or no fences, those horses would arrive in the space of a couple of hours, and she needed to be as prepared as possible for them. She'd thought she'd be further along. She was willing to admit it was taking her longer to perform what she'd expected to be simple ranch chores—chores she'd performed hundreds of times when she'd worked on ranches before. She hadn't allowed for the extra time it would take when she was working with rundown or missing equipment and no extra sets of hands. If she'd made mistakes—and she privately admitted she had—she would work it out.

She had to.

What she *didn't* have time for was to deal with this giant of a cowboy making fun of her and her work.

"Don't cry," he murmured, reaching out for her and then awkwardly dropping his arms again. "Please. I really didn't mean to—"

"I'm not crying," she snapped, dashing the wetness from her cheeks.

Stupid tears.

A muscle in the corner of his jaw ticked as his gaze followed the path of her hand. Clearly, he wasn't convinced. And why should he be?

He didn't believe anything about her—not that she was happy living simply for the time being while she funneled all her time and resources into her horses, or even that she was capable of running this rescue at all.

Maybe he was right.

The niggling doubt that haunted her late at night when she couldn't sleep worked its way into her chest, pressing into her lungs and making it difficult for her to breathe. Adrenaline coursed through her, the fight-or-flight instinct that challenged her to run away from the difficult and unknown.

She chose Door #1. She would fight. She would not run. She would do this thing, and no cowboy—or a whole herd of them—was going to convince her otherwise.

She was just barely managing to tamp her hidden anxieties back into the recesses of her mind when a shiny new red truck pulled into her driveway, hauling an incongruently beat-up two-horse trailer.

Oh, no.

Panic revved Faith's pulse even more, charging it into overdrive, and heat flushed her face.

They were here. Her first rescue horses were here.

She had Alban, her riding horse, already stabled. These were her mustangs. Wild and untamed and Faith planned to let them stay that way.

Marta Stevens from the Mustang Mission in Wyoming waved out the window and then pulled her truck around, slowly backing the trailer toward the side corral gate.

Faith had thought she would have a bigger window of time before Marta arrived. Two hours wouldn't have been enough, of course, as Jax had so handily pointed out. But—

"Your horses, I presume?"

Faith expected Jax's voice to be laced with sarcasm, but surprisingly, it wasn't. Not too much, anyway. Mostly, he sounded only vaguely amused and very tired.

Of course he was tired. What was he even doing here with her? She felt suddenly guilty that she was asking him to spend his day mending fences for her. Why he was helping her out when he'd no doubt spent the weekend getting to know his twins was beyond her comprehension. He must be exhausted beyond belief, and yet here he was.

With her. And her horses.

"You ready?" he asked, leaning an elbow against the corral fence.

All she could do was nod. Words escaped her. There

was no way to describe what she was feeling right now. She was so excited she thought her heart might burst. She'd dreamed of this day for so long that it hardly felt real. Her whole life culminated in this moment.

Past, present and future converged.

Her feet were frozen to the spot, and she was unable even to breathe. She should probably be doing—something. She wasn't sure what.

Jax watched her, his gaze unreadable. "Give me a second, will you?"

He stepped to the side and fished his cell phone out of its holder. She assumed he was checking on his twins.

She shifted her attention to the trailer, and she surveyed the corral with a critical eye. There were a couple of loose beams, but it wasn't as bad as it might have been. If a horse wanted to get out, it would. No question. But there was at least the hint of containment. Faith prayed that would be enough.

"How are they?" she asked as Jax returned to her side.

"What? Who?"

She raised her eyebrows. "Why, Rose and Violet, of course. Who did you think I was talking about?"

He chuckled. "Oh, yeah. Right. My mom is having the time of her life with them. They're doing great. But she's not the only one I called. My brothers, Slade and Nick, are on their way over to work on your fences for you."

"They are?" Her throat tightened with emotion. Jax didn't have to be here today, and he could have driven off without a word. After all, she'd ordered him to do so.

Instead, he was calling in reinforcements. She'd never be able to aptly express her gratitude, much less repay him for his kindness.

"I'll take care of the fences around the front pasture," he said. "Between the three of us we ought to be able to get it in working order within a couple of hours. Not perfect, mind you, but serviceable for the moment."

Faith sent up a silent prayer of appreciation.

"But the horses are already here. I'm sure they aren't comfortable in the trailer." If she could hear the discouragement in her tone, she was positive he did. After all, she was pretty much admitting she was everything he thought she was.

Flighty. Foolish. Unprepared.

"Yes, the horses are here," was all he said. He shoved his hands into the front pockets of his jeans and rocked back on his heels. He glanced down at her expectantly.

As if she knew what to do and he was just waiting for her to do—whatever. But she *didn't* know what to do.

Was he *smiling*?

She couldn't quite be positive because of the scar, but still. His expression was both annoying and unfair.

Annoying, because he knew more than she ever would about raising horses and he knew it, and unfair because—because of the butterflies his hint of a grin sent whirling through her stomach, made more intriguing by the mystery inherent in his smile.

"Marta must have made exceptionally good time. She wasn't supposed to be here for a couple of hours yet," she said with a defensive tilt of her chin.

"And yet, here they are."

She narrowed her gaze on him and he chuckled.

Marta hopped out of the red truck's cab and rushed toward Faith, laughing and enveloping her in an animated hug, nearly knocking both of them off their feet in her enthusiasm.

"Your first horses," Marta exclaimed, continuing to hug the stuffing out of Faith. "Trust me, you'll remember this day for the rest of your life."

"I'll say," Jax said under his breath, a low rumble emerging from his chest.

Faith rolled her eyes at him. "Marta, this is Jax. Jax, this is Marta from Mustang Mission in Wyoming."

Jax extended his hand, but Marta was slow to respond, staring at Jax's scar. Jax uncompromisingly met her gaze, and she winced and quickly averted her eyes.

His shoulders tightened and his brown eyes flashed with anguish as he dropped his arm to his side. Faith glimpsed one second of the depth of the pain he was experiencing and then it was gone, hardening along with the line of his lips. Clearly this wasn't the first time someone had been taken aback by his injury.

Personally, Faith didn't get it. The scars showed that he was strong—a survivor. How was that a bad thing? And anyway, a man was made by his heart, not his face, and from what she knew of Jax, he was pure gold. She'd never been the type of person who averted her gaze from someone with an injury or disability. Jax might look like a bear of a man, but he had feelings, too, even if he kept them well under wraps.

"I can't wait for you to meet my horses," Faith said a little too brightly, desperate to distract him. "The mama is Willow and her colt is Pilgrim."

Jax turned his attention to Faith, allowing her to drag him to the rear of the trailer. He unlatched the hook and carefully opened the doors to reveal a bay-and-white pinto mare and her nearly identical offspring.

The skittish colt bucked his back legs and tossed his head. When he turned to look at her, Faith was startled to find he had one brown eye and one blue. How beautiful and rare he was. Her heart leaped into her throat, overflowing with the joy of discovery. Her first horses, and she'd managed to score a gorgeous, unique mustang beyond what she could ever have imagined. How blessed she was.

Her joy quickly muted when she caught sight of the mare's stark condition. Her entire rib cage was as visible as a xylophone, and her flanks poked nearly out of the skin. The poor thing had very little flesh on her bones at all. Her coat was dull and patches of hair were falling out. It was a wonder she'd birthed a healthy foal at all in the shape she was in.

"Do you see?" she whispered, laying a hand on Jax's elbow. "Do you understand now?"

He looked down at her and nodded. "I see why you're rushing things. Do you mind?" He gestured toward the mare.

"Please."

Jax spoke to the horse in a low, rich, lyrical tone. The mare pricked up her ears. Faith thought she might spook as the colt had done, but she just shivered.

"Easy there, girl." Jax's voice held such a calming effect that even Faith felt soothed by the gentle vocal caress. "You don't want to upset your little one. It's all good. We're going to take care of you. No worries. You're home now."

Home.

Faith's chest was full to bursting. These horses were home, and they would benefit from every bit of her time and attention. With her help, Willow would regain the weight she'd lost and her coat would turn shiny and beautiful again. Her colt would grow up happy and free.

Free to live.

Free to run on Faith's thousand acres.

Free to flourish as wild horses should, with no man-made expectations or agenda.

It was only a few more minutes before Jax's brothers arrived. Slade perused the front meadow and made the same estimate Jax had—one or two hours of labor at the most. Tools in hand, he and Nick headed out to the fence line.

"I think we can unload the horses into the corral now," Jax said, unhooking the rope strung across the back of the trailer. "I'm sure they want to stretch their legs."

Faith agreed, but she was bumping up against her fear and her inexperience. Back in Wyoming, where she'd worked as a volunteer, she'd rarely dealt with the newly arrived horses—settling them in was left to the more experienced staff, who would be better prepared to deal with any problems. On top of that, Marta's trailer was an older model. It didn't have a side door to disembark the horses. It didn't even have a ramp in the back. She'd somehow have to convince the horses to back out of the trailer, and she wasn't even sure if they would take a halter.

There were so many things she didn't know. Embarrassment coursed through her. She cast her gaze downward, afraid Marta, or worse, Jax, would see the panic in her eyes. Her pulse was pounding so hard she thought they might be able to hear it.

She needed help but she didn't know how to ask for it.

How *did* one unload a wild mustang from an old trailer?

She glanced up and found Jax staring right at her, his gaze narrowed as if he was trying to figure her out.

Fat chance of that.

She was an enigma even to herself at times, now being one of them. She was at once as excited and as scared as she'd ever been in her life. She couldn't imagine the plethora of expressions that must be flittering across her face. It was no wonder Jax was staring.

Jax's eyes glittered as he opened the corral gate adjacent to the rear of the trailer, effectively creating one side of a chute.

Marta moved to the other side and widened her arms

to block off that path as best she could. Jax briefly caught Faith's gaze and tipped his head, encouraging her to do the same.

Faith held her breath as Jax strode up to the trailer, his voice and his steps slow, even and confident. She marveled at his rich, melodious tone. She didn't think she would ever get tired of hearing Jax speak, at least to the horses.

The mare tensed when he laid a gentle hand on her flank, but she didn't buck or try to bolt. Jax took his time, talking, talking and talking some more as he slid his palm up her back and onto her neck.

He stopped for a moment and allowed her to get used to his presence and his scent. He wasn't in a hurry. He appeared perfectly at ease, intently attuned to the animal, communicating with words and without. It was a wondrous sight to behold, and it took Faith's breath away.

When Jo had said Jax was a genius with horses, she hadn't been kidding. Faith had never seen anything like it.

After another minute had passed, Jax slipped his arm under Willow's neck and pressed gently, urging the horse to step backward. Every time she balked or protested, every time her nostrils flared or her ears pinned back, Jax would stop and wait until she was once again calm and in tune with his own serenity. He displayed endless patience, coaxing Willow backward and chuckling when the foal nudged his thigh with his muzzle, impatient for it to be his turn for attention.

He backed the mare up until her rear legs were on solid ground. Willow shifted and tossed her head but Jax took it in stride, his melodic murmuring never ceasing.

"One more step, girl. You can do it. I know you can. And then you and your little one will be free to run."

If Faith didn't know better, she would have thought that the mare understood Jax's words, for in a moment more he had her off the trailer and into the corral with her colt right on her heels.

"Success," Marta cheered, closing the gate behind Faith, who had followed the horses in. "You've got a good one there, Faith."

"I know." She smiled at her friend and mentor. "I appreciate you bringing her out to me. I promise I'll take good care of her."

Marta laughed and nodded toward Jax, who was still by Willow's side, running his hands down her neck and head. "I meant *him*."

Heat rose to Faith's cheeks. "Oh."

Marta's chuckle turned into a full-blown laugh. She was right, though. Jax's way with horses was nothing short of extraordinary. She'd never seen anything like it. The Lord had truly guided her hand—or rather, her pocketbook—when she'd bid on Jax at the auction.

But she certainly didn't want Marta to get the wrong impression.

"Jax?" Faith tried to sound surprised. She waved off-handedly. "He—he's just helping me out today. Those are his brothers out there mending the fences."

Marta's green eyes gleamed at her. "Is he married?"

"What? No." And with what had just happened to the poor man on the home front, Faith doubted he'd be remotely interested in *that* particular institution in the near future.

Or ever again.

And neither, for that matter, was she.

But Marta already knew Faith's story, and Faith had no business discussing Jax's, so instead she just smiled and let Marta think whatever she wanted to.

"You've just brought me the true loves of my life," she

reminded her friend. "Willow and Pilgrim. I'm sure they're going to keep me plenty busy."

And Jax?

She didn't know what he was. Helpful, maybe. Useful, sometimes.

But mostly, he was a complication she simply didn't need in her life. And she'd keep telling herself that until she believed it.

Chapter Four

Jax yanked the last corner of a yellow fitted crib sheet over the mattress until it finally slipped into place. He grunted with satisfaction.

One crib down, one to go, and finally the twins would be able to graduate from the bassinet and into the cribs in their nursery. In the three weeks since they'd been dropped on his doorstep, Rose and Violet had flourished. They were already growing like nobody's business, and Jax couldn't be prouder.

From her view in a nearby bouncy chair, Rose babbled at him as if providing him with instructions, her chunky arms pumping in delight. Violet, whom Jax had quickly recognized as the quieter of the two twins, sucked on her tiny fist and stared at him with her wise brown eyes.

It was hard to believe that he ever had had trouble telling these two beautiful babies apart. Now he recognized both on sight and could tell one from the other as much by personality as by looks.

"You think so, huh?" he asked, addressing Rose. He chuckled. Look at him, talking to a newborn baby as if she could understand his words. As if he understood her replies.

In the most peculiar way, he kind of did. In the three weeks he'd had the children, he'd learned how to interpret their sounds and cries. He could differentiate between whether they were wet, needed a bottle or if their little tummies were hurting them.

Sometimes it was none of the above. Sometimes they were scared or lonely and just wanted to be held, and he was okay with that. He liked snuggle time. One cowboy and two babies didn't seem like much of a fair match, but he thought he was managing surprisingly well, all things considered, and even more surprising, enjoying every minute of it.

This was uncharted territory, after all.

Most folks had nine months to prepare for a newborn. He hadn't had a single second, which explained why he was just now completing the transition of his spare room into a nursery. His mother had decorated the place with pink frilly curtains and pink and white kittens on the wall. He drew the line at pink crib sheets and had chosen a more neutral yellow color.

A man could take only so much pink, after all.

Like Jax, Faith was treading new ground. He often thought about her out there all by herself with her horses. He still meant to find her a couple of teenage wranglers. It had been on his to-do list since day one, but he simply hadn't found time, what with taking care of the twins and all.

He'd been over to Faith's place a few times over the past weeks, not so much out of obligation as curiosity. She had officially released him from his commitment to her, so that wasn't a factor, and yet he kept finding reasons to go visit her.

Untamed Mustang Refuge, she'd named the place. She planned to advertise the moniker with a large post sign at the front of the driveway, but paying for something like that would be a long time out yet. She did have funds—she'd explained to him about all the money she'd saved over the years, looking forward to this dream—but she was spending it only on things that directly benefited the horses. Stubborn woman still refused to put any time and effort into her own house or any part of her property that wasn't specifically mustang related.

She was all about her horses. He had to give her that.

"I hope you and your sister grow up to be as tough and resilient as Faith Dugan," he told Rose as he picked her up and offered her a bottle.

Every time he'd come by to visit her, she'd been out with the mustangs—mending fences, pitching hay and toting water from the well pump to the trough. Hard labor, especially for a woman who, for the past few years, had been able to do this kind of work only by volunteering a few hours a day on weekends. Nonstop physical work, day in and day out, was new to her. He'd noticed the blisters on her hands and the sunburn on her cheeks. But she never complained, and she never slowed down. Nothing put her off course. He wouldn't be surprised if she ate her own meals out in the meadow with her mustangs.

With his help, and the aid of Nick and Slade, who'd come out a few more times, she'd managed to mend most of the major fences around her property, although it would still be some time before she would be able to address every beam and pole on her thousand-acre spread. But she'd done enough to give the mustangs plenty of room to safely run.

Willow was already looking markedly better. Her ribs weren't showing as much, and her coat was quickly regaining its shine. Faith had mentioned something about adding to her herd soon—well, a mare and a foal hardly constituted a *herd*, but he knew what she meant.

His lips curved upward and he shook his head. He didn't know why thinking about Faith and her hobby horses made him smile. It just did.

She did.

His phone rang, and he fished it from its holster, expecting it to be his mom or one of his brothers checking up on him. They'd all been hovering over him the past few weeks to the point where he was beginning to wonder if they all thought he was completely inept at being a father.

He glanced down at the screen, and his gaze widened.

Faith?

Why was she calling him? He'd given her his number in case she wanted to consult him about any of her ranch projects, but she'd never reached out to him.

"Hey, Faith. What's up?" he asked, shifting Rose to the crook of his elbow and propping the bottle with his chin while he used his other hand to hold his phone to his ear. Violet fussed from her chair, so he bounced it with one foot. All he needed was a stick and a plate to balance on the other foot and he'd be a regular circus act.

"Jax!"

The panic in Faith's voice brought him to instant alertness. Electricity popped through him. He must have jerked his head, because the bottle slipped from under his chin, hit the floor by his boots and rolled underneath the crib.

He grumbled something unintelligible.

"What's the matter?" He stooped and reached for the bottle. Rose screeched her discontent. Even Violet jumped into the fray, and he went from feeling as if he finally had it together with the twins to a total loss of control in half a second.

And then there was the woman on the other end of the

line. Faith sniffled and swept in a shaky, audible breath. Jax's protective instinct sparked to life and swirled through his chest, lodging in his throat.

"What's wrong?" he asked again when she didn't immediately answer.

"I'm s-sorry. I can hear that you have your hands full with your babies. I just— I didn't know who else to call."

"Faith." He stated her name firmly and calmly. She had to get her emotions under control, or he would never be able to figure out what was going on with her. "Tell me what has you so flustered."

"I called the vet but he's out of town."

"A problem with one of the horses, then?"

"Yes, I—" She paused and hiccupped. "My new stallion. Fuego. I only just brought him and a couple of other horses up to the ranch over the weekend. I thought everything was going remarkably well. The herd accepted him immediately as their leader and he acknowledged them as his band. But then today—well, I'm trying to build a shelter in the front meadow so the horses have plenty of shade. There's lumber everywhere. I didn't even think about..."

Again she paused. He lowered his brows. She wasn't making any sense.

"The herd usually keeps its distance, especially when I'm working on a project. I'm not very good with a hammer and I make an awful racket. So it didn't even occur to me to worry about closing the gate to the front meadow. And then Fuego—I don't know why, I didn't provoke him, but he charged me. Straight through the pile of lumber."

"Are you hurt?" he demanded, already buckling a still-crying Rose into her car seat and tucking her bottle into the nearby diaper bag.

Adrenaline pounded through him at the thought of Faith being injured. Wild stallions were nothing to mess around with, and Faith had no one out there to keep her safe. She loved those silly horses so much, he knew she'd put herself into the path of danger before she risked hurting one of the mustangs.

Just how bad had it gotten this time? He clung to the thought that she was well enough to call him—and that she was allowing herself to ask for help. It was a start.

He only hoped she wasn't too late in asking.

"Me? No. No. I'm fine. Don't worry about me." She sounded confused that he'd even asked the question. "The thing is, Fuego never made it to me. His hooves got tangled up in some lumber, and he fell onto his back. He's not getting up, Jax. What if he— Oh, Jax, I—"

Jax's jaw tightened with strain. He hoped the stallion wasn't as bad off as all that, but if the injury was as serious as it sounded, this was going to be an especially rough day for Faith, who wasn't ready for the harsher realities of ranch life. Putting down an injured animal was a difficult but sometimes necessary part of living in the country.

Sometimes the best thing for the animal was the hardest for the human being involved.

Especially a woman with a heart as sweet and tender as Faith's.

He clenched his jaw. He hated to be the one who might have to introduce her to the severe side of the life she'd chosen for herself, but it couldn't be helped.

She needed him. Now more than ever.

"I'll be right over."

"Thank you."

"And Faith?"

"Yes?"

"Please don't do anything until I get there. Do you understand? Stay right where you are and don't move." Pictures of Faith being taken down by a terrified, injured stallion flashed across his mind.

"Yes, Jax. I will. Just please. Hurry."

She didn't have to tell him twice. He couldn't get to Faith's ranch fast enough. His mother was out shopping in San Antonio, and there was no time to call in his brothers, so he was on his own with the twins. He strapped Violet into her car seat, then jogged around the house frantically grabbing whatever baby items he thought might be necessary and jamming them in the diaper bag. He slipped the strap over his head and onto one shoulder and grabbed both car seats, one in each hand.

It took him longer than he would have liked to figure out how the car seats snapped into the base. He really should have paid more attention when his mother was showing him how it was done, but until now she'd always been there to help him.

Once on the road, he forced himself to drive the speed limit for the twins' sake, but his heart was thumping heavily in his chest like the beat of a clock. The stallion's condition might be worsening with every second that went by—and that was to say nothing about Faith's safety.

She'd promised him she'd wait for him to get there, but he knew it couldn't be easy for her, standing around and doing nothing while one of her beloved horses suffered.

He was afraid the worst part was yet to come.

Faith breathed a huge sigh of relief when Jax strode up, a car seat in each hand and a diaper bag slung over his shoulder. She'd never been happier to see someone in her entire life. To think he'd dropped everything and rushed over with two babies in tow. Gratitude welled in her chest, mixing with the anxiety already lurking there.

She felt horribly guilty that she'd had to interrupt his

day with his children, but she hadn't been joking when she'd said she knew of no one else to call. It was the first time she'd truly felt alone on her ranch.

And worse than that—*helpless*.

She'd almost had a heart attack when Fuego had gone down, and the sound he made— She hoped she'd never have to hear anything like that ever again.

He'd rolled from side to side a couple of times, snorting and flailing his legs, but in the end he hadn't stood up. He'd shaken and shivered and whinnied in distress but had not regained his footing.

Faith feared for the worst.

What if Fuego's leg couldn't be mended, even with surgery? She'd have to put the beautiful silver stallion down, and it would break her heart. Nothing she'd ever experienced on a ranch could have prepared her for a situation like this.

Jax would know how to proceed. He would be able to determine if the stallion could be saved. She trusted him to do what was best.

Big, strong, solid, dependable Jax.

He hesitated, glancing down at his daughters, fast asleep in their seats. "Can you watch these two sweethearts while I—" He gestured to the half-built shelter. "I'd rather keep them safely away from the drama, if you don't mind."

When she nodded, he placed the car seats in the shade next to the barn and strode toward Fuego, a frown creasing his brow. He stood silently for a few moments, his hands on his hips, evaluating the stallion.

She didn't know what she expected—for Jax to run straight for the horse and help the stallion regain his feet on sheer strength alone? Was that even possible?

Jax was a large man, but even he didn't have enough muscles to lift a thousand-pound animal, especially a frightened one that would be thrashing and aggressive. She thought maybe he might examine Fuego's legs with his hands to try to determine if there was any serious damage, but if he got that close, then he'd run the risk of getting kicked by those vicious hooves.

He didn't try to right the horse, nor did he check Fuego's legs for wounds. Instead, he slowly and steadily walked around the lumber pile, occasionally pushing a beam aside with his boot. He assessed the situation without approaching the wild-eyed animal. He spoke to the horse in the rich, lyrical tone Faith now thought of as his horse-whisperer voice, although she knew he would pitch a fit if she ever said such a thing out loud. But that was what it was. It reassured and calmed even the most frightened or spooked of horses.

Even with Jax there, Faith wasn't convinced all would be well with Fuego, but her heart responded peculiarly to the tenor of his voice. It had the same effect on her as it had on the horse. Calming. Hypnotic. Lulling her pulse to a gentler, steadier rhythm.

He crouched by the horse's head and stroked its neck. Fuego thrashed and made another terrifying, heart-rending squeal. Jax adjusted his position so he wouldn't get kicked but left his hand on the stallion's shoulder.

"Easy there, boy," he coaxed. "You've got yourself into a real pickle this time, haven't you? Serves you right for trying to charge a pretty woman. You should know better. Just be your handsome self and the women will come to you."

The horse slowly stilled under the sound of Jax's voice. "Let's have a look at those legs, shall we?"

Violet made a mewling sound that caught Faith's attention. She guessed the baby had been woken by Fuego's disturbance. She unbuckled the infant's car seat and sheltered the infant in her arms.

The act of soothing the child had the additional benefit of calming her, as well.

"Your daddy came to the rescue," she informed little Violet in a whisper. "He'll be able to help Fuego. I know he will."

She stared down at the wide-eyed infant, and her heart welled with compassion for the little one. "I know your life hasn't always been ideal, but you've got your daddy now. He'll do right by you, you know. And you've got—" She stopped herself before she could say the words hovering on her lips. *You've got me.*

No.

These two little girls were coming to mean so much to her—too much. But she could not let herself get involved, not without risking her whole world imploding.

Hadn't she learned anything from last time?

With effort she willed her emotions back, folding them up and tucking them deep inside her heart. She would not come to care meaningfully for these children. She could not. They would be a neighbor's children and that was all. She had no place in their lives and they had no place in hers. And neither did their father.

She'd called upon Jax because he was an expert with horses and because he was still one of only a few townspeople she'd met so far. In an emergency—and this definitely qualified as one—she hadn't known whom else to call.

It had nothing to do with the spark of attraction that surfaced between them every time their eyes met. It wasn't because the reflection in his gaze suggested that the chemistry she felt might be reciprocated. It wasn't because of his tenderness or thoughtfulness, nor even that he'd offered his time and talents even when she'd assured him it wasn't necessary for him to do so.

And it had nothing to do with the way he'd dropped everything to come to her rescue.

What sent a jolt of dread skittering from nerve to nerve until her whole frame was quivering was the way she couldn't stop her chest from expanding when she gazed down at Jax's two precious infants.

She didn't dare make a connection, come to care for these tiny pieces of humanity. These soft, sweet, innocent twins.

She wiped a hand across her suddenly wet eyes.

No. She couldn't do this, couldn't become involved.

She had her reasons—good ones—and one of them was Jax himself, embroiled in a bizarre and complicated relationship with his ex-wife.

And then she had her own issues. She knew her limits. Caring too much was her Achilles' heel. It invariably got her in trouble.

She invested her heart in the wrong places—in the wrong *people*. It had taken an utter heartbreak for her to learn that hard truth, and it was the reason she had chosen to go it alone with her wild-horse rescue.

Except she wasn't going it alone.

Jax was here.

He'd turned his attention from the stallion to the piles of timber surrounding him, hemming him in. Still speaking in low murmurs, he moved beam after beam, tossing them to the side to give Fuego more room to move.

Why hadn't she thought to do that?

He'd nearly cleared a path for the stallion when suddenly the horse neighed loudly and rolled, unaided and snorting, to his feet. He shook his mane and bucked twice.

Faith breathed a sigh of relief. Clearly Fuego's legs weren't broken. All was well.

And then, in the blink of an eye, the stallion put down his head and charged. Faith's adrenaline roared to life, and yet events seemed to unfold in slow motion.

"Jax!" she screamed.

Jax had his back to the horse. He didn't even see it coming. He dropped the beam he was holding and half turned toward her—and away from the horse. She'd unwittingly made his situation worse.

Fuego hit Jax with a momentum that would have sent most men sprawling in the dirt. It was almost as if Jax sensed the thousand-pound collision just moments before it happened. He ducked and dodged to the side.

The horse hit his left shoulder. Jax staggered and his hat hit the dirt, but he kept on his feet in the shuffle, running several steps to regain his balance.

Faith's heart was beating frantically in her ears.

Oh, Jax.

He could very easily have been trampled under the powerful stallion's hooves, and all because she'd messed up. She was the one who had placed the lumber where the horses could potentially hurt themselves. Jax wouldn't be here if it wasn't for her.

Another epic failure in a long stream of them, it seemed, one of many in the weeks since she'd arrived in Serendipity. Compared with her much smaller list of accomplishments, she was feeling rather low and pathetic. And she needed to apologize to Jax once again.

It was becoming a habit she would rather break.

Jax stooped to retrieve his hat, and Faith realized that Rose had woken. Both babies were howling in protest, playing off each other to see who could cry the loudest.

Her attention had been so rapt on the interplay between Jax and Fuego that she hadn't even heard the poor darlings.

It was no surprise that they were bawling. In pure terror, Faith had just screamed their father's name loud enough to wake the entire town, and these poor little babies were well within hearing distance.

No infant should have to wake up to that.

"It's okay, my sweethearts," she cooed. She considered trying to remove Rose from her car seat, but she was already holding Violet, and it would be difficult to unlatch the buckle with one hand. Plus she'd have to juggle two babies at once, which she wasn't certain she could do.

She could only imagine Jax's learning curve with his twins. How did he manage caring for two babies at once?

For the first time since she'd arrived in Serendipity, she regretted that her house was a certified wreck. It wasn't fit for adult visitors, much less a couple of newborn babies. She couldn't invite them in and let the little ones down on the floor anytime soon.

Jax flashed a smile at Faith as he reached the barn and effortlessly scooped Rose into his arms. Rose immediately quieted, even before he spoke to her.

"It's okay, little darlin'," he murmured, brushing a soft kiss over her downy forehead. "Daddy's fine. Fuego is fine. Everything is okay now."

Faith breathed a silent prayer of gratitude.

Jax turned to plant a kiss on Violet's forehead, and Faith's gaze narrowed on the sleeve of his navy blue T-shirt. Fabric hung in tatters over the shoulder and a copper-red stain was spreading in uneven patterns across the surface.

Faith gasped and reached for his elbow to still him. "Jax! You're not fine. You're bleeding."

Chapter Five

Jax glanced at his left arm and shrugged. "Don't worry about it. It's nothing."

The expression on Faith's face was priceless—going from startled to confused to angry in a matter of seconds. Her face flushed from peach to cherry red. Her expressions were so distinct from each other that they reminded Jax of one of those old flip comic books that demonstrated basic animation.

When she gathered her brows over her eyes and her expression slammed to a halt on *determined* with a dash of *stubborn*, he knew he was in trouble.

He'd seen that look before, and it didn't bode well for him. He didn't see why she was making such a big deal out of the gash, anyway. It was just a little blood. He'd had worse.

Much worse.

"I'd better be going," he said, rather than allowing his mind to dwell upon the *worse*. "The babies need to be fed. I think Fuego is out of the woods now, but keep an eye on him and call the vet for a follow-up appointment just to be on the safe side. Watch for any signs of lameness."

"If the babies need to be fed, we'll feed them here, together, but there is no way I'm letting you drive off this property in that condition."

She seemed determined to bandage him up, and he couldn't restrain the shudder that went through him at the prospect. This wasn't about the gash or the blood or even the pain. This was about him leaving before she got a good look at his upper arm.

Her grip on his elbow tightened. "Come inside. My house is not pretty but it's functional. You can feed the twins while I gather some bandages and antibacterial ointment." She frowned. "I think I know where my first-aid kit is. I've had to use it often in the past few weeks on my own splinters and blisters."

She was rambling, more to herself than to him, and for some reason he found her little quirk amusing, like a mama bird chirping over her chicks. He just wished he wasn't the injured chick. She was about to see more than she bargained for.

"Sit down," she encouraged him, nodding toward a burnt-orange armchair that had clearly seen better days. It was probably older than Jax was, but he found it surprisingly comfortable when he sank back into the cushion and crossed his left ankle over his right knee. Having had much practice recently in the art and craft of child-propping, he deftly supported Rose within the triangle of his legs.

"Here we go, then," he told Rose, wishing he felt as confident as his tone. He was surprised his voice wasn't shaky. "Apparently your auntie Faith is going to patch up Daddy's owie."

One of them, at least.

His entire life had changed for the worse because of the accident, because of these ugly scars he carried on his body and in his heart. Some were visible to the eye. Others were known only by him. His family might suspect that the damage ran deeper than what he'd admitted aloud, but he tried to keep the bulk of his pain and shame to himself.

He didn't care to share either his inward or outward disfigurement with anyone. That Faith was about to discover a hidden wound somehow made it all that much worse. They were friends, he thought, and it was only recently that he'd realized he had far too few of those. It was his own fault. He'd alienated those who'd reached out to him after his accident. He didn't want to ruin his newfound friendship with Faith.

She wasn't a superficial woman. She seemed to be able to see beyond the puckered scar on his face and glimpse the man within. But maybe it was only that she was too wrapped up in her own problems to look—really *look*—at him.

And that was about to change.

He knew how irrational his emotions were. The physical scars were inconsequential. They shouldn't matter, but the pain of Susie's revulsion was still too fresh in his mind. He remembered in vivid detail the day—

"I found it," Faith said, sounding out of breath as she burst into the living room with Violet in one arm and a white tackle box–looking thing in the other. "This has a little bit of everything. I bought it at Emerson's Hardware the first day I was in town. I was stocking up on supplies and wasn't sure what I needed. That Eddie Emerson is such a sweet guy. He walked me through the store and made lots of suggestions."

Sweet guy.

Jax didn't know why he bristled at the words. He had no claim on Faith, nor did he want to.

Eddie was, in fact, a good guy, at least as far as Jax could discern. He worked hard at his family's store, he attended church every Sunday, and he was popular with the ladies. If Faith was interested in him, she could do worse.

Jax's gaze swept over Faith and abruptly changed his mind. Eddie was too young for her. He was still figuring out who he was. Faith had lived with the harsh realities of real life. She hadn't spoken of them, but he could see it in the way her eyes glazed over sometimes as memories overtook her and in the sad shadows that sometimes accompanied those moments.

Faith placed Violet in her car seat and then rummaged through the diaper bag and withdrew two empty bottles and a can of formula.

"That's the difference between a small town and a big city," she informed him.

He wondered if she realized she was carrying the whole conversation on her own. Jax was afraid anything he said right now would come out sounding bitter, so he remained silent.

"Back in Connecticut, where I was born and raised, shopping experiences are on the opposite side of the spectrum. Most often you can't find a store employee to help you even if you're looking for one, and if you do somehow manage to flag one down, they drag their feet and don't give any more assistance than absolutely necessary." She paused and gave this cute little feminine snort. "And don't even get me started on trying to find someone to help you carry out a large load of material. It would be better if we didn't even talk about the headaches you'll find there."

Okay.

He grinned. He wasn't *talking* about anything. She wouldn't let him get a word in edgewise.

She disappeared into what he assumed was the kitchen and reappeared moments later with two warm bottles of formula.

"I tested the temperature on the inside of my wrist. That's right, isn't it?"

He chuckled and nodded.

She already knew the answer to her question—she was just giving him the opportunity to show off his new daddy knowledge. "Okay, good. Anyway, back to Emerson's." She picked up the conversation right where she'd left off. Jax wondered how rude it would sound to tell her he didn't want to talk about Eddie Emerson anymore.

"I couldn't believe it when I walked in the door. Eddie came right around the counter with a welcoming smile on his face and didn't leave my side until he was satisfied I'd found everything I needed."

Jax had been born and raised in Serendipity and had worked the family ranch all his life. He visited San Antonio for supplies when he absolutely had to, but mostly he kept to himself and shopped in Serendipity.

He liked the country. He'd never once considered leaving the town, but he had to admit he'd never taken the time to see it through a newcomer's eyes. Faith was beaming, and in the oddest way, it made Jax proud to call Serendipity home.

"That looks terrible," Faith said, moving to his side to examine his bloody sleeve. "Do you think you can mind both babies while I tend to your injury?"

He chuckled. He'd learned to do a lot of things in pairs since his daughters had come into his life.

"Observe," he said mildly.

Faith set Violet into the curve of his right arm and he propped her bottle with his left hand, then gestured for Faith to hand him the other bottle in his right. Exhibiting yet another circus-worthy feat, he aimed carefully and managed to connect the tip of the bottle with Rose's smacking lips.

He grinned in triumph.

"I am duly impressed." Faith laughed and applauded. "Well done, Daddy."

She perched on the corner of the coffee table and rummaged through the first-aid kit, removing gauze, alcohol swabs, tape and antibacterial ointment.

"Let's see what we've got here," she said, reaching for the sleeve on his T-shirt.

A monster.

He strove to hold himself steady as she rolled up the sleeve, bit by excruciating bit, apologizing profusely when he sucked in a ragged breath. The stupid scar tissue was ultrasensitive, and despite what he'd told Faith, the gash he'd gotten today was fairly substantial and it hurt like the dickens.

She rolled the sleeve to his shoulder and gasped. There it was, then, the same reaction Susie had had the first time she'd looked upon her husband's scarred body.

He knew what he'd see when he saw Faith's expression—horror and revulsion. Morbid curiosity followed by disgust.

So he didn't look.

He kept his head low and his gaze averted. How had she managed to talk him into this, anyway? He could clean his own wounds at his own house, secure and isolated.

Alone.

And yet here he was, under Faith's gentle ministrations, hating every moment of it but conversely not so much.

She made an exclamation, but it wasn't shock. It was compassion. "You poor thing."

"What?" Her response wasn't what he'd expected at all, and it took him a moment to recover. Was it pity he was hearing?

Anger welled in his chest, and he grasped at it, needing

it to cover everything else he was feeling. He didn't want her to feel sorry for him. He didn't want her sympathy.

Her reaction was at least as bad, maybe worse, than her turning away in revulsion, because it jabbed at his insides and made him *feel* things. At least he'd learned how to shield himself to those who turned away at his physical scars.

This, he was defenseless against.

With effort, he hardened his heart. His shoulders tightened with strain. He would not give in.

"I know it hurts, but try not to tense up on me," she gently coaxed. "If you can, try to distract your mind with something." Squinting, she examined the wound, her bottom lip caught in her teeth.

He stared at her full lips so he didn't have to meet her gaze. That was distracting enough for him. He knew by now that biting her lip was a sure sign she was fully concentrating on something, but right now it annoyed him.

She didn't have to be so cute about it. He had plenty to keep his mind on that had nothing to do with the pretty lady tending to his wound—the two babies in his arms, for instance. But no matter how he tried, his babies weren't distracting him, and he didn't like it one bit.

"This has to hurt. How did it happen?"

His fists tightened involuntarily, and he lost his hold on Violet's bottle. He scrambled to readjust, but the bottle rolled from his grasp. Without a word, Faith retrieved it for him, smiling softly as she pressed the container back into his hand. Her gaze shifted from Violet's eyes to his.

She was asking about his scars.

No one asked about his scars. They stared. Gaped. Whispered.

But no one asked.

Where did he even start? And did he want to get into this with her at all?

"I feel so bad about this. I saw Fuego connect with your shoulder, but I didn't see him bite you." Her tone sounded as if she was going to go reprimand the stallion for his bad behavior. "There's no doubt about it, though. I can clearly see the bite marks."

Huh? His mind fogged. What was she talking about?

He'd been thinking about the hideous scar that covered his upper arm all the way to his collarbone. They'd had to graft his skin, and he'd been in the hospital for a long time. It wasn't pretty to look at.

There was some irony in that. As a teenager and young adult he'd never given a thought to his appearance, except for the cocky, youthful knowledge that he was considered attractive by the girls. Now he was suddenly hypersensitive to Faith's eyes on his ugliness.

"He caught me on his way out," Jax explained, still wondering why they were talking about the bite and not his scar. "I was mostly able to roll away from him, but he still managed to take a chunk out of my arm."

"I'll say. I don't think you'll need stitches, but you probably ought to have your doctor take a look at you just to be on the safe side."

He scoffed and shook his head. "I have every confidence that you can patch me up just fine."

She tore open a couple of packages of alcohol swabs and laid out some gauze.

"This is going to hurt," she warned him.

He set his jaw and didn't flinch when she gently dabbed the alcohol on his skin.

"Sorry. I know it's painful. This is the worst of it, though. I just want to make sure I clean the wound well so there's no chance of infection."

"I can handle it. I'm a big boy." He was too tough to let a little swab get the best of him, even if it was drenched in liquid fire. He tried to smile but grimaced instead.

She laughed, which somehow put him at ease. "No argument there. They grow men large out here in Texas." She spread a big glob of antibacterial ointment over the wound, covered it with gauze and then ran the one-inch-wide self-sticking elastic tape around his biceps several more times than Jax thought was necessary. A little more and he'd practically have a cast.

"Are you current on your rabies vaccine?" she teased.

He snorted. "Fuego had better be the one worried about that."

She laughed as she took Violet from his arms and settled herself on the burnt-orange sofa across from him. She shifted the baby to her shoulder and gently patted her back.

"I'm sorry my horse went after you that way," she said, her smile faltering. "And after you came over here specifically to help me with him. I can't believe he bit you."

"I won't press charges."

She swept in a surprised breath, and her gaze widened. She looked as startled as if he'd just slapped her.

"You wouldn't—"

"No, of course not," he hastened to say. "I was just kidding. It's not the first time a horse has charged me, and I'm sure it won't be the last. I didn't mean to upset you."

"You didn't. I'm sorry. It's been a really tough day for me and I'm probably overreacting. It's just that Fuego is on his third strike."

"His what?"

"If he doesn't work out here he'll be put down. That's why your remark shocked me so much."

He caught her gaze and held it steady. "You don't ever have to worry about me, Faith. Trust me. I would never do anything to purposefully hurt you or put your rescue in jeopardy. How did Fuego get himself in so much trouble, anyway?"

She shrugged. "I don't know all the details. Probably displaying much of the same behavior as he did today. Possibly acting aggressive." She pinched her lips into a hard line. "I don't want anything to happen to him, but I can't keep a horse who poses a threat to the rest of my herd, or to people who visit the rescue."

She looked so brokenhearted that Jax's gut flipped like a pancake, soaring up, over and then right back down onto the hot griddle. What she lacked in know-how she more than made up for in heart and determination.

"He's not a bad horse. He's a wild stallion. Aggression is to be expected. And I suspect he may not have had great experiences where people are concerned."

Faith nodded and straightened her shoulders. "I was afraid of that."

"Being wild and being gentle aren't mutually exclusive, you know. Would you like me to help you with Fuego?"

Her eyebrows rose, and her eyes gleamed with unshed tears. "Even though he took a chomp out of your shoulder?"

"Especially because he got his teeth into me," he assured her. "It's not just visitors to the rescue that I'm worried about. What if he does something to hurt you? I'll do whatever it takes to keep that from happening."

Relief flooded her gaze. "I feel like I owe you more than I can ever repay. You've done so much for me. And you keep offering."

"Goes both ways. You helped me get on my feet when Rose and Violet got dumped on my doorstep," he reminded her. "Besides—you bought me, remember? Five hundred dollars, I think it was. That's a lot of man-hours."

She chuckled wryly. "I don't own you, Jax."

He grinned.

Maybe she didn't own him, at least not in the technical sense of the word. But he still wanted to help her, protect her and see her dreams come true. And in a way, wasn't that the same thing?

Faith's strategy—staying as far away from Jax and his babies as possible—was failing miserably. In the three weeks since Fuego took a chunk out of Jax's shoulder, Jax had used his training as an excuse to visit her ranch nearly every day, often bringing his daughters along with him.

Faith's favorite times were when his mother, Alice, accompanied him. Faith and Alice would sit and visit and take care of the twins while they watched Jax run Fuego through his paces. Without so much as a lunge lead, he encouraged Fuego to run around the perimeter of the corral, keeping him trotting as much as possible. Faith didn't really understand the process, but Alice assured her she'd get it when Jax was finished.

Honestly, she didn't really care how long Jax took. She enjoyed sitting on the porch, rocking the babies on one of the dual rocking chairs Jax had bought for Faith under the guise of needing to make sure his mother was comfortable. Faith knew it was as much for her as for his mother's ease.

Alice regaled Faith with stories about Jax and his brothers when they were growing up. Not surprisingly, they'd been a handful, getting in trouble in turn and sometimes all three together.

Alice beamed whenever she spoke of her family. She was proud of all her sons. She couldn't say enough good things about Jax's gift with horses. And then there was Slade's bull-riding achievements and Nick's dedication to the ranch. Sometimes she even spoke of Jenson, her late husband.

Jax had shared with Faith how much of a hit his mom had taken when Jenson had passed away after a forty-eight-year marriage. The once-social woman had hidden away in her home and had stopped attending community functions.

Seeing Alice's bubbly and outgoing personality, it was hard to imagine her under the heavy cloud of depression, but Faith knew just how hard grief could hit a person, taking her completely off guard and off grid.

Alice really was a lovely woman. Faith was grateful that Rose and Violet had brought new light into the woman's life and knew that Alice was good for the babies, as well.

"He's amazing," Faith said, watching Jax run the stallion around the corral. "When he started, Fuego wouldn't come within twenty feet of him. Now look at them."

The horse was still skittish, but every day seemed to bring Jax one step closer.

"You haven't seen the half of it," his mother assured her. "He'll have that stallion literally eating out of his hand before he is through. Right now he's teaching the horse to trust him—his scent, his movements, his voice."

She wondered if Alice was aware of the heat that crept up Faith's face at those words. If she did, she was too nice of a person to show it.

Fuego wasn't the only one who responded to Jax's leathery scent, his smooth, muscular movements and that *voice*.

Every time she looked into the depths of his dark, chocolate eyes, all the promises she'd made to herself before moving to Serendipity just whisked away like dandelion seeds on a breezy Texas afternoon.

She knew all the reasons why a relationship with Jax McKenna could never be, but there were an increasing number of moments when it would have been all too easy to set reason aside.

She was grateful for the babies. They were good, natural interruptions that kept things light between her and Jax. And she needed all the help she could get.

After Jax was satisfied with Fuego's progress, it would probably be better if he stopped coming by to check on her entirely, but she would miss Alice. And the babies.

And Jax.

When Fuego was settled, there would no longer be a reason he needed to come by. With a donation she'd received from a recent benefactor, she had been able to hire a couple of teenage wranglers—two girls who came highly recommended by Jax and were especially good with horses. The kids had to balance their ranch work with their schoolwork, but Faith thought it was the perfect solution to a very messy problem.

"Jax was my quiet one," Alice said, smiling softly at the memory. She rhythmically patted Violet's back with each creak of the rocker. "He's the middle child, you know.

"Nick is the textbook firstborn—walks the straight and narrow, strives for perfection in everything he does and really puts his heart into it."

She chuckled. "Slade bothered Nick to no end before he found his way to God and really started growing up. His best friend, Brody, was killed while bull riding, God rest his soul. Such a terrible loss, but I think it forced Slade to take a hard look at his life in a way that he needed." She frowned and shook off the memory. "Slade is settled down now—at least as much as a man like Slade will ever be."

Alice appeared to be meandering in her thoughts. Even though Faith was most curious about Jax, she let Alice continue at her own pace.

"And Jax? He's always been about the horses he trains.

He helps Nick with the cattle and daily chores around the ranch, of course, but I think if he had his way, he'd sleep in the stable. Even more so now that—"

She paused. Her gaze darkened. Alice's bottom jaw jutted out under her top one for a moment as she struggled to regain her composure. At length, the older woman scoffed and shook her head.

"I'm sorry, but when I think about what *that woman* did to my son, it makes me angry enough to spit nails. If ever there was a woman set out to try my temper, it is *that woman*." She wouldn't even say Susie's name.

Faith didn't want to pry, but clearly Alice needed to talk about it. She prayed she'd be a good sounding board and that Alice would realize she was trustworthy.

"You mean Susie? Are you talking about the way she dumped the twins on him?"

"Well, yes, there're the girls, of course. There is no excuse for that but—"

Faith didn't realize Jax had stopped calling and nickering to the stallion until he strode to the fence and braced one foot on the bottom rung, leaving Fuego to his own devices on the far side of the corral.

"You're staring at me," he accused, lifting his hat by the crown and wiping the sweat from his brow with the fabric at the bottom of his T-shirt. "Are you two talking about me?"

"I was just about to show Faith your baby pictures," Alice teased. "I've already told her lots of stories about you."

Scorching heat flooded straight to Faith's cheeks. Jax caught her gaze and he raised one eyebrow. Silence stretched between them for what seemed like forever. Her heart pounded so furiously she thought he might be able to hear it.

Then he grinned, that heart-flipping half smile yanked up by his scar. And he winked at her.

Winked.

While Alice was sitting right there in their midst. His mother had surely seen the exchange.

Just when Faith thought the level of her mortification could rise no further, Jax found a way to increase it. Her head was likely to pop off from the pressure of the heat between her ears.

"All good things, I hope." He included his mother with his statement and the wide grin that accompanied it. "I would hate to think you were talking trash about me."

"I've been telling her what little terrors you and your brothers were when you were children. These gray hairs?" She pointed to her shoulder-length hair, still a deep black spun with shades of silver. "Every single one of them has your names on it. Nick. Jax. Slade." She pointed them out one by one. "You're blessed, young man," she continued, wagging a finger at Jax. "You have daughters."

Jax threw back his head and laughed. Faith smiled. It was the most carefree she'd ever heard him. He was always so tense, and with good reason. She was glad he could loosen up around his mother.

Fuego neighed and snorted.

"I'd best get back to the stallion. No rest for the wicked, right?"

Alice scoffed. "Don't let him fool you," she informed Faith. "He's a good man, that one, right to the core. He has a heart of gold, broken though it is. He just needs the right woman to mend it up for him."

Alice looked directly at Faith and raised her eyebrows. Asking? Insinuating?

Faith cleared her suddenly tight throat and swallowed hard to relieve the pressure.

To distract herself, she laid a plastic pad across her lap and made a big production out of changing Rose's diaper.

Alice was still peering at her inquisitively. What in the world did Jax's mom expect her to say?

She knew what she *should* say.

I'm not interested in Jax in that way.

Well, that would be an outright lie, because how could she not be interested?

There's nothing between us.

Still not quite right. After what had happened the day Fuego had taken a bite out of Jax, she could hardly say they hadn't shared anything emotional. And the chemistry was undeniable.

There will never be anything serious between Jax and me because I won't ever let there be.

It was as close to the truth as she was going to get in her confused state of mind.

It was also something she could never tell Jax's mother.

"Susie was Jax's high school sweetheart." Alice picked up the thread of the conversation as if she'd never left it. "You know how it is in a small-town ranching community. Since most of the kids already know what they are doing with their lives, those who pair up tend to stay that way—after high school they marry off and have families right away.

"Susie wasn't like that. She had aspirations that went beyond Serendipity. Which was okay, in theory. She went away to college while Jax remained home tending the family ranch."

Alice shook her head, remembering. "When Susie returned to Serendipity, she was a different girl. Worldly and bitter. Life hadn't quite worked out the way she'd anticipated. She didn't ever get her degree. I don't know what she was doing all that time away.

"Whatever she got into, it changed her, and not for the better. The only one who couldn't see it was Jax. Or maybe he was just set on honoring his commitment to her. You know how Jax is. Honestly, what I can't figure out is why Susie married him. She was never happy, even before…" Alice's sentence trailed off.

"Before the accident?"

Alice pressed her lips and nodded. Her gaze flickered to Jax and then back to Faith again. "Jax should probably be the one telling you this, but he'll never do it and I don't believe he can move on until he gets past the tragedy of what happened. And that's not likely to occur if no one besides his own family knows what truly went down that night."

Faith was at once honored and terrified that Alice had bestowed on her the gift of her trust. She knew the woman wasn't giving it lightly, not when it had to do with her son.

"He told me he was injured in an accident, but he never said any more than that."

"He doesn't like to talk about it. He was returning to Serendipity from watching Slade compete in an out-of-town rodeo. He'd asked Susie to accompany him, but she no longer cared for *country* activities. She'd seen how the other half lived, apparently, and wanted Jax to move to the city."

Faith kissed Rose's downy head and watched Jax work, his strength and confidence matching the stallion's. It was hard to believe that a vulnerable heart beat in that big old chest of his, a heart that could be injured by one thoughtless woman's words and deeds. But she'd glimpsed enough of Jax to know how badly Susie had hurt him.

"On the highway on his way home, a car in front of him blew out a tire and went headlong into a tree. Jax immediately pulled to the side of the road and called 911, then rushed to see if he could help. You know Jax. He's not the kind of man to stand around and do nothing."

That sounded exactly like the Jax Faith knew.

"The driver had hit her head and was barely conscious, so he wrapped his jacket around his arm and broke a window out and then dragged the woman and her six-year-old son to safety."

Faith gasped, then frowned in confusion. The jagged scar on his face might possibly have been caused by a sharp piece of glass, but his shoulder told another story.

"What happened to his arm? That doesn't look like an injury consistent with a wound caused by sharp glass. I'd have guessed it was a burn scar."

Her eyes grew wide. "You're right—it is from a burn. I have to say, I'm surprised he showed you his arm. It's one of his big secrets."

She sniffed. "Oh, believe me, he didn't want me to see it. I kind of forced the issue. Fuego took a bite out of his shoulder, and I insisted that I be the one to patch him up, since it was my fault it happened."

"Still…" Alice stopped her rhythmic patting on Violet's back and tilted her head, analyzing Faith. "He's very sensitive about that scar."

"It doesn't bother me. Honestly. But I'm curious. How'd he get burned?"

"The car was on fire when he went to rescue the woman and her child. He went back to make sure there weren't any other people left in the car. The driver had been dazed and kept saying something about her baby—turned out later that she meant the six-year-old, but Jax believed another child might still be caught in the wreck."

"There wasn't, I hope."

"No. But the engine exploded before Jax could clear away. The car rolled with him in it. He was badly burned and had to have skin grafts on his shoulder. And he lost most of the hearing in his left ear, you know."

Faith hoped Alice didn't hear her gasp. Jax was deaf in one ear. That explained a lot. "Praise God he's still alive to tell the story."

"Indeed."

Faith reached out to squeeze Alice's hand. The poor woman had been through so much recently. First she had lost her husband, and then the near death of her son so soon afterward. What a nightmare. It certainly put Faith's meager problems in perspective.

"Come on, boy." Jax's deep, lyrical voice reached Faith's ears, and she turned to watch him. "Get up, now. Show me what you're made of."

"He rescued those people. He's a hero," she whispered.

Alice nodded. "Everyone thinks so but him."

"I don't understand. He threw himself in harm's way for people he didn't even know. In my book that makes him a Good Samaritan, and he has the scars to prove it. How could he think any differently?"

"He hates those scars."

"But—why?" It wasn't even that she respected the scars now that she knew the story behind the wounds, that he had been performing an act of mercy when he received them. Even before she'd known what caused them, the scars hadn't bothered her. Particularly that jagged scar on his temple. Hadn't anyone ever told him it gave him a rugged, bad-boy appearance? Women ate up the tough-guy image. She had to believe she was not the only one who thought Jax McKenna was a good-looking man.

Alice snorted. "In a word—Susie. She completely shattered his self-image. On the day the doctor removed his bandages, she took one look at Jax and walked out of his life. Poof. She was gone. He came home from the hospital to an empty house. Susie had cleaned out her drawers and taken most everything of value. Divorce papers followed a week later."

"A *week*?" Faith was aghast.

"Right? If you ask me, those divorce papers were in the works well before the accident happened."

"Clearly."

"But Jax doesn't see it. To him, his scars ruined his marriage. He looks in the mirror and he sees himself as a monster. So he hides himself away at the ranch, trying to make the outside world go away. As if it ever does." She sighed and paused to deposit a now-sleeping Violet into her car seat.

Rose was still fussing, so Faith continued to rock her, receiving as much comfort from the rhythmic motion as she was giving to the baby.

"He rarely goes into town for any reason other than to attend church, and even then he never stays to socialize. The Bachelors and Baskets auction was actually the first community event he's attended since his injury."

That was odd. "Pardon me for saying so, Alice, but why did he choose that one? If he doesn't like being on display, putting himself up on an auction block for everyone to see would be his worst nightmare."

"Believe me—it was. At least until you stepped up with the winning bid and rescued him out of his misery. He was your first official wild rescue." Alice smiled at her joke but quickly sobered. "You see, his father passed away in a hospice in San Antonio. He needed round-the-clock care and there simply wasn't a closer facility. The boys took turns driving me back and forth to see Jenson, and it was hard on all of us. Nick missed his father's passing, and he's never forgiven himself for that. Jax and Slade were there, but that didn't make it easier for either one of them.

If there had been a hospice here in Serendipity—well, that would have changed everything."

Faith nodded.

"So you see, Jax would do anything for the cause—even put himself on display."

"That was very brave of him. I can't even begin to imagine the pure torture he must have been feeling, standing up there on that grandstand. He probably thought everyone was looking at his scar."

"Interesting how our perspective changes based on where we are sitting, isn't it? Now that I think about it, I suppose I've done the same thing I've accused Jax of doing. After Jenson died, I retreated to the ranch because of my broken heart."

"That's understandable, Alice," Faith assured her. "Everyone grieves differently."

Different perspectives.

Faith had grieved by running away to the country and hiding out among her mustangs.

"Well, the twins have certainly shaken things up around here." Alice laughed, a clear, happy sound that made Faith smile.

"That's one way of looking at it. Your family's whole worldview has shifted. But from what I've seen, Jax is handling it tremendously well. He's definitely daddy material. Those girls are blessed to have him, and anyone can tell how much he loves them."

"I can't say I mind spoiling these two little sweethearts myself. They make my heart sing. The way all this came down on us was definitely less than ideal, but in this case it's the end result that matters. Rose and Violet have a family who loves them. Jax will give them a good, stable Christian home. All of us will."

Faith sighed inwardly. If only every child was so blessed

as to have a man like Jax for a father. Her own dad had been more interested in climbing the corporate ladder than in praying with his only daughter before she climbed into bed for the night.

"When Jax finishes gentling Fuego, we'll have to have a party to celebrate," Alice announced, with so much excitement in her tone that Faith knew she wasn't going to turn Jax's mom down, whatever she offered. "Dinner at my house. We'll raise a toast to Jax for his labor, but you and I both know it will be for much more than that. We'll be celebrating his courage and his future with his two beautiful daughters."

Alice looked as if she was about to say more, but then she abruptly closed her mouth and shook her head.

"You'll come, won't you?" she asked after an extended pause.

"Yes, of course." Faith tried to smile but it felt shaky at best.

She would show up and do her best to look happy, but she wouldn't be celebrating the end of Jax's work with Fuego—she'd be grieving the loss of his friendship.

Because she couldn't continue to be friends with Jax McKenna. Not without getting her heart woven up with him and the twins. And that was something she simply could not allow herself to do.

The party had given her an extension—a few more days to spend with Jax, assuming he continued to show up at her ranch—but she wouldn't let herself think beyond that.

"Look there," Alice said, nodding toward the corral. "This is what he's been waiting for. Watch."

Jax slowed Fuego's pace and then turned his back on the horse. He stood stock-still in the middle of the corral, his arms hanging loosely at his sides and a confident, expectant look on his face.

Faith held her breath. She had no idea what would happen next, but she instinctively knew it would be beautiful, a moment to savor.

Fuego snorted and threw his head, stepping toward Jax and then bucking and backing up again, turning indecisively in a tight circle.

Still, Jax did not move.

"Come on, Fuego," Alice whispered, leaning forward in her chair.

Tentatively, the stallion started back toward Jax, and this time he did not startle or turn away. He stopped just behind Jax and sniffed at his neck and shoulder, nickering as if accepting the man's scent as trustworthy.

"That's my boy," Jax murmured, turning with a slow, even motion and running a reassuring hand down the horse's muzzle. "See now? Everything is okay."

He continued to stroke Fuego's head and neck, speaking in the lyrical voice that mesmerized horses and humans alike, as butterflies fluttered through her stomach.

Amazing.

Jax was simply amazing.

Faith's heart welled. His patience with the wild stallion had paid off in spades. Without so much as a halter, Fuego willingly followed Jax to the gate that emptied out into the front meadow, nickering when Jax opened it.

"Go on now, boy," Jax said, running his hand down the horse's neck one last time. "Your band is waiting for you."

What Faith had just witnessed was beyond anything she could have imagined when she had first conceived of rescuing horses. Jax had opened a whole new world to her.

She wanted to thank him but knew he'd act as if what he'd done was just another day's work. He strode up to the porch two steps at a time and took Rose in his arms, nuzzling her neck and making her pump her arms and gurgle in delight.

"Fuego will be approachable now." He smiled, and for once Faith didn't see a shadow of pain in his eyes.

"Amazing." Faith could find her voice for only the one word. She had a hundred words in her head, but they were all verses of the same song.

"That's my son," Alice agreed, a proud smile splitting her face. "Absolutely amazing. It looks like we're going to have that celebratory dinner sooner than we expected."

Jax's eyebrow rose. "What are we celebrating, or do I want to know?"

Alice flashed a wink at Faith and smiled at Jax. "Why, you, of course."

Chapter Six

*A*mazing.

If Jax heard that word one more time, he was going to knock his head against a wall. The day he'd finished Fuego, Faith had repeated the compliment at least five times that he'd counted.

Every day for the rest of the week he'd been working at her ranch, and he'd heard it over and over again.

Amazing, amazing, amazing.

Good grief. The woman couldn't get over it.

His mom was not helping. She had come through on her threat to throw a celebratory dinner over the weekend. He suspected it was more for Faith than it was for him, though his mom said otherwise. He had a close family, but they didn't get together every time one of them did something worthwhile.

He hated the thought that he was going to end up the focus of the evening. It made him itchy all over to think about what fun his brothers were going to have with all this. He'd never hear the end of it. And on top of their teasing, he still had to deal with Faith's praise.

All he'd done was gentle her stallion. She was acting as if he'd flown her to the moon and back.

He smiled. He had to admit she was good for his ego. She seemed genuinely appreciative of the work he'd done around her ranch, especially with Fuego. That was probably part of the reason he kept going back. She asked a lot of questions, sometimes curious, always learning—so many queries that he would definitely have been annoyed by them if they'd come from anyone but her.

Faith was different.

Most telling of all, she didn't seem to be the least bit put off by his scarred body. After the afternoon she'd patched up his shoulder when Fuego bit him, she'd never mentioned his injuries again, and it hadn't changed their relationship at all. If anything, it had brought them closer.

Sometimes—sometimes—he thought he caught her staring, but it wasn't the way others gawked at him.

Her gaze was sweet. Tender. It made his gut feel all fluttery. He wondered…

His chest tightened. He was reading too much into a simple look. Faith wasn't good at shielding her emotions, which was good, because in general he was lousy at reading them. Even though she never talked about it, he knew she had her own issues from her past.

Could she get beyond them?

Could he?

No.

Those thoughts were leading him down a path he could not afford to tread, not only because Susie had trampled on his heart and left it in shreds by the roadside, but because his focus needed to remain entirely concentrated on raising his daughters.

On the other hand, it was true that Faith wasn't anything like Susie.

He trusted Faith implicitly. She would never belittle anyone for any reason. And she was a wonder with the twins. Sometimes he'd covertly watch her with one of the babies and wonder why she wasn't married with a family of her own. She obviously loved kids.

Maybe that was part of the grief she carried in her eyes. He wouldn't pry, but he hoped he'd proved she could count on his friendship. If she ever wanted to open up to him, he would listen.

Faith was the first guest to arrive at the house, bearing two pies that she promptly admitted she did not bake. Phoebe Hawkins at Cup O' Jo's Café in town was a world-class baker.

"I don't even want to try to compete with that," Faith said, laughing. She set the pies on the sideboard and turned to Jax.

He chuckled. "My mom ordered our chicken from the deli. She likes to say, 'Why should I slave away in a hot kitchen when there're so many other nice things to do?' But the truth is, cooking is not her forte."

"I'm with her on that. Besides, I'm too busy with the horses to mess around with culinary endeavors. And my kitchen isn't exactly well equipped. The appliances aren't in very good shape. Now, what can I do to help you?"

"Um—set the silverware, I guess."

Jax had the oddest sensation that the atmosphere of the house had lightened the moment Faith walked in. Maybe it was because of the way her smile seemed to brighten up any room she entered. Maybe it was knowing he could be himself around her without worrying about what he was saying or doing, or that she was staring at him for all the wrong reasons.

He was, after all, *amazing*.

He grinned. Whatever it was, he liked it. She made him feel less burdened. More secure. He couldn't wipe the smile from his face if he tried.

Which was kindling for a very large fire. He might as well just hand Nick and Slade a pack of matches and be done with it. They were going to take one look at his face and off they'd go, razzing him to no end, assuming there was something romantic going on between him and Faith.

And worse yet, they would give Faith a whole lot of the same kind of trouble.

For his part, he could handle it. He'd been picked on enough growing up with his two rough-and-tumble brothers that there was nothing they could say or do to ruffle him. But how fair was that to Faith? She didn't deserve the ribbing that was most certainly coming her way. He was pretty sure she didn't want to hear his brothers' teasing suggestions about romance or anything else.

Jax was so busy worrying about what his brothers could or would say that he didn't notice how many pieces of his mother's best silverware Faith had laid out at each place setting.

"Whoa, whoa, whoa there, cowgirl," he said, throwing up his hands. "How many forks does one man need to eat his meal?"

Three, apparently. At least Faith thought so.

She looked at him in dismay. "I was just trying to make it look fancy. Do you think it's too much, then?"

"Believe me—one knife, one fork and one spoon is all we'll be needing," he advised her with a smile. "Any more than that and my brothers will take to creating such a ruckus over it that you'll never hear the end of it."

Alice entered the room, wiping her hands on a dish towel. "Why, Faith dear, I didn't hear you come in."

"She brought pies," Jax said, patting his lean middle.

"Phoebe's pies," Faith qualified.

"The table looks lovely, honey," she said, addressing Jax. "I especially like what you've done with the silverware." Alice flashed Jax a crafty smile before returning to the kitchen. The Cheshire cat couldn't have done a better job of it. Jax thought he might even have caught a wink.

Jax met Faith's eyes, and they broke into smothered laughter.

"Guess we're keeping the silverware," Faith said, covering her mouth with her palm as another giggle escaped.

Jax shook his head. "Don't say I didn't warn you. There will be a food fight before the night is over."

"Don't worry about me. I can take anything your brothers sling at me. Even peas. And I give as good as I get."

He choked on his laughter. She probably could, Jax realized. Maybe his brothers ought to be the ones to look out. Faith was strong and sure of herself, able to take life as it came to her. But that didn't mean he wasn't going to do his best to shelter her from the worst of the familial fallout.

The doorbell rang repeatedly, as if someone was holding the button down. Jax's first thought was of his sleeping babies, followed by thunderous intentions toward whichever idiot brother thought ringing the doorbell was a good idea.

Somebody's head was going to roll.

"I'll get it," Faith said. "You'd better check on the twins."

Jax growled in agreement and crept down the hallway, gingerly avoiding the loose floorboards that creaked when he stepped on them, like a soldier in a minefield. He'd often stayed at his mother's during those first few crucial days with his girls. Long nights pacing the hallway had taught him where each and every creak and squeak was located.

He peeked into the portable crib, where Rose and Violet were napping. Happily, the doorbell hadn't wakened either baby. He wanted them to get as much rest as possible before chaos reigned supreme in the house.

He watched Violet sleep for a moment, measuring the

rise and fall of her chest and smiling softly at her sweet little face and the way she sucked noisily on her fist in her sleep.

Happy dreams, little ones.

He tiptoed out of the room and closed the door so it was open only a crack. His mother had installed a baby monitor, but he was still in that first-time parent freak-out-at-the-tiniest-little-noise phase, which his mother often teased him about.

So he was a little overprotective. He wasn't sure he would *ever* get over that phase. Look out, teenage boys wanting to date either one of his daughters.

Still grinning, he turned the corner of the hallway into the family room, where Faith was standing at the front door, her mouth agape.

"Jax?" she squeaked in a high, tight voice.

He immediately went on full alert, adrenaline shooting through his veins. Faith's defensive posture and the fact that she was literally blocking the doorway was a clear signal that it wasn't one of his brothers standing there, but who—

"Jackson?" a shrill voice called, sending a chill down Jax's spine. "This *woman* will not let me in the house. Tell her to get out of my way. I want to see my babies."

At the sound of Susie's voice, every muscle in Jax's body tightened to the point of pain, but the angry haze in his mind made him oblivious to it.

This was *so* not happening. And if she thought she was going to waltz in and see the twins, she was highly mistaken.

Faith, bless her courageous little heart, hadn't budged from where she blocked the doorway. The set of her shoulders suggested she wasn't taking this unwanted invasion any better than he was, but she was tough and determined and he was glad he had her fighting on his side—on his children's side.

Forcing himself to take a deep breath, he moved into the doorway behind Faith and laid a reassuring hand on her shoulder.

Calm. Cool. Collected.

He'd been fervently praying to be able to forgive Susie for all of her thoughtless actions, but then the second he saw her face it all came rushing back—the humiliation, the pain of rejection. The grief caused by the death of a marriage. The shock when he'd suddenly discovered he was a father twice over and that his babies had been unfeelingly dumped on his front porch.

Surprisingly, though, there was one key emotion missing from the equation. Susie no longer had the ability to break his heart. Not because it was already broken beyond repair, but because it had healed—and it no longer belonged to her. His love for her was truly in the past.

"What are you doing here, Susie?" he demanded. "Circle M isn't your home anymore."

He swept his gaze across his ex-wife. The long brown curls she'd once put so much stock into had lost their bounce and sheen. Her eyes were glassy and the pupils dilated to the point where her normally blue eyes appeared nearly black. Susie had always been slender, but now she looked skeletal. The woman who had always been so particular about her appearance was gone, replaced by a stranger Jax barely recognized.

He narrowed his eyes on her. "You didn't drive here on your own, did you?"

She scowled and crossed her arms, the long orange sleeves of her shirt flopping over her wrists. "So what if I did?"

So what?

She was clearly on something, making driving a vehicle both dangerous and illegal.

She scoffed. "If you must know, my boyfriend, Michael, drove me here. He prefers not to see you, so he's waiting for me in the car." Her scowl deepened. "Don't judge, Jax. You have no idea how difficult it was for me to come here today."

Jax wondered if this Michael fellow was in any better condition to drive than Susie, but he didn't ask. Maybe it was better not to know.

"Come in." Jax sighed and stepped aside, sliding his hand from Faith's shoulder to her waist, keeping her close to his side. As much as he would have liked to believe he was somehow offering her comfort with the physical contact, he knew better.

Faith was his rock.

Jax gestured Susie to the armchair and guided Faith to the couch. He drew her down beside him and rested his arm over the back of the sofa after they sat. To his relief, Faith didn't protest. She seemed to understand that he wanted Susie to know he'd moved on with his life—although probably not as far as Susie might interpret, given Faith's presence and their body language toward each other.

Susie gave Faith a pointed look. "Jax and I need to talk. Alone."

He stiffened and slid his arm firmly around Faith's shoulders. "Faith stays. Anything you have to say to me you can say to both of us."

And to his mother, who was standing just out of sight in the space that separated the family room from the dining room. Jax had seen her when he'd turned around to let Susie in.

He figured she would make her presence known if and when she wanted to, and in the meantime, she had as much a right to hear this conversation as anybody present.

"Make it quick," he said. "My brothers will be here in a few minutes for a family dinner."

"Oh! And how are Nick and Slade?" Susie's voice was animated, sounding as if they were old friends engaged in small talk.

He raised his brows. As if she cared.

"Get to the point." Maybe his voice was a little too abrupt, but what did she expect? He was coping the best he could, given the circumstances.

"Okay." Susie smoothed her palms on her jeans and pulled her mouth into a pout, an expression that used to work especially well on Jax. Now he felt nothing other than mild annoyance and the urge to roll his eyes.

"Well, then, if we're not going to talk, I'd like to see the babies now." The cavalier way she referred to her children made him sick, and even worse was the way she shifted her gaze to Faith. "Why don't you be a dear and go get them for me?"

"No." He wasn't going to beat around the bush with this, and he wasn't about to give in to her demands. "You are in no condition to see the twins right now."

He was torn. In a perfect world, the twins would be raised by both a mother and a father, and neither parent would ever have to be separated from them. But he had to do what was best for his babies. Even were Susie not as high as a kite, she was still the woman who had had the gall to dump Rose and Violet on his doorstep. He couldn't trust her to be someone whom the twins could count on, and he wouldn't risk hurting them by letting her back into their lives. Not when there was every chance she'd just let them down again.

He suddenly wished Faith was the twins' mother. She would never put her own needs above the girls', and under her gentle guidance his babies would each grow up to become a strong, independent woman, as Faith was.

He didn't even realize he was squeezing her shoulders

until she cleared her throat and glanced up at Jax, her gaze silently asking him if it was okay for her to speak.

Of course she should speak her mind. He nodded briefly.

"Honestly, Susie," Faith began, "I think you lost your rights to Rose and Violet the moment you left them on Jax's front porch and walked away."

"Who? And who cares what you think, anyway?" Susie crossed her arms and glared at Faith.

"I care," Jax assured both ladies. "As for the nicknames, we didn't know the twins' names when you left them with us. If you recall, you didn't even bother to include that information. I tried repeatedly to get a hold of you, but you refused to pick up your phone or reply to any of my messages. So we nicknamed them Rose and Violet. They are a good fit for their individual personalities."

"We?" Susie glared at Faith, but Faith didn't respond in kind. She kept her spine erect and her chin high. Jax could feel the tension in her shoulders, but it didn't show on her face.

"You let some woman nickname *our* babies? Their names," Susie informed them, "are Elaine and Patricia."

"Fine. Elaine and Patricia. Good to know. Birth certificates would be nice." So now he knew the twins' legal names. But he was still going to call the girls Rose and Violet. He couldn't and wouldn't change that now. Their names wouldn't change, and neither would their living situation.

"What *is* your plan?" Faith asked. "For after you see the babies, I mean?"

Susie shrugged. "I haven't thought that far ahead. I guess Michael and I will take them back to our place."

"I see," Faith said drily. "You have cribs? Diapers? Formula? You've babyproofed your home?"

Susie looked unsure of herself. "Well, no. We live in a trailer, but it can't be that hard to—"

"You need plug protectors for every outlet." Jax pushed his advantage. "All of your *medicine*—" he emphasized the word "—has to be locked away."

"All of your cabinets and drawers need child locks," Faith added.

"They're only tiny babies. They can't even crawl yet," she argued. "Why would I need child locks?"

Jax wondered if she still pictured the children as she'd left them. Didn't she realize how much they'd grown in the two months he'd had them? "They can roll over," Jax said proudly, feeling the accomplishment just as strongly as if he'd done it himself. "I do tummy time with them every day, and they are really strong. They can even sit up with help."

"Tummy what?"

Jax wasn't about to go into all the details of child rearing—or any of them, for that matter—because he'd already decided it wasn't in his children's best interest to have Susie in their lives. Not until she'd cleaned up her own life. If that ever happened.

"Did you not read any baby books during your pregnancy?" Faith asked in astonishment.

Susie snorted. "Not that it's any of your business, but I didn't want to be pregnant in the first place. So no, I did not read any baby books."

The pained expression that crossed Jax's face nearly ripped Faith's heart out. He might have been caught completely unaware on the day he found the twins left on his doorstep, but from the very first second, he'd loved those girls with every part of his heart and soul. For him to hear that Susie had never wanted them in the first place...

Since she'd abandoned them, it wasn't a huge stretch for Faith to believe it, but she knew it had to hurt Jax. For his babies' own mother to treat them with such a blasé attitude was beyond the pale for any man.

"I was going to give them up for adoption to some needy couple like you see in the movies," she said, sounding completely juvenile and at the same time self-righteous, as if someone ought to crown her for her thoughtfulness and charity. How far was that from the truth? "But then after I had them I thought it might be kind of fun to be a mom. So I kept them instead."

"But you didn't keep them," Jax reminded her, his jaw clamped so tight he was speaking through his clenched teeth. "You left them on my front porch. What happened, Susie? Motherhood wasn't all you thought it would be? Did it become too inconvenient for you? Were the kids cramping your style?"

His tone was laced with sarcasm, but Faith couldn't blame him for that. His muscles were pulsing, tightening in on themselves, like a cougar ready to spring on its prey.

She laid a gentle hand on his knee, reminding him of her support—and that it wouldn't do any good to argue with Susie. Not in her current state. He appeared to understand her unspoken gesture, taking a deep breath and covering her hand with his own.

"The first day was okay, but after that it got bad. Michael didn't like all the noise. He was complaining constantly, and he wasn't helping me at all. I didn't see why I had to do everything. I figured you have your whole family to help you out."

"And he does," Alice said, suddenly deciding to make her presence known. Faith hadn't actually seen her up to now but had assumed she was somewhere just out of sight, listening in on the conversation. "Those precious girls have us, and they have Faith."

Faith's heart welled. She'd never been included in a

family before. When she was growing up, it had just been her and her dad, and he'd never taken much interest in her. She'd spent enough time with Keith's son to fall in love with him, but Keith himself had never introduced her to his parents, which she now realized should have been a glaring neon sign to her that something was not right—much like the one Susie was holding up now.

Parts of Susie's story didn't add up. "Wait. So you want to take the babies back, right? But you said you're still with Michael."

She shrugged. "I am."

"Then what do you imagine is going to be different this time around?" Faith's patience was wearing thin, and she was struggling to keep a grasp on her temper. The last thing Jax needed now was for her to come unglued on him.

"The babies are older, right? Like Jax said. Almost sitting up and all that? They won't bawl like they did at first. They'll be easier to take care of."

"I've got news for you." Jax scoffed. "Babies cry. Even three-month-olds. That's one of the primary ways they communicate."

"Oh." Susie pursed her lips.

Jax blew out a breath. His hand slipped underneath Faith's, palm to palm, and he linked his fingers through hers. She gave his hand a reassuring squeeze.

"Susie, I've got to be honest with you, and you need to be honest with yourself. You're in no condition to care for the twins. You need some time to figure out your own life. Get yourself clean."

"But I want to see the babies now. Tonight."

"That's not going to happen." Jax was firm but gentle. Faith admired his self-control. She wasn't sure she would have behaved as well as he was doing. "Not in your present condition. I'm not trying to be unreasonable, but I don't want the children to see you this way."

"They're just babies!" Susie wailed, loud enough to *wake* the babies.

"Nevertheless, this is nonnegotiable."

"I have rights."

"I don't think you do. You gave up your rights the moment you abandoned your children. Your current lifestyle doesn't lend itself to a family. Take a look at yourself. Think about Michael. You two don't want to be burdened with children. I, on the other hand, have a quiet lifestyle and my family's support. The girls need to stay with me. Please don't try to fight me on this."

Faith had to admit Susie looked legitimately crestfallen, the way a child would if her ice cream fell out of her cone and landed on the hot sidewalk. In that moment, she genuinely felt sorry for Susie, who'd somehow strayed far from the path of her youth. Faith prayed she'd find God's redeeming grace.

But Faith was firmly with Jax where the welfare of the babies was concerned. Susie was in no way a fit mother. Not now, possibly not ever.

"If and when you clean up your life, I'll be happy to meet together—just the two of us—and reevaluate how you might fit into the girls' lives. But even then, you have to realize that you'll need to make many changes to accommodate the twins, and I'll have to be sure you're making a permanent commitment to them. No disappearing for months at a time and then suddenly reappearing, deciding you want to play mommy again. It's not fair to the girls for their emotions to be jerked around like that, and I'll not allow it."

Faith's heart turned over. Big, strong Jax at his best, protecting his two little sweethearts, who had become his world. He'd learned how to feed them, change them, wash them and rock them to sleep, but the most important thing of all—loving them—he hadn't had to learn. He'd done it from the start.

Clearly there was nothing left to say to Susie, so Jax stood and pulled Faith to her feet, keeping hold of her hand. Susie also stood and stepped in front of Jax, gazing up at him with a mixture of sadness, resentment and contempt in her expression.

Her brow lowered and she lifted a hand, tracing her finger down the scar on Jax's face.

He shuddered. Faith tightened her grip on his hand.

Susie still has the power to get to him.

Of course she did. He'd been married to her for years, and it hadn't been his decision to split with her. His heart was probably breaking all over again, and looking at his miserable expression, Faith's heart broke for him.

She cared for Jax, probably a great deal more than she should, and she didn't like seeing him hurt.

"I think it's time for you to leave now." Faith's voice held an edge to it, and her proverbial claws sprang out. She'd had enough of *that woman* for one evening.

Susie's gaze flashed to her and she scoffed. "Excuse me?"

She might still have some influence over Jax, but if Susie thought she was going to intimidate Faith, she had another thing coming.

Susie turned back to Jax. "Honestly, I don't know how your little girlfriend here can even stand to look at you."

Jax looked as if he'd been slapped. Faith couldn't believe the woman could be so intentionally hurtful. She grabbed Susie's elbow and none too gently turned her toward the door.

"Go. Now," she demanded.

Susie tried to jerk her arm away, but Faith held it tight

until they reached the door. She was just reaching for the handle when the door opened from the outside, nearly plowing both women down.

Nick, Slade, his wife, Laney, and their toddler, Brody, barreled in the door, talking and laughing, their arms laden with food.

Nick and Slade froze in shocked silence when they realized Susie was in the room.

"What's *she* doing here?" Nick growled.

Faith waited a moment for Jax to respond, but he didn't appear to be able to find his voice.

"Susie was just leaving," Faith informed them, ushering her through the open doorway and watching until she and Michael drove out of sight.

When Faith turned around, she realized everyone's eyes were on her. Heat flared to her cheeks. She had no right to tell anyone to come or go. This wasn't her house, nor was it even her fight.

Suddenly the room burst into spontaneous applause.

"Well done," Slade cheered. "Way to put Susie in her place."

The protective gleam that Faith had so often seen in Jax's eyes was now reflected in his brothers' expressions, and she decided she liked them very much.

"I don't know," she said, dropping her gaze. She really hadn't done anything special.

"I do." Jax's usually clear voice was husky.

The monitor crackled to life with the sound of hungry, babbling babies. Jax and Faith looked at each other and laughed, the tension broken.

"Shall we?" Jax smiled and offered his arm to her. Her heart inflated and her stomach felt giddy.

Laney cleared her throat, and the room burst into action.

Chatter resumed as Jax's brothers moved into the dining room with their offerings for the party.

Jax and Faith walked in companionable silence to the nursery Alice had set up in her spare room.

Faith was lost in her thoughts—or rather, her feelings. She was trying to contain the quivering that came after an adrenaline rush. She was greatly relieved that the whole ordeal was over—for tonight, at least. She was sad that it would never really be over for Jax and the children. And—

Jax whirled around so suddenly that she nearly walked into him.

"Faith, before we go in and get the babies, I—I just want to tell you—" He paused and swept in a ragged breath, his Adam's apple bobbing. "That is, I—"

His lips were on hers before she knew what was happening. Soft, warm, sweet. His reassuring scent wrapped around her senses, a heady combination of leather and the countryside that was uniquely Jax.

His fingers threaded through her hair, drawing her nearer, while his other arm stole around her waist. He groaned her name and slanted his head, deepening the kiss, and she wrapped her arms around his neck, welcoming him into her heart.

After a minute Rose's babble became a wail, and Jax broke off the kiss, leaning his forehead against hers, their breaths mingling.

"I have to—" he started, then kissed her again.

She smiled into his lips. "I know. Go. I'm right behind you."

He brushed his palm down her cheek.

"No," he whispered softly. "You're not behind me, sweetheart. You're right by my side, and for that I'm eternally grateful."

Chapter Seven

Sunday morning, Jax attended church with his family. Faith was there, but she stayed chatting within a crowd of single women until the service was ready to begin, and then she sat on the opposite side of the sanctuary.

Little more than an awkward smile had passed between them the whole morning. The atmosphere wasn't companionable between them as it had always been before. She wouldn't even look him in the eye, and he had no doubt she was avoiding him.

He just didn't know why.

Thanks to Susie's inopportune visit, the celebratory dinner had been a little less animated than it might have otherwise been. His mother, Faith and Laney had tried their best to redirect the atmosphere and the conversation, mostly citing all the exciting things that were happening at Untamed—the repairs on the outbuildings, Faith's ever-growing herd and Jax's success gentling Fuego.

Jax appreciated the women's efforts to make things better, but he couldn't shake his myriad thoughts, which were traveling at the speed of light with a variety of emotions tagged to their backs.

He'd known Susie would return some day, asking for

the kids, but he hadn't been prepared for it to be so soon. Susie was a loose cannon. He would never know when she might appear to shoot things down again. He was just getting used to having his daughters here, and Susie could potentially ruin that.

And now he feared Susie had somehow damaged his relationship with Faith. Or was it the kiss they'd shared that was the reason she was avoiding him? But that left a lot of questions, and he knew the only way to get answers was to go to Faith and ask her straight-out what was bothering her.

Whatever she was feeling, he wanted to reassure her that last night's kiss wasn't a fluke. He needed time to put his head and heart in order, but if she was willing to wait for him, he'd like to see what they could have together. Would she be willing to wait? Was she even interested?

As soon as he got home from church, he asked his mother if she could watch the twins. He threw together a turkey sandwich and headed out to saddle his favorite mount, a blood-bay mare named Calamity, who'd earned her name with more than one fiasco over the years.

He took off down the trail at a gallop. Riding usually helped him clear his head. He could communicate with horses without the strain of lipreading and guessing at human body language. With people, he was always wondering if his responses were appropriate to what had been said. He always knew if his horses understood him or not.

Today the tension didn't leave him, no matter how hard he rode. Calamity could feel his anxiety and was skittish, throwing her head and bucking when he reined her in.

He ran a gloved hand down her neck. "Easy, girl. It's not your fault I'm antsy today." He dismounted and slid the reins over Calamity's head to lead her on foot.

"Maybe I can walk off some of this pent-up energy instead of making you do all the hard work," he told the horse, who nickered in response. "No sense transferring all my worries to you, right?"

How had his life fallen apart so quickly—and just when it was starting to make a little sense for once? He could only hope that he was misreading Faith's signals.

But could he really ask her to get in the middle of his mess of a life? She'd already done so much for him. How could he ask her for more?

He wasn't foolish enough to believe he'd seen the last of Susie. She'd get drunk or high and forget what a disaster last night had been, forget that he'd forbidden her to return until she got her life together. She'd pop up whenever and wherever she wanted.

He felt confident he could protect the twins while they were still babies, but what would happen later, when the girls were old enough to interact with her?

How would he be able to protect them then?

The alternative was taking legal measures, but he wasn't sold on that avenue, either, not when there was the possibility of the courts giving Susie custody. They couldn't see what he saw. There was just too much at stake.

His boots were giving him a blister on his ankle. In total opposition to the country song that suggested otherwise, his boots *weren't* meant for walking—at least for the distance he had gone today. He had to be several miles outside Serendipity town limits by now.

He groaned. Walking away from his problems wasn't going to make them go away. He needed to turn around and face them like a man—and in this case, a very special kind of man.

A daddy.

He mounted Calamity and turned her back toward town, letting her pick an easy gait and giving her her head. She knew the way back to the ranch without him directing the way. Slumped in his saddle and lost in thought, he didn't realize where Calamity had taken him until he saw the brand-new sign proudly marking Untamed Mustang Refuge.

Apparently, he'd been unconsciously directing the horse, after all.

He reined in, hesitating. Faith hadn't seemed too keen on seeing him this morning. She hadn't even come over to say hi to him. Of course, he hadn't approached her, either, having felt the unspoken tension between them.

He didn't get it. Last night they'd seemed so close. Now he felt as if there was a chasm between the two of them and neither of them knew how to cross it. *He* certainly didn't have a clue what had changed. The aisle that split the church sanctuary might as well have been the Grand Canyon.

Now that he thought about it, she'd started acting peculiar just after they'd stolen that moment together. She'd been gracious to a fault and genuinely appeared to enjoy interacting with his family. She'd even handled his brothers' teasing remarks about all the forks, giving every bit as good as she got. She'd insisted on helping clean the dishes, even though Alice had protested heartily that she was a guest in the house.

But she'd avoided being alone with him again. He'd had every intention of walking her out to her truck, where he hoped he might steal another kiss, to re-create the emotions he'd felt the first time. He didn't know where it would lead, if anywhere, but for the first time in years he'd seen a glimpse of something positive in his life.

First the twins.

And now Faith—except that she'd skipped out on him when he'd gone to change Violet's wet diaper. He was out of the room for no more than two minutes, but when he returned, Faith was gone. She'd left without giving him as much as a wave goodbye. He thought he deserved that much, at least, for all they'd been through together that evening.

Then again, maybe he was imagining the whole thing and he was the one creating the tension and the chasm. Maybe he was making a big deal out of nothing. He was probably being hypersensitive because seeing Susie again had brought back all of those bad memories.

The physical pain. The horror. The shame.

But that was the past, and the past was over.

Sitting here at the entrance of Faith's ranch wasn't going to do anybody any good, least of all him. He wouldn't know how Faith was feeling until he asked her. He needed to stop hesitating and start acting like a mature man instead of a brainless teenager.

Even though it was a day of rest, Jax knew he wouldn't find Faith in her still practically unlivable house. Ranch work didn't take a Sabbath, and though he'd helped her hire a couple of responsible teenage wranglers to assist her, she wasn't the type of person to delegate everything to someone else.

No—she'd be in the barn or the corral or the meadow, or maybe riding her gelding Alban around her thousand acres checking her fences for breaks. Even if she had nothing pressing to do, she would want to be out with her horses. They were her happy place.

He looped the reins back over Calamity's neck and led her out to the pasture to graze, then turned back toward the barn.

He'd reached the entrance and was waiting for his eyes to adjust to the dim interior when a shadow came whirling like a Tasmanian devil out from around the corner of the door.

Faith was walking backward, hauling heavy buckets of feed and overcompensating on the weight. Before he knew what was happening, her back had collided with his chest.

He reacted instinctively, wrapping his arms around her waist to keep her from falling, but he could do nothing about the buckets of grain she was carrying.

The aluminum buckets clanged to the dirt, and the oat mixture exploded into the air as if it had been set off by a detonator.

Faith shrieked in alarm and turned on him, a hand over her heart and her face flushed pink with exertion.

Or maybe anger.

"*What* do you think you are doing here?" she demanded, glaring up at him. "You nearly scared the life out of me. And just look what you've done to my feed!"

So—it was anger, then.

"I was getting ready to call out for you," he said, grabbing one of the buckets and crouching to scoop the oats back into it. Most of the feed was salvageable, although some of the grain would be lost in the dirt. "I was just letting my eyes adjust to the darkness first."

She harrumphed and grabbed the other bucket, scooping up the nearest pile of grain and tossing it inside.

"I apologize, Faith. Really. Come on. I didn't mean to startle you."

"No biggie." She didn't meet his gaze. Instead, she tossed more oats into her bucket with a little more fervor than was strictly necessary.

Jax sat back on his heels and braced his hands on his thighs. He waited for her to stop her frantic activity, but it was almost as if she didn't see him there.

Except he knew she did.

"Faith," he said, reaching for her elbow. "Will you just stop for a second?"

She brushed her hair out of her eyes with the back of one hand and finally met his gaze. "What?"

"Why are you mad at me?"

She stood and shook her head. "I'm not mad. You startled me. That's all." Her eyes narrowed on him. "Why are you here on a Sunday, anyway?"

Jax sighed inwardly. Stubborn woman. He wasn't talking about their little run-in in the stable just now, and she knew it.

"You were avoiding me in church this morning. Do you want to tell me what is going on with you?"

"No, not really."

She stood and grabbed Jax's bucket from him, striding off to the corral. He followed close behind, jamming his hands into the front pockets of his jeans so he wouldn't give in to the sudden urge to throttle her.

She hung the buckets on a hook in the corral. Two black-and-white pinto yearlings huddled as far away from Faith as possible until she tapped her hand against one of the buckets.

"Come on, guys. This is the good stuff."

She leaned her elbow against the corral fence and waited. Jax thought her posture was a little too stiff and was fairly certain he was the cause of it.

He still had a pretty major learning curve where women were concerned, especially Faith, but he knew enough to know that now might not be the best time to mention anything posture or tension related. He didn't have a death wish.

The colts snuffed and snorted, but eventually the idea of a gourmet meal won out over having to eat it with a strange human standing next to them.

"They're beautiful," he remarked when the horses were well into their dinner.

"Aren't they? It's hard to believe they were considered expendable. Some cattle ranchers didn't want the wild horses grazing on public land near their ranches. Grass guzzlers, they call them. So when new foals are born, it doesn't go over very well with those ranchers. These two sweet colts were in what they call *temporary holding*, although it's rarely temporary. More like a way to thin out the herd."

"They look like they're in pretty good condition." Slowly and smoothly, he moved closer to them to get a better look. One of the horses briefly pinned his ears back, but Jax's presence didn't stop him from eating. What was one more human in the big scheme of things?

"They are. The vet gave them both a clean bill of health. I'm just giving them a little extra nutritional head start. I've been introducing them to the herd a few horses at a time while you were out working with Fuego. They're doing well. Willow seems to have taken a special interest in them. I think they're about ready to be able to taste full freedom, or at least as much as I can offer them."

Faith appeared to have lost the tension in her shoulders. She was breathing easier, and her hazel eyes were gleaming, a beautiful mixture of greens and golds, just as they always were when she talked about her herd.

Horses.

Jax realized with a sudden burst of inspiration that horses were their bridge to communication, the one thing they had absolutely in common. No matter what else was going on between them—and he was still completely in the dark as to what that might be—they had horses.

"Look, I don't want to push you, but—"

"You already did, remember?" she said with a strained laugh. "You nearly knocked me down back there in the barn."

"Hey. You ran into me, remember?" he protested.

"Only because you were looming in the doorway as silent as a mouse."

Jax smiled and relaxed a little. He'd never been compared to a mouse before. A monster, maybe.

Anyway, if Faith was bantering with him, it couldn't be all bad, could it? Did a man have room to hope?

"Can I help you with your chores?" he offered. He figured he might as well stay on neutral ground, at least for the time being. Eventually the serious conversation would have to happen, but it didn't have to be right this second.

She shook her head, and Jax felt her refusal like a punch in the gut. She'd always been happy to have his help before. For her to turn it down now must mean that she had decided to push him away. The kiss last night, and the comfortable companionship they'd built over the preceding weeks—she'd decided she didn't want that. Didn't want *him*.

Her rejection hurt. Really hurt. He never should have let himself become vulnerable to another woman. He shouldn't have allowed her to get close to him. Hadn't he learned anything from Susie?

"Okay, well then, I guess I'll—"

"No—I mean, I've finished with all my chores for now," she qualified.

He let out a breath he hadn't even realized he'd been holding, but it caught tight in his throat, giving it a ragged quality.

"If you want to take Calamity's tack off and give her a quick rubdown in one of the stalls, I'll go up to the house and make us a pot of coffee." She glanced up at the sky to the gray clouds rolling in. "It looks like it might rain."

"A hot cup of coffee would be nice but…" He paused,

unsure how he should frame his question without heading down the wrong path again.

"But what?" She tilted her chin and regarded him calmly. There was no anger or frustration in her expression. In fact, Jax couldn't read it at all. He had no idea what she was thinking.

That was unnerving.

He cleared his throat. "I was just wondering—why the sudden change of heart? Last night I thought we were—" He paused to find the right word. "Close. This morning I had the distinct impression you were avoiding me."

She sighed with so much emotion that all he could think of was how much he wanted to wrap her in his arms, tuck her head under his chin and hold her until the world went away.

But he knew better than to try that right now, not when something was so obviously bothering her—something that involved him.

So it was coffee, then. For now.

She still hadn't responded to his question, and he thought perhaps she wasn't going to. She ran a hand across her cheek, leaving a tiny trail of dirt.

Jax's gaze seized on it, and he clenched his fists to keep from following the line with his finger.

Finally, she spoke. "Ignoring this—*problem*—isn't going to make it go away. We both live in the same town, attend the same church. You're right. We need to talk. Now is as good a time as any."

Problem?

So she thought he was a problem. Well, it wouldn't be the first time. His chest tightened defensively over his heart. The emotional shields dropped into place.

Faith might not care about his outward scars, but it sounded as if she was about to add to his inward ones.

Even if she didn't mean to, and even if she didn't understand what she was doing, her words had the ability to pierce him straight through to his heart.

Because there weren't walls high enough or armor strong enough to protect him from Faith. He shouldn't have let himself develop feelings for her, but he had.

He wouldn't survive another broken heart.

Faith scooped four measures of hazelnut-flavored coffee into the coffeemaker basket, added water and pressed the on button. She had about five minutes max to gather her thoughts, to be able to give Jax a coherent explanation for her completely inexplicable behavior.

She knew what Jax had been through, understood that, especially after the kiss they'd shared, the way she was suddenly backing away from him was hurting him.

She would never in a million years have wanted to be someone who could cause Jax pain, but that didn't change the fact that she was in that very place now. She'd let herself grow close to him, had somehow even encouraged him to have feelings for her. She didn't even know exactly how that had happened, but when he'd turned around and planted one on her, there was no doubt that it *had* happened.

She wished she had been transparent about her past from the get-go. Then he'd understand why the recent events had affected her the way they had.

But she hadn't shared her past with him, and now it was too late. There weren't words to make this better, and there were no excuses. *I'm sorry* wouldn't be good enough. She had to get some distance from him, and no matter what she said, how she tried to explain, he would take it as a rejection—not of their relationship, but of *him*, his very essence, of who he was as a person.

Which was the furthest thing from the truth. It was because she cared for Jax and his sweet, darling baby girls that she could not let herself become more involved with him.

More than anything, she wanted to communicate that message to him, but no matter how she phrased it, she was going to come out sounding trite and clichéd.

It's not you, it's me.

The truth. And the ultimate brush-off.

She heard the screen door open and slam shut and then Jax stomping his boots on the welcome mat. He knew there was no need for him to take his boots off in her house. The stained pink carpet was well beyond repair and would have to be replaced—eventually. Sometime down the road, when she finally got around to repairing the house. And who in their right mind had originally chosen to cover their floor in garish pink carpet, anyway?

"Faith?" Jax called.

"In the kitchen."

He appeared in the main doorway before her statement was finished, which meant he'd been standing right there all along. She raised a brow.

"Last time I didn't call your name fast enough," he explained with the familiar half grin that made her heart dance. "So I thought I'd better be extra careful this time around, just in case you were—you know—walking backward carrying a couple of cups of hot coffee or something. Getting doused with oats is one thing. Scalding-hot liquid is quite another."

"Oh, you," she said, swatting his arm.

He laughed and ducked out of her reach.

Then their eyes met, and their amusement flickered to life, turning to something more akin to a warm fire in a hearth on a cold night.

Oh, why did this have to be so difficult? She'd never felt as much at ease with anyone as she did when she was with Jax. She could be herself with him. He understood her, and she believed she understood him, as well. Their friendship was rock solid.

If only it could remain a friendship.

But it couldn't. There was no possible way of it now. The kiss they'd shared the previous evening had taken the strength of their friendship and woven all kinds of new emotions into it, in a way that she knew they could not now unweave. It was the kind of experience she'd always dreamed of and yet never truly imagined existed.

Chemistry? Undeniable. There were stars and fireworks galore. But as deep as that was, their physical attraction to one another only scratched the surface of their interchange. It was like the lyrics to a song. The accompanying emotions were the music, the melody and harmony weaving in and out of her heart.

And ruining everything.

He pulled out a chair for her at the kitchen table and gestured for her to sit.

"Mugs?" he asked.

"Right above the coffeemaker."

"That's a sensible place to keep them."

"You make it sound like *sensible* is unusual for me."

He poured two cups and set one before her and one across the table before seating himself.

"I would never say any such thing. I'd never even think such a thought. Cream or sugar?"

She shook her head. "I take mine black."

"Yeah. Me, too." He cupped both hands around his mug. "I could never figure out why people dump so many extra calories into a perfectly good zero-calorie beverage."

She choked on a sip of coffee. "Right. Because you're so

calorie conscious. I guess you have to watch your weight, don't you, to make sure you still look cute in your skinny jeans?"

He barked out a laugh. Jax was a big man, but he didn't have an ounce of fat on him. He was pure, unadulterated muscle from head to toe. And his jeans looked mighty nice on him, even if they weren't of the skinny variety.

"I'll bet you don't even exercise."

His brow rose. "You mean like running? Or going to work out at the gym?"

She shrugged. "Something like that."

"I hate to break it to you, but there's no gym in Serendipity."

"That's a real shame."

"Not really. I wouldn't use it if there was. And running? Forget that noise. You won't see me running unless I'm being chased by a grizzly bear. And it'll have to be a big bear."

She chuckled. "Wow. And here I figured if you ran across a grizzly, you'd stick around and wrestle the thing."

"Only if you were watching." He winked at her. "Would that impress you?"

"Everything you do impresses me."

His gaze widened, then narrowed. He reached across the table and took her hands.

"You say that," he murmured, distracting her by rubbing his thumbs against her palms in small circles. Plus he was using that *voice*, the one that made Faith melt into a puddle of goo.

How fair was that?

"Something has shifted between us since last night," he continued. "I don't have a clue, but I'm pretty sure you know what it is. Tell me what's bothering you."

She dropped her gaze to where her hands lay in his. How could such big hands be so gentle?

"It's because I kissed you, right? It was too soon? If it was, I apologize. I got so caught up in the emotions of the night that I—"

"Don't apologize," she interrupted. "It wasn't the kiss, exactly, or the timing."

"We can take a step back," he continued, his voice low and urgent. "I can go as slow as you need me to, Faith, but you've got to talk to me. Please tell me what you need."

"I need you to leave me alone." She hated the way she'd blurted it out, but if she hadn't, she knew she would have forever lost her courage.

His gaze clouded and he swallowed hard. He let go of her hands and laid his own flat on the table, staring at his fingers as if they would give him the answers he was seeking.

Faith knew there were no answers. Not for this.

She expected him to make a hasty exit, but when he looked up she could see the determination lining his gaze. He wasn't going anywhere. Not without a better explanation, which she didn't know how to give him.

"No." He frowned and shook his head. "I refuse to believe that. Not after last night. What we have here growing between us, it's real. It's good. You know it and I know it. But you're afraid. Why? Is it because of Susie? Because—"

"It's not Susie. It's the babies."

He rocked back in his chair, clearly stunned.

"Rose and Violet?"

"I love those two little girls more than you can possibly imagine."

He let out a breath, reminding Faith of a deflating balloon. Relief flooded his expression.

"What did you think I meant?" she asked in alarm. "Surely you couldn't possibly think that I disliked them?"

"Two babies are a truckload of work," he said. "Some women would consider that a lot of baggage."

"Well, I'm not *some women*."

"No. You're not. You're special." Their gazes met and his eyes flamed.

"And so are your children. Don't you ever let anyone tell you those babies are anything other than the biggest blessings in your life. If a woman doesn't get that, she's not worthy of you."

He nodded. "I agree. But you love my babies and you are definitely a worthy woman and yet you don't want to be with me. Is that right?"

She pinched the bridge of her nose. "I do want to be with you. Very much. That's the problem."

"Because…?" He frowned over the rim of his coffee cup, his dark brow crinkling over his nose.

"Before I came here, I was in a relationship with a man who—" She paused. This was going to sound like a scripted reveal episode on a reality television show, but it was her story and it was her own fault for waiting this long to tell him the truth.

"Keith had a six-year-old son named Trevor. He introduced me to the boy just a few dates into our relationship."

"How long did it last?"

"Two years. I thought I was in love with Keith, although now, looking back at it, I realize I had no idea what true love was about. There were signs from the beginning that it wasn't a healthy relationship.

"To tell you the truth, I think I stayed solely because of Trevor. His life wasn't remotely stable, and he needed an adult he could trust, not to mention a female role model in his life." She sniffled. "And I loved him."

Tears burned in her eyes despite her best effort to keep them at bay.

Jax picked up his chair and brought it around to her side of the table and then pulled her into his arms.

She didn't stop him, even though it was hardly consistent with her intention of backing away from him. If anything, she was getting more and more involved by the second.

"Keith was never responsible as a man or as a father. I knew he was seeing multiple women, and yet I stayed to keep Trevor out of the cross fire.

"Until one day, out of the blue, Keith told me he never wanted to see me again. I don't know why he waited so long, or why he chose right then to kick me out of his life. I only know that he—he told me I was lousy mother material and that he'd never even consider having me raise his son. I knew in my heart that it wasn't true, but his words still stung and it crushed me that I'd never be able to see Trevor again."

She swept in a deep breath and shrugged helplessly. "That's it, in a nutshell—why it's just me and my horses out here on the range."

At least it had been, until she'd gotten all tangled up with Jax. If only she hadn't attended the auction, or if she'd bid on some nice old married rancher with twenty grandchildren. Why had she gone and bid on the most appealing man on the block?

Jax's growl surprised her. "Keith is the biggest fool who ever walked the planet." His voice was thick with emotion. He leaned back and took her face between his palms, gently stroking away her tears with the pads of his thumbs. "Listen to me, and listen to me good. There is no woman I've ever known who more deserves to be a mother. You will definitely be the greatest mom ever. I completely trust my babies with you. One hundred percent. Do you hear me? Those girls already understand that you are someone special in their lives.

"And in my life, too, Faith. I care for you."

She pulled back and crossed her arms as a shiver ran through her. "I know. I believe you. You know as well as I do that I've already developed special feelings for Rose and Violet, and I know they recognize that in me. But I can't risk going through that kind of experience ever again, Jax.

"You already have the power to break my heart. Every day I'm with you I grow closer and more attached to Rose and Violet. If we ever ended our relationship, I'd be ending my relationship with the twins, as well. I can't do that. I just can't. It wouldn't be fair to them, and it would be devastating to me. And before you say it, I don't think I can just be your friend. Not after last night."

She knew she should stand up and move away from him. She needed to put some physical distance between them. She couldn't think straight when she was looking into his warm chocolate eyes.

She knew that in her head, but she couldn't seem to make her limbs cooperate. She did not protest when he leaned in closer, even when he bent his head to brush his lips over hers. She laid her palm flat against his chest, but it was not to push him away.

She wanted to feel his heart beat.

"I understand," he murmured against her ear. "I do. And I don't claim to know what the answer is right now. I only know I can't let you go. We will find a way, Faith. I promise you that. Do you trust me?"

She nodded and laid her ear where her palm had been, listening to the steady, reassuring thump of his heart, breathing in his familiar scent.

She did trust him. He'd won her over the same way he'd

done with Fuego. With lots of patience and hard work. She believed him. She believed *in* him, probably more than he believed in himself.

They were a fine pair, the two of them, each broken in their own way.

"I'm sorry, Jax. This was a bad time for me to wig out on you this way, what with Susie coming by and all. I didn't mean to add to your grief."

He let out a deep breath and combed his fingers through his thick, dark hair. She sat back in her chair and brought her knees up to her chest, then picked up her coffee cup and took a long, satisfying sip of the now-lukewarm liquid. The hint of hazelnut lingered on her tongue.

"I've been thinking about the situation with Susie. I think I may have to take legal action," he said, stroking a hand down the stubble on his jaw. "I don't know how else to keep her away. But honestly, I hate to go that direction unless I have to. I can give the twins everything they need without a government document telling me to. But I don't trust her to keep her distance, just because it's the right thing to do. Getting custody officially will let me protect the twins from her. I'll get a DNA test done to prove my paternity in case my name isn't listed on the birth certificate."

"That's a good idea."

"And I'm going to do everything I can to keep interacting with Susie on my own terms. I hope—I pray—she wises up and gets the help she needs."

Faith put her hand on his. He linked their fingers.

"What happens if she keeps coming back?"

His lips thinned. "That thought occurred to me. I can't let it keep me up nights, or it will make me crazy. I've got too many good things going on in my life right now to let endless negative possibilities put a damper on it. I'll hire the best lawyer on the planet and fight tooth and nail for the twins. I don't know what I would do without my girls."

"I'm sure you will be able to—"

Her sentence was cut off by the eerie sound of a horse's scream.

Chapter Eight

Jax was on his feet in an instant, rushing toward the door. Faith knocked her cup over and righted it again, not bothering to wipe up the black liquid spreading across the table.

Rain was coming down in sheets, and thunder and lightning boomed and crackled. Jax knew the herd would probably be a little skittish because of the storm, but it shouldn't have put them in an all-out frenzy. Something else was wrong. He could feel it in his gut.

Faith grabbed his elbow, and he shot a glance back to her.

"What's happening?" she asked frantically, and he knew it wasn't the first time she'd asked. Stupid hearing loss.

"I don't know." He held out his hand to her. "Come on. Hurry."

Jax couldn't immediately see what was causing the herd to act up, but clearly something had majorly spooked them. It was only after they'd turned the corner of the barn that Jax realized what was happening.

Fire.

His scar tissue sparked to life with a scorching itch as if the flame was right on top of it, attacking him again.

The memory was as intense as the lightning above them. It came in short, sharp bursts like photographic images.

He sees the accident take place in front of him as if it plays out in slow motion. He watches the car's taillights gleam as it flies off an embankment. He hears the sickening crunch of the front end plowing headfirst into a tree.

The shrill horn peals and peals. He wants to cover his ears against the sound. It makes his ears hurt.

He reaches for his cell phone and calls 911, giving his location in a shaky voice.

He runs out in the rain, ignoring the downpour.

The car is on fire. How can it be on fire in the rain? The driver is slumped over the wheel and doesn't appear to be conscious.

He checks the driver's side door. It is locked. He runs around to try the passenger door. It is also locked.

He wraps his coat around his hand and punches through the passenger side window.

Once. Twice.

The shattered glass mirrors a spider web but does not break through.

Another punch. He's through. He trips the switch, unlocking all the doors.

The woman in the driver's seat is partially conscious after all, but she's nearly unresponsive. There's a kid who looks to be five or six in a booster seat in the back. He reaches for the booster seat first, unbuckling the belt. He carries the little boy, up the ravine, placing him in the safety of the truck until the paramedics arrive to help him.

He slides back down the ravine to rescue the woman. He knows it's not safe to try to move an injured person, but the car is still on fire. Do cars explode in real life like they do in movies?

He doesn't know. Can he wait, not knowing for sure?

The police are almost here. The fire department. Para-medics. They will know what to do.

But the fire.

The fire.

"Ma'am?" he yells. "Can you walk, if I help you?"

She nods and mumbles something in his ear but he can't understand her. Reaching under her shoulder, he supports her while she climbs out of the car. He walks her step by careful step up the embankment.

She's repeating something over and over, but the rain washes the sound away.

"What?" *He leans closer.*

"My baby. My baby."

A baby. Is there a baby in the car? Or is she talking about the little boy?

He slides down the hill and forces himself into the back-seat of the car. The storm is dark. There is no moon. He searches blindly with his hands for another child.

The engine explodes. The car lists and then overturns. Jax is flung forward, rolling over the backseat and into the front. His head strikes something hot. The last thing he remembers before passing out is the searing pain of skin on hot metal.

"Jax!" Faith was pulling on his arm, desperately trying to get his attention. He didn't know how long his shock had lasted. A few moments at least. "Do you see it? The fire?"

He nodded. The grass fire looked to be somewhere around the third meadow, probably caused by lightning. It might be hampered by the rain, but it was a real threat nonetheless. Fires like this could flare out of control within minutes.

And fire was Jax's worst nightmare come to life.

"What should we do?" Faith asked, wringing her hands. "I'll call 911 as soon as I get back in the barn."

"Yes, that should be the first order of business. I think the fire department should be able to take care of this grass fire fairly easily, but fire is a tricky thing. It's unreliable and has a mind of its own."

Unconsciously, he ran a finger across the scar on his face.

"Oh, Jax." She laid her hand on his scarred cheek and then hugged him fiercely.

"I'm fine. Look, we've got the rain in our favor. I'll get the Bobcat going. I don't know how much trenching I'll be able to do but every little bit helps, to keep the fire from crossing the line and destroying more of your land. And if you can find me a shovel, that will help, too."

"Should I go with you?"

"No. You need to look after the horses. Take Alban and see if you can find the herd and drive them into the corral. They'll be frightened so they may be more difficult than usual, but I know you can do it. It's time to prove your skills, Faith. The horses are going to be pretty stressed. Do whatever you can to keep them calm so you can get them where it's safe."

Faith stepped inside the barn and pulled out her phone, speaking with a 911 operator at the same time she retrieved a shovel for Jax.

He had the Bobcat running by the time she returned. He couldn't tell whether the moisture on her face was from the rain or from tears. He wiped her cheeks with his palms and kissed her forehead.

"Your horses will be fine, Faith. And don't worry. I'll save as much of your property as I can."

She squeezed him so hard he lost his breath.

"I don't care about my stupid land," she said with a sob. "Promise me you'll stay safe. Promise me, Jax."

He framed her face with his hands. "We'll get through

this, Faith. Together. God didn't bring us this far to leave us hanging now."

She nodded and set her jaw in determination. "Go."

He hopped into the Bobcat and made it about five feet before he stopped the vehicle again. He strode back to where Faith was still standing and kissed her long and hard.

"I love you."

She placed a palm on his cheek. "Go."

This time he continued down the road on the Bobcat, wishing the vehicle went faster. His good ear strained to hear anything above the roll of the storm and the hum of the engine, trying to make out the sound of stray horses or the sirens of rescue vehicles.

But all he could hear was his own ragged breathing cutting up the night air, growing shorter and more rapid as he drove closer and closer to the one fear he could never quite overcome.

He might not be able to do much to save the land, but he refused to quit now. He would fight with everything in him and do whatever he could. Faith had worked too hard to lose it all now.

And he wasn't going to allow himself to think about what would happen afterward.

He had declared his love for her, which had surprised him as much as it must have done her. She hadn't said she loved him back. He refused to be crushed by that knowledge. She had good reason to guard her heart. He hadn't yet offered her anything permanent and stable that she could trust, that she knew she would be able to depend on forever.

But he would—even if he had to walk through fire to do it.

Faith spent more time than she should have watching Jax leave, bobbing down the road in the little tractor. *Cou-*

rageous didn't even begin to describe his efforts, heading off to face his worst fears straight on.

She didn't have that strength. She had waited until Jax was back in the Bobcat before she'd whispered her own vow—

"I love you, too."

There was no way he could have heard it, and that was for the best.

She shook her head to regain her focus and ran back into the barn to grab her horse. She didn't bother tacking Alban up. She bridled him as fast as she could and mounted bareback. It would be a slick, dangerous ride in the pouring rain, especially in the dark, but she had to make sure her horses were safe and there was no time to spare.

She clicked her tongue and urged Alban into a gallop as soon as she had passed through the corral gate. She wished she'd thought to bring a flashlight, but she wouldn't have wanted to take the time to run back to the house to try to find one. She wasn't even sure she owned a flashlight.

Yet another mark on her record. Her learning curve was atrocious.

The storm clouds covered whatever moon there might have been, but the sky lit up with lightning often enough for her to find her way. She knew her property like the back of her hand, so even in the dark she felt confident in her direction.

Hearing the frightened nicker of a horse nearby, she pulled up, trotting toward the east fence where she thought she'd heard the sound.

She suspected it would take her a long time to round up all the horses, especially if they'd spooked and scattered. She prayed none of them had been caught up by the fire.

And she especially prayed for Jax, who had put himself directly in the path of those dreadful flames, just to help her. The physical part of it was bad enough without considering the fight of his life he was probably battling inside his head.

She'd seen his expression when he'd first caught sight of the fire, and she'd recognized the way his gaze faded into the past.

She'd lost him for a good minute as he'd probably relived the horrors of his accident. And now he was facing a fire again. A different sort of fire, and hopefully not one that would put him in personal danger, but as he'd said, flames were unpredictable and could take on a life of their own.

What if Jax got caught up out there?

If something happened to him, she would never forgive herself. He already had enough scars—inside and out—to last him a lifetime.

He had to stay safe. He'd told her he loved her, and she knew he didn't take those words lightly. It was hard for her to believe she'd even heard him right.

But she couldn't afford to think about that at the moment. His declaration had caught her completely off guard, and it had probably surprised him, as well. It would take her whole mind, body, soul and spirit to work through all the implications.

Right now she needed to keep her head in the game. She had to save her horses and hopefully most of her land.

The sky lit up, and she saw a flash of silver moving in the distance near the east fence in the second meadow, right near where she'd thought she'd heard the sound of horses. The area was about as far away from the fire as the horses could get without access to the corral.

Fuego.

She nudged Alban forward, happy to see her herd's stallion safely out of the way of the fire, even if she wasn't entirely certain he would take her direction to get back to the corral. She wasn't sure she possessed that skill level yet.

But she was all Fuego had, and she would have to be enough.

As she drew nearer she realized it wasn't just Fuego but her entire herd huddled together, with nearly every last horse present and accounted for.

Thank You, Lord.

Performing a quick head count, she realized there was only one horse missing, and she wasn't immediately sure which one. She wouldn't have time to do a full equine roll call until she had them all locked safe in the corral.

Fuego was running around the outside perimeter of the herd, neighing and snorting and keeping his mares and foals all together.

"Well done, Fuego," she said, although she wasn't sure he could hear her voice over the sound of the wind and rain.

Now was the hard part—communicating to the wild horses that they needed to be moved to the corral for their own safety until the fire was extinguished and they could return to the land.

If Fuego bucked her authority, the others would most certainly follow his lead.

She gritted her teeth. If that was the case, then she couldn't let him challenge her.

She adjusted her reins and pulled up beside Fuego, holding out her free hand for him to sniff. She could see the whites of his eyes and realized how close he was to spooking. His grunting was just short of frantic.

She held her breath and ran her palm down his neck. "It's okay, boy. We've got this all under control. You and I have to get your mares and foals to safety. You know that, right, Fuego? This is your band. It's up to you."

She didn't possess Jax's lyrical voice, but Fuego pricked

his ears and tossed his head, making snorting noises that almost sounded like speech.

"All right, then. Let's go." She rode to the back of the herd and waved her hands in large back-and-forth motions. "Let's go. Let's go now."

She weaved Alban back and forth a few times and managed to get the herd trotting in the right direction. Fuego seemed to be leading, although he occasionally swung around to urge a straggling colt or mare along.

They made surprisingly good progress, and it wasn't long before they crossed into the first meadow. Now was the hard part. The corral gate didn't have a big enough opening to accept all the horses at once, and she didn't have any help to keep them in any sort of line. She'd have to herd in a few at a time and hope the others didn't wander away.

But it turned out she *did* have help, after all. As she worked, Fuego watched over the rest of his band, keeping them together in a loose circle. It was almost as if he understood what she was doing and he was working with her.

It took her a few minutes, but she was finally ready for the last three horses—Willow and Pilgrim, the first two horses she'd received at Untamed, and Fuego himself.

But when she turned to herd them through the gate, only Willow and Pilgrim remained.

Fuego was gone.

Chapter Nine

Jax stood with his back against the Bobcat and watched the Serendipity Fire Department put out the last of the flames. Though he was standing in the rain, sweat drenched his forehead and salt stung his eyes. The sun was just starting to peek over the horizon, making the smoke look like a misty haze instead of the deadly threat it had felt like last night.

He'd used the small tractor to create as long of a trench as he could and as fast as possible to keep the fire from spreading. He had continued to help once the fire department arrived, but by the end of the night he could see what little good it had done. Despite his best efforts, Faith had still lost close to a hundred acres of grazing turf to the fire. It made him sick to think about.

Chief Jenkins, the fire chief, assured him that if it hadn't been for his efforts, the damage might have been a whole lot worse.

Jax wasn't satisfied with that answer. The damage was bad enough, and it would set Faith back substantially. If he'd been able to move faster, or if he had carved his trenches closer to the base of the fire…

"I'm going to drive the Bobcat back and check on Faith and the herd," he told Chief Jenkins, who shook his hand.

"You did well, Jax. We appreciate your efforts. The department will finish up things here, and then I'll come up to the house and let Faith know how things stand."

"Thanks for all you've done. I know Faith will want to express her gratitude, as well."

The Bobcat moved at a snail's pace, unlike the previous evening when it seemed to carry him to the fire much faster than he could handle. His heart had been beating out of his chest last night, trying to get to the fire and stop it from attacking Faith's property even as every instinct in his body told him to get as far away from the flames as he could. Now his heart was aching even worse, knowing he had to tell her the bad news about the destruction of her land before Captain Jenkins beat him to it. Better that the information come from a friend than from the fire chief.

He wondered not for the first time how Faith was handling dealing with the herd. He had every belief in her abilities. He just hoped she was aware of how good she was.

He hadn't seen her since they'd split the evening previous, nor had he spotted any stray horses lingering around, so he hoped all had gone well in that regard.

At least God had seen fit to save the house. And hopefully all the horses.

And most important of all, Faith herself.

He'd meant what he'd whispered into her ear the night before. It wasn't some kind of disaster declaration, made only because of adrenaline and the drama of the moment.

He was in love with her. It had started the moment she bid on him at the auction, even if it had only been because she felt a backward sense of compassion for his sorry mug. She'd been by his side through every catastrophe since then—one after another—and they'd had a few beautiful moments, too, such as the times they'd spent together with the twins and the incredible kiss they'd shared.

He'd grown used to having her in his life, helping her with her burdens and letting her help with his, being by her side, enjoying the way she offered up her own brand of strength and compassion, whether he asked for it or not. She was always there for him, no matter what.

And he wanted to be there for her, to protect her, provide for her and love her with his whole heart. If she'd let him, he wanted to take the savings he'd earned over the years as a horse trainer and partner with her to make Untamed everything she imagined it could be, and then some. If it was in his power, he wanted to make her dreams come true.

He also wanted to give her a family no one could take away from her—the family she'd always dreamed of. Wanted to fully entrust to her the care and love of Violet and Rose, giving her the opportunity to open her heart up to the children she'd longed for, completely without fear. He wouldn't be opposed to hearing the pitter-patter of even more little feet somewhere in the future, babies with Faith's hazel eyes and sweet smile.

He wanted to give her the world.

But was she willing to accept it from him? Did fear have too strong a hold on her heart for her to consider opening it to him? She didn't seem to want to fall in love again—and who was he to change her mind? A battered, scarred wreck of a man. But a man who loved her with all his heart. Would that be enough?

With nowhere else to turn, Jax decided to hand the situation over to God. When he'd become a father, it had given him a whole new outlook as to who God was as a Father, and Jax found himself turning to the Lord more often for help and guidance.

He prayed now as he drove, asking God for all the right

words to express the feelings in his heart. All of this meant nothing if he couldn't convince her she could trust him with her heart, if she couldn't finally lay her past to rest and realize she could truly hope for the future with him and the twins.

He of all people knew how hard it was to keep the past in the past, especially since *his* past seemed to keep popping back up in his life. But he also knew he couldn't let fear keep him from living his life to the fullest.

Last night Faith hadn't shared his sentiment, or at least she hadn't said the words aloud. It was his own fault that he'd picked the least opportune moment possible to make such a declaration.

His hopes were sky-high as he approached the ranch house, but he also felt as vulnerable as he'd ever been in his entire life. Faith was a kind woman, but even a compassionate rejection might be more than he could handle right now.

He was tired of hiding from life for fear of rejection. And Faith held that in the palm of her hand. If she didn't love him, then so be it. He would have to try to find satisfaction in being her friend. And he would keep trying to earn her trust and respect.

Just as long as she stayed in his life.

He spotted her long before she saw him. She was leaning against the corral fence, speaking to the horses. Alban's back was bare and his reins loosely tied to the fence.

At first glance it looked as if she'd managed to round up the entire herd. He was impressed with her skills, but then, he'd known she could do it. Even in the dark, and even in the pouring rain. When she set her mind on something, she accomplished it.

Just look how fast she'd learned how to handle running the ranch. For someone who'd not grown up with horses, she displayed considerable finesse with them. She had adapted far more gracefully than he had taken to caring for his twins. He still felt awkward sometimes when he was faced with daddy duties.

As soon as she saw him unfold himself from the Bobcat, she jumped down off the fence and ran to him, throwing her arms around his neck and squeezing him so hard she was choking him. He laughed and grabbed her waist, whirling her around and around.

He was so happy it took him a second to figure out she wasn't laughing with him. She was shaking so hard her teeth were chattering.

He pulled back to look at her face. He was surprised to see tears pouring down her cheeks. His gaze met hers.

"Sweetheart, what's wrong? Are you hurt?"

"I'm just so happy to see you."

"Well, that's good to know." He grinned and shook his head. He'd never understand why women cried when they were happy.

She touched his shoulder, his face, his ear, gently running her fingers against his scars. In some ways it was the same thing Susie had done, but it was such a different kind of caress that it was like night and day. There wasn't disgust or pity in her fingertips, nor even kindness or compassion. It was as if she was reassuring herself of his reality by touching those marks that were uniquely his to bear.

She sighed and brushed her palm down his whiskered cheek. He laid his hand over hers, holding her to him. "The fire is out, Faith. It's over."

He was about to tell her about the damage to her property, but she spoke first.

"I lost him."

What? Lost who? Had one of the horses perished in the fire?

"I'm sorry, Jax. I don't know what happened."

"To…?"

"Fuego. And after all you did for him. It was the weirdest thing I've ever experienced. And then to have it end like this—it just hurts my heart."

She took Jax's hand and threaded her fingers through his, drawing him toward the corral.

"By the time I found the horses, Fuego had rounded up practically the whole herd and had driven them to the eastern part of the second meadow."

"About as far away from the fire as he could get. That's my smart boy."

"I was shocked. He seemed to know what he needed to do to preserve the band."

"As I'm sure you're learning, horses are intelligent."

"I've always known that."

He smiled down at her. Maybe not always, but she certainly knew now.

"I herded the mares and foals back to the corral just like you told me to do. Fuego helped me, nudging the foals along and rounding up the occasional straggler."

She groaned in dismay. "I got them as far as the corral without any problems. I knew I was one horse short when I did a head count in the field. I couldn't take the time to figure which horse I was missing until I got them all rounded up in the corral. It broke my heart to even think about leaving a horse out there on its own, but I knew I had to put the well-being of the band over that of the one horse.

"The corral gate isn't big enough for me to be able to herd all the horses at once, so I rounded up three at a time. Fuego kept the rest of the band together while I did the herding. It was as if we were working as a team."

He nodded. "You were."

Her smile was tired, and though her tears had slowed, they hadn't stopped.

"Near the end I had three horses left—Willow, Pilgrim and Fuego. But when I got ready to herd them in, I discovered Fuego had disappeared. I looked around and he was just—*gone*."

"Hmm. That's odd."

"The horses in the corral were spooking all over the place. My presence seemed to calm them. I just couldn't justify leaving an entire herd of frightened wild horses cooped up in a corral by themselves to look for Fuego, even though I knew that's where they'd be safest."

"So you stayed with them," he guessed. "It was the right thing to do."

"But Fuego—"

"Is probably fine," Jax finished for her. "You said it yourself. He's a smart horse. He managed to get all the rest of the herd away from the fire. I doubt he'd go charging into it himself."

"I just keep thinking about how he got caught up in the lumber. If anything else happened to him, I'm not sure my heart would be able to stand it."

"I'll go look for him," he assured her. "Or better yet, we can go together. The horses will be fine unsupervised for an hour now that the fire is out and the sun is up. We'll put them in the first meadow and they can graze. Did you ever determine who else was missing?"

"A pregnant mare. Prada. She's close to her time. I'm praying nothing bad happened to her."

"We'll look for her, as well." He ran his gaze over her mount. "Please don't tell me you rode Alban bareback last night." He knew he sounded like a badgering schoolteacher, but he was soaked and exhausted beyond belief from staying up all night, and the thought of Faith galloping around bareback in the dark with slick rain pelting her and her wet mount was more than he could handle.

Didn't she know she could have hurt herself, fallen off and hit her head on a rock? His chest tightened at the thought.

She frowned. "I didn't want to take the time to tack up. As far as I was concerned, every second counted, and I still stand by that decision."

"Except that a horse's bare back is especially slippery when it's wet, and it would have taken all of five minutes to put a saddle on him. What would have happened if you'd hurt yourself?" His voice rose. "Did it even occur to you that you might be putting yourself in danger?"

She scoffed. "Of course it did. And I didn't have a lot of time to think through all of the implications. But now that I'm looking back on it, I would do exactly the same thing again, so stop bugging me about it."

Jax growled in frustration. Stubborn woman.

"Well, we're saddling him this time. Did you get your second riding horse in, or are we doubling up on Alban?"

"*Thankfully*," she said, emphasizing the word, "he showed up the day before yesterday. He's a beautiful quarter horse named Brobie. I'm warning you—he's only green broke. I'm not sure he's ready to ride in the open country yet."

Jax didn't care one whit if the horse was green broke or purple broke or if he had ever seen a saddle at all. Grumbling under his breath, he tacked up both horses. The woman was riding with a saddle this time.

He mounted Brobie and waited for her to mount Alban. "We should check the east fence where you found Fuego and the herd last night," he decided, knowing he sounded like a dictator but unable to temper his tone.

She lifted her chin and glared at him. "I agree."

Hmmph. Well, at least they agreed on something.

He led them at an easy lope, just fast enough that talking was difficult. He should probably be telling her all he knew about the fire and the damage to her land, but that news wasn't going anywhere. He'd let her regroup from one crisis at a time.

And try, this time, not to be so grumpy about it. He owed her an apology for being so short with her. She was still new to ranches and horses. So she'd made a mistake. Nothing bad had come of it. She was fine. *He'd* been the one to make a big deal about it.

He scowled, angry at himself. After today, with his huge display of bad temper, it would be a wonder if she agreed to marry him.

Marry him?

Yes. That's what he'd been dancing around when he'd been thinking of babies and families and offering Faith security and safety. He just hadn't formulated it in words, so much.

Now that he had the idea in his head, though, he liked it. What said *forever* like a diamond engagement ring?

Aaaand now he was starting to sound like a jewelry shop commercial. He wanted to provide a permanent commitment and express his love, but he hoped he wouldn't get as sappy as all that.

Was he getting ahead of himself? Probably. Just the previous night, he'd told her he loved her—and had then walked off without giving her a chance to respond. Maybe she was just waiting for the crisis to pass before letting him down gently. He knew with a bone-deep certainty that he wanted to spend the rest of his life with her. On the other hand, he had no idea what she wanted.

He just hoped it was him.

And he also hoped that she wouldn't stay mad at him

after their little spat this morning. He was glad to know she wasn't the kind of woman who held grudges.

But he wasn't about to propose out in a field on horseback while they were missing horses and they were both soaked to the bone and she was still mad at him for something stupid he'd said. He'd wait until today's chaos was in the past, and then he'd tell her everything—how much he loved her, how he wanted to build a life with her, how beautifully he thought their hopes and dreams for the future could mesh together. And then he'd ask her to marry him.

But none of that was going to happen today.

Faith surged ahead of him and cantered to the fence line, riding a few hundred yards before pulling up and returning to his side. He was struggling with the green-broke colt, who wanted to bolt instead of stand still.

"This is where they were last night, but I don't see any sign of Fuego or the mare."

"Then we've got to keep riding." Rats. He sounded like a dictator again.

Way to go, King Jax.

Thankfully, Faith didn't recognize his tone, or else she chose to ignore it.

Faith's land was fairly flat with only minor hills and ridges and a few random trees in the whole thousand acres. The horses had to be somewhere out of sight. He refused to think of any other outcome for them. Not until he had to.

"What about the copse of trees over by the stream?" she suggested. "I know some of the mares and foals like to hang out there."

That area was fairly close to where the fire had been. Too close, by Jax's estimation. Fuego wouldn't have gone that near to the flames. Unfortunately, it was more likely that he'd found a break in the fence and was long gone by now.

And the pregnant mare? She was anybody's guess. A crazed mare about to foal might have run straight into the fire.

Jax didn't want to suggest either of these possibilities. Not yet. But he didn't have any better alternatives to offer her, so he agreed with her suggestion and trailed her to the water. They followed along the streambed for about fifteen minutes before they heard distressed whinnying coming from the very copse of trees where Faith had guessed she would be.

Prada was lying on her side, her body covered with sweat. Her skin shook and she grunted and snorted and threw her head, clearly straining with the effort of pushing out the foal. Jax didn't know how long she'd been there, but it appeared a new life was about to make its entrance into the big wide world.

With a little cry of distress, Faith slid out of the saddle and ran toward the mare.

Jax wanted to call out to her, but before he had a chance, Fuego came out of nowhere, neighing and bucking angrily. The stallion had appointed himself protector of the laboring mare, and he wasn't happy about humans coming anywhere near her.

Jax knew his green-broke horse would be useless in this situation, and he had only seconds to spare before the stallion charged Faith.

He threw himself off the colt as if he were bulldogging, landing halfway across Fuego's back. He grabbed a handful of mane and struggled to pull himself onto the horse's back. Fuego turned his head and snorted, then threw his weight to one side and then the other, rearing to the front and then the back, turning in tight circles and trying desperately to dislodge his unwelcome rider.

"Easy, boy," he called, but the horse was too wound up to listen to his voice.

Jax somehow managed to stay on Fuego's back. He'd never had any inclination to try to ride a wild mustang stallion, bareback or otherwise, and he didn't want to now, but when the alternative was seeing Faith plowed down by an overprotective band leader, he'd do whatever he had to do. He wanted to yell at Faith to get away from the mare, to go back to Alban where she'd be safer, but Fuego's bucking kept jolting the breath out of him before he could speak.

Faith was hunched over by the mare's side, stroking her neck and speaking to her in soft tones. She seemed entirely unaware of the explosion of silver stallion going on behind her. The stream was rushing loudly beside them, swollen from the previous night's storm. The sound of the frothing water, on top of the mare's pained grunts, must have been enough to block out the noise of Fuego's temper tantrum.

"Faith!"

She turned in his direction and her eyes widened, her mouth gaping in fright.

Jax could feel his grip on Fuego faltering and knew he wouldn't be able to keep the stallion away from the mare—and Faith—for much longer. He opened his mouth one more time to try to warn her, but his words were lost at the same time he lost his seat.

He landed hard on his bad shoulder, and the pain of his scar roared to life, but he ignored it, pushing himself to his feet and running full force toward Faith.

He couldn't see Fuego but knew the stallion must be right behind him. Faith's eyes were still glued to his.

He charged forward and scooped her up by the waist. She screamed in alarm. He twisted hard, just barely missing the angry muzzle of the charging horse.

"Run," he said, pushing her in the direction from which they'd come. "Run and don't look back."

She cast a look over her shoulder and apparently saw Fuego and realized what danger she was in, because she actually listened to him. She tucked her head and ran, following the path of the streambed.

Jax turned back to the stallion, who was stomping and snorting, the whites of his eyes a reflection of his defensive frame of mind.

Jax slowly raised his hands. "Easy there, boy. Faith didn't mean to interrupt. She just wanted to see how Prada was doing. No harm, no foul."

Fuego snorted again but didn't charge him.

Progress. Jax let out his breath and calmed his posture. Fuego would sense any stress or tension Jax carried in his body. They'd already had quite a run-in today. He knew he probably wasn't on top of the stallion's friends list right now.

He backed up until he was even with Alban. If he could somehow manage to get mounted, he'd hopefully be able to handle Fuego and watch the mare for signs of distress, but it was a risk. Fuego could very easily charge him and prevent him from ever mounting Alban.

"It's okay, boy. Remember, we're the good guys," he said, keeping his voice low and even as he hooked his hand over the saddle horn and put his foot into the stirrup. "We're glad to see you both are safe, you know. The three of you, I mean. And I totally get why you'd want to keep an eye on one of your mares. You're a good boy."

Jax swung his leg over Alban's body and shifted his weight in the saddle.

Fuego hadn't moved but was still eyeing him warily.

"Let's just make sure everything is well with the foal,

and then I'm out of here," he promised, carefully watching Fuego's body language for any sign of a sudden movement.

He glanced behind him, but Faith was out of sight. He hoped she'd keep on running and wouldn't get it in her head to turn back over a mistaken sense of obligation toward him or the horses.

He watched the mare for a few more minutes until two wet legs appeared. Good. It looked as if the foal was in the right position for an easy birth. It would have been even easier for Prada if he was able to get down and offer her a bit of assistance, but there was no way he was going to put Fuego to the test again. That was a battle he knew he would lose, and he respected the stallion for that.

"Come on, girl," he cheered quietly. "You can do it."

The mare snorted, and with another big push the foal emerged and immediately started wriggling around. Prada whickered and rolled to her feet, nudging for her little chestnut foal to do the same.

Jax chuckled as the wobbly-legged foal struggled to follow its mama's lead. Fuego snorted and trotted back and forth around the area, acting like a proud papa even though it wasn't his foal.

I know how you feel, buddy. I've got a couple of kids myself. And even though I didn't know them before they were born, I couldn't be prouder of them.

Jax watched Fuego for a few more minutes and observed the mare and foal. He probably wouldn't have kept a stallion in the same meadow with a mare about to foal, but in this case it had turned out fine. Better than fine. All three horses were thriving.

And his job was done, at least for the time being. He had to find Faith before she managed to jog all the way back up to the house by herself. He nudged Alban's side and reached for Brobie's lead, frankly impressed that the green-broke colt hadn't bolted off somewhere during all the chaos. He'd be a good horse and a fine addition to Faith's stable. It would be nice for her to have more than one riding horse, if nothing else than for emergencies such as this one.

He leaned forward and all out galloped, enjoying the wind in his face, which, now that he thought about it, must look smeared and sticky from smoke and sweat. It was a wonder Faith hadn't said anything about it. She'd looked at him as if he was the most handsome man she'd ever seen.

So he was deaf and she was blind.

He caught up with her less than half a mile from the house. She wasn't running, but she was…*striding*. Stomping, maybe, her arms flinging back and forth as if she were punching the air.

He reined in beside her and dismounted, pulling the reins over Alban's head and handing them to her. She took them without slowing her pace or speaking to him. She hadn't even glanced at him since he'd ridden up.

So she was still mad at him, then.

He supposed he deserved it. And she might very well have misinterpreted his earlier actions with Fuego. She'd been concentrating on the mare. She probably hadn't seen him wrestling with the stallion or realized the possibility of her getting trampled under Fuego's mighty hooves.

And then there was the issue of him scooping her up like a cowboy loading a sack of oats in the back of his pickup truck. He'd tossed her around with just about as much finesse.

She whirled on him and pounded her fists into his chest. "What in the world were you thinking?"

Jax opened his mouth, probably to try to explain his side of things, but Faith was too angry to let him get a word in edgewise.

"You could have been killed, you crazy cowboy. And it would have been all. My. Fault! I can't believe I did something so stupid."

"It wasn't stupid. You were only thinking about the welfare of your mare."

"Right. And not that Fuego wouldn't be happy about me messing with one of his mares. Or that you would jump in to save me, putting yourself at risk, like you always do."

He had put his arms around her waist, and now he tightened his grip on her, tilting his head so his gaze caught hers.

"Did you even know Fuego was there?"

"Well, no. But that's beside the point. I put you in mortal danger."

He laughed.

Laughed!

Faith found nothing funny about this situation. She'd almost lost the love of her life before she'd even gotten to tell him he was the love of her life.

"I have to admit I never wanted to be a bronc rider. Now I'm certain I don't ever want to rodeo. I'll leave that kind of craziness to my ex-bull-riding brother."

"I can't believe you actually got on Fuego's back," she breathed. It was totally wrong in a million different ways, and she'd been scared out of her mind, but she had to admit it had been magnificent to watch—now that it was over and Jax was safe in her arms.

"And stayed there." He puffed out his chest and flexed his biceps. "For a minute, anyway."

"Yeah. Long enough for me to realize what a terrible mistake I had made. He didn't hurt you, did he? After I took off running? I know you took quite a sharp fall. You don't have any new bites for me to bandage?"

He kissed her forehead. "Other than a couple of bumps

and bruises, I came out unscathed. Alban helped me out when I needed him."

"He's a good horse."

"So is Fuego."

"I know. He was just being a wild stallion, right?"

"The best kind."

"How is Prada? She looked pretty awful when I was there with her."

"That's because she was just about to give birth. She's fine now, and you have a new little sweet chestnut filly in your herd."

"Oh, Jax." She tightened her arms around him. "I thought maybe there was something wrong with Prada. Or the baby. And I was so afraid Fuego was going to go ballistic on you." She shuddered and tears poured from her eyes.

She dashed them away with the back of her hand.

"I never cry when I'm frightened," she said. "Although admittedly I've never been *this* frightened before. Lately it seems I cry at the drop of a hat, but usually I only bawl when I'm angry about something."

He nodded solemnly. "Good to know. So if I see you crying, I should turn and walk the other direction."

She swatted his shoulder. "Stop giving me a hard time. I was really scared for you."

"Hey, who would tease you if I wasn't around to do it?"

"Exactly my point."

"Then I guess I'd better stay."

"In one piece, thank you."

"If you insist." He lowered his head and brushed his lips across hers. "We need to talk."

"Didn't we start last night with this same conversation?"

His eyes widened. "I hope not. I thought you were going to dump me."

"I was."

"Then I guess it's a good thing that the fire interrupted us." Jax paused and lifted his head. "Whoops. I forgot you have company."

"Company?"

"Chief Jenkins. He said he was going to come up to the house after the fire department was finished on your land. He wants to give you a report of the damage. It's not as bad as it could have been, but—"

"Jax. I can't believe you didn't mention this earlier. Here we are meandering along, and the fire chief is probably sitting on my front porch. What am I going to do? I can't invite him inside. My house is…"

"Unlivable?" he supplied for her.

"I was going to say *messy*, but I guess *unlivable* is another way to put it." She tossed the reins over Alban's neck. "I've really got to go if he's waiting."

Jax sighed heavily and shrugged his shoulders as if he was carrying a great weight upon them. "Every time I think we have a minute to finally talk, something happens."

"I know." She blew him a kiss. "Tomorrow. I promise."

They had a lot to talk about, but it was only after she'd ridden away that she realized she hadn't told Jax the one thing that really mattered most.

She hadn't said *I love you*.

She hadn't said *I love you*.

Jax had hoped he might hear those words from her lips, especially after he'd bulldogged-slash-bronc ridden a wild stallion on her behalf.

She'd been grateful enough, and her kiss had been both sweet and thorough. Sweet and thorough enough to banish nearly all of his doubts about her loving him back, after all.

But she hadn't said the words.

So did he wait until he was sure about her feelings before he proposed?

He didn't want to wait. He wanted to get back up on that stupid makeshift auction block in front of the entire blinking town and announce over the loudspeaker that he'd fallen in love with one very pretty mustang rescuer.

But that was out, so he had to come up with something a little cleverer to surprise his hopefully soon-to-be bride. Something that he could share with the whole world and yet would be personal, just for her.

He had the perfect plan in mind, but it was going to take some juggling on his part to pull it all together. He started by talking to his mom, his brothers and Laney, who all agreed they couldn't think of a better way for him to pop the question.

From there it was just a matter of spreading the word to everyone in Serendipity that Faith needed a bit of assistance around her ranch. It was actually Jax who needed the real help, but he couldn't carry out his plans without the town's full support.

Everyone had heard of the grass fire, so it was no great stretch to visit Cup O' Jo's and plant the seed in Jo's ear that Faith's house could really use an overhaul. And telling Jo was just about the same thing as telling the whole town. That woman could spread the word like nobody's business. He arranged for everyone to meet at Faith's ranch on Saturday, and on the off chance Faith visited town, asked his neighbors and friends to be hush-hush about it.

He wanted this to be the surprise of a lifetime.

He spent the week making lists and ordering materials. He even made a special trip into San Antonio for a ring. He still preferred to shop in Serendipity over a larger city, but a man had to make an exception once in a while, such as for the woman he loved.

He called Faith on Thursday evening to set the stage for the Saturday event. He wanted it to be a surprise, but he didn't want to accidentally catch her airing her literal laundry or anything embarrassing like that.

He intended to tell her that he and the vet would be coming by to check up on the new filly, but when Faith answered the phone, he didn't get past hello.

"Where have you been? I thought maybe Fuego caught up with you and stampeded you, after all."

"What?"

"You were the one who said we needed to talk. Wasn't that supposed to happen Monday?"

Jax frowned. His brain wasn't catching up as fast as Faith was speaking. He was feeling all happy and giddy and barely able to contain himself from belting out his love for her, and she was mad at him?

"I—er—"

"You can say anything, Jax. That you got busy at the ranch. That the twins caught pinkeye. Just please give me one good reason why you've left me hanging for nearly a week, or I'll hang up this phone right now."

Because I've got a ring in my pocket?

No. He couldn't tell her that. He *wanted* to tell her that, but it would ruin the surprise.

"I was busy. I *am* busy with something important that just couldn't wait. I've got some—*construction* issues I've been dealing with. Nothing I'd want to bother you with."

Until Saturday.

Her silence was deafening. It was worse than her expressing her hurt feelings.

"Look, I didn't mean to neglect you. I forgot we even had something going on Monday."

"Every week, Jax. Every single week you are over here all the time, helping out with the horses or fixing my fences or *something*. And then suddenly, this week of all weeks, when we're supposed to sit down and have a serious discussion, you are gone, like you dropped off the face of the planet. What am I supposed to think?"

He didn't know how to answer that question.

"You could have called me."

"I shouldn't have had to."

He sighed. "You're right. I should have called. But I'm not avoiding you." He kind of was, but not for the reasons she thought. "I'll make it up to you, I promise."

"Really?"

"Yes, really. Or don't you trust me?"

She mumbled something under her breath.

"What was that?"

"Yes, Jax, I trust you. I'm asking myself why at this point, but I trust you."

"Good. I'm glad to hear it."

"So are we ever going to have that talk, or have you moved on to bigger and better things?"

He started to laugh and then quickly smothered it.

Bigger and better things. Definitely.

"I called because I wanted to bring the vet out to see the little chestnut filly of Prada's. You know, just to make sure she's faring well?"

"I've been keeping an eye on her. She's nursing well and Prada is a good mother. But I won't say no to the vet taking a look at her."

Whew. His ruse was going to stand, then. For a second there he'd been worried. He hadn't thought about what he was going to do if she'd said no.

"Okay, I'll see you Saturday morning. Say about seven o'clock? We can talk afterward if you'd like."

"Sure. And Jax?"

"Hmm?"

"If you don't mind, will you bring the babies? I miss them almost as much as I miss you."

"Sure. I can bring the babies."

And my family, and everyone else in town.

Jax hung up smiling.

Chapter Ten

Faith was dressed and ready at five thirty in the morning on Saturday. She'd put on a new blouse and had spent extra time on her hair.

To meet with the vet. Jax was going to razz her for sure, even if he knew perfectly well that the extra effort was on his behalf.

She was still mad at him for ignoring her the whole week. She supposed it was past time he focused on his own life rather than rushing around to take care of hers. But it had still stunned her when he didn't show up on Monday.

They'd talked about Monday, right?

Not really. She'd blown him a kiss, that was all. She'd been the one to mention Monday, and only because she could hardly wait to say the words.

Jax, I love you.

She'd recited them enough times. Surely they'd come out of her mouth this time, and hopefully somewhat coherently. But then Tuesday, Wednesday and Thursday had gone by and she'd heard nothing from him. She couldn't bring herself to call him. She didn't know whether to be relieved or furious when he'd finally phoned her on Thursday evening. She'd responded with a little of both.

Yes, it was the twenty-first century and she had a cell phone. She could just as easily have called him, or shown up at his ranch, for that matter. But something felt different. She couldn't put her finger on it, but she could sense it and it made her feel that the decision to reach out had to come from him.

She was half-afraid he was going to rescind his feelings for her. Maybe that's why she never quite pushed the call button when she started to dial Jax's number.

She checked the clock on the stove. A quarter past six. She still had some chores to do in the barn, and she wanted to bring out some oats for Prada. Being a new mommy, the mare could use the extra nutrition, and Faith figured she might as well spoil Prada while her filly was being examined by the vet.

She looked at her cell phone only a half dozen more times before seven o'clock rolled around—and then passed by. The clock displayed one minute past the hour, then two.

Jax was late, and he was never late. Maybe the vet was one of those guys who was never on time, or maybe there had been some kind of animal emergency.

And then she heard the roaring of dozens of truck engines coming down the road that bordered her house. She frowned, hoping the noise wouldn't bother her herd.

What was going on, anyway?

She was even more surprised when the trucks started pulling into her driveway, all laden with two-by-fours and circular saws and huge cans of paint. Someone had made a big mistake. They had to be looking for a neighbor's house. It looked as if everyone in town was going to this shindig, and she wondered that she hadn't heard about it. She'd been to Cup O' Jo's twice this week. That's usually where she heard all about the latest upcoming social event.

She went out to tell someone they were in the wrong place when Jax strode up, a baby car seat in each arm.

"Sorry we're late. It took me a little longer than usual to dress Violet and Rose."

She glanced down at the babies, who were each covered with frills and ribbons. Rose in a rose-colored dress and Violet in violet.

"Making it easy for the neighbors?" she teased.

He grinned. "Something like that."

"Well, they look very nice. But speaking of neighbors—do you know where all of these people are headed? They mistakenly pulled into my driveway, and I'm not sure where to direct them."

"Oh, don't worry about that. I've got it covered."

She raised a brow. "Meaning?"

Alice approached with a wide smile. "Come on, Faith, darling. You're the guest of honor." Alice laced her arm through Faith's and led her away from Jax, who just stood there grinning like an idiot.

She looked at Alice, who led her up to one of the rocking chairs on the porch. "I don't know what that means."

"What that means, my dear," said Jo Spencer, pressing Faith into the chair, "is that you get to sit back and watch while we fix up this ol' house of yours."

"I'm sorry?" She couldn't help but stare at the gregarious redhead's T-shirt, which read My Horse Is a Mustang.

"It's our latest community service project. We've got everything—the tools, the materials and, most important, lunch."

She was about to say she didn't take charity, but Untamed Mustang Refuge actually *was* a charity, so technically that wasn't a feasible argument. A workday on the land or fence-mending might be in order, but—

"My *house*?"

"You'd be surprised at what the townspeople can do in one day. We'll have it looking as good as new," Alice assured her. "Jax even bought some new furniture."

"He did what?"

"Oops," Jo said, covering her giggle with her palm. "I guess we let the cat out of the bag. Was it supposed to be a surprise?"

"This whole thing is a surprise."

"My son did well, then." Alice's voice was full of pride, and Faith supposed it should be, if Jax had organized the entire event.

She was glad she was sitting down because she was beginning to feel a bit overwhelmed. She pressed her palms to her eyes, wondering if someone had a paper bag she could breathe into.

"You don't look so good. Are you feeling okay?" Jax's lyrical voice actually sounded worried.

"I'm feeling overwhelmed, is what I'm feeling. You didn't think it might be a good idea to mention the *entire town* was going to be visiting me today?"

He gave her a once-over and smiled appreciatively. "What are you worried about? You look great today."

She blushed. She *had* dressed up for him. A little. It was nice that he noticed.

"You don't have to worry about a thing. We've got it all under control."

"I can see that," she replied wryly.

He ignored her tone. "The ladies will be setting up lunch pretty soon. I can guarantee you it will be the best country cooking you have ever tasted."

"This is all nice. But why me?"

"Why not you? You put every bit of your effort into your horses. The least we can do is see that you and your home are taken care of, as well."

His gaze warmed and so did her heart. She'd known she belonged in Serendipity from the very first day she was here, the day she'd bid on a big, brooding cowboy with a heart of gold.

"I have to go now since I'm—" He paused. "Kind of in charge of organizing this." Before she could get a word in, he said, "But I'll be back as soon as I can. In the meantime, grab yourself a lemonade and try to enjoy the day."

"Jax?"

He turned back to her.

"What about the vet? Is he even coming, or did you just make that up?"

"Oh, he's coming. Around lunchtime, I think. He loves a good meal."

"But he'll look at the filly, right?"

Jax smiled. "Of course. I'm not going to let that little girl down. I had the privilege of seeing her be born. Have you named her yet?"

"No. I thought maybe we could name her together."

"Great idea. I'll see you at lunch."

She watched Jax walk away, but she lost track of him soon after that. It was hard to make out anyone in particular when everyone was wearing a cowboy hat. At length she took Jax's advice and got a glass of lemonade. She tried to offer to help at the food tables but was promptly turned away.

Everyone seemed to know that this was *her day*—even people she hadn't met before. She wondered exactly what Jax had told them. Whatever it was, it must have been good.

She wandered around, watching folks thatching her roof and painting her barn. It actually looked quite nice after it had been painted in the red and white colors it was supposed to be. Almost like something off a country calendar.

She was surprised when Frank Spencer, Jo's husband, approached her and pulled her aside.

"Now, I know you have a nice big sign out in front of your ranch," he said in a gruff but friendly voice. "But I thought maybe you'd like to have something to hang over your barn, so I—uh—well, here. Take this."

He pointed to a large, tissue-wrapped package lying next to the side of the barn and walked away without another word. Curious, she pulled back the tissue to find a handmade burned-wood carving.

Untamed.

She swallowed hard but the tears still came. This wasn't about fixing up an old house or painting a barn. It was about a community accepting her as their own, and not just her, but the horse rescue she represented.

She was certain there was no better feeling in the world.

She tried to find Frank to thank him for his thoughtful gift, but he had disappeared. A few minutes later, Jo pulled her aside, letting her know lunch was about to begin.

"Folks," she called, loud enough to get the attention of those closest around her. From there, people continued calling and whistling until everyone was looking at Jo— and at Faith.

She was beginning to understand how Jax must have felt up on that auction block.

"Today we're celebrating with our new neighbor, Faith Dugan. As most of you know, she has put a great deal of time and effort into getting this here mustang refuge up and running. I'm sure I can speak for her when I say she appreciates all that you've done for her today. And if you're feeling so inclined, she could also use a little cash to help with the horses' upkeep and in fixing up her land that was recently burned. She didn't ask for that, by the way. I extemporized." Jo laughed heartily at her own joke, but Faith noticed that Frank had reappeared and was passing his hat. People were reaching into their pockets just as surely as if it was a Sunday morning offering.

"I know everyone is ready to dig in to all this great food," Jo continued, to a big round of applause. "But there's one more item on our agenda."

The crowd parted, and Faith saw Jax at the corral gate. He and the vet were crouched over the little chestnut filly. Jax looked up and grinned, then motioned for her to join him.

She held her breath. How could the newborn foal have anything to do with—*whatever* was going on?

"Vet says she checks out good," Jax told her, loud enough for everyone to hear.

She questioned him with her eyes, but he was giving nothing away. He just kept smiling.

"That's—nice." She wished she'd read this script in advance. She had no idea what she was supposed to say.

"I was thinking we might want to name her. This seems like as good a day as any." He said it in such an offhand way she would have believed he was just making casual conversation, except for the fact that they were surrounded by the entire population of Serendipity and they were all watching avidly.

"I thought maybe Rose and Violet could help us pick out the perfect name."

"O-kay."

"Mama? Jo? Will you please bring the babies out here?"

The two ladies didn't need to be told twice. She'd never seen Jo Murphy walk so fast, and even Alice, with her arthritis, was moving at a clipped pace. The animation in their faces was a dead giveaway to—something.

They put the babies down in front of Faith and stepped away. She looked at Jax, wondering what she was supposed to do. It wasn't as if the babies were going to tell her a name.

Or were they?

She remembered the first time she'd seen the twins, so sweet and vulnerable as they waited for their daddy to come rescue them.

They hadn't had names. She and Jax had searched them for notes. She bent down and brushed her hand through Rose's ruffled dress.

Sure enough, there was a note there, folded in half and fastened with a diaper pin. She laughed as she removed it and waved it for the crowd's benefit. She was about to open it when Jax stopped her.

"Wait. Get Violet's note first. It'll make more sense if you have both of the notes together."

This whole thing was making less than no sense to Faith, but she went along for the ride, feeling as if she was taking part in some larger-than-life baby-shower game, with diaper pins and newborn foals.

She stood with a folded note in each hand. "Can I open them now?"

Jax jammed his hands into the front pockets of his blue jeans. "Yeah. Yes. Open them now."

Faith didn't know what she expected, but she thought the notes would at least be in English. Or maybe they were, but there was only a single letter on each note.

V.

V? V.V.? What was that supposed to stand for?

"You want to call the horse V.V.?" she asked, confused.

Jax burst into laughter. "They aren't letters, Faith. It's a picture."

She looked at the notes again, trying without success to figure out what in the world he was talking about. She glanced up to ask Jax to give her another hint, but he was no longer standing.

He was kneeling, with a diamond ring in his hand.

"Get it?" He grinned.

She glanced around her, totally flustered. Every eye in the place was on her. She didn't know whether she should address the notes in her hand or the name of the filly or—

Oh.

Jax was still on one knee.

The two notes—put them together and they made a diamond.

Jax stood and took her hands in his. As always, the gentle giant.

"I don't care what you call the horse," he said, his voice making every nerve in her body sing. "I just want to hear you tell me you'll be my wife."

He held her left hand and poised the ring, then looked at her expectantly.

"I'll be your wife."

He slid the ring on her finger and kissed her, and the entire town cheered for them.

The next half hour was a blur. Jo and Alice physically placed them at the beginning of the lunch line, and they had to accept the well-wishes of everyone.

"We'll have to do this again in—a month?" he whispered suggestively.

"Three. It takes time to plan a wedding."

"Two."

"Deal. You know, though—I'm not sure this is all on the up-and-up, technically speaking."

"How do you figure?" His brow rose upward, as did the adorable half smile that was pulled by his scar. "What did I miss?"

"I *think* you actually didn't ask me to marry you. Technically speaking. It was more like a demand."

"Yeah, that dictator thing. I'll have to work on that."

She kissed his cheek, right over his scar. "I'll help you. I'm sure Rose and Violet don't want a daddy who bosses them around all day."

"You're probably right." He slid his cheek until his lips met hers. "But you missed something, too. I don't think I've yet heard those three little words."

"Wait a sec."

He shook his head. "No, that's not quite right."

"No. I mean, wait a sec. I want to get my head and heart together before I say this. I've been waiting a long time."

She took his head in her hands and brushed her thumbs against the soft whiskers on his cheeks. "Jackson McKenna, I love you, and there is nothing I want more in the world than to become your wife and the stepmother of your children."

His smile made the wait worthwhile.

"Mother," he corrected. "You are the girls' mother."

"I accept," she whispered, thinking that at that very moment, her life was absolutely perfect.

Except for one thing.

"You know," she said, "we forgot something else in all this excitement."

"What's that? I've got my future bride by my side and my beautiful daughters making the rounds with the neighbors. What else could I possibly want?"

"You did say we were going to name the filly. I think we ought to make that official, too, don't you?"

"Right. The filly. So what do you want to name her, sweetheart?"

She took her time with the answer, simply enjoying the warmth radiating from her future husband's chocolate-brown eyes. Basking in the feeling of loving completely and being loved completely in return. Scars and all.

"Are you going to tell me or do I have to guess?" he prompted between repeated kisses.

"Why, I thought you already knew," she said with a laugh. "Her name is Diamond, of course."

* * * * *

A DAD FOR HER TWINS

Lois Richer

But the person who trusts in the Lord will be blessed.
The Lord will show him that he can be trusted. He will
be strong, like a tree planted near water that sends its
roots by a stream. It is not afraid when the days are
hot; its leaves are always green. It does not worry in a
year when no rain comes; it always produces fruit.
—*Jeremiah* 17:7–8

Chapter One

Cade Lebret wished he had a woman with him as he steered his truck through the tiny Canadian town of Buffalo Gap, Alberta. Maybe then the locals on coffee row would talk about her instead of him. But romance was never going to be part of his life again because he wasn't the type women loved, at least not with a forever kind of love.

So he drove through town, staring steadfastly ahead, ignoring the curious stares of bystanders, knowing exactly what they'd say to each other over at Brewsters, the local coffee shop.

Guess who I saw today? Cade Lebret. Remember how his old man always chewed him out? Chewed me out, too, more than once. Nasty temper that Ed Lebret. Poor Cade.

For as long as Cade could remember, he'd hated being "poor Cade." So now he came to Buffalo Gap only when necessary, did his business and left fast to avoid the sympathy the townsfolk had showered on him for most of his thirty-one years. They all thought his father's vitriolic outbursts had ended when his dad had a stroke.

Cade's lips tightened. Even loss of speech and paralysis hadn't stopped the simmering disapproval in his father's eyes or his constantly accusing glare. It made for a trying life at the Double L. But Cade had promised he'd stay until he'd turned the ranch's red ink to black and he wouldn't renege on his promise, though it was proving to be extremely difficult to keep his word.

Thankfully Cade wasn't stopping in Buffalo Gap today. His business was in a cemetery outside Calgary and it wasn't the kind of business that could be rushed.

Having escaped the town limits, Cade hit the accelerator. His truck's powerful engine ate up the highway, easily pushing back arctic gusts of January air that swept through the valley nestled in the foothills of the Rockies. He flicked the heater up a notch but in spite of the warmth pouring out, Cade shivered. Hot, sunny days were the only thing he missed about Afghanistan.

Well, the heat and Max—Maxwell McDonald, the best friend Cade ever had. Max with his exuberant laughter; Max who found joy in a desert sandstorm. Max who'd once saved Cade's life, then lost his own over five months ago on a mission that Cade had refused to accept. He'd received a hardship discharge because of his father's strokes, and despite the military's offer of a one-time premium payout, he couldn't go back. The big fee showed how badly they wanted his specialized skill set of breaching enemy defenses. He could have used that money, but not enough to suppress his fear of dying in that war-torn country. Finally they'd accepted his refusal and Max had left without him.

Memories of past missions braided with guilt in Cade's head for the entire half-hour drive. Why hadn't he just gone? Why hadn't he been there for his best buddy? Why was he such a weakling? By the time he pulled into the winding road of the cemetery and made his way to where

Max's grave marker thrust out of the snow, a familiar anger festered inside.

Why Max, God? Why not me?

The question died in his throat at the sight of a small, huddled form kneeling beside his grave. Abby, Max's wife.

Cade hesitated, not wanting to interrupt her. But the winter afternoon light was already fading because he'd been later than planned getting away from the ranch. Now there were clouds forming in the west, suggesting his drive home might be stormy. He waited several minutes, then switched off his truck, grabbed his gloves and stepped down, following small, feminine footprints through deep drifts of snow. Gasping sobs made him stop just behind the diminutive brunette.

Feeling like an intruder, Cade fiddled with his hands. He should have left this morning's fence mending till tomorrow. If he'd arrived earlier he could have avoided Abby.

"I failed, Max. I've failed so badly." Her weeping wrenched at Cade's heart. He almost decided to go away until she finished her private mourning, but changed his mind when the wind whipped snow around them and she shivered.

"Abby? Are you okay?"

She twisted her head to look at him.

"Hi, Cade." She forced a smile, but her pale skin, sunken eyes and too-prominent cheekbones shocked him. She looked nothing like the full-of-life beauty Max had loved, but then she wouldn't. Almost six months ago she'd lost the man she'd been married to for four short months. She swiped a hand over her cheek to erase the tears. "It was nice of you to come. He would have liked that."

Her awkwardness when she tried to stand surprised him. Cade reached out a hand to lend support, then gulped hard when she rose. Abby McDonald was very pregnant.

"I didn't know—" He stopped, swallowing the rest of his comment.

"You couldn't," she excused him with a faint smile.

"I should have called you." Guilt ate at Cade. He hadn't visited her since the week after the funeral because seeing her roused a tickle of envy. Why hadn't he ever met someone like Max's Abby? Someone to love?

"Cade?" She'd obviously said something he hadn't heard. "I'm all right."

"That doesn't excuse me. Max would have wanted me to make sure you were." He watched as she placed a tender hand on her abdomen and smoothed circles. "Is everything okay?"

"With the babies? Yes." She sounded guarded, which bothered Cade until his brain clicked in.

"Babies?" he gasped. "As in more than one?"

"Twins." Her glance slid to the gravestone and her smile seemed to drain away.

"Congratulations. When are you due?" Though he felt awkward asking something so personal, Cade was determined to make up for his neglect. Ensuring Max's beloved Abby was all right was the very least he owed his friend.

His conscience reminded him that it couldn't make up for the guilt of not accompanying Max on that last mission, the one that had cost his buddy his life. Cade should have been there to protect him.

"The babies will arrive in three months, give or take." Abby's black calf-length coat didn't fit around her bulk. She dragged on the lapels, trying to close the gap and shuddering as the January wind sucked at them. She didn't look directly at him. That bothered Cade.

"It's too cold for you out here." He flicked his key fob to remote start his truck. "Let's sit inside."

"Ok-kay," she stammered. She took one step toward him and slipped.

As Cade reached out to grab her, Abby fell forward into his arms. The breath squeezed from his lungs at the contact. He held her until she was stable but he couldn't stop staring.

"I'm sorry," she gasped, her green eyes at his chin level. "I'm not as agile as I used to be."

"No problem." He tore his gaze free and drew her toward the truck, moving slowly, his hand firmly anchoring her. But when he threw open the door, Abby just stood there, looking from it to him helplessly. That's when he realized she couldn't manage the high step.

"Hang on." Without asking permission, Cade scooped her into his arms and lifted her until both feet were on the truck step.

Abby gasped a thank-you before scooting inside the cab. As she drew off her gloves, Cade noticed their thin shabbiness. Her snow boots looked worn-out, too, the leather battered and nicked, the heels run-down. He remembered how her glossy brunette curls used to bounce with life. Now the lank strands were scraped back from her face and tied in a ponytail. The only color she wore was an emerald-green wool scarf twined around her neck. It matched her eyes.

Abby looked nothing like the vivacious blushing bride he remembered and yet he couldn't keep from staring at her.

Cade closed her door and walked to the other side of his vehicle. He climbed into his truck, trying to imagine what could have caused such change. Not that Abby wasn't beautiful. She would always possess the timeless lines and angles that neither time, worry nor age would ever diminish. But today she looked drained, careworn, and Cade had a hunch it wasn't all due to her pregnancy.

He cursed himself for not checking on her with more than a monthly phone call.

Cade had missed Max's funeral because of his dad's second stroke. To make up for his absence, he now visited the graveyard every month. He'd gone to see Abby twice, but she'd seemed so shattered during those times that Cade had made do with phone calls from then on, unwilling to interrupt her grieving. Now he realized he should have done more. He should have gone to visit Abby every time he came to town. She'd always said she was okay, but he should have made sure.

Of course, Cade *had* been preoccupied with the ranch, trying to wrest every acre of land and animal from the fiscal chaos his father had created. Abby had known his phone calls were only duty calls, even made light of them, teasing him about his commitment to Max. She kept insisting she was fine and Cade had accepted that because the one thing he didn't need, didn't want, was responsibility for something or someone else.

Judging by what he now saw, Abby was not fine.

She held her bare hands in front of the heating vents. He noticed with some surprise that the diamond solitaire and matching gold band Max had given her were absent from her pale ring finger. Her shoulders slumped and her eyes closed, as if she'd lost her last ounce of strength. Was her pregnancy so difficult?

"Max was such a good man." Abby stared out the side window at her husband's grave, then, after a moment, turned to look at him. "I know God directed his every move." Pain wove through her words. "I can't understand why he had to die."

"I can't, either." Cade could do nothing about the bitter sound of those words. He'd been asking God that same question ever since a military buddy had called to tell him of Max's death. "A whim of God, I guess."

"Cade!" Abby's eyes widened. "God doesn't have whims. He has plans to prosper us and not to harm us." A smile lifted the corners of her mouth. "I keep repeating that to myself when these little ones kick me in the ribs."

"Do you need help with that? I mean, uh, someone to be there with you when—it, the babies come?" The personal questions seemed too intrusive. He and Abby were little more than strangers. The only thing they'd had in common was their love for Max.

Anyway, Cade had his hands full with the ranch and his father. He barely had a moment to call his own. Still, he wasn't going to leave her like this. He needed to help her, somehow.

"I'm fine, really." Abby turned again to look once more at Max's grave. She sighed so deeply it seemed to sap all her energy. "I should get home. There's supposed to be a storm tonight."

"I didn't see your car." Cade glanced around. "Where's it parked? I'll drive you to it."

"I sold my car a while ago, when I couldn't fit behind the wheel anymore. I came here on the bus." Her chin thrust up when he blinked at her in shock.

"But there aren't any buses that come all the way out here! You must have walked miles." He knew he was right when her green eyes suddenly swerved away from his. A spurt of anger bubbled inside him. "Should you be doing that, in your condition?"

"I'm pregnant, not disabled," Abby said, her tone firm. "It's good for me to walk."

"But it's so far and it's cold out." Cade clamped his lips together to stem his words when she shrank against the truck door. Arguing with her wouldn't help. "You have to take care of yourself, Abby," he said in softer tones. "Max would want that."

"I'm fine, Cade. Truly. I just got a little chilled sitting there in the snow." She laid her fingers on his arm and held them there until he looked at her. When she drew them away he felt somehow bereft. "I'm warm now. If you could drop me at the bus stop I'd appreciate it." Her heart-shaped face with its dark widow's peak looked forlorn.

Cade's heart, hard and frozen cold inside him since Max's death, thawed just the tiniest bit. He'd lost his best friend, but she had lost her husband, her life, her future.

"I'm not leaving you at a bus stop, Abby. I'll take you home."

"Oh." She let out a pent-up breath, probably in relief. "Okay. Thank you."

"You're welcome." Taken aback by her lack of argument, he pulled into the circular road that took them out of the cemetery and back into the city. Before turning onto the main freeway, he paused. "I don't remember your address," he admitted in embarrassment.

"It's been a while, hasn't it?" There was nothing in her tone to accuse him but Cade felt guilty anyway. "It will be easier if I direct you," she murmured. And she did.

By the time Cade pulled up in front of her tiny white bungalow, the afternoon sky glowered a dark, burgeoning gray. Snowflakes seemed imminent. The sidewalk to the front door had been shoveled clear, but there was nothing else to show that anyone lived here, no welcoming light on the front porch, no snowman lovingly created on the snow-covered front lawn, no leftover Christmas decorations waiting for removal. The place looked as forlorn as Abby.

"Stay put until I come around and help you out," he ordered. "It's icy. I don't want you to fall."

"Wait!" Abby grabbed his arm, her fingers tight, forcing him to pause. "I can manage. There's no need for you to fuss, Cade," she said in an almost desperate tone.

"I insist." He held her stormy gaze with his, refusing to back down.

"Fine," she finally conceded. "You can help me to the door if you must." Her green eyes narrowed. "But that's all. I'm sure you have things to do. You don't have to babysit me and I don't want to bother you any more than I already have. Just to the door," she repeated.

During his five-year stint in the military, Cade had risen up the ranks of the Canadian Special Forces unit quickly. Much of that was due to internal radar that told him when things weren't right. At the moment his personal detection system was on high alert. Something was definitely wrong with Abby. Her body was tight with tension. Clearly she did not want him inside her home.

Why? Though Cade was loath to cause her more stress, he owed it to Max to find out.

It felt good to lift Abby out of the truck and support her over the slippery sidewalk to the front door. As he did, Cade considered and discarded a hundred reasons she might not want him here but found nothing that would explain her oddly unwelcoming manner. He waited as she fished in her pocket for her key, wondering if she'd change her mind about him coming in. But she did not open the door. Instead she turned to face him, blocking the entry.

"Thank you for your help, Cade. I appreciate you remembering Max today. And I really want to thank you for the ride home." A tiny smile danced across her lips. "I *was* tired."

Cade didn't move. Abby's eyebrow arched.

"I can't leave until I make sure you get safely inside."

Though she tossed him a frustrated look, Cade didn't budge. "Want me to open the door for you?"

"No, I don't. Thank you." Her green eyes blazed at him for a few seconds more. Then with a harrumph that expressed everything from exasperation to frustration, Abby stabbed the key into the lock and twisted it. "See? Everything is fine. I'm fine. Thank you."

Cade had never felt less certain that everything was fine. Maybe it was rude and pushy, but this was necessary. He reached past her and twisted the door handle while he nudged his booted toe against the door. Abby made a squeak of protest and grabbed for the doorknob. But it was too late.

"Abby?" He let his gaze travel twice around the empty interior before returning to her face. "Where's your furniture? Where's…anything?"

"I'm—er—moving," she stammered. With a sigh she stepped inside and urged him in, too, before shutting out the cold air. "This place is too big for me. I'm moving out today." Her chin thrust upward. Her voice grew defensive. "I've decided to make some changes."

"Now?" Cade gaped at her in disbelief. "Three months before your due date?" He shook his head. "I can't believe that. What's really going on, Abby?"

She turned away from him to remove her coat and toss it over a packing box. He wondered why, since the room was quite chilly. Confused and troubled, he waited for her answer, stunned when her narrow shoulders began to tremble. Her muffled sob broke the silence and made him feel like a bully.

"You need to sit down and relax," he said with concern. But where could she sit? There was no furniture, nothing but a derelict wooden chair that looked as if the slightest whoosh of air would send it toppling over.

"I'm fine," she whispered. But she wasn't and they both knew it.

With his gut chiding him for not getting here sooner, and at a loss to know what to do now that he was, Cade gently laid his hands on her shoulders and turned her to face him.

"I just want to help, Abby. Please, tell me how." He waited. When she didn't respond he softened his voice. "I couldn't help Max," he murmured, his breath catching on the name. "I will always regret that. Please let me help you."

Abby edged away from him, moved behind the kitchen counter and leaned one hip against it. In that moment her mask of control slid away and he saw fear vie with sadness.

"I've lost the house," she whispered. "Our dear little house, the one Max and I bought together, the one we had such dreams for—I've lost it."

"Lost it?" Cade frowned. "What happened? Why didn't you come to me?" he demanded, aghast.

Abby's head lifted. She pulled her hair free of the hair band, tossed back the muss of curls that now framed her face and glared at him.

"Come to you?" Her green eyes avoided his. "You dutifully phone me every so often like a good friend of Max's would, and that is wonderful." Her chin thrust out. "But even if I could have found you, I didn't want to bother you."

"So you wouldn't have called me no matter what." He blinked. "Why?"

"Because I'm managing, or at least, I thought I was." Her chin dropped and so did her voice. "It doesn't matter. Nothing matters now."

The pathos combined with a lack of expression in her words told Cade he needed to act.

"Do you have any coffee—or tea?" he revised, think-

ing that in her condition she probably didn't drink coffee.
"Or have you packed everything?"

"I used up the last of the groceries. Everything I own
is in those two boxes over there." Abby pointed. "That's
what's left of my life." She looked around. "I sold the rest
because I needed the money."

Cade knew how that felt. He'd come home to find the
ranch hugely in debt because of his father's mismanage-
ment. Only recently had he begun to crawl out. But how
had Abby gotten in that condition? A second later he decided it didn't matter. The petite woman the bowed
shoulders and exhausted face touched a spot deep inside
his heart. There was no way he could leave her to manage on her own.

"Tell me what happened so I can help," he coaxed softly.

"You can't. The bank has foreclosed on the house. If
I'm not gone by six today, they have a sheriff coming who
will come forcibly move me out." Her breath snagged but
she regrouped and finished, saying, "I've done everything
I can to make things work. But they *don't* work."

"Abby." Someone else needed him. He wanted to turn
and run away from the responsibility but then he looked
at her, and her amazing green eyes clutched onto his heart
and refused to let go. How could he leave her alone?

"I'm homeless, Cade." Her voice dropped to a whisper. "I don't have a home for Max's babies. I may have to
give them up."

Though a whisper, the words echoed around the empty
room. Cade stared at her in disbelief, everything in him
protesting.

"You can't," he finally sputtered.

"I might have no choice."

Something flickered in the depths of Abby's amazing
eyes. Hope? In him? "A friend of mine will let me camp

on her couch but she's no better off than me and I can't stay there long. She's moving, too."

Promise me that you'll be there if ever Abby needs you, Cade.

I promise, Max.

Cade sucked oxygen into his starved lungs, pressed his lips together and muttered, "Okay, buddy."

"What?" Abby stared at him frowning.

Cade ignored her, walked to the corner, hefted the two boxes into his arms and carried them outside to his truck. When he returned, Abby was still standing where he'd left her, frowning. She watched him, that faint glimmer of hope draining out of her eyes. Her defiance had withered away, leaving her small, huddled and, he sensed, very afraid. No way could he leave her like that.

Cade picked up her coat and gently helped her into it.

"What are you doing, Cade?"

"Say your goodbyes, Abby." He fastened the top two buttons of her coat before moving his hands to her shoulders and gently squeezing. "We're leaving."

"To go where?" She eased free of his hands. Her eyes searched his for answers.

"We'll talk about that after lunch. I'll wait for you outside. Don't be long." Cade pulled the warped front door closed on his way out, guessing it was another of the projects Max had planned for this old house.

As Cade stood on the doorstep waiting for Abby, his mind tied itself in knots. What was he to do with her? He had no money to give her, he knew no one in the city with room to take her, and he was fairly certain she wouldn't stay with a stranger in Buffalo Gap.

He thought about what Abby had said earlier about God having a plan.

"Would You mind clueing me in?" he muttered. "Because I haven't got any idea how to help Max's wife. A little divine intervention sure would come in handy."

Past prayers hadn't brought many answers for Cade. As he waited for Abby, today didn't seem any different. The only solution he could think of was to take Abby back to the ranch, and Lord knew how that would turn out.

Putting a delicate pregnant widow under the same roof as his bitter, angry father? That was asking for trouble. But what choice did he have?

Cade figured that with Abby at the ranch, he'd be calling on God, a lot.

From the moment Max had introduced his best friend, Abby had realized that Cade, like Max, was a man who seized control. Today she was going to sit back and let him.

What else could she do?

She'd prayed so hard. She'd trusted and waited and prayed. Now she'd run out of options. Maybe Cade was God's answer to her prayers. If Max's buddy could think of a way to help her out of this mess, she'd grab it with thanks because she'd used up all the options she could think of and she was too tired to do anything more.

Aware of Cade's presence just outside the door, Abby pressed her knuckled fist against her lips to muffle her sob of loss. A memory of Max's booming voice echoed through her mind.

This is our home. You and I together will make it so.

Only it never had been. From the first day of their impetuous marriage she'd known something was wrong between them. Max had been generous, loving and kind but he'd never really let her get truly close, never let her help when the night terrors woke him or a sound made him startle. Too late, Abby had realized that Max had chosen her because she was safe; he'd called her his refuge. She'd stayed with him because she'd promised to love him forever and Abby, the missionary's daughter, could not break that promise.

Stiffening her shoulders, Abby walked through the rooms as fragments of memories flooded her mind. The windowpanes she'd scrubbed free of paint. The old wooden floors they'd refinished. The mounds of wallpaper they'd raced to remove. But memories were a blessing and a curse, so finally she returned to the front door, shoulders back, exhaling the past. She'd cried enough over her failure to be what Max needed. Whatever solution Cade offered, it had to be better than the misery and fear she'd endured here since Max's death.

"Goodbye, Max," she whispered, tears rolling down her cheeks. "I'm sorry I failed to love you the way you needed. I know it was my fault. I'm not the kind of woman you should have married. I didn't have enough strength to force you to get the help you should have had. If I had, maybe you would have retired or opted out of Special Forces into some other branch of service instead of going on that mission to Afghanistan. Maybe then you wouldn't have died."

She gulped, swallowing the last of her regrets because there was nothing she could change now.

"I won't make that mistake again, Max. I'll focus on loving our babies. Maybe then I can make up for failing you." Then she walked out to meet Cade.

"Ready?" He waited for her nod, his face implacable. "Let's go, then."

He closed and locked the front door. But this time when he scooped her up and set her inside the truck, Abby was prepared. Even so, her breath caught when his face loomed mere inches from hers and his breath feathered over her cheeks. She told herself her reaction was purely hormonal, that she'd missed that kind of male strength.

Abby composed herself as Cade drove her to a warm, homey restaurant with tantalizing aromas that made her stomach growl. Relieved he'd asked for a table instead of a booth where she wouldn't fit, Abby snuggled a mug of steaming peppermint tea in her palms as they waited for their food order to arrive.

"I know Max didn't have any family left but he never told me much about you, Abby. Do you have family?" Cade asked.

"None that I know of." She smiled at his questioning look. "I was three when I was adopted. My parents were older, very strict and the most loving people I've ever known. I adored them. To me they're my true parents. I never wanted or needed anyone else. I guess that's why I never felt compelled to discover my birth history."

"I see." Cade sipped his coffee thoughtfully. "Your adoptive parents are gone now?" His brows drew together when she nodded. "So there's no one you can contact for help?"

"I'm afraid not." Warmth rose at the concern Abby saw on his face. How wonderful it felt to have someone worry about her, even for a moment. "I'm not your problem, Cade. I'll figure out something." As if she hadn't tried. He didn't need to know that, although he'd probably guessed she was out of options.

"Max said you were a social worker."

"I am." Abby leaned back, closed her eyes and smiled. "The day I learned in third grade that not every kid had parents like mine was the day I decided I was going to be the one to help kids find the best parents they could. It's a job I love. I'd still be doing it, too, if the government hadn't cut back and laid me off."

Abby could feel his sympathy, could see it in the softening of his baby-blue eyes. The rancher was big and comfortable and—nice, she decided, choosing the simple word. Cade was genuinely nice.

"I'm sorry," he murmured.

"I'm sorry, too," she said, trying to disguise the sourness that sometimes bubbled inside. "There aren't any less children who need help. And there are even fewer workers to handle all the cases. But—" She shrugged. "What can I do? I was out of work and I couldn't find another job, no matter how hard I looked."

"And then you learned you were pregnant." Cade looked straight at her. "That must have been a frightening time, to be alone, without a job, knowing you're going to have twins. I wish you'd told me when I called. I would have come to help you, you know."

"I do know." Touched, she reached out to brush his hand with her fingers, to comfort him. "But I felt I had to handle things on my own."

Abby's heart melted as she watched Cade helplessly rake a hand through his very short black hair. His lean, chiseled face had lost some of its harshness, though the lines around his eyes and full lips remained and the cleft in his chin deepened with his frown.

"It's okay, Cade," she murmured.

"It isn't okay at all. Max would never have allowed you to handle this alone." His voice tightened, dropped to a low growl. "I'm so sorry I wasn't here for you, Abby."

"It's not your fault. It's not anyone's fault. It's just a problem I have to figure out." She was glad their server brought their meals just then. Maybe eating would ease the strain that was building and help them both avoid awkward, useless moments of regret. She scrounged up a smile. "I haven't had a turkey dinner in aeons," she said, licking rich gravy off her fork.

"Christmas wasn't that long ago." Cade paused, lifted

his head and stared at her. His pupils widened. "You didn't have Christmas dinner, did you?" He closed his eyes and groaned. "Oh, Abby."

She'd made him feel guilty again. She knew because she carried her own load. But she didn't want Cade's guilt. So what did she want? Because Abby didn't want to explore that thought she set down her fork and reassured him.

"Actually I did have Christmas dinner, Cade. I've been volunteering at a kids' shelter and they served a lovely meal." She chuckled. "But I didn't have much time to enjoy it."

"Why?" Cade crunched on a pickle as he waited for her to explain.

"One of the kids ran away, so we went looking for her." Abby liked the way Cade chewed slowly, appreciating the nuances of flavor in his food. "Searching took most of the day. By the time we found her, I was too tired to eat. Anyway, everything was cold."

She picked up her fork and chose a square of dark meat. Fork midway to her mouth, she blinked and paused, suddenly uneasy under his scrutiny. "What?"

"Can I ask you something?" He waited for her nod, forehead furrowed, his left hand, the one lying on the table, clenching and unclenching. "You spoke of giving up Max's, er, your babies?"

Abby swallowed the lump in her throat and nodded.

"But—you can't!" he protested, his voice sounding loud in the almost-deserted dining room. His eyes narrowed and his mouth tightened into a grim line as he spoke in a lowered tone. "Abby, you cannot possibly be considering giving away Max's children!"

"Do you think I want to?" she gasped as tears welled. "These are my children, part of me." She set down her fork, no longer hungry. Emotions rose through her like a tidal wave but she forced them back in the struggle to make him understand. "These children are the most precious thing in my life. I would do anything, *anything*—" she emphasized "—to give them the best life they can possibly have."

"Then why in the world—"

"The best life," she repeated softly through the tears filling her throat. "Max's children deserve that. But homelessness, lack of money, a life on the street—that is not the best life for them. Yet, at the moment, that's all I can offer them." She shook her head. "No child deserves that. I have to at least consider foster care."

"Lack of money?" he said, honing in on her words. "But won't Max's military benefits cover everything you need?"

"I haven't received any."

"What?" Cade stared at her in disbelief. He shook his head. "Why?"

"The military says he never informed them he was married, never filled out the forms. He was also behind on paying his insurance premiums, probably because of the down payment we made on the house," she said with a sad smile.

"But it's been months since—" Cade clamped his lips together.

"Since he died, I know." She sighed. "I sent them a copy of our marriage license, but they say that until they are able to verify its authenticity or legality or something, I can't receive any funds. That's why I didn't have enough to pay the mortgage or power bills or…" Tears erupted in a flow Abby couldn't staunch. She bent her head and let them fall, ashamed of her weakness but utterly weary of fighting.

Cade fell silent. After she regained control, Abby peeked through her lashes and found him staring at her, his blue eyes brimming with anger or perhaps disbelief? When he opened his mouth, his voice emerged in a squeak of protest that Abby shushed by reaching across and grabbing his clenched fist.

"It's true," she assured him.

"I know you're not lying, Abby." He drew his hand away as if he didn't like her touching him. He leaned back and thought it over for several moments, then jerked his head in a nod. "It's just that I never heard of the military withholding benefits when…"

"Well, that's what they've done." Abby sighed. "I think it might kill me to give up my babies, even for a short time," she told him. "But I have to face the facts, and that's a choice I might have to make if I can't give them a home, food, safety. I have no intention of failing my children." *As I did Max.*

Cade studied her for several long minutes. She knew something had changed when his broad shoulders went back and determination welled up in his blue eyes. He reached across the table, his hand closing around hers, squeezing tightly. Abby could only stare at him as the rough calluses on his skin brushed hers and wonder what the rush of emotions across his handsome face meant.

Was Cade God's answer to her prayers?

"You have another choice, Abby," he said in a clear, firm voice. "You can come to the ranch and stay until the babies are born. There's plenty of room. Mrs. Swanson, our housekeeper, will be on hand if you need anything. You won't have to lift a finger. You can rest and give the babies a rest, too. Stay as long as you need to get back on your feet." His blue eyes locked with hers and held.

"But I can't pay you," she whispered.

"I don't want anything," Cade said in a brisk but firm voice. He stopped, shook his head. "Actually I do," he corrected himself. "I want you to wait until Max's children are born, to take some time before you make your decision about your future and theirs. Okay?"

Abby couldn't believe it. God had sent her a place to stay, to wait for her babies' arrival without fearing someone would hassle her about her bills, moving and everything else she'd been fighting. A little window of hope, that's what Cade was offering. All she had to do was accept.

And yet, there was something in the depths of his kindly eyes, something that tugged at one corner of his mouth—something that made her stomach tighten with worry.

"What aren't you saying, Cade?" she murmured.

Shutters flipped down over his eyes. He eased his hand from hers and leaned back, his big body tense.

"Come to the ranch, Abby. It's better if you see the way things are for yourself. Then you can decide whether or not you want to stay." He lifted one eyebrow. "Okay?"

Abby sat silent, thinking. God had opened this door, she knew it.

Max had trusted Cade with his life.

Maybe she was being weak by accepting this opportunity. Max would have expected her to handle her life without revealing that he'd left her unprotected. If he'd known she was pregnant he wouldn't have left, but on the day she'd kissed him goodbye, the morning after she'd comforted him through a terrible nightmare, he went back to active duty in Afghanistan without knowing he was going to be a father. Neither of them had known what the future held.

She had no alternative but to accept Cade's offer, just until the babies were born. Then she'd get on with her life, alone except for her babies.

"I'm ready," she told him. "Let's go to the Double L."

Chapter Two

"You don't have to do this, Cade. I'll find another way. I'll figure out something." Abby's voice broke through the silence that had reigned since they'd left the city behind. "There's no need for you to put yourself out like this."

Abby's words drew Cade from his morose contemplation. He suddenly realized she thought his silence meant that he didn't want her at his home.

"What other solution do you have in mind?" He drove silently, waiting for her response with undiluted curiosity.

"I could sleep on my friend's couch while I think of the next step." Those green eyes of hers squinted at him with defiance. "Isaiah 62:7 says, 'Put God in remembrance of His promises.'"

"Uh, okay," he said, clueless as to her meaning.

"It means that if I keep praying, I know that eventually He will give me an answer."

"Until He does, maybe this is His answer—coming to my place, I mean." Cade didn't actually believe that, but Abby's certainty that God would help her intrigued him. He'd never known anyone so confident in God.

"It's not His answer if it's going to put you out or make things difficult in your home."

"Things are already difficult in my home." The words burst out of him. As soon as they were said he wished he could retract them but, of course, Abby's curiosity was obviously pricked.

"What do you mean?" she asked with a frown.

How to explain? Cade tossed around several responses. There was no easy way to say this.

"I got leave from the military because my father had a stroke and couldn't run the ranch himself. In fact, he was on the verge of bankruptcy." Cade licked his lips, mentally framing his explanation. "The day of Max's funeral, Dad had a second stroke. That's why I wasn't there."

"I heard." She blinked and nodded. "Go on."

"The stroke not only paralyzed him and took away his speech, but it left him locked inside his anger."

"Anyone would get frustrated in such a condition," Abby murmured.

"Trust me, he was frustrated long before he had a stroke," Cade muttered. "My father is a very angry man. He's been that way for as long as I can remember. It's my fault. He hates me."

"That can't be true," Abby gasped. "I'm sure your father doesn't hate you."

A faint smile twisted Cade's lips. Max was the only other person he'd told his life story to and he'd shown the same reaction.

"He hates me because I killed my mother." Why did the knowledge still hurt so much? "She died giving birth to me."

"Oh. I'm sorry." Abby's hand touched his shoulder, then fluttered away. Her voice dropped. "But even so—it can't be true. You must have confused something. He probably got so caught up in his own pain and didn't know how—"

"No." Cade heard the sharpness in his own voice, felt

his jaw tighten. "You can't romanticize it, Abby. Even if he was decimated by grief, it's been over thirty years and his attitude toward me hasn't changed one iota. His anger and the way he took it out on me for my entire life is the reason I left home and joined the military."

He swallowed the rest of what he wanted to say. His fingers gripped the steering wheel as he turned off the highway and into Buffalo Gap. It struck him that he'd received his wish. A woman now sat beside him. The rumor mill would be rampant with speculation.

Cade with a woman? He hasn't brought anyone to the Double L since that woman, Alice, and Ed chased her off pretty quick.

Again Cade pretended he didn't see the curious stares. He drove stoically through the small town.

Cade didn't get involved in Buffalo Gap. He didn't have time for it. The constant mental battles with his father left him beaten and worn down, as did the challenge of constantly avoiding another misstep that would take the ranch to financial ruin. He didn't have time to socialize with the townsfolk.

Max had told him once that women could sense the anger festering inside him and so they steered clear of him. Cade now knew that was true. In his life he thought he'd loved only two women and both of them had dumped him after a visit to the ranch. Cade had blamed his father's anger and rudeness, but he knew the truth; he simply wasn't the kind of man women cared for. He lacked the softness that having a mother would have given him. Now Cade no longer wanted the complication of romance in his already uncomfortable world.

But with sudden awareness, he now realized that to expect Abby to endure the simmering discontent of his father was a bad idea. She said she had a little more than three months to go before the twins were due; three months in which she should be pampered and soothed to prepare for delivery. Cade was no expert on human birth, of course, but he'd helped deliver hundreds of calves and about the same number of colts, and he knew giving birth was hard work for any mom.

"Cade?" The softly voiced query drew his attention to Abby. "I don't have to stay on your ranch. I could go to my friend's or a shelter, if that would be better for you. I don't want to cause you problems."

"You can't stay in a shelter. Max would never have allowed it and neither will I." Admiration for her pluck drove off the brooding that always enveloped him when he thought of his father. Cade focused instead on the small woman in the opposite seat.

"But I need to prepare you for what you'll find. And I want to ask you to, as much as possible, avoid my father. He's very unhappy with the way I've been managing the ranch and with the decisions I've made. He refuses to work at his physiotherapy. He often won't eat the meals our housekeeper, Mrs. Swanson, prepares. He deliberately knocks things over and bangs his cane against anything to express his anger."

"Oh, the poor man." Abby's eyes welled with tears. For some reason that made Cade very angry.

"He's not a poor man. He's unhappy, as he's always been, and he's trying to make everyone else feel the same." Cade had to force his fingers to relax on the steering wheel as he drove the gravel road toward the ranch. "I have only one rule for your stay on the Double L, Abby. You must avoid my father. I won't risk anything happening to you or to Max's babies."

Abby's eyes widened before she turned to look out the window. Cade hated the worry he'd glimpsed there, but he was issuing the warning for her sake.

"Maybe I should go somewhere else—" she began.

"I've made you afraid." He cut off whatever else she'd been going to say, mentally stewing over his lack of subtlety. "Don't be afraid, Abby. Physically, you will be perfectly safe at the ranch." He used the gentlest voice he could muster but mostly Cade was out of touch with gentleness.

"But you said—"

"My father has never deliberately physically harmed Mrs. Swanson or me. He uses words instead." Cade pushed ahead with his confession. "His negative state can be very depressing. I don't want you to be depressed or unhappy. For that reason I want you to avoid him, as much for your sake as for his."

Cade pulled up in front of the big white farmhouse that had been home for his entire life. He switched off the truck. Then he turned to look at Abby. She returned his stare, her clear gaze direct and unflinching. Her hands smoothed over her bulging stomach in a protective shield before she spoke.

"I'm here as your guest, Cade. I'll do whatever you ask. I don't want to cause any problems for you or your father." She smiled and Cade noticed the faint trace of dimples in her cheeks. "I'll try not to be a bother to anyone."

"You could never be that, Abby. Just be advised. Don't expect a nice, kindly old man. He's not."

Clearly she didn't believe him. Abby was sweet and good, everything he'd missed from life, everything he craved but couldn't have. He tore his thoughts away from that thinking and turned his attention to the front window. His father sat there, watching. Cade knew the time for talking was past.

"Welcome to the Double L, Abby." He climbed out of his truck, walked around to the other side and opened her door. "I'll introduce you to my father and Mrs. Swanson. Then you can settle in."

"Thank you." She held out her hand so he could help her down, letting out a tiny squeal of surprise when he simply lifted her and set her on her feet on the snowy pebbled driveway. Her cheeks grew warm when she noticed surprise on the housekeeper's face where she stood in the open doorway. His father was there now, too, his usual scowl deepening in disapproval.

Cade's fingers curved around Abby's arm. He knew she could feel the tension rippling through his body. Absently he noticed that his boots crunching on the stones made the only sound in the crisp winter air.

"Come in, the pair of you." Mrs. Swanson's round face beamed. She pulled his father's wheelchair backward. Cade urged Abby forward so he could close the door behind them.

"Mrs. Swanson, Dad, this is Abby McDonald. She's my friend Max's wife. You remember Max? He used to visit when we had leave." Cade's voice tightened. He paused, then resumed speaking, this time in a firmer tone. "Abby's going to be staying with us for a while."

"It's very nice to meet you." Abby stepped forward, hand outstretched. It was obvious that she remembered too late that Cade had said his father was partially paralyzed. Both his hands lay in his lap. Abby bent, covered his fingers with hers and gently squeezed, smiling in spite of his fierce glare. Then she moved to the woman who stood next to Mr. Lebret's chair. "Finally I meet the legendary Mrs. Swanson. Max talked a lot about your amazing apple pies."

"Ah, the dear, dear lad." Mrs. Swanson's faint Scottish brogue died away as she sniffed. "'Tis sorry for your loss I am. Max was a good man. He'd wrap me in those gigantic arms of his and swing me around till I was dizzy."

"Me, too," Abby whispered with a watery smile.

"I think Cade brought him here to fatten him up. Never saw a man who could eat like your Max did and not gain an ounce." She slid an arm around Abby's waist and urged her forward. "Come, my dear. You've had a long drive. It's tea you'll be wanting to revive you."

"Tea would be lovely. Thank you."

Cade almost laughed aloud at the expression on Abby's face. She looked as though she was being swept along by a tidal wave.

"But I can make tea myself," Abby protested. "I don't want to be a bother. You don't have to wait on me."

"'Twould be my pleasure to care for Mr. Max's wife and her wee bairn," Mrs. Swanson assured her, patting Abby's stomach gently.

"Bairns," she corrected. "I'm having twins."

"Well, glory be!" Mrs. Swanson chuckled again, then urged her forward.

Abby glanced back once, just in time, Cade knew, to see the word his father scrawled with a fat felt marker across a pad of paper lying on his lap.

No!

There was no subtlety in the stark, one-word comment. Cade met Abby's gaze, saw the question in her eyes. He shook his head once firmly, then smiled, a tight, controlled twist of his lips. Anger tightened his shoulders. He spoke in a careful tone.

"You go with Mrs. Swanson, Abby. Dad and I will join you in the kitchen for tea in a minute." When she hesitated, he nodded at her as if to reassure her.

After a second check of Cade's face, Abby gave in. Judging by her expression, she understood he didn't want her to overhear his discussion with his father. A wave of sympathy rolled through her vivid green eyes before she walked back to him, stood on her tiptoes and murmured for his ears alone, "Max always said you were the most caring man he'd ever known. He told me stories of how you encouraged and praised the men in your unit." She touched his arm, squeezed. "Now I've witnessed your kindness for myself. You don't have to shield me, Cade. I'm tough. I'll be fine."

"Thank you for understanding." Cade felt the warmth of her smile touch his cold heart, but as she and Mrs. Swanson left the room, the warmth faded. He chose his words carefully, using a measured voice to explain Abby's situation to his father, leaving out the worst details and making generalizations that would save her embarrassment.

"She will stay for as long as she needs to. I owe Max that."

His father glared at him, then shoved his pen in his shirt pocket.

Cade pushed his dad's chair into the kitchen. As they drank Mrs. Swanson's tea he thought how perfectly Abby fit in. It would be nice to have a friend like her. But when Abby teared up as she answered Mrs. Swanson's questions about Max, Cade snapped back to reality. It was clear Abby wasn't nearly over mourning his death.

Cade was pretty sure Abby wouldn't want a friendship with him, not when he should have been there to protect her husband.

Nothing was going the way Cade hoped. As they sat around the dinner table, he appreciated Abby's valiant efforts to make the meal enjoyable. She told them amusing stories, complimented Mrs. Swanson on everything she served and asked him questions about the ranch.

But through it all, his father sat at the head of the table, grim-faced, his fists clumping on the table when he was displeased, fingers clenching around his black felt marker to scroll a series of angry commands across his writing pad.

Cade was utterly embarrassed and deeply ashamed of his parent by the time the meal was finished. He could hardly wait for Mrs. Swanson to push his father's chair to the television room so he could apologize to Abby for his father's behavior.

"I'm so sorry," he said when they were alone in the dining room. "I expected him to fuss about having you here, but—" He shook his head. "I've never seen him as full of rage as he seemed tonight. I apologize for his making you feel unwelcome. If you'd rather leave—"

"Stop apologizing for something you can't change, Cade." The twinkle in Abby's green eyes surprised him as much as the smile twitching at the corner of her lips. "Anyway, I think tonight was good for him."

"Good for—" He gaped at her. "I don't understand what you mean."

"Did you see the way he kept grabbing that pen and writing on the paper?" She spread her small, delicate hands wide. "You told me he hasn't been doing his physiotherapy. But he was sure giving those fingers a workout tonight." She rose, walked to the end of the table where his father had been sitting and gathered the scrunched-up pieces of paper from the floor. Then she laid them on the table, one by one on top of each other, looked at him and grinned. "See?"

Cade moved to stand beside her. He sifted through the sheets of paper, each with an angry word scrawled across it.

No! Won't have it! Quiet! Stop. Some of the words were repeated. There were fourteen sheets in all. It was the biggest effort Cade had seen his father make since his stroke.

He lifted his head to stare at her, confused but somehow more lighthearted than he'd been in years.

"Maybe my being here isn't so bad after all," Abby said timidly, "if it forces your father to fight, and by that I mean put out some effort. Isn't that good for him?"

"Abby, your being here isn't bad at all. You bring lightness that's been missing from this place for a long time." As he said it, Cade realized the truth in his words. She'd been in his home only a few hours but already Abby made things seem bearable, though he wasn't sure exactly how she did it. "I'm glad you're here," he said quietly.

"I am, too." Her lovely smile flashed at him. "Maybe God can use me to help you, as you're helping me."

"God again." He frowned. It was a recurring theme with her.

"He's part of my life, part of everything I do, part of every decision I make." Abby tilted her head to one side and studied him. "I trust God."

"Such unshakable faith. I wish I had it," he said, and meant it.

"I don't know that it's unshakable," she told him thoughtfully. "But you can have it. Faith is yours for the taking. In Ephesians 1:19 Paul prayed we would understand the incredible greatness of God's power for those who believe. But the power is only activated *when* we believe, so that's where I put my focus."

A hundred questions buzzed through his head, but just then the doorbell rang. Cade glanced at his watch in surprise. It was late for visitors and highly unusual for anyone to just show up at the ranch. Abby followed him to the entry. Cade blinked when the town's mayor, Marsha Grant, surged through the open door and shoved it closed behind her.

"Mayor Grant," he said, taken aback as he always was by her forwardness.

"Good evening, Cade." She smiled at him, then turned to Abby. "And you're Mrs. McDonald, correct? Abby McDonald?"

"Yes." Abby blinked and glanced at Cade, who shrugged. "How do you—"

"My daughter used to work with you. She saw you ride into town with Cade. She tells me you're a social worker." The mayor tilted back on her heeled boots. She removed her thick glasses, polished them with her vivid purple scarf and returned them to her face. "I'll explain that later. I'm here about something else."

"Would you like to come in? I can make a fresh pot of coffee." Cade didn't like the flicker of fear he saw cross Abby's face. Perhaps she was in more trouble than he realized. His protective instincts pricked as his mind ran scenarios. Perhaps...

I trust God, Abby had said. Dare he do the same? But God hadn't come through for Cade, not once in all the years he'd prayed for reconciliation with his dad.

"Can't stay, thanks. Emergency." Mayor Marsha's short staccato sentences were simply the way she always spoke, but Cade interpreted Abby's frown as concern.

"What kind of emergency?" he asked.

"You have acted as a child's special advocate before, have you not?" Marsha focused on Abby, ignoring him.

"Yes," Abby agreed. "But I haven't been in social work for some months. I was laid off and—"

"Yes, yes," the mayor said impatiently. "But your credentials are all active? You could return to work anytime you choose, correct?" Marsha's stare was relentless.

"Yes, but I'm going to have twins in three months. I doubt anyone would hire me in this condition, especially knowing I'd soon be taking time off to be with my children." Abby shook her head. "I doubt I can be much help to you."

"Oh, yes you can." Marsha chuckled. "You can be a very big help to me tonight, if Cade's agreeable." Finally she turned her attention back to him. "I have a situation."

"Okay." Cade pulled forward a small chair from near the entry door and urged Abby to sit. "We're listening." Her smile of thanks sent a feathering of warmth through him.

"There was a serious accident tonight," Marsha explained. "Two people died, the parents of young Ivor Wynne, age ten. Buffalo Gap is his community, his home, the only place he's ever known. But I'm afraid Children's Protective Services will take him to a home in Calgary until next of kin can be contacted and decisions about his future made." Mayor Marsha's gray eyes grew steely. "Unless I can change their minds."

"I'm so sorry," Abby whispered.

Cade's heart also contracted with sympathy. Poor kid.

"I will not have that child taken from here." Marsha insisted. "I need someone who has the credentials, someone who knows what to do in these situations, to act for him so he doesn't have to leave the only place he's ever known as home."

"You want Abby to be in charge of him?" Cade shook his head, irritated that she'd asked and more annoyed that Abby seemed to be considering it. "She can't. She's pregnant and tired. She needs to rest."

"I could do it, Cade," Abby said very quietly. "It wouldn't be hard on me to help this boy through such desperate circumstances. But I'd want *your* agreement."

"Mine?" He frowned. "Why?"

"Because he'd have to stay here. Unless you'd want

me to take him somewhere else?" Abby's big green eyes brimmed with compassion.

"But—this is a working ranch." Cade gulped, desperate to avoid getting involved. He didn't want another kid to experience his father's vicious temper, to feel as stupid and useless as he had. He turned to Marsha. "This isn't really a place for kids. Besides, my father is an invalid who needs constant care. Mrs. Swanson has her hands full. Who will look out for this boy when Abby needs to rest?"

"He's ten, not an infant, Cade. But we can work all that out." When Abby gazed up at him like that, Cade's anger dissolved. "I trust God to help us," she added quietly.

How could a guy argue with that?

"I'd like to know a little more about how your daughter knows Abby, that she's a social worker." He waited for Marsha's response, grabbing at anything to stall the inevitable.

"My daughter visited me today for lunch. We were just coming out of the restaurant when you and Abby drove through town. My daughter waved but I guess neither of you noticed." Marsha turned to Abby. "She used to work in your building. She said you even shared a few cases." The mayor smiled at Abby's surprise. "My daughter is Cindy Sharp. She's in Legal Aid."

"Cindy is your daughter?" Abby's grin spread. "How is she? I always enjoyed working cases with her. She has such common sense."

"She's fine. Anyway, she'd just arrived back home in Calgary when she heard about the accident. I told her I wanted Ivor to stay in Buffalo Gap and she suggested you might help make that happen. Cindy says that when it comes to protecting kids, you're like a tigress." Marsha's gaze held Abby's. "That might be what I need to keep Ivor in this town."

"Why is it so important he stay here?" Cade interrupted the knowing glance shared between the women.

"Aside from the fact that Buffalo Gap is Ivor's home?" Marsha's intense gaze shifted to him. Cade nodded. "We need him to stay because showing we have the wherewithal to handle these kind of challenges is one way of moving forward with an idea I've been hoping to initiate."

Another of the mayor's "ideas." Cade had heard about many other impractical plans. He stifled his groan.

"I want us to open a placement plus adoption agency in Buffalo Gap," Marsha said.

"Really?" Abby leaned forward and said in an eager voice, "Tell me about it."

Marsha's idea took a while to explain. Cade found another chair and set it so Marsha could be seated without having to remove her boots. Then he leaned his shoulder against the wall, waited and listened.

"Buffalo Gap is a small town and like most other small towns, we're shrinking. We don't have the economic base or the industry to draw people here. Besides, Calgary's barely half an hour away. It's nothing for folks to drive there and back for what they need." Marsha paused. A twinkle lit her eyes when she smiled at Abby. "But we have two important assets—lots of land with lots of families."

"I don't see—" Cade paused when Abby interrupted.

"I think I do. Your town can offer foster homes for displaced kids with families who have lots of land for them to run free on, animals to care for and an atmosphere that offers respite from whatever the troubled kids might be suffering." She said it thoughtfully while staring at some distant point. "On ranches like this one." She turned her head to look at Cade. "It's a marvelous idea," she told him. Then she frowned at Marsha. "But I don't get the adoption angle."

"A small town has great connections. Everyone knows someone. A friend of mine used to run an adoption agency down east. She gave that up when she moved here to marry but she's continued to help find homes for children. The difference is, she's been doing it unofficially."

"I see." Abby nodded.

"It gets better." Marsha leaned forward. "Recently, six separate couples have come to her asking for help to adopt a child because they heard about her success. So now she wants to open a formal adoption agency."

Abby nibbled on her bottom lip as she listened. She looked so cute. Cade refocused.

"My friend's husband died about eight months ago. She's got the time and the money but she's near retirement and doesn't want the responsibility of opening an agency on her own," Marsha explained. Her gaze narrowed on Abby. "You'd be a perfect partner."

"Abby's going to have twins," Cade interjected without thinking. The words sounded silly even to him. He hadn't really wanted to bring her here to the Double L but now that Abby was here, he didn't want her to go?

"I'm not giving birth for a few months," Abby said sharply with a sideways glare at him. "That doesn't make me helpless in the meantime."

"But—"

"Look, we can argue about my fragile state another time," she said, cutting him off briskly. "The one to focus on now is Ivor. Can Marsha bring him here?"

All Cade had wanted was to help Max's wife out of a tough situation. Even that was only meant to be a temporary solution. Now they were asking him to take on a grieving boy, too, to open his home to someone else who would witness his father's hate toward his own son?

"Please let him come, Cade," Abby whispered. She rose,

walked toward him and grasped his hand in hers. "I'll keep track of him. I promise he won't go near your dad. I can help him. I know I can," she said, her voice impassioned. "Please let me be useful again."

How was he supposed to argue with that logic?

"He can come," Cade said gruffly, too aware of Abby's small hands still clutching his. "But only for as long as it takes to find him another home. This isn't permanent—"

"Oh, thank you, Cade." Abby flung her arms around him and hugged him. "Thank you for giving Ivor a chance."

"Yeah, sure," he said into her hair, his hands moving automatically around her waist. His nose twitched at her soft lilac scent.

"Ahem." Marsha's voice broke into his reverie.

"Oh, I'm so sorry." Abby pulled away from Cade. She kept her eyes downcast but her cheeks were hot pink. "I, um, I just wanted to thank you."

"You did." He grinned when she peeked up at him through her lashes. "Very nicely, too." Her eyes widened at his teasing tone, as if she didn't expect him to have a sense of humor.

"So I'll go get Ivor and bring him here," Marsha asked, glancing from Cade to Abby, a question on her face. "Okay?"

Abby stared at Cade. "Okay?" she murmured.

Cade exhaled, straightened his shoulders and nodded.

"We'll get a room ready for him. But he only stays as long as absolutely necessary," he emphasized. "Agreed?"

"Oh, absolutely," Marsha said. She rose, buttoned her coat and walked to the door. "I'll be back in half an hour."

Cade nodded, let her out and then closed the door behind her with a sigh.

"You're doing the right thing, Cade. God will bless you for it," Abby whispered.

He wasn't sure about God or blessings, but he was pretty sure his dad would hate him for it.

Still, Cade mused as he walked with Abby chattering madly beside him, how could you possibly refuse a woman who wanted to help some hurting kid? Her sweetness, her gentleness, her care and concern were part of her nature. Those were only some of the things he liked most about Abby McDonald.

Maybe if he'd met a woman like Abby—

Cade immediately eradicated those thoughts. Romance wasn't going to be part of his life. He didn't have what it took to be a loving partner. And anyway, he wasn't free to get involved, even if he wanted to. He had his father to think of and to plan a future for.

Cade was not going to let his heart get involved with anyone, but he was also determined never to end up bitter and angry like his dad. With Abby here, maybe that would get easier.

Chapter Three

"You must have been starved," Abby said, watching Ivor inhale the two sandwiches Mrs. Swanson had made for him. "Would you like something else? I don't think Cade ate all of that delicious chocolate cake we had for dessert."

She hadn't finished saying it before Mrs. Swanson set a huge piece in front of the boy, patted his shoulder and clucked sympathetically. Then the housekeeper said good-night.

Cade sat on the other side of Ivor, nursing a mug of steaming coffee, broodingly silent. Abby saw his head jerk upward as the sound of his father's motorized wheel-chair drew near. Every muscle tense, Cade shoved to his feet, his eyes dark, his brows lowered. Abby thought the frown spoiled his very handsome face.

Thump! His father banged his cane on the tiled floor to gain attention as he glared at Ivor first, then Cade. Even after all these years his father still needed to look in control. Only difference was, now he used a cane to do it.

Who's he? he scrawled on his notepad.

"Dad, this is Ivor. He'll be staying with us for a while." Cade leaned down and murmured something in Ed's ear, then straightened. Ed glared at him, then reached out with his cane and nudged Ivor's leg.

"Dad!" Cade's cheeks flamed red. He grabbed at the cane but Ivor beat him to it.

"Is there a hidden point in this thing?" Ivor peered into the end. "I saw canes like those at the nursing home where my grandma used to live." He let the cane drop. "She's dead, too," he mumbled before returning to his cake. But instead of eating it, now he just picked at it.

Much more gently this time, Ed poked his leg with the cane. When Ivor turned to look at him, Ed grinned and shook his head. *No point*, he scrawled on his sheet. Ivor grinned back.

Abby saw shock fill Cade's face. He stared at his father, then turned his attention to Ivor, obviously puzzled by the unspoken communication the two were sharing.

"You should watch where you're pointing that thing," Ivor warned. "Someone might poke *you* with it." Ed chuckled out loud. "Do you know how to play chess?"

Ed nodded vigorously.

"He's very good at it," Cade warned the boy. Abby knew he was trying to protect Ivor, that he feared his father would misbehave and somehow hurt the boy, not physically but mentally, the way she figured Cade must have been hurt.

"I'm pretty good at it, too," Ivor bragged with ten-year-old bravado. The lost look on his face drained away. "Want to have a game?"

Ed jerked his head in a nod, beckoned to the boy and led the way out of the room. When they were gone, Cade turned to Abby.

"Maybe I should go with them, make sure everything's okay," he said, his voice halting, unsure. "I don't want the kid to get hurt. Not that Dad would purposely hurt him, but he's not very careful about feelings."

"Let's give them a chance." Abby smiled. Under that veneer of gruffness, Cade was a big softie. "Do you have to go and care for your cattle tonight?" she asked to change the subject and to learn more about her new home.

"I have a hired man. He would have taken a couple of bales of hay to their pasture this afternoon," Cade explained. "I'm sure he's fed the horses, too."

"Horses?" Abby gasped, staring at him, eyes wide. "You have horses?"

"Most ranches do," he teased, one eyebrow arched. "Why?"

"I love horses." Abby squeezed her eyes closed and silently whispered a thank-you to God. If she had to leave her precious little home, coming to a place with horses was the next best thing. "Can I see them?" she asked eagerly.

"Well, maybe not tonight." His crooked smile teased her. "I'll show you and Ivor around tomorrow. Do you—did you ride?" he asked. Abby noticed the way he glanced at her stomach, then slid away.

"Oh, goodness no," she said with a laugh. "I don't know the first thing about horses."

"Then how can you love them?" Cade looked totally confused. The look was so cute on him.

"I've always been infatuated with horses." She shrugged. She thought a moment, searching for a way to explain. "They're so—pretty," she finally managed.

"My horses are not pretty." Cade snorted his indignation. "They're strong, capable, well trained, but pretty? No." He frowned at her. "You sound like a city girl."

"I *am* a city girl." She giggled when he rolled his eyes. "You and Max share that same macho characteristic. He always teased that I was naive." She sobered suddenly. "I guess I was naive," she murmured, remembering how her husband's romantic dreams had melted away in the face of his post-traumatic stress issues and how he'd refused to accept his illness.

She glanced up and found Cade watching her, a curious look on his face.

"Max had no idea of the ugliness I've seen through my work," she said quickly. "City or country, ugliness always rears its head."

Cade nodded but said nothing.

When the moment of silence her words brought had stretched too long, Abby cleared her throat. "What do you raise your horses for?"

"We sell ours for riding of all kinds, but rodeo stuff mostly. There are a lot of families in the area who are involved in 4-H." Cade raised an eyebrow as if to ask if she knew what that was.

"4-H. A group for kids to learn skills," she shot back with a grin, anxious to show her knowledge. "Lots of involvement in gymkhanas which means riding and training a horse and participating in judged events."

"Very good." Cade grinned back. She could tell he loved verbally sparring with her. "A lot of the dads around here buy their kids horses from me, which means they have to be broken and properly trained before the boy or girl ever gets on. We also dabble a little in pedigreed horses."

"And the cattle?"

"Our cattle are Black Angus, raised strictly organic, prime Alberta beef. We also have a few pigs because I like ribs, a few dozen chickens because Mrs. Swanson likes her eggs fresh and natural, and some sheep who supply her with enough wool to knit her scarves and mitts for the street kids in Calgary." A smile played at the corner of his lips. "We also get a few ducks and geese on the pond in the spring, the odd coyote or wolf after our cattle and some owls in the woods. That about covers the animals on the Double L."

"Why is it called the Double L?" Abby asked. The moment she said it, she knew she shouldn't have. A dark, brooding look filled Cade's face.

"My great-grandfather homesteaded the land, then my grandfather and father."

"And now it's passed on to you," she said with a bright smile, trying to understand his odd manner.

"For the time being," Cade said, then pressed his lips together and stared at her.

"That's nice," Abby said. "After my parents died, I had to sell their place. They had some serious bills from the nursing home they stayed in." She blinked when Cade suddenly jerked upright.

"Did your parents choose to go into the nursing home?" he asked in an intense tone.

"Yes." She nodded. "It was the best option for them. I was at university and couldn't always be there when they needed me. They both had mobility issues because of lung problems. In the nursing home they got the care and support they needed to enjoy their lives." She couldn't help wondering why he'd asked.

Cade said nothing but a raised eyebrow told her to continue.

"They served overseas in Africa when they were young and got some virus that affected their lungs," she explained. "That's why they eventually came home. But the virus never went away."

"I'm sorry, Abby." His hand brushed hers, then drew away.

"It's okay. They were both strong in their faith. I know they're in heaven, waiting to see me. It's just—" She paused a moment, sucked in a breath of courage to chase away her sadness and summoned a smile for him. "I get lonely now with Max gone, too."

A crash from the other room cut off whatever Cade had been going to say. They glanced at each other, then hurried to see what had happened. Abby could tell from Cade's face that he expected the worst. What they found were Ivor and Ed laughing. The chess board and pieces were spread all over the floor.

"Sore loser," Ivor said to Ed, who simply grinned. Then he saw them standing in the doorway and the laughter stopped to be replaced by the scowl he habitually wore.

"What happened?" Abby asked when Cade remained silent, his gaze locked with his dad's.

"I told Ed that cane would be the death of him," Ivor explained. "He keeps waving it all over. Finally it caught on the board." He shrugged. "We were finished anyway. I won."

Cade began picking up the pieces. Ivor knelt to help him. "Do you play chess with your dad?" he asked innocently.

"No." Cade gave no explanation, simply set the pieces back on the board and rose.

"I think it's time I went to bed," Abby said before Ivor could ask more questions. "This has been a busy day for me." She walked over to Ed, bent and brushed her lips against his leathery cheek. "Good night," she whispered. She managed a quick hug for Ivor.

"Want me to walk you to your room?" When he shook his head firmly she recognized that he didn't want to be seen as a baby and it was too early for him to accept someone else doing what his mom had done. She nodded, then looked up at Cade. "Thank you again," she murmured, keeping her voice low enough so the others wouldn't hear. "Good night."

His eyes held hers for a long moment. Finally he said good-night, but as she walked out of the room, Abby could feel three sets of eyes boring into her back and was grateful Mrs. Swanson had already shown her the way to her room. Abby scurried down the hall, grateful the house was ranch style with only one floor. She didn't think she could manage stairs tonight. She was just too tired.

She was tucked up in bed when she heard the others go to their rooms. Cade's calm, level voice penetrated as he wished Ivor good-night. She couldn't decipher what he was saying to his dad but Ed's cane made several loud thumps, which were soon silenced. Sometime later she heard Cade say "Good night, Dad." Then a door clicked and the house settled down.

Abby lay on her big, wide bed and marveled at the lovely room. It was twice the size of the one she'd shared with Max. There were huge windows opposite the bed. Come morning she would probably have a view of the entire ranch, maybe even the horses. God had certainly taken care of her. For now.

But what was she going to do about getting a permanent home for the babies?

Abby smoothed her hand over her bulging stomach as she pressed down the rush of panic that threatened to overwhelm her.

"God will provide," she whispered. A tiny unborn foot in the center of her midsection kicked her hand. She smiled. "For all of us," she said. But how? That question haunted her. While the babies went through their nightly calisthenics routine, she picked up her Bible, flipped it open and began reading in the Book of Psalms.

God adopts us as His very own children.

Abby smiled to herself. Here was a promise she could cling to. God had adopted her. She was His. He'd used Cade to bring her here, to give her a home, even if it was temporary, and she had new friends in Mrs. Swanson, Ivor and Ed, not to mention Cade.

For a moment her thoughts got caught up in the strong, handsome rancher, in his gentleness to her, his protective attitude and the way he'd insisted on rescuing her. Poor Cade. He was trying to do the right thing here, too, but his father certainly didn't make it easy on him.

An idea blossomed. Maybe that's why she was here, to help the two of them mend their relationship. Despite Ed's crankiness, Abby had seen a glint in his eyes when he'd surreptitiously watched Cade. She was certain father and son loved each other. They'd just gotten off track.

She could never repay Cade for all he'd done for her. Except, maybe she could help him find his way back to the man he clearly loved.

Show me, Father, please? she prayed.

Then she put her head on the pillow and closed her eyes. As usual, her fingers closed around the tiny locket she wore, the one precious thing she couldn't bear to sell. She popped it open and stared into Max's eyes. For the first time in months, tears didn't well up. She traced his features with a forefinger.

"Your friend's taking care of us," she murmured. "We're fine. And you're at peace now. I'm sorry I couldn't do more to help you. I'm sorry I failed you. But I promise I will not fail our babies. Cade will help us."

But just how much help could she take from the handsome rancher with the deep blue eyes?

In all his years on the ranch, Cade had never had a more frustrating day. His two best bulls had broken through a fence last night and it had taken forever to round them up, get them back with the rest of the herd and fix the fence. It had to happen on the day he'd given Garnet Jones, his hand, the day off. The drifts were so deep he'd had to use the snowmobile. Ivor had seen him and rushed out, eager to try the machine.

Cade wanted the kid to feel at home, even to enjoy himself. Since he hadn't had much luck interesting Ivor in anything else the past three days, he figured the snowmobile might act as a kind of bridge between them. That was before Ivor had raced the machine too close to the pond and broken through the ice on the edge.

"It could have been worse," he told Ivor after he'd pulled the snowmobile out with his four-wheel drive.

"How?" Ivor glared at him.

"If you'd gone further, you'd have sunk in completely and taken a cold bath. And you'd have ruined my machine." He studied his snowmobile and sighed. "Not that it won't take a fair bit of work to dry it out and get it running now."

"It's really old. You should probably buy a new one," was Ivor's only comment before he wandered back to the house.

"Why didn't I think of that?" Cade muttered as he towed the snowmobile into his machine shed, dismayed that his attempts to bond with the boy had gone so poorly.

Things got a little better after lunch when Abby insisted on seeing his horses. She crept up to the stall as if in fear for her life, but when Liberty, his favorite mare, stuck her head over the gate and whinnied, Abby seemed to forget her inhibitions. She reached up a hand and gently brushed it over Liberty's golden-red mane. A moment later the two were holding a mutual admiration meeting. Abby's green eyes grew huge with wonder when she looked at him.

"She's beautiful," she murmured.

"She's a sucker for apples." Cade handed her one of two he'd tucked into his pocket earlier.

"Does it have to be cut up—oh!" Abby blinked as the horse nipped the apple from her fingers and chewed the treat. She looked at her hand in wonder. "She didn't even touch me."

Cade laughed.

"Liberty's an expert thief. Sometimes she searches my pockets for carrots when I'm cleaning her stall or feeding her and she always finds them." A sudden rush of satisfaction filled him when Abby began to caress Liberty, which made Cade wonder why it seemed so important she was comfortable with his animals.

How at home do you want her to feel? He ignored the voice in his head.

"Liberty loves her treats almost as much as she loves being brushed," he explained. "Want to try?"

Abby studied him for a few minutes, then slowly nodded. Cade went to the tack area, grabbed Liberty's favorite brush and carried it to Abby. Carefully he opened the gate and positioned himself by Liberty's side so he could show Abby how to brush. When his fingers covered hers, Cade's heart rate giddyapped, just as it had right before he'd shot out of the chute on an ornery bronc when he competed at the Calgary Stampede.

As soon as Abby had the motion memorized, Cade let go and stepped back, trying to even out his erratic breathing. What was wrong with him today?

Liberty shifted and whinnied. Abby backed away with a frown. "Did I do it wrong?"

"No. You're doing it right. That means she likes it."

Cade smiled. "She won't hurt you, but she might not want you to stop," he warned.

"Do all her noises have meanings?" Abby resumed her work.

"Not always, but you'll know if she doesn't like something. She's not subtle." He couldn't tear his gaze away from Abby's face and the pure joy that radiated from it as she curried the horse.

"I hear you had some trouble with Ivor this morning." She gave him a quick sideways look.

"We don't seem to be hitting it off," Cade admitted. "He won't listen to anything I say. I tried to tell him to keep the snowmobile away from the pond but—" He shrugged and let the rest of his sentence die.

"Ivor doesn't come from a ranch family, does he? I think Mrs. Swanson mentioned his dad was some kind of mechanic." Abby moved to Liberty's other side. Cade followed and stayed close, just in case she needed him.

"Maybe Ivor worked with him," Cade said dourly. "Then he could help me fix my sled."

Abby chuckled, then smoothed her hand between Liberty's eyes, whispering soothing words. She winked at him.

"Maybe Ivor would like to brush a horse," she mused in a speculative tone.

"I'm not sure he likes animals." Which was a relief since Cade wasn't sure he wanted Ivor anywhere near his prized horses. Sensing that Abby was wearying, he called a halt and put Liberty back in her stall, placating her whinny of complaint with another apple.

"It's coffee time," he said as he closed the stall door. "Let's go see what Mrs. Swanson baked today."

"Does she bake a lot?" Abby asked. She slid her hand through the arm he offered and daintily picked her way over the snowy path toward the house.

"She usually makes something special every day. It's her way of trying to tempt my dad to eat a little more," he told her.

"Has she been here a long time?" Abby wondered.

"Since my mom died. She practically raised me." He cleared his throat and said the words that had nagged at him for hours. "You were with my father for a long time this morning. I really think it's better if you stay away, Abby."

"Your father and I were playing games." She stopped when he paused outside the back door and studied him. "Ed seemed to really get into them, so I didn't want to cut it short. But if you'd rather I didn't interact with him—" She stopped, waited.

"I don't want you hurt," Cade said firmly. "I heard his cane banging several times. When he gets riled he sometimes loses control—"

"He wasn't riled." Abby laughed. "He was celebrating. He beat me at every game of checkers. Ivor told me he'd lost to Ed earlier, too."

"He didn't get upset?" Cade frowned when Abby shook her head.

"Your father seems to enjoy winning."

"Yeah, he loves winning," Cade told her with an ironic grin. "Understatement of the year to say he loves winning. My father *has* to win."

Winning was all that mattered to Ed. At least it was all that seemed to matter in his relationship with his son. Since Cade had often overruled him in regard to decisions about the ranch, he'd assumed that accounted for his father's worsening behavior.

Confused by the different view of his dad, Cade held the door for Abby to precede him inside. They shed their outer clothes and boots in the mudroom that adjoined the kitchen.

"Something smells wonderful," Abby said, following her nose. "I can't believe I'm hungry again. I ate a huge lunch."

"Ranch life does that to you." Cade accepted two cups of coffee from Mrs. Swanson and set them on the kitchen table. "It's the fresh, unspoiled air."

"It's also the wee ones wanting a snack," Mrs. Swanson said with a knowing glance at Abby's midriff. "Some cinnamon rolls might quiet them."

"They certainly would." Abby sat next to Cade, then accepted a steaming cinnamon roll. She nipped a bite between her pink lips, closed her eyes and smiled. "Delicious," she said, much to Mrs. Swanson's satisfaction.

A few moments later Ed and Ivor joined them. Ivor pushed Ed's chair to the table as if he'd done it a thousand times before. As they all sat around the table sharing the delicious treat, Abby teased Ed about winning and then Ivor about almost sinking the snowmobile.

For the first time in memory, Cade realized that he and his father were seated together at the table without the usual tension. Everyone seemed to find harmony, fun and pleasure in one another's company. Cade had no doubt that was Abby's influence on them. She seemed to bring out the best in everyone she met.

Cade's gaze slid to Ivor. According to Marsha's call this morning, the kid was going to be here a while. None of the relatives she'd spoken to seemed ready to add the orphaned boy to their menageries, which meant Cade needed to find a way to connect with Ivor. His horses had reached Abby. Maybe they would Ivor, too.

Cade spared a moment to wonder why it was so important for him to connect with Ivor, then decided he was just being a good host.

"Maybe tomorrow you'd like to go for a horse ride," he offered. "I could teach you if you don't know how to ride."

"No, thank you." Ivor didn't even look at him. He did turn to Ed and ask him for a rematch. The pair left the kitchen with Ivor teasing the older man and Ed thumping his cane as he rolled along in his wheelchair, just for effect.

"Well, that went well," Cade muttered, embarrassed that Abby had witnessed the brush-off he'd just received.

"Don't get discouraged," she encouraged, patting his arm. "Ivor's hurting. He's found a safe place with Ed. Let him savor that for a bit."

"He seems to reject almost everything I suggest." He grimaced. "Except for the snowmobile, and look how that turned out."

"He'll come around. You're doing fine, Cade." She leaned back, cupping her coffee cup against her cheek as she studied him. "Kids are unpredictable, especially when they've suffered such a big loss. I heard Ivor weeping last night. He sounded like his heart was breaking." She sighed. "I wanted to go to him and comfort him, but I didn't because I believe he needs those moments to release the miasma of emotions he's got whirling inside."

Cade listened, trying to grasp what she wasn't saying.

"Ivor would never weep in front of us," Abby explained. "It would embarrass him. But in private he can express his feelings without feeling judged."

"I wouldn't judge him," Cade objected.

"No, but he *thinks* you would." Abby smiled. "You're a big tough cowboy. You run a ranch with a lot of land and animals and you stand up to Ed. In Ivor's eyes, you're too tough to cry. He's intimidated. Give him time to find a real bond with you. Don't force it. He'll share your horses when he's ready."

Abby made it sound so easy to relate to Ivor. Cade didn't think it was going to be, but for now he'd take her opinion on the matter. After all, she was the kid expert.

"What do you think about Mayor Marsha's plan for the adoption agency?" He watched her pretty face, trying to decipher the emotions that fluttered across it.

"I think it's great," she enthused, eyes bright. "I'd love to help create a sanctuary for women who are in a situation like mine. And to help find homes for kids like Ivor would be very fulfilling. I see lots of potential."

"Is that because you're getting bored with us?" he asked. Surprise flared in her eyes before she looked down.

"That would be rude of me after all you've done."

"Hardly. Living out here is nothing like living in the city. I get that." Cade grinned when she finally looked at him. "I'm used to the slow pace of life around here, but you're not. If you can fill in the time till the babies come by getting involved in the adoption agency, then I think that would be good for you."

"You talk as if I was living the high life in Calgary," she said and made a face. "Hardly. I'll be happy to help out however I can. But it's hard to get an agency going." Abby's green eyes darkened to match her serious tone. "Most have years of reputation that clients can trust in. Of course, offering expectant mothers a place to stay until they give birth could be a major draw for this agency. I might suggest that. Also, I think Marsha's friend could have even more impact if she specialized in placing 'special' kids."

"You mean mentally handicapped children," he said, mulling over her words.

"Or disabled children. Or older children. Many adopting parents aren't prepared to take an older child until someone tells them how much difference they can make in that child's life," she explained.

"I guess," he said, thinking of his own past and what a difference feeling loved would have made to him.

"In social services we always had a long list of kids like that waiting to be adopted. Like everyone, they desperately want to be loved." A haunting note filled her voice. "If Marsha's friend's agency specialized in adoptions for children who are hard to place, she would quickly make a name for herself."

"And the agency would get more business." Cade nodded. "I see."

"It would also be a big hit with the government," Abby explained. "Most social workers simply don't have the time or resources to search for families with the references and skills to take those kinds of children. Mayor Marsha's friend would have business from day one."

"Great idea!" Cade studied Abby with new respect. "You should think about going into business with this woman," he said. "You have a lot of knowledge that she could use."

"Actually I am considering it. If my money would come through I could use some of it to buy in." Abby studied her hands. After a moment she lifted her head and looked at him, her smile self-mocking. "I can't stay here forever."

"Well, don't rush into anything. Stay as long as you want," Cade offered. He hesitated, then added in a low voice, "If you like, I could try mediating with the military for you. There's no reason they should be stonewalling you about money you're owed."

"Thank you. I accept your offer," she said promptly. "I have had zero success with them. They intimidate me, just like you intimidate Ivor. He hasn't figured out yet that you're a teddy bear inside." She brushed his cheek with her fingertip, smiled at his grunt of disgust, then added, "It's very nice of you to give me shelter, Cade. But my stay has to be temporary. I've got to get a job so I can make a home for my babies. If I can't do that—"

Abby didn't say the rest. She let her words drain away to silence, but it was clear to Cade that she was considering a number of options, including some last resorts to give her twins security.

"I'll get in touch with the military tomorrow morning if you'll give me the information. For now you'll have to excuse me," he said, rising. "I have an appointment with someone this afternoon. He should be arriving soon and I have a couple of things to do to prepare."

"Sure. I'll go dig out my records. Thanks for the trip to see Liberty," Abby said.

Cade hurried back to the barn. Truthfully, he had an hour before the scheduled meeting and he'd already done as much as he could to get the ranch into the black and thereby prepare it for this prospective buyer who would see that it was profitable. But he wanted to be alone to think about what Abby had said and wonder why he'd wanted to protest when she'd talked about leaving. Why did her staying matter so much?

Cade knew why. Because with Abby here, the ranch felt like home. Because with her in the house, people laughed, enjoyed each other. Because there'd been no bickering with his dad since Abby's arrival.

Because he liked her company and wanted her to stay.

Cade figured that was really stupid of him, given that even *he* wasn't staying. Sooner or later the ranch would have to be sold. It was the only way he could think of to pay for his dad to get into one of those seniors' places

where Ed could make friends while getting special attention from staff physiotherapists who would get him back
on his feet, walking.

Abby couldn't stay here. Neither could Cade. They both
needed to move on.

Chapter Four

Abby's feet ached, her back hurt and her head whirled from too many introductions. The funeral for Ivor's parents had been somber and quiet, but the luncheon following the interment was everything Ivor had said his parents would like. The community had gathered to support him and re-affirm their connections with each other. It was wonderful to be part of it all, but she desperately needed to rest.

"Sit down before you fall down," a brusque voice ordered from behind her. Cade, who'd seemed a bit distant since they'd left the ranch, dragged a chair forward. "Rest a bit. Then we should leave."

"Leave?" Abby frowned at him as she sat down. "Why?"

"Because Ivor's as worn out as you. Look at him." He inclined his head in the direction of the bereaved boy. "He needs to get out of here."

Abby was about to protest. But then she observed the way Ivor forced a smile to his lips as one after another of his parents' friends came to speak to him. When one woman threw her arms around his shoulders and hugged him, Ivor's eyes met Abby's and she saw something she thought was desperation creep in. He endured the embrace for a second longer before he drew away, struggling to mask his emotions.

"Did he tell you he wants to leave?" she asked Cade.

"He didn't have to. I can tell from his body language that he wants out of here. I'm going to have to do something to initiate that. Excuse me." Cade strode purposefully across the room. He said something to the crowd surrounding Ivor, then drew him away.

Abby had felt Cade's withdrawal the moment they'd left the ranch for town. It was much like Max's withdrawal from her when his PTSD had overtaken his nights and she'd been unable to help him.

Cade's withdrawal had increased through the afternoon and nothing she'd done had alleviated it, either. Abby had already gathered he was uncomfortable around the townsfolk and wondered at the reasons. Maybe that's why it seemed all the more touching when Cade rescued Ivor with everyone watching.

As Cade now spoke to Ivor, a kindly look softened his expression. Whatever he said brought a wash of relief to the boy's face. Ivor nodded and then strode to the food table where he picked up a steaming cup and two sandwiches wrapped in a napkin and carried them toward Abby.

"Cade said you need these." He set the food on a chair beside her.

So he'd been thinking of her, too. How kind of him.

"Is that tea?" At his nod, Abby took the cup, sipped from it and sighed. "He was right." She smiled at him. "Thank you."

"You'd better eat something, too. Cade said we're leaving soon." He inclined his head toward the sandwiches, then sat down on her other side.

"It's been a long day for you." She touched his shoulder, drawing his attention from the tall, lean rancher. "Are you okay?"

"I don't know. It's weird. I know they're gone but I keep expecting to…" Ivor shook his head and gulped. "I'm fine," he muttered.

"After my parents died," she told him, dredging up the memory because it might help Ivor, "it took me forever to stop reaching for the phone to call them when something happened in my life."

"And your husband, Max?"

"When Max died, I thought I'd died, too. Sometimes I still feel like that." Abby forced a smile and ignored the familiar rush of guilt. "You'll always miss your parents, but I promise that it will get easier after a while," she said softly.

Ivor stared at her for a few minutes before he nodded, then turned away. He said nothing. Abby picked up a sandwich and chewed thoughtfully. Her gaze returned to Cade, who was now speaking with Mayor Marsha. Whatever he was saying, the mayor obviously agreed, for she clapped a hand on his shoulder and nodded her head wholeheartedly.

She moved quickly around the room like a practiced politician, saying something here, chuckling at something there. Moments later Abby noticed that people began to drift out of the community hall. Abby knew Cade had asked Marsha to encourage that.

"Time for us to go." He held out Abby's coat, waiting for her to slide her arms into it.

It felt good to slip her coat on without struggling, to feel the comfort of Cade's hands on her shoulders, settling the garment there before he drew away his fingers. It seemed like forever since she'd felt so protected.

Surprised by that thought, she walked between Ivor and Cade to the truck, lost in her thoughts. Had she not felt protected with Max?

At first, perhaps. But then their roles had reversed and she'd been the one to protect him, silly as that sounded. She'd protected him by nurturing him through his darkest moments, but not contacting the military to tell them Max needed help. Maybe if she had—

Once again Cade lifted her inside the truck. Though Abby was prepared, that didn't stop her heart rate from accelerating or her breath from catching in her throat at the contact with him. But she did manage to control her expression as she settled herself in the seat, pretending calmness.

As Cade drew out of the parking lot and headed toward the ranch, Ivor leaned forward.

"I never said that I'm sorry about Max," he said. "He sounds like a good man."

"He was—" She turned to stare at him. "How do you know about Max?"

"From Ed," Ivor explained. "He told me Max was the only one who understood what it was like for him to be stuck in his wheelchair after he had his first stroke."

Abby happened to glance at Cade as Ivor said it and saw the way the corner of his mouth tightened. Not in disapproval, but...she couldn't quite define it. She had the oddest feeling that Cade envied Ivor for the solid relationship he was building with Ed because he'd never been able to attain that. Maybe deep inside, Cade also felt a nub of hurt that his own father felt Max understood Ed better than Cade ever could. Why had they never been able to connect as father and son?

When they arrived at the house, Ivor went to find Ed, to tell him about the funeral, Abby guessed. Cade's father had awoken with a cough and neither Mrs. Swanson nor Cade would even consider allowing him to brave the frigid air to attend the ceremony.

Abby sat at the kitchen table, grateful that Mrs. Swanson had a pot of tea ready because she hadn't finished her earlier cup. She was doubly glad when Cade sat down across from her. The housekeeper went to make some phone calls, leaving them alone.

"Are you okay?" Cade asked, examining her with an appraising look.

"Just need to catch my breath." Abby decided to risk being rebuffed. "You didn't like being there today, did you?" she asked. His lips tightened and he looked everywhere but at her. "In town, I mean."

"It wasn't because of the funeral," he said.

"Because being around the townspeople bothers you," she guessed.

"I—don't go to town much," he said after a small hesitation. His long, dark lashes fanned across his cheekbones as he stared at the table. Then he lifted them and stared straight at her. "Most of them think of me as *poor Cade.*"

"Because?" He just kept looking at her, so Abby stretched out a hand and touched his arm. "Is it because of your dad?"

"He wasn't—isn't an easy man," Cade murmured with hesitation.

"He was hard on you as a kid?"

"I'm sure you must have noticed by now." He barked a laugh that held no mirth. "Ed is hard on everybody. At one time or another, I suspect the whole town has felt the lash of his anger and felt sorry for poor Cade."

"The whole town?" She shook her head in disbelief. "I'm sure his temper embarrasses you. But he is the way he is, Cade. It's nothing to do with you and I doubt anyone in town holds his outbursts against you. But I think there's more to your aloofness."

Cade simply looked at her without saying anything.

"I know I'm new in town, but when I hear people talk about you, there is a tone of respect in their voices," she said sincerely. "They know you served your country and they're proud of you. I don't think they think of you as 'poor Cade' at all. Even if they did, if you gave them a chance, once they know you better—"

"I can't get involved in town affairs, Abby." He pushed to his feet. "I haven't got the time. I have too much to do around here."

"I know." She smiled and let go of the topic. For now. "Especially with two more of us here. Are you sure that if I got involved in the adoption center, taking me to town for meetings wouldn't be too much? I mean, you've already agreed to pester the government for Max's insurance and stuff."

"I'll manage." He moved toward the porch, then stopped. "Did you get your papers together?"

"I left the folder on your desk," she told him and added, "Thank you."

"Don't thank me yet," Cade said, then lifted an eyebrow. "I overheard Marsha telling someone there's a meeting at the seniors' hall about the adoption agency tomorrow afternoon. You never said anything about it. Why?"

"I thought maybe I wouldn't go." Abby nibbled her bottom lip. "It's bound to be mostly organizational. I know you're busy, and anyway they just want ideas from me. I can do that over the phone."

She ducked her head. Cade was already doing so much for her. She didn't want to inconvenience him, especially now that she realized what long hours he put in around the ranch.

"Abby." Cade waited for her to look at him. "I said it wouldn't be a problem to take you and I meant it. I promise that if I can't do it, I'll let you know and we'll figure out something else. Okay?"

She nodded, reassured by the quiet competence in his voice.

"Trust me," he said.

Abby couldn't tear her gaze from his. "I do," she whispered.

Cade kept looking at her. Finally he broke the silence between them with a nod. "Good. I won't let you down."

"I know," she said in total confidence.

Then he was gone.

"Dad, you've got to do the exercises." Cade smothered his irritation and strove for calmness. "The medication can't do it all. The doctor said you have to help your muscles recover by moving them."

Fat lot you know, Ed scrawled across his pad with a guttural growl, then ignored Cade to concentrate on his game with Ivor.

Cade opened his mouth to protest, then gave up. If his father couldn't motivate himself, he would hardly listen to his son. He never had before. It only reaffirmed Cade's decision to sell the ranch to pay for a place with an emotionally uninvolved staff that could coerce and coax Ed back to health.

"Cade?" Ivor motioned him over, pointed to the pad where his father had written *Foals?* in big, scrawling letters.

"Not yet," he told Ed. "The vet says Blue Girl isn't ready yet, but he's keeping a close eye on her. It won't be long for Recitation, though." He knew his father worried about his favorite mare. "I think after she foals we'd better make sure this is her last pregnancy. She's getting too old."

Ed frowned but for once he didn't argue.

"I have to take Abby to town for her meeting. Will you two be okay?" Ed glared at him and Ivor rolled his eyes. Cade sighed. "I'll rephrase. If you need anything, Mrs. Swanson is in her room. Call her."

He left the room knowing the housekeeper would check on them. The two males would be well looked after. It was just that he had a constant, nagging need to be sure he'd covered every detail. He didn't want Ed having a relapse on his watch. The responsibility weighed heavily.

Abby waited in the kitchen, bundled up in a thick, warm coat his housekeeper had found for her. Cade escorted her to the truck and soon they were on the road.

"It's going to be hard on your father when Ivor returns to school," Abby mused.

"When will that be?" he asked.

"Ivor seems to think the sooner the better. I overheard him ask Marsha if he could go back tomorrow. I didn't realize she's his temporary guardian." She nodded at Cade's look of surprise. "I expected her to have made me his guardian but apparently she sees this as some kind of test case with the authorities."

"So why didn't she take Ivor to her house?" Cade asked.

"With her husband so ill, Marsha can't take Ivor home. But she did tell him today that the bus will pick him up for school at the end of our lane. I'm sure she'll phone later to let us know the rest of the details."

Cade nodded.

"I didn't get the impression that the relatives he was with over the weekend are stepping up to take him." Abby tilted her head to one side. "I think the routine of getting back to normal at school will be good for him."

"I don't know how normal his life will be, but he's welcome to stay on the Double L," Cade told her. "He's good for Dad. Somehow the two of them really communicate. I wish I could manage that feat with my father." He couldn't mask his wistfulness.

"Why can't you?" Abby grinned when he rolled his eyes. "I didn't say it would be easy, but if that's what you want, you have to at least try." She tilted her head so she could study him. "You should make the first move, Cade."

"How?" he demanded.

"You know him better than I. You'll figure out something." The way Abby fiddled with her seat belt told him she wanted to ask him something. It wasn't long before she said, "Did you, uh, find out anything about my money?"

"Not yet." Trying to get answers about Abby's money had gone as badly as his meeting with his potential buyer. But getting passed around the various government departments forced Cade to appreciate what Abby had gone through. "I'm still working on it."

"Thanks." She stared out the window, blinking rapidly. He hated seeing Abby so emotional.

"Can I ask you something?" When Abby looked at him with her expressive green eyes, a cinch tightened around Cade's heart. *It's none of your business.* "Never mind."

"No, go ahead. Please ask me whatever you want." She waited, her glossy walnut curls sparkling in sunshine reflected off the snow.

"Why don't you wear Max's rings anymore? Is it because they remind you of him too much?" Cade wished he'd kept silent when devastation filled her eyes. "You don't have to tell me."

Abby remained silent for several moments. When she spoke, her voice was so quiet, he wasn't sure he heard her correctly.

"I pawned them. Isn't that awful?" she whispered, tears shining in her eyes. "I pawned my dead husband's rings."

"Abby, I—" Cade was so shocked he couldn't think what to say.

"They were my dearest link with him." She stared down at her knotted hands. "But I had no money and I had to pay the bills or they would have turned off the gas. I kept the thermostat as low as I could, but the house was old and drafty and it cost a lot to heat, especially since this winter has been so cold."

She was apologizing for keeping warm! Cade's anger ballooned. If he'd toyed with any doubts about trying to recover her money, they now dissipated. But he didn't say a word. He simply let her talk.

"I've only got a month left before the man at the pawn-shop is legally entitled to sell the last of my stuff," she continued in a very quiet voice. "I keep hoping and praying my money will come in time to recover my most precious things, but— I'm leaving that up to God." She gulped, surreptitiously brushed away a tear and forced a smile. "Tell me about your horses that are having babies."

So for the rest of the journey into town Cade babbled about mares and foals and how he raised them, but his mind wouldn't let go of the grim fact that she'd had to pawn her jewelry to stop from freezing to death.

Cade figured he must have told a good story about ranching because by the time they arrived at the seniors' center, Abby's eyes danced with anticipation.

"I want to be there when the horses give birth," she insisted. In the short time she'd been on the ranch the sallow tone of her skin had been replaced by a lovely rose that gave her cheeks a healthy glow. The big, generous smile he remembered from when Max had introduced them seemed back to stay.

Cade still had doubts about bringing Abby to the ranch, but at the moment he was fiercely glad he'd taken her away from her drafty house, the bill collectors and those who smeared Max's sacrifice by withholding the payments she was due.

"Looks like half the town's here," he said, irritated that he couldn't park nearer the entrance.

"Good. It'll be even more fun if the whole town gets involved in making the adoption agency happen." She gathered up a stuffed satchel she'd brought and reached for the door handle.

"Wait," he ordered. "I'll help you." But by the time he got to the other side of the truck, Abby was reaching down with one toe, trying to feel her way onto the truck's running board. "You are a stubborn woman," he told her as he helped her descend.

"That must be hard for you," she agreed, grinning as she peeked through her lashes at him. "Especially since you're just as stubborn."

Cade couldn't stifle his shout of laughter as he walked her inside the building. A second later he choked it back, intimidated by the group of people who turned to stare at them.

"Abby, I'm delighted you came. And you brought Cade. Just the man we need for several jobs." Mayor Marsha swooped down on them and drew them both forward.

Cade almost groaned. He didn't want any part of this. He had his own work to do, including finding a buyer for the ranch. But how could he refuse to repair the loosening banister the mayor showed him? Or ignore the loose carpet corner that very well might trip Abby? Seniors needed those things in a center they used frequently and Cade couldn't find any excuse not to complete the other items on the list the mayor handed him.

It would be churlish to refuse and downright silly to drive all the way back to the ranch and then return to pick up Abby, so Cade got to work. But in spite of his refusal to get involved, he couldn't help listening to the discussion as he worked.

"I want to announce that Wanda Scranton has purchased the old hotel with the intention of opening an adoption agency which will also be a place where moms-to-be can come as a sanctuary, a kind of home to stay and await the birth of the child she wishes to give for adoption," Marsha informed the group after she'd called them to order.

Applause mingled with surprise and almost everyone clapped.

"As a building, it should work very well. The rooms are a nice size with those big, old-fashioned windows that let the sun in," Marsha continued. "Wanda is already speaking with builders about renovations the government requires. She's hoping it won't cost too much to make changes."

A sense of excitement rippled through the room. Abby, head bent, doodled on a pad she'd brought along.

"On the staffing side, Holly Janzen, our nurse practitioner, has agreed to act as midwife if the birth mom wants that rather than hospital. Holly's fully qualified, of course, and she can call Doc Treple for backup. He's agreed to that. Wanda will need other personnel, of course, but for now she'd like suggestions on what you think needs doing to make her agency a Buffalo Gap success."

"I think it will take work to make that place homier, less institutional," Karina Denver said. "I had this idea that handmade quilts might lend that touch to the rooms. Maybe we could even give them to the birth mom or send them home with the child." She grimaced and shrugged. "Of course, I have no idea how to make quilts."

Muted laughter filled the room.

"I know how. I could teach you," Abby volunteered. "I've quilted since I was eight."

"You're sure it's okay in your condition?" Karina asked with a tentative glance at Abby's stomach.

Cade frowned. Everyone in town knew how badly Karina wanted a baby. But she and Jake were childless and Abby was obviously pregnant. Wouldn't working with Abby make it harder for Karina? His reservations were smothered by the excited responses of others gathered around the table at the mention of quilting.

"I'm perfectly fit to quilt," Abby insisted, her cheeks bright pink now that everyone's attention was on her. "There are many patterns to choose from. How many rooms will there be?"

"Twelve." Mayor Marsha frowned. "But I don't know if Wanda can afford fabric for that many quilts."

"Maybe she won't need to." Abby remained silent for a moment, then smiled. "Why not put out a call for leftover fabric? We can make scrap quilts."

"That's a lot of quilting," someone else said, echoing Cade's reservations.

"It is. I wish I still had my mom's long-arm quilting machine," Abby mused, a faraway look in her eyes. "It would make the quilting part go much faster."

Just by glancing at her face, Cade knew she'd pawned it along with her rings. His gut burned at the thought that she'd been forced to part with things she must treasure. But Abby didn't look gloomy or depressed.

"We'll have to leave it with God and see what He works out." That sparkle was back in her eyes. "Or..." she dragged it out for maximum impact. "We could have quilting bees." She grinned at the others' obvious approval. "We could set up a frame at someone's house and get together to quilt like they did in the old days. With all of us working together, it won't take long."

"Years ago we had a group like that in Buffalo Gap but

we kind of lost interest." Mayor Marsha was obviously intrigued. "Do you have a quilting frame, Abby?"

"No." Abby's head lifted and her eyes met Cade's. "But I know someone who could make one." She winked at him. "Leave it with me."

Cade added *build a quilt frame* to his to-do list.

"Those are wonderful ideas. Now let's move on to the next piece of business," Mayor Marsha decreed.

Cade had no idea what a quilt frame even looked like, let alone how to build one. But thanks to Abby, he had an idea about how he could find common ground with his dad.

"So I thought maybe we could figure out a way to get back Abby's rings and her mom's quilting machine," Cade said to his father later that night after everyone had gone to bed.

How? Ed scrawled across his pad.

"That's the part I need your help with," Cade admitted. "But it seems to me that since Max gave his life for our country the least we should be able to do is help out his wife. So will you think about it, let me know if you come up with any ideas?"

Ed studied him for several minutes, then shrugged and nodded.

"Thanks, Dad. And don't tell anyone. I'd like to keep this between us if I could. Abby's proud. I don't think she'd want anyone to know she had to pawn her things." Cade sipped his coffee, knowing he couldn't stay much longer. He had to get back to the horse barn. "It looks like we're going to have a new foal tonight," he told Ed.

For the first time in ages Cade actually felt comfortable talking ranch with his father. Maybe Abby was right; maybe this relationship could be salvaged.

Raise the foals? his father wrote on the pad.

Cade shook his head.

Why not?

"Justine Brunfeld has already given me a deposit for the first six foals we get that aren't thoroughbreds. She's asked me to halter break them. She intends to add them to her riding academy." Cade hadn't promised because he wasn't sure he'd still be here. He sighed as his father jerked upright in his chair. "I know you don't want to sell, Dad, but we need the money."

We need the foals to build our herd.

The herd we're going to sell? Cade didn't say it because of the carved lines of age and worry deepening around Ed's dark eyes.

"The Double L has always raised thoroughbreds. I don't want to weaken our brand and the foals aren't thoroughbreds," Cade explained. But it was no use. His father didn't feel that should be his decision alone. They'd been over this topic a hundred times before. "I have to go back to the barn," Cade said, rising. "We'll talk about it more tomorrow."

I decide. Ed shook the yellow tablet to emphasize his displeasure.

The truce was over. There would be no reconciliation this night.

"You can't run the ranch until you're up and walking, Dad," Cade said in his quietest voice. "And if you won't do your exercises we both know that isn't going to happen. So in the meantime, I'll decide. You gave me control, remember?"

His father's face turned red and he opened and closed his mouth powerlessly.

"I'm doing what I think is best," Cade told him. "I'm sorry if that's not good enough." While his father stabbed the black marker against the yellow pad in a series of angry words, Cade turned away. "Good night, Dad," was all he said before he walked to the kitchen.

He rinsed his coffee mug in the sink, wishing it didn't have to be this way, wishing God would change something. But then God hadn't answered his prayers in a very long time.

"Bad night?" Abby sat wrapped in a blanket on the corner window seat. "Coffee won't help you sleep."

"I hope not." He smiled at her curious look. "I'm drinking it to keep me awake. I think we'll have some new foals by morning."

"Can I come and see?" Her emerald eyes stretched wide with excitement. "Please, Cade? I promise I won't get in your way."

"Abby, it's cold out there—" But she cut him off.

"I'll dress warmly and bring a blanket. I've never seen anything born." Her voice was part awe, part reverence. "And I want to so badly. Please let me come, Cade."

Against his better judgment he acquiesced. How could he deny such a simple pleasure to this woman who'd had to give up so much?

"Go put on the warmest clothes you have," he ordered. "I have to gather some stuff. Meet me back here in ten minutes. Okay?"

"Yes." She rose, her smile huge. "Thank you, Cade," she said before she hurried from the room.

How did Abby's smile have the ability to thaw the part of his heart that had always been frozen, the part that had always yearned for love?

Chapter Five

"You're going to take pictures?"

Abby smiled when Cade's wide-eyed gaze swung from the camera around her neck to her face.

"I want to capture every marvelous moment of this birth," she explained. He didn't say a word but his expression spoke volumes. "If I get anything good, I might blow it up. Maybe we could use it to decorate the walls in the adoption agency. I'd call it *Moms and Babies*." He just kept looking at her. It unnerved Abby. "You think I'm being silly."

"I didn't say that." He dragged open the door and waited for her to enter the barn.

You didn't have to, she thought. *I'm beginning to understand what your expressions mean.*

"I don't know how good your photos will be because you'll have to stay outside Recitation's stall," Cade warned. "For your safety. I piled up a couple of bales for you to sit on so at least you can put your feet up."

"Thank you." Abby accepted his hand to climb onto the thick blanket he'd spread over the bales. A feeling of coddled protectiveness swelled as he laid another blanket over her legs and tucked it around her. "I'm warm as toast," she told him, deeply touched by his consideration.

"Good." Cade's gaze rested on her stomach for a moment, lifted to meet hers, then slewed away. He turned, opened the gate and stepped inside a large pen in which an anxious black horse paced. "Hello, beauty," he said, his tone oozing reassurance.

The horse pricked her ears as she looked at him, snorted once, then bunted him with her sweaty head. Abby snapped a shot. "She doesn't look upset."

"She isn't." Cade twisted his head to grin at her when the horse whinnied. "The lady has done this before. She's reminding me she wants peace and quiet while she's preparing for birth."

Cade's blue eyes roved over the animal while his big palms gently smoothed over her flanks, checking for signs that the birth was progressing normally. All the while he murmured soft encouragement. When the horse nudged him away, he stepped back.

"Is she okay?" Abby asked anxiously.

"She's fine, though she'd prefer Dad to be with her right now. He raised Recitation from a filly so she favors him. Guess she'll just have to tolerate me instead of Dad tonight." Cade sat down on a bale in the corner. "You're doing well, Mama, so I'll leave you alone," his voice brimming with affection.

"Leave her alone? That's it?" Abby flushed when Cade chuckled at her disgusted tone.

"I don't like intervening with foaling unless absolutely necessary. Recitation knows what she's doing." He shrugged. "I'm here just in case."

But despite those words, Abby noticed Cade didn't really sit and wait. Every so often he approached the horse using a soft, calming voice as he slid his hands over her to assess her progress. Entranced by the evident bond between them, she snapped pictures of the laboring mare from many angles, waiting patiently until Cade stood just the right way with the light on his face so she could include him in the frame. Through the lens, Abby saw the gentle man her troubled husband had spoken of so affectionately.

The more Cade worked with the horse, the more his demeanor changed. His face lost all signs of the stress it usually wore. The standoffish belligerence he'd used like a shield to keep people away when he'd taken her to the meeting in town evaporated. Now a warm glint lit his eyes and the sternness of his features melted, giving way to a boyish grin and a smothered chuckle when Recitation eased her head under his hand for a pat.

Cade seemed to forget Abby was there so she used the opportunity to take many pictures, trying to capture his pleasure in this moment.

"Okay, girl, we're getting down to business now, aren't we?" Cade moved beside the horse, his sensitive fingertips assessing her burgeoning midsection as she strained and grunted.

He seemed unsurprised and stepped nimbly out of the way when Recitation suddenly lay down, rolled, then regained her footing only to nuzzle around in the hay, making nests.

Confused, Abby finally asked, "Is something wrong with her?"

"She's getting ready. It won't be long now. I think the human equivalent is when pregnant women clean the house." Cade spared her a grin before his attention returned to the horse. "It will happen quickly so have your camera ready."

Cade's words continued in a soft drawl, leaving Abby amazed at his communication with Recitation, as much through a stroke here and a caress there as by any words he spoke.

"Watch," Cade ordered as the mare's legs strained. Moments later a soot-black foal was born. Recitation proudly cleaned off her baby and nudged it to its feet. Cade leaned against the pen, beside Abby, his smile huge. "Isn't he a beaut? Big and strong. He's great Double L stock even if he's not a thoroughbred."

"But he's not breathing." Abby held her breath, concerned that she could see no sign of movement in the small chest.

"He's breathing. He's just tired. He worked hard to get here." Cade touched Recitation's head with an affectionate brush. "So did you. Good job, Mama. You're a real trouper." Recitation nuzzled his chest and Cade laughed. "Yes, I have a treat for you." He held out a carrot. The horse quickly nipped it out of his hands, drawing more laughter from Cade. To Abby he looked as proud as any father.

"What happens now?" she asked, utterly awestruck by the amazing spectacle she had just witnessed.

"They bond. You can come in the pen now. Recitation wants to show off her new son." He opened the gate, then waited.

Abby slid off the hay and walked toward him. She stepped inside the pen hesitantly, awed by the strength and power of the horse.

"Don't be afraid." Cade slid his hand under her elbow, his fingers firm as he drew her forward.

"I'm not afraid." And she wasn't, at least not afraid of the horse.

But Cade, like this, soft, gentle, tender—that sent a confusing shaft of fear through her. Was she letting him get too close?

For some reason Abby's skin grew warm under Cade's fingers though it couldn't possibly be from his touch because there were layers of clothes between it and her arm.

And the way her breath snagged in her throat had nothing to do with the horse and her colt.

"She's beautiful," she finally managed, tears welling as she thought of her own children's births to come and wondering if she would do as well in labor as Recitation. Would Cade be there to help her? She glanced up and found him staring at her.

"Are you crying?" he asked in disbelief.

"How can I not?" she asked, half embarrassed by the tears tumbling down her cheeks. "Birth is such an affirmation of everything God gives. Max never understood—" She bit her lip, unwilling to let Cade see the troubled side of her marriage.

Guilt overwhelmed her and suddenly Abby was incapable of suppressing her sobs. She stood there, helpless and hurting. A moment later Cade's arms closed tentatively around her shoulders. After a second of hesitation, he gently drew her closer and brushed away her tears with his thumbs.

"Max wouldn't like these," he said, his voice low.

"No. He hated tears. Said they made him feel helpless," she agreed with a sniff.

"I know exactly how he felt." Cade said nothing more but he didn't have to. His comfort, the willingness to let her stand there until she could regain her composure, said more than any words could have.

Abby reveled in feeling cherished, protected, confident that if she leaned on Cade he would always support her. Only thing was, she could not let herself get used to leaning on him. She had to stand on her own two feet.

Once she'd regained control, Abby stepped away and swiped the back of her hands across her cheeks. She ignored the immediate sense of loss that washed over her.

"Sorry. That doesn't happen as often now, but—"

"Sometimes his loss still catches you unprepared." She was surprised by Cade's nod of understanding. "I miss him a lot, too," he said quietly. "He was my best friend." After a moment he drew her nearer to the colt that now stood on wobbly legs beside his mother. "Recitation has produced our best colts for years. She's an amazing horse."

The tone of his voice, the way his eyes glowed, the fierce pride in his words made Abby study his face more closely.

"You really love all this—" She waved a hand. "Ranching, I mean. The land, the animals—all of it. This is where you belong."

"Do I?" Cade twisted his head to stare at her, his expression altering into the familiar mask that hid his emotions better than a shield.

"I think so. I can see it in the way you relate to the animals." Cade's lips tightened and his body stiffened slightly but Abby continued to speak, certain she was right. "I don't know much about ranching," she admitted, "but I don't need to in order to see how you feel about Recitation and the others. They're part of you. This place is part of you. No wonder you're working so hard to keep this legacy of your father's going."

He blinked, his eyes glowing with intensity as they studied her. His lips parted as if he would speak but then he clamped them together, cutting off whatever he'd been about to say.

A sadness washed through Abby. For a moment she had felt so close to him, hoped he might open up to her, let her see what was beneath the brooding anger he kept so tightly bound, as Max never had. But then Cade's shields went up. He shut her out and she didn't know why.

With a sigh she turned her focus on Recitation and her foal.

"The Creator made us just as He made this colt. He

knows everything about us. It reminds me of that passage in Luke where Jesus is talking about our daily needs and He says not to worry about getting what we need because God knows exactly what we need and that He will always provide."

Cade's whole body jerked.

"I wish He would," Cade muttered as he turned away. He checked the feed bag and water trough, then motioned for them to leave Recitation's stall. Abby followed pensively.

"What makes you think He hasn't?" she asked when they were standing outside the stall. "You live on this amazing place, which you share with your father. Your animals are reproducing. Mrs. Swanson says your beef is in high demand. Your life seems on track here."

"Maybe it looks that way," he said brusquely.

"Your life isn't on track?" she asked curiously. "Why? What do you need?"

"Maybe a way to make my father better." Cade turned on her, his blue eyes shooting sparks. "Or maybe a way to get him to look at me as his son instead of the dumb hired hand who can't take two steps without fighting for some respect." He clamped his lips together.

The pain underlying those words helped Abby understand. Cade wanted what his father gave so freely to Ivor; he wanted to be appreciated, loved.

"This might sound counterintuitive to you, Cade," she said, wishing she knew how to heal his hurting heart. "But I don't think your father argues with you because of who you are or because of anything you've done."

He lifted one eyebrow in a question, waiting for her to continue.

"I think Ed fights with you because he's angry at himself, at what he can't do and feels he should. I think he feels he's putting all the load of running this place on you." Abby shifted, a little unnerved by her temerity in broaching such a sensitive subject.

"Then why doesn't he work harder at his exercises so he can get better and take back the reins of this place?" Cade demanded in a tight, hard tone.

"What if he does that and nothing changes?" Abby asked softly. "What if he invests every ounce of courage and strength he has in trying to recover and it doesn't happen?"

Cade studied her with a frown.

"Don't you see, can't you understand?" she asked, irritated by his blindness. "Your father is desperately afraid that even if he does everything he can to recover, he might still fail. I believe he fears that if that does happen he'll lose you, the ranch, everything that matters most to him."

Cade lifted his head and stared at her, locking his gaze with hers. Abby shivered at the intensity reflected there but her heart bumped at the flicker of hope that danced to life for a few brief moments.

Until Cade said, "Not possible. I never mattered. And my father was never afraid of anything." He added with conviction, "Never."

"Maybe once, he wasn't. But the strokes stole his confidence, Cade. Now he can't do the simplest thing he never gave a thought to doing before." Abby let a smile curve her lips when he shot her an indignant glare, as if to ask who she was to believe she knew his father better than he did.

"I'm not sure—"

"It's a kind of role reversal," she said. "You're the strong one now and he needs you. I think Ed's afraid that he'll never be the dad you remember, the strong, capable man who was always in control. And that terrifies him."

"Really?" Surprise made Cade's eyes widen for a moment. Then he frowned and shook his head. "I doubt that."

"Think about it," she coaxed. "He's gone from being strong, independent and running the ranch on his own, to having to write his needs on a pad of paper. He must chafe at the dependency that now rules his life."

"So we're back to my original question. Why doesn't God do something to make him better?" Cade's frustration was obvious.

"I don't know. Maybe He is doing something. Have you talked to Him about it?" Abby inclined her head, waiting.

"I don't speak to God," Cade muttered.

"Then how can you fault Him for not helping you?" Abby walked to Liberty's stall and petted the horse. She chuckled at the snickered response. "Yes, I brought an apple." She let the horse snatch it out of her hand before looking straight at Cade. "Your response is irrational. Not talking to God is like expecting Ed to do something without ever talking to him. That's not a relationship."

"I used to talk to God," Cade said in an edgy tone. "When I was a kid and my dad had just reamed me out for something, Mrs. Swanson said I should pray. So I did. A lot. But nothing ever changed. And it still hasn't."

"You don't know what God is doing," Abby insisted. "You can't see inside your father to know his thoughts and feelings and since you don't talk to him about that, how will you find out?"

She would have said more but the clanging of a bell caught Cade's attention.

"That's Mrs. Swanson's signal for me to get back to the house fast," he explained, her eyes narrowing with concern. "It could be Dad."

"Let's go." Abby waited till Cade tugged open the big door. As soon as he'd closed it behind them, she slid her arm through his. "I can go faster if I hang onto you," she explained, wondering if he got the same jolt of awareness that she did when their bare hands touched.

If so, Cade didn't show it, or maybe he was too preoccupied. All he did was lead her back to the house.

Six hours later Cade closed the door on the last guest and sighed his relief that they'd finally gone, leaving the ranch house to return to its solitude.

"Wasn't that fun?" Abby's green eyes sparkled with excitement. "I never imagined they'd all show up here to discuss the agency, but it wasn't a bad idea, was it?" She searched his face, a question on her own. "You didn't mind?"

"Only when I thought I'd have to go hunt down a cow to feed them all," he teased, refusing to acknowledge the rush of fear that had filled him at the sight of so many people invading his home, people he usually avoided when he was in town. "Once they brought out all those goodies for a potluck it was okay."

"It wasn't the potluck that made you feel better," she said indignantly. "It was the sight of Mayor Marsha's raspberry pie." Abby shared a grin with Mrs. Swanson.

"I didn't think Ed was going to get a taste, let alone Ivor." The housekeeper chuckled.

"It was an excellent pie," Cade said, ignoring the burn on his cheeks. He hadn't been that greedy, had he? He turned to Abby. "Are you pleased with the decision to proceed with the adoption agency even though all the funding isn't yet in place?"

"I think it's a great idea." She nursed a mug of peppermint tea between her palms, letting the steam bathe her face. "It's troubling to find out that Wanda doesn't have sufficient funds for a contingency plan, but I believe God will bless Family Ties. We just need to be prepared for when He answers our prayers."

As usual, Abby's faith in God was irrepressible.

"Family Ties?" Cade couldn't help appreciating how lovely she looked in the soft light of the kitchen.

"Everyone seemed to think it's an appropriate name." That was her modesty talking, not taking credit for a name that had been her suggestion.

Mrs. Swanson swished her dishcloth over the counter one last time before wishing them good-night. But she paused in the doorway, speaking hesitantly.

"I think having those people come out here for their meeting was a great idea," she said, facing Cade. "Ed loved playing host and he enjoyed listening to the men's discussion. The guys who drove their wives here had their heads together about something. Whatever it was, it seems to have put a light in his eyes. I think they should come again—only could you tell me first? I nearly died when they all drove into the yard and I had nothing prepared." Then she turned and quickly left the room.

Cade glanced at Abby. Her lips twitched.

"Mrs. Swanson thinks we arranged that gathering," she said in a choked voice.

"Actually, for a few minutes, I thought *you* had," Cade admitted. "You didn't seem all that surprised to see them."

"Well I was. But I'm glad they came. The more people we get working on this, the sooner we can get Family Ties operational." She sipped her tea, her gaze resting on him thoughtfully. "You know a lot of people around here, don't you?"

"I know what you're thinking, Abby." Cade held up his hand while shaking his head. "No. I haven't got time to take on more."

"I was only thinking you might make a few phone calls

to help with fund-raising. It wouldn't take that much time," she coaxed. "Since you'll be driving me into town anyway, you could make them on your cell while you wait…"

Cade kept shaking his head but deep inside he knew that eventually he'd make those calls. He was putty in her hands and the thing was, most of the time he didn't mind helping because he liked being around Abby, enjoyed seeing her happy smile stretch across her lovely face. But he also enjoyed teasing her so he shook his head.

"No."

"Fine," she finally conceded. "Be like that. But you'll wish you'd joined us when we have the grand opening."

"Poor Max," he said softly. "He must have been terribly henpecked."

"How well did you know him?" Abby shot back right before a huge yawn stretched her lips. "Max never did anything he didn't want to. Even when it would have been better for him to listen to someone else."

There was a certain asperity in her voice that made Cade frown. What wasn't Abby saying? She seemed lost in the past, her face closed up, a hint of—pain? flickering through her lovely eyes. He waited, hoping she'd say more.

Since Ivor was away on a visit to another extended family member and Ed had already retired, Cade lingered despite Abby's obvious weariness. He enjoyed sitting with her in the silent peace of the cozy kitchen.

But when her head began to nod he rose.

"You'd better get some sleep if you're going to church tomorrow."

She jerked upright, a tentative smile lifting her lips. "You'll take me? You don't mind going to church?"

"I'll take you," he agreed.

"Are you going to start talking to God?" she asked, then added, "If that's not too personal."

"I'm going to take you so I can take Dad, so he can be among other people," Cade told her without answering her question. "Mrs. Swanson's comment makes me realize Dad needs the sociability that church offers. He's been isolated out here with me too long."

"Good idea." Abby's green gaze held his.

"Mrs. Swanson deserves the change, too. She's had to miss a lot of Sunday services because of my ranch work."

"Uh-huh." Abby just kept watching him. Cade shifted uncomfortably under her assessing gaze. He was not prepared for her next comment. "Your dad, Mrs. Swanson, me, Recitation and the other animals." Her voice dropped to a soft, thoughtful tone. "You take great care of all of us, don't you? But who takes care of you, Cade?"

"I don't need taking care of. I can take care of myself," he said gruffly.

"One thing I learned from Max is that sooner or later we all need someone to be there for us, even if it's just to listen to us. Those people in town want to be your friends," she told him, her voice very gentle. "They want you to be theirs. Don't shut out everyone, Cade. Someday you might need them."

He didn't have the time or the fortitude to be involved. But Cade didn't say that because Abby was moving as if she was going to rise. He held out a hand to help her up. Abby smiled her thanks as she stepped away from the table. Cade couldn't tear his gaze from her when she lifted one hand to her stomach and brushed her fingers lightly across her abdomen.

"Twins acting up?" he asked, then wished he hadn't. It was none of his business and far too personal. Apparently Abby didn't think so. She grinned at him.

"Nightly calisthenics," she complained, but her chuckle

belied her complaint. "Good thing you have a substantial library on the ranch. At least I can read while they bounce."

"Help yourself to anything in it," he told her. "Do you need help to your room?"

"Not yet, thanks," she said, her laughter echoing around the room. "But be careful what you offer, because that day may come and I can almost guarantee that I won't be nearly as calm as Recitation when I go into labor." Her face softened with her smile. "In fact, I'll probably be a complete nuisance."

"We'll deal with it," he said, not knowing what else to say, slightly concerned by her words yet oddly eager to be there for her if she needed him.

"I know you will." She nodded, her face totally serious now. "You'll deal with that as you do everything else. You're good at dealing with things, Cade. That's a trait God can always use in His kids. I often wished Max had that calm ability to work through an issue." She said goodnight, then turned and walked to her room.

What issue? Cade didn't understand. Had things gone bad between them? If he'd been more involved with his buddy, maybe he could have helped. Yeah, right. He'd had that chance when he'd been asked to accept the special mission. He'd refused and because of that, Max had died. Abby was speaking through her grief, that's all.

But she kept harping on God, as if God cared about Cade Lebret. He switched off the kitchen lights and walked to his study, which Abby called the library. He sat down behind his desk and pulled out his record book, noting the date and birth of Recitation's foal. That brought to mind Abby's reaction and the memory of holding her in his arms to comfort her.

Hard as he tried, Cade couldn't suppress the wiggle of yearning that memory revived. He shoved it out of his mind to concentrate instead on what Max would have done to help Abby through the rest of her pregnancy, because knowing Abby, Cade was positive she was going to throw herself into Family Ties. Someone had to ride herd on her, make sure she didn't overdo or take on too much. And, as she'd said herself, Cade was good at dealing with things.

Except that watching a mare give birth was an entirely different matter than human birth. He knew less than nothing about that. Cade turned on his computer, pulled up an online bookstore and began researching books on pregnancy and birth. He scribbled down the names of several.

Tomorrow he'd phone the library in Calgary and see if they had the books. He could pick them up on Monday when he took Abby to her doctor for a checkup. While she was busy with that, Cade intended to meet his buddy who thought he'd found the pawnshop where Abby had hocked her rings and her quilting machine and who knew what else.

Funny, but her comments about talking to God had him thinking. Maybe instead of skipping out on church, he'd sit beside her and listen. Maybe God would finally show him a way to help his dad.

Abby had been right about one thing—he did love this ranch. He'd just never realized how much the place meant to him, how many dreams and goals he'd built up until she reminded him. For a few moments today he'd even wondered if he should reconsider selling. Abby was the only one besides Max who'd ever understood the fulfillment he found here. Her encouragement had reignited his old daydream of carrying on the Double L with someone like her by his side.

But that was just a daydream.

There wasn't anyone else like Abby, and even if there were, what would they want with Cade? He didn't have the ability to love somebody like her, not the way she deserved. And how could she love him after loving Max? It was a silly dream and yet he couldn't quite shake it.

Maybe tomorrow when everyone else was praying he'd ask God about that.

Cade reached out to put away his record book. His fingers brushed the forms he'd received from the government about Max's death benefits. Just another area where he was unsuccessful, but he wouldn't give up. Abby needed that money for her kids and Cade was determined to get the government to pay her.

For the first time, Cade criticized his buddy. Why hadn't Max taken care of things?

Unable to find an answer, he switched off the lights and walked to his room. But sleep was elusive. As he lay wide awake, his thoughts returned to Abby. Had he done enough for her? Was he missing something?

By the time the grandfather clock in the living room chimed two, Cade decided he might as well help the town do a little fund-raising. That way he could keep a closer eye on Abby, make sure she didn't overdo.

Though how in the world Cade would stop Abby once she made up her mind to do something was a puzzle that kept him awake far into the night.

Chapter Six

"Seems like this is your day to visit doctors." Abby glanced at Cade, hoping her teasing comment would help relax the edges of strain on his face. "First Ed, now me. What did Ed's doctor say?"

"That he needs more physiotherapy sessions." Gloom darkened Cade's expression. He seemed taken aback by the friendly hands waving hello. "I guess they're waving at you," he mumbled, staring straight ahead as they drove through the town.

Abby's heart ached for his self-imposed exile. She yearned to help him and Ed but the gulf between them seemed so great, filled with unspoken things. So like Max. She hadn't been able to help him, either.

"I'd gladly take Dad for them, but Buffalo Gap only has a part-time therapist. She's heavily booked and doesn't have any extra sessions available, even if Dad would agree." Cade heaved a sigh of frustration. "Anyway, Dad's not high on the list for extra time from her because he refuses to work hard. According to Doc Treple he isn't progressing quickly enough."

"I'm sorry." Abby grimaced. Sorry was such a weak word. "I could try encouraging Ed some more."

"I think that right now it might only alienate him. You've already gone above and beyond by persuading him to repeat the lists of speech patterns his therapist gave him." Cade did glance at her then. "Thank you for trying to help him."

Abby nodded. Since Cade didn't say anything else, she, too, fell silent as the truck ate up the miles toward Calgary. After a moment her thoughts drifted to the constant problem that now nagged at her: how could she get enough quilts made from the mass of donated fabric Mayor Marsha was collecting to supply the orphanage? Her mind drew on her work with her mother, searching to remember the simplest patterns. Cade's voice jerked her out of her daydream.

"I can tell from that blissful look on your face that you're thinking about quilts," he teased, amusement threading his tone. "I heard rumors you're looking for people to cut out pieces for them."

"A few women have offered to do some cutting at home," she told him. "Mostly they're former quilters, so they'll do fine. Even so, we'll need a lot of help. I think we'll stick to simple patterns like the nine patch or flying geese variations."

"I have no idea what you're talking about," Cade said with a blank look. "But I am wondering how and where you'll put all the pieces together."

"I haven't worked that out yet," Abby admitted. "I really wish I had my sewing machine."

"Mrs. Swanson has one."

"I know. She's already hard at work piecing." She frowned. "She's a great help, but I have a lot of spare time right now and if I had a machine I could be working, too…" She let it trail away. After all, her lack of funds wasn't Cade's problem.

"I made a few fund-raising calls for your project," he

said, his voice sheepish. "But I didn't do very well. Buffalo Gap is a small community, mostly made up of ranchers like me, struggling to keep going. Nobody's wealthy in anything but cattle and pasture. In fact, the only person I can think of who'd have cash to spare is Hilda Vermeer. But I doubt she'd contribute."

"Why not?" Abby could hardly control her curiosity. Small towns were so interesting once you unraveled their history.

"Hilda's—uh." He frowned, searching for the right word. "I guess you'd say she's rigid in her beliefs. She'll likely be against the adoption agency. Still, if you want a seamstress, she's your lady. She used to design fancy clothes so she certainly has the equipment." A little smile curved his lips upward, making him so attractive that Abby's heart began to thud. "In fact, Mrs. Swanson used to envy Hilda her fancy sewing machines."

"Really?" Abby forced her focus off Cade's handsome face. That was getting to be more of a struggle each day she stayed on the ranch. "Tell me more about the lady."

"Hilda's father made his money in the oil fields. As his only child, she inherited everything. She's very—uh, frugal, I guess you'd say," he added, mouth pursed. "She's also become quite reclusive. Not that she was ever very sociable."

"Is that all you can think of to tell me about her?" Abby pressed when Cade stopped.

"Pretty much." He glanced at her, scrunched up his face and finally said, "I was in her Sunday-school class when I was a kid. The thing that sticks with me is that she was heavy on rules."

"It's sad when people get so caught in obedience that they forget about God's love," Abby agreed. "But Cade, how could Ms. Vermeer possibly object to an adoption agency?"

"I think she just would. On principle or something." His face wore a funny look. "Never mind. I shouldn't have said anything."

"Why not?" Abby stared into the distance, her brain busy with possibilities.

"Because you're going to talk to her, aren't you?" He groaned and shook his head. "Don't bother, Abby. She'll only put you down. Her community spirit is even lower than mine."

"Then I'll have to work on both of you," Abby told him with a smile. His answering grin lit a puddle of warmth inside her. "On a different subject, have you heard anything from the government?"

"Nothing. I think I might have to resort to talking to the media," Cade said. "If word got out the government was abandoning the widow of one of their top soldiers, withholding what is rightfully hers and leaving her penniless, the politicians would trip over themselves trying to rectify the error. Maybe that's the way to go."

"You won't ask me to do interviews or go on television, will you?" Cade looked so delighted with that idea that Abby had to burst his bubble. "Because I can't."

"Why not?" He looked irritated by her comment.

"I'm as big as a house, for one thing," she mumbled, wondering suddenly what Cade thought of her ungainly body. "And getting bigger."

"So? Adds more pathos to your claim. 'Needy Mom of Twins Ignored by Military.'" Cade looked ashamed when she hissed her breath between her teeth. "Okay, maybe that's not politically correct or very sensitive, but being pregnant does add immediacy to your need to get the claim settled. And besides," he added after taking a swig from his coffee cup and returning it to the holder on the dash. "You'd look beautiful on television."

"I wasn't trying to squeeze a compliment out of you," she blustered. "You don't have to lie."

"I'm not lying." He glanced at her, brows uplifted. "If you don't believe me, ask Dad when we get home. Or look in a mirror. You're a beautiful person, Abby."

"Thank you." Somehow the words left her feeling deflated.

Being a beautiful person wasn't quite the same as being called beautiful by a man like Cade, and for whatever inexplicable reason hiding inside her, Abby wanted him to see her as beautiful. Silly. Cade was just a friend and friendship was all she wanted, wasn't it?

"I don't want to put myself on show or have the world know I'm destitute. I just want what belongs to me so I can get on with building a home for myself and my kids."

"Doing my best," he said, his lips tightening.

"I know you are, Cade, and I appreciate it very much. Thank you." Abby brushed his arm with her fingertips, trying to express her gratitude. But she worried that her comments had hurt him. Recently she'd begun to realize that under that bravado and assurance hid a very sensitive man. "What will you do while I see the doctor?" she asked curiously.

"You're sure you don't want me there?" he asked.

Abby had been shocked when he'd suggested it before they left the ranch, before she realized that was all part of the care and concern Cade lavished on everyone.

"I'm sure," she said firmly. No way did she want him present when the doctor scolded her for gaining too much weight. "Anyway, I'll have to wait for lab work and stuff. That would be boring for you."

"Then I'll probably call up an old buddy for coffee." The

way he said it so nonchalantly made something inside her prickle with warning. But when he turned his head and met her gaze Abby decided she was being overly sensitive.

"Good. You probably miss connecting with your buddies. Max didn't—" She frowned.

"Max didn't what?"

"He didn't seem to want to get together much. He'd become very—introspective," she said finally, wishing she'd kept quiet.

"He let the work get to him." Cade nodded. "Something that's really hard to learn but totally necessary is to let go of the mission when you come home. Max struggled with that, relived his decisions. It's hard not to do, but it drives you nuts."

"Yes," she whispered, relieved that he understood. "I think he had PTSD," she murmured.

"Max?" Cade shook his head then frowned. "Why?"

Abby told him about the night sweats, the screams of terror-filled nightmares, the startling when a car backfired.

"It preyed on his mind constantly. I think that's why he forgot to do some of the things he should have," she murmured.

"I'm sorry. I had no idea." Cade shook his head. "I should have checked on him more before he went back."

"He wouldn't have talked to you, Cade," Abby told him quietly. "He wouldn't even talk to me. Mostly I guessed what was wrong."

"Still." He was silent for so long Abby felt compelled to change the subject.

"I'm stuck on where we're going to put together all that donated fabric," she said when some time had passed.

"Marsha mentioned the seniors' center as a project place, but she said they use the big tables there almost every day, which means you'd have to put your stuff away after every session, right?" Cade asked.

Abby nodded. "It's not even close to ideal but if that's all we have…"

"I might have an idea. Let me think about it for a bit and I'll get back to you," Cade said, his brow furrowed in thought.

"I appreciate any help you can give," she said and meant it. Trust Cade to want to help with that, too. The soft spot for him grew. "Creating quilts for the center makes it concrete, like we're taking the first step toward actually achieving the goal of the adoption agency."

"Is the agency that important to you?" he asked with a sideways frown.

"Yes, because it could mean a job for me. A future. But it's not only that." A feeling of selfishness that she'd mentioned her own reasons first swept over her.

"What else?" he asked.

"An adoption agency could bring added business to the town. Adoptive parents will need somewhere to stay, so the motel will get increased business," she elaborated. "They'll need to eat, so the cafés will need to hire more employees. These types of offshoots from the agency could really give a boost to the local economy."

"You've certainly given this a lot of thought." Cade sounded surprised.

"It's something my mom taught me," she explained. "If you intend to do something, think through all the ramifications of it and then explore how you could make even more of an impact."

"Good plan," was all Cade said as he steered into the city toward her doctor's office. Somehow he maneuvered his hulking truck into a tiny parking space. "Wait," he ordered before he jumped out on his side and went around to assist her in alighting from the vehicle.

Abby gladly took his arm as they navigated the icy sidewalk to enter a tall stone building. She pointed to her doctor's name on the plaque between the elevators.

"That's where I'm going but I'm supposed to have an ultrasound before I see the doctor. That will take extra time. I'll be at least a couple of hours," she reminded him.

"Here." Cade handed her a cell phone. "It's an extra one I keep at the ranch. You can reach me by pressing this." He showed her. "Call me and I'll get here as fast as I can."

"If you're doing something important, I can always wait in the little coffee shop they have here." She grinned when his forehead furrowed. "I won't even have to go outside."

"Good." He checked his watch. "So unless you call and tell me otherwise, I'll be back in two hours. Okay?"

Abby nodded and watched as he sauntered away. He'd left his Stetson in the truck but even without it, anyone would know Cade Lebret was a cowboy. It wasn't just his long-legged stride of confident assurance, or the way his jeans, though faded and worn, fit him like a second skin. It wasn't even his battered leather jacket with its sheepskin lining that made her think of the open range.

It was all of those things and something else, some intangible aura that exemplified strength and self-reliance and poise under the most difficult of circumstances. Looking at Cade, having him near, made her relax because she knew she could count on the rancher.

Maybe it was silly, but with Cade she had no worries that he'd suddenly step away from her. Cade wasn't fighting the same terrors Max had; neither did he seem to need her. Perhaps it was foolish but Abby felt as if Cade was more of a partner.

Abby gave herself a shake and pressed the elevator button. She was spending far too much time thinking about Cade Lebret. As if to emphasize that, as the elevator doors opened, one of the babies kicked her in the side.

"Point taken. But you can't deny he's a very good-looking man and ultra nice besides," she reminded them.

A man tossed her a wary look before stepping into the elevator with her. He stabbed a button before retreating to the farthest corner. Abby suppressed a chuckle. That's what came of letting yourself daydream about your husband's best friend.

But the reminder sobered her. Cade was a wonderful friend, a truly decent man who was doing his best for her. But he didn't know that she'd failed to help Max, that their marriage hadn't been as carefree as Max made everyone believe. Now that she was having his children, she couldn't afford to get sidetracked by another romantic dream of love.

No matter how nice a guy he was.

Cade stepped inside the pawnshop and let his curious gaze rove around the building.

"If she pawned something, this is probably the place," his friend Serge said sotto voce. "It's the closest one to where she lived and the owner's the easiest to deal with of all the people I talked to."

"Did you ask him about a quilting machine?" Cade finished his survey, then turned his attention back to his old military buddy.

"No. I'd do a lot of things for you, Cade, but asking about quilting isn't one of them." Serge ignored Cade's snicker. "I'm going to look around. Why don't you do the same? Then *you* can ask the guy about quilting or sewing or knitting."

Cade was about to retort when his attention snagged on

an old sewing machine, its plastic yellowed, sitting on a table against the far wall. A sign on it said twenty bucks.

"Does this thing work?" he called to the owner, pointing to the sewing machine.

"Guess so. That's what she said, anyway." The old man sauntered over and laid a fond hand on the machine. "Should be selling it as an antique," he muttered. "It's got to be over forty years old. Bought it from an old lady who was cleaning out her house, getting ready to move into the nursing home."

"I'll take it," Cade told him, somehow certain that Abby would know how to operate the machine. "But if it doesn't work, I'm bringing it back."

"For twenty bucks?" The old man snorted. "Cost you more to drive here."

"Do you have any quilting machines?" Cade figured it was best to just blurt it out. "I think they're called long-arm."

"Got one. Over here." After a speculative glance at Cade, the man led the way to a corner where a big metal machine stood. "You don't look like no quilter I ever saw." He chuckled, amusement lighting up his eyes.

"It's for a friend. She came on some hard times and had to pawn her mother's quilting machine. Turns out she could really use one now," Cade explained, his heart dropping when he saw the price tag dangling from the machine.

"You know Abby McDonald?" The man's eyes lit up when Cade nodded. "How is she? I haven't seen her for a while. Nothing's wrong?" he asked anxiously.

Cade explained that Abby was now living on the ranch. Then he shared her idea of making quilts for the adoption agency.

"It's a relief to know someone's watching out for her

and those babies. Max should have done that but he had too many problems, I guess."

What problems? Cade wanted to ask but the old man didn't even pause to take a breath.

"I'm Boris, by the way." He held out his hand to shake Cade's. "You give Abby my best. She was a real blessing when my wife was passing. Checked in on her every day for seven months straight. Most of the time she stayed long enough to make some soup or bake some biscuits. Later, when Max went overseas, she'd stop by with what she called leftovers but I knew she'd made them especially for me. She's a wonderful woman."

That was Abby, caring for people wherever she went. Cade felt his lips curve in a smile as he imagined her taking Boris and his wife under her wing.

"I hated to see her pawn this machine," Boris said sadly. "Particularly after she showed me the beautiful things she and her mom had made with it. But I knew she was desperate because she'd already pawned her rings. At least I could give her a good price."

Cade's heart took a nosedive. So he would never be able to retrieve the rings Max had chosen for Abby even if he could find the money. *I'm sorry, buddy.*

"When her husband's money still didn't come through— well, she was desperate, begged me to help. There's not much of a market for this stuff," he said with a flick of a finger at the quilting machine. "I scraped together all I could to help her out but I figured that cash wouldn't last long, not with paying for the funeral and everything." Boris's eyes narrowed. "You get that money thing fixed for her?"

"Not yet." Cade shifted under the reproach in that piercing gaze. "I'm working on it." He slid his fingers over the handles of the quilting machine, his mind sketching a mental image of Abby bent over it. He could see her green eyes shining like emeralds at the return of her precious legacy. "Would you take less for this? I want to buy it back for her."

"Wish I could," Boris told him with a rueful shake of his head. "But I'm too invested. Besides, I've got a grandson who needs some special surgeries out of country. He's only six. I'm trying to get enough money to send his mom with him. Provincial health care won't cover her expenses." He named the amount he'd accept for the quilting machine. It was way beyond anything Cade could manage.

Cade shook his head ruefully. "Sorry."

"I have to get at least that much back to recover what I gave Abby and I'm only giving up the commission because it's for her," Boris said apologetically.

"I understand." There was no way Cade could afford to buy the quilting machine. Frustration grew. Abby believed in God, trusted Him for everything. Why couldn't God do something to get this machine for her? It was for the adoption agency, not for herself. Didn't God know that?

"Can I at least give you a deposit to hold it, until I can figure a way to buy it for her?" he finally asked.

"Abby's special to you?" the pawn shop owner asked. The intense look Boris gave him made Cade shift uncomfortably.

"She's special because she's the wife of my best friend. I owe it to Max to help Abby," he said finally.

At least, that's what Cade kept telling himself—he was doing what he did for Abby for Max's sake. But that wasn't the whole truth and he knew it. He struggled on a daily basis with the fact that Abby's growing importance in his life had less and less to do with the past and more to do with who she was and how she made him feel. Which was?

Cade skittered away from answering that. Once or twice

recently he'd fallen into daydreams about Abby in his life. But those dreams had quickly ended because he knew he wasn't the kind of man Abby needed. He wasn't strong and dependable like Max had been. He'd be useless as a father because he'd never known the kind of fatherhood he knew Abby wanted for her children.

Feeling Boris's scrutiny he repeated, "Will you take a deposit?"

"I guess that'd be okay seeing as how I don't have many requests for a quilting machine, specially a top-of-the-line one like this." Boris wrote him a receipt for his paltry down payment and added Cade's cell phone number to his copy. "I'll give you a call if I have any buyers before you get back."

"Thanks." Cade wrote out a check for the deposit. It would drain his account to near zero. He hoped he wasn't making a big mistake but knowing it was for Abby, how could that be a mistake? He lifted the sewing machine he'd bought and found it substantially heavier than he'd anticipated. "This thing better work," he muttered as he walked to the door.

"It will. You tell Abby I said hello. Let me know when she has the babies. I have something special for them," Boris called. "I'm glad you're there for her. After her trouble with Max and losing her job and all, she deserves some special attention."

"Yeah," Cade grunted as he waited for Serge to open the door. *Her trouble with Max?* "I'll do that."

He had no intention of telling Abby he'd been here. Not yet. Not until he could get that quilting machine, but he was going to ask her about Max.

"You're going to learn to sew now?" Serge asked, brow uplifted, lips twitching in amusement as he watched Cade store the sewing machine in the truck box.

"I already know how to sew. I stitch bridles and saddles and reins by hand. The machine is for Abby." He'd already told Serge about Abby's problems with the government. Now he explained about the adoption agency but he left out Boris's comment about Max. First he needed to learn more.

"Me and the guys were talking about Abby. We want you to give her this." Serge thrust out a handful of cash. "Max meant a lot to all of us. You take care of her. If she needs more, you let us know and we'll see what we can do."

None of his buddies had money to spare. Everyone had their own issues. And yet they'd come together for Max's wife simply because they'd all loved Max. Cade felt a spurt of emotion build inside. He explained about the long-arm quilting machine.

"It's very special to her because her mother gave it to her. She was dead broke so she pawned it. I'm trying to get it back. Can I use your gift for that?" he asked Serge, then added, "Actually I'm pretty sure she pawned a lot. When I moved her all she had was two boxes."

"Use it for whatever you think best," Serge told him gruffly. "How much more do you need to get this quilting thing?" He whistled when Cade told him the amount. "That's a lot."

"I know." They were both silent for a moment, then Serge said he had to leave for his son's hockey game. Cade thanked him for his help and watched him walk away. Seeing his friend again hadn't been as awkward as he'd expected. Maybe Abby was right and he could let other people into his life.

He glanced down at the cash, then walked back into the store and put it on the tab for Abby's quilting machine. It made a very small dent in a very large number. Cade left the store trying to conjure up a way to find another nine thousand, five hundred dollars. He spent a few moments in his truck surfing the net on his phone to check on prices for a new machine and quickly learned that Boris hadn't been wrong. Abby's machine was top-notch for commercial-grade quilters. To replace it would be impossible for her and would cost way more than Boris was asking.

Somehow Cade had to get Abby's machine back.

God wants to help us in every situation. All He's waiting for is us to ask Him. Abby's words from one of the meetings he'd taken her to flickered through his mind.

"Can You help me get her machine back?" he asked hesitantly, feeling awkward and uncomfortable about talking to God. "She deserves it. She's one of Yours." He didn't get any answer but he felt a little better for having left that problem with God.

But Cade couldn't dislodge his questions about Abby and Max. He needed to figure out what had gone wrong. He puzzled over this while he finished his other errands, then drove to the doctor's office. Since Abby wasn't in the coffee shop, he went upstairs to wait for her in the doctor's office. His stomach rumbled, reminding him that he'd missed breakfast. He'd wanted to clean out Liberty's stall himself this morning, though his hired man was certainly capable enough. But Liberty was special.

And like that the idea hit Cade.

Over the years he'd had lots of offers for his favorite horse. If he sold Liberty, he'd have more than enough to buy Abby's machine. All he had to do was give up the one living thing that he'd been able to freely love.

Liberty had been part of his heart from the moment she'd been born. In Liberty had rested Cade's hopes and dreams for the future of the ranch. Liberty's progeny could bring big dollars if she was sired with the right stallion. In

Liberty he clung to the last thread of hope that he could keep the Double L and keep the Lebret legacy alive.

Surely God could find another way to make Abby's wish come true? Surely He didn't expect Cade to give up the only thing he had left to love?

Chapter Seven

"Feeding me must be costing you a mint." Abby leaned back in her chair, replete from the potpie lunch she'd just eaten. "Lately it seems like I'm always hungry." She glanced around the room, then focused on Cade. "I lived in Calgary for years. How is it I never found this place?"

"Mama's Diner is owned by the parents of a guy I served with." Cade's mouth tightened, then he said in a low, tight voice, "Lanny never made it back from Afghanistan, either."

"I'm sorry." Abby reached across the table and covered his fingers with hers. Immediately a rush of warmth spread from her fingers up her arm. She was shocked by the intensity of her reaction and quickly drew her hand away, trying to expunge the flutter of longing to draw Cade into her arms and comfort him.

"Thanks," he said in the gruff kind of voice he used to hide his emotions.

"You must miss him," she murmured, glancing around the room. "Is that why you come here, to feel closer to him?"

"Yeah." His eyes narrowed as he studied her. "You're perceptive. I guess a mother has to be. You'll make a great one. The way you talk about your mother makes me think she was one of those women who are constantly hugging their kids."

The wistfulness in Cade's voice surprised Abby as much as his words.

"You think my mom was a hugger?" She laughed heartily when he nodded. "She wasn't. She was straight to the point, businesslike. She'd tolerate a hug now and then but she wasn't what you'd call warm and snuggly. And yet everyone loved her." She fell silent for a moment, thinking. "I guess they loved her honesty. If you were messing up she told you straight out. She didn't bother to hint when she told you that you needed to do better."

"You make her sound like a tartar."

"She sort of was," Abby told him, smiling as Cade's eyes grew wide.

"And here I've been envying you those childish times I missed, like listening to stories from your mother's lap," he grumbled.

"My mom did read to me a lot," Abby agreed. "But it was a means to an end—she wanted me to learn how to read as soon as possible. She believed reading for yourself was the best way to plant God's word in your heart. She started teaching me the day after I arrived at their house."

"At three?" Cade blinked his surprise when she nodded.

"She had this idea that a person was better able to judge truth if they were well-read." Abby smiled. "Don't look so shocked. She was an amazing woman, but she was not the type of mother about which fairy tales are written. She had a solid code of belief and needed to ensure that I knew and followed it." Abby paused to sip her tea before continuing. "That's what I tried to do as a social worker and that's what I want for the kids who'll be adopted through our agency. I want those children to have parents who will fight to give them every opportunity they can to make the world better." The fierce rush of feelings exploding inside surprised her. "That's the legacy my mom left me," she murmured.

"Huh." He thought about that as he ate the last of his lunch.

"Do you ever wonder what your mother was like, Cade?" Abby asked quietly into the silence that had fallen.

"Sure." He played with the tablecloth. "Dad would never say anything about her and he got mad when anyone else did. After a while I suspected his anger was a habit but I'd faced it too often and soon learned to quit asking." He shrugged. "Mrs. Swanson has told me little bits now and then, but even she seemed reluctant to talk about my mom."

"You must have felt cheated," Abby mused, lost in her thoughts of a lonely little boy, bereft, without a mother to comfort him.

"At first I didn't realize I had been," Cade shot back, his lips twisted in a self-mocking smile. "I had Mrs. Swanson. For a long time I didn't know the difference between her and a mom. She took good care of me, shielded me from Dad when he got angry or depressed. It was only when I went to school and saw and heard what moms did that I realized I was missing out on some things."

He pushed back from the table and motioned for the check, making it clear that he didn't want to discuss his childhood anymore. But Abby felt compelled to say something more.

"I probably made my mother sound brisk, even harsh, but that didn't mean she didn't love me. She did but she didn't always know how to say it." She inhaled and prayed for guidance. "Max was a bit like that. He struggled to express the feelings inside. It was as if he was afraid to give them free rein. Maybe it's like that with Ed. Maybe he doesn't know how to express what he is feeling inside."

"He never had any trouble expressing his anger," Cade scoffed.

"But maybe that's the shield he hides behind because he's scared to reveal the fear he keeps tamped down inside." After sipping the last of her peppermint tea, Abby dabbed at her lips, giving him a chance to consider what she'd said.

"Why do you keep harping on what my father feels?" he asked.

"Because you need to know so you and he can reach each other," she said quietly. "You can't help another person unless you can figure out what they feel. I should know." She paused, then smiled at him. "Rebuilding the connection between you two is important."

"You can't rebuild what was never there." His voice was edged with what Abby diagnosed as pain.

"If you can't rebuild, then build a new connection." She leaned forward, knowing he wouldn't like hearing the next part but compelled to say it anyway. "You and Ed don't have forever, Cade. Nobody but God knows how long you have together."

"You're thinking of Max."

"Yes. There were a lot of things I should have said to him and didn't. I'll always regret that." She sighed. "I know you have questions you want to ask Ed. Why not do that while you can instead of imagining something that may not be true? Twenty years down the road," she added with a last, desperate effort, "it might be too late."

"Maybe I don't want to hear his answers to my questions," Cade said tightly.

"Maybe the answers will surprise you," she answered, praying silently for the troubled father and son.

"Maybe." He shrugged. "Do you want dessert?"

"No, thank you." Abby patted her bulging stomach.

"And even if I did, I can't have it. I'm under strict orders to keep my weight down. I've put on some pounds since I arrived at your ranch."

"Oh, so it's our fault?" How she loved the way his eyes crinkled at the corners when he teased her.

"Of course it's your fault," she shot back with a pseudo glare. "And Mrs. Swanson's with all that good cooking. You both spoil me."

"If you don't mind my asking, is that all the doctor said?" The intensity of Cade's voice and the expression on his face told her of his concern. A rush of warmth suffused Abby's insides. It was nice to have someone fuss over her.

"He said I'm fine, the babies are fine. Everything's fine. Except I'm too fat." She made a face at him.

"I doubt he said that. But I'm guessing he did say you need to get a little more exercise." When she blinked at him in surprise, Cade shrugged. "Just a guess. Everyone needs more exercise these days."

"I am supposed to walk more," Abby admitted. "Though how I'm to do it with so much ice around is a mystery." She saw the interest in his eyes and blushed. "Everything seems to be progressing well. I want a natural delivery and he thinks that's possible. I'm to see the local doctor next week."

"Doc Treple?" Cade gaped at her. "But—but—he's not a specialist!" His tone dropped. "Abby, you need to be near someone who can make sure everything will be okay. You can't take any risks."

"I'm not taking a risk. He's a doctor, Cade," she said. It sounded as if he was trying to get rid of her. A new thought dawned. "Are you worried about the babies being born?"

"Yes," he admitted candidly. "Or rather I'm worried about something going wrong before they can be born. I've been reading and…" Cade let it trail away. Red spots appeared on his cheeks. He ducked his head and lowered his voice. "There are so many things that could happen."

"Yes, there are," she agreed, touched that he was worried about her and relieved that he was willing to discuss it instead of stuffing his worry inside where it would fester and grow. "But I'm in God's hands and He will take good care of me and of the twins."

Cade opened his mouth as if to say something else, but closed it. Abby decided he must be champing at the bit to get back to the ranch.

"Shall we go?" Abby stifled her laughter at how quickly he rose, schooling her features as she waited for the wonderful familiarity of his strong fingers beneath her elbow. "That was a delicious lunch," she said as he held her coat. "Thank you."

"You're welcome, though I think we're way past lunchtime." Cade helped her to the truck. When they were belted in he asked, "Can you busy yourself at the mall for half an hour? There's something I need to do there."

"Sure." Actually Abby was delighted by the opportunity to pick up a few personal-care items. Curiosity nagged at her about Cade's mission, but Abby chided herself for it. *He's got his own life*, she reminded herself.

By the time the half hour was up, she was waiting for him on a bench, too tired to visit any more stores. He came sauntering toward her, blue eyes lighting up when he saw her. He held a bag with the label of a chocolate store and another with the name of a bookstore.

"Mrs. Swanson's sweet tooth and some reading for Dad," he explained. "And you?" One eyebrow lifted when he spotted the bag at her feet.

"Shampoo, lotion and some new pants," she told him, flushing as she looked at him. "My old ones are too tight."

"I see." His eyes crinkled at the corners when he

grinned and held out a hand to help her up. When they were in the truck, their packages stored on the backseat, he turned to her, his face serious. "Do you mind if we stop by to see Max?"

"That would be great." She didn't want to visit her husband's grave because she felt irrationally guilty over her move from the past, from him and the unhappiness she was beginning to shed. But this was another example of Cade's thoughtfulness so she busied herself counting the many ways Cade had made her transition to the ranch easy.

The Double L had begun to feel like home. Maybe that's why she couldn't suppress a flutter of guilt when they arrived beside Max's headstone. It was getting harder to remember all the details about him that had seemed so terribly distinct a mere month ago. His voice, his laugh— it wasn't that she'd forgotten any of that. It was just that sometime in the past few weeks she'd finally accepted that what they had was over. Max was gone and he wasn't coming back.

She could feel the change within herself. She'd begun to feel alive and vital and free of the burden of trying to escape a marriage she now knew she'd rushed into too hastily.

"Abby?" Cade's quiet voice broke into her reverie.

"I'm okay." Knowledge slid through her, filling every cell of her body. "It's over," she whispered to herself. "There's nothing more I can do for him."

"Abby, I—" Cade stopped speaking when she turned her head to look at him.

"I tried my best, you know. I did everything I could think of." A tear slid out and tumbled over her cheek. "But he wouldn't admit he was suffering. He couldn't claw his way out of the remorse long enough to know something was wrong." She exhaled.

"What are you saying, Abby?" Cade's voice emerged in that careful tone he used when he didn't want to upset her.

"Max's PTSD was worse than I let on." She looked at him. "It made him fearful. He couldn't sleep or relax. The nightmares ate at his confidence. I know I should have stopped him from going on another mission, but he wouldn't listen. I think he was almost glad to escape."

"But—the twins?" Cade stared at her, aghast.

"He didn't know. Neither did I. Not then." She touched her abdomen, felt the response of two sharp kicks and smiled. "I tried my best to love Max, but I don't think it was enough for him. I never quite became his other half. He wouldn't allow it. He considered it weakness to depend on me."

Cade looked stunned by her words.

"I realize now I should have ignored his request for privacy. I should have told someone, forced him to get help. And I didn't. I'll always have to live with that." She didn't even try to stop the tears now. "Something went wrong with our marriage, Cade. Something I couldn't fix. I can't mourn that anymore. I have to let go of the past and push ahead. For the twins' sake."

"And so?" Poor Cade sounded utterly confused.

Well, why wouldn't he be? She'd been a little confused herself but now understanding dawned, clarifying that verse she'd puzzled over this morning.

"That's what it means in Philippians. Chapter 3," she said to herself, amazed by the simplicity of it. "'But this one thing I do, forgetting those things which are behind, and reaching forward to those things which are before, I press toward the mark for the prize of the high calling of God in Jesus Christ.'" Abby grinned at Cade. "It won't be easy but chapter 4, verse 13 says, 'I can do all things through Christ who strengthens me.'"

"Abby, are you saying you didn't love Max?" Cade asked.

"I loved him the best I could," she said, meeting his stare. "I don't think it was enough, that I was enough. I failed him and I will always regret that. And I will not make the mistake of believing a fairy tale is real love again. I must get on with the challenges God has set before me."

"Which are?" He gazed at her, wide-eyed.

"Preparing to be a mother, making a home for my children, getting a job and doing my part to get the adoption agency going. That's my world now." She looked out the window at the grave marker once more, then turned away. "Let's go home, Cade."

After a long moment of confused silence, Cade flicked the key in the ignition. In the deepest recesses of her heart Abby apologized to Max for failing him. Then she pushed back her shoulders and stared straight ahead.

The Bible said God had plans for her, plans to prosper her. It was time to find out what those plans were. Once or twice Cade tossed a surreptitious glance her way, clearly worried by what he'd heard.

A new thought dawned in Abby's mind. How did Cade fit in with the plans God had for her? And why was she so nervous around him?

He's a friend, that's all. A good friend. But he can never be anything more.

Something was different about Abby.

Cade didn't know exactly what it was or how to explain it. He couldn't comprehend what he'd heard her say at the cemetery. But this Abby was far different from the woman he'd brought into his home five weeks ago. When they returned home from her doctor visit, he'd shown her the sewing machine, utterly unprepared when she threw her arms around him and hugged him. Hugged him! A week had passed and he still couldn't get over it.

"As if I did you a big favor by spending a few bucks on that old wreck," he'd sputtered when at last she pulled away from him.

"It isn't a wreck," she'd insisted and brushed away the glitter of tears on her cheeks. "It's a wonderful blessing, Cade. Thank you. It's going to help me do what God has planned."

He still didn't understand her strange words about Max, or her claim that he'd suffered from stress disorder. He'd replayed them often in his mind, searching for some clue yet unable to find it. Max was tough, strong. He'd never been afraid in his life. She had to be wrong about him.

But Abby had been Max's wife. She would have known. Cade had stifled all his questions until a later date, but he couldn't forget what she'd said.

Half an hour after he'd set up the sewing machine she got busy oiling and coaxing it into a perfectly humming appliance. Since then she'd spent hours in front of it, stitching tiny bits of colored fabric shapes into the most glorious quilt tops that would cheer even the crankiest of souls. Even his father's notes had teased her about her changed attitude.

"You can't just sit there watching me, Ed," she'd told him with a grin. "You've got to dig in and give us a hand, be part of our project."

Cade couldn't believe his father had agreed to help. Now every day found Ed clutching some tool called a rotary cutter in his good hand and using the other to hold a ruler, trimming lengths of fabric as instructed by Abby. Whenever Cade came into the house he heard Ed and Abby laughing, teasing and sharing, as they worked together. His father stumbled and halted as he tried to form the words, but at least he was trying. For some reason having his father spend all that time with Abby made Cade slightly jealous.

"'Tis a blessing she is to us," Mrs. Swanson murmured from behind him, bringing Cade back to the present. Her accent always became more pronounced when she was emotionally touched.

Cade glanced at her over one shoulder, surprised to see her so affected. Then he turned back to watch the pair laugh at something.

"She won't let your pa cut an inch until he's done his exercises to her satisfaction," Mrs. Swanson said after clearing her voice. "And I'll tell you, she's not easily pleased. Our Abby made Ed repeat his routine twice this morning and he was *laughing* at the end."

Our Abby. It seemed everyone had adopted her. The house phone rang constantly as folks from around the area asked for a few moments to consult with Abby. Sometimes it was about the adoption center, but other times she grew silent as she listened, her brows drawn together in concentration as she tried to help.

Cade tried to resist the sprout of envy that grew inside. Everyone hogged her time. He seldom found a spare moment with her alone anymore, unless the babies kept her awake at night. Then he'd come upon her, snuggled in the kitchen window seat, one of her own quilts wrapped around her as she pored over her Bible.

"Hello, Cade. I thought you'd gone out to the west pasture or something this morning." Abby's words drew him out of his introspection. His breath caught as she lifted her glossy head and smiled at him, the familiar slash of white teeth across her pretty face setting his heart pumping faster. "Was everything all right out there?"

"Fine." Her hands hovered above the machine as she

studied him. "I'm about to take a coffee break. Can you join me? I have something to share."

"Sure." She left the fabric where it was, flicked off her sewing machine and rose. Despite her ever-expanding stomach, Abby walked with grace, stepping easily past the mounds of fabric that lay scattered in color-coordinated piles on the carpet around the room. "Come on, Ed. You need a break, too."

Bossy. Ed showed Cade the word he'd written and added a grumpy face beneath, but he obediently laid down his cutter and turned his wheelchair. Unfortunately one wheel caught in some fabric and he couldn't turn around. *More room*, he scrawled.

"That's what I want to talk to you about." Cade quickly freed him and stood back so his father could roll his machine into the kitchen. He easily adjusted his body to balance himself for the turns and twists. Cade knew that was because of Abby's insistence on Ed's exercises. They were slowly paying off.

But Cade also knew it wasn't enough. Abby would leave eventually and Ed would lapse into his old ways. He needed to be in a place where the staff wouldn't allow that to happen. Somewhere like the local nursing home. Yet, Cade still needed a buyer for the ranch. When was God going to answer that prayer?

When Ed and Abby were seated at the table with steaming cups of coffee and fresh doughnuts piled on a plate in the middle, Cade waved to Mrs. Swanson.

"You're part of this, too," he insisted. He sipped his coffee as he waited for her to sit down, noting the way Abby's curious green gaze kept flicking over his face. He suppressed his grin because he knew it made her more curious. "I've had an idea about a sort of workshop area for the quilting," he explained at last.

"Really?" Abby's big smile beamed at him. "How wonderful. Tell us."

"Years ago, before I joined the military, I used to run a riding school. Since I left, the building's been used mostly for storage."

This was the hardest part, knowing his father would object to his idea. Though Ed got along great with Abby, he continued to dispute almost everything Cade did. Still, Cade pressed on because this was for Abby.

"I've spent the past few months cleaning it out, getting rid of junk and repairing things." Ed opened his mouth. Cade hurried on before he could interrupt. "It's a very large area. I thought it might be just the place you need to spread out and work on your quilts."

Ed smacked his cane on the floor when the words he wanted wouldn't come out of his mouth. He scrawled across his pad and held it up. *Dirty*.

"Yes, it was," Cade agreed. "But I've cleaned it thoroughly."

Too cold was Ed's next objection.

"We put water heat under the floor, remember, Dad?" Cade felt his idea was beginning to lose some of its shine but he pressed on anyway. "It hasn't been used in a while, but it should still work. If Abby thinks the place will be suitable, I'll hook up the water heater and test it out."

"I think it's wonderful, Cade. It could be the answer to our prayers." Abby pushed away her mug and the plate with her untouched doughnut. "Can we go look at it now?"

Cade glanced regretfully at his still-full coffee mug and half-eaten doughnut. Mrs. Swanson's doughnuts were his favorite and she didn't make them often.

"I guess we could," he agreed with an inward sigh.

"Finish your coffee," Abby said, retaking her seat. Her eyes twinkled. "I'm sure you haven't eaten since we enjoyed Mrs. Swanson's massive breakfast—what was it? Two hours ago? You must be starving," she teased.

"Actually, I am." Cade was about to take another bite of the doughnut when he noticed his father's crestfallen appearance. "Are you coming with us to look, Dad?" he asked, stuffing down the regret that he'd be giving up the private moments he could have shared with Abby. "You and Mrs. Swanson need to come."

How? his dad scrawled, hope vying with frustration in his eyes.

Cade thought about it for a moment, then grinned.

"I'll take you all in the sleigh," he said. The warmth glowing from Abby's eyes made him feel like he was part of the group again.

Funny how that seemed so important.

"We'll have to be quick," Mrs. Swanson said. "You've that meeting in town after lunch. Ivor's going to meet us there after school. I'm glad he came back yesterday. I've missed him."

"We might just make it if we eat lunch as soon as we come back," Cade said, checking his watch so they wouldn't notice how relieved he was that he wouldn't have to contend with the boy for a while. It was getting harder to reach Ivor. Five times he'd returned from relatives that didn't want him and with each return he seemed less reachable.

"Maybe you should save that for dessert?" Abby suggested, gazing meaningfully at the remainder of the doughnut he held.

"I guess." He relinquished the tasty morsel to his plate. "I'll go harness the horses and bring the sleigh around. You guys get on some warm clothes."

Cade rose to leave, but as he pulled on his jacket he felt

the weight of someone watching him. He turned to find Abby gazing at him with her sweet smile.

"Thank you for trying to help by thinking of the building, Cade," she murmured. "I believe God will bless your efforts."

As he walked to the horse barn, Cade couldn't suppress feelings of shame. Abby put herself last in order to help others. Compared to her, he'd done little to help the adoption agency progress. Why would God bless his measly offer of an unused building?

As usual, Cade stopped by Liberty's stall to offer a pat and a carrot. The idea that plagued him day and night returned. To get the quilts completed, Abby needed that long-arm quilting machine. Getting it for her might be something God *would* bless.

"But even if I sold Liberty, I need the money for the ranch," he said aloud. "I can't afford to give away that much cash."

Sale of the ranch wasn't progressing. With such a cold winter, buyers seemed uninterested. Cade had to scrutinize every cent he spent to make sure he got the most value for his dollar, even more so now that he'd discovered how much paying for extra sessions for his dad, even if they could get them, would cost.

As he harnessed the horses to the sleigh the question that had been building inside now demanded an answer. Dare he sell his precious horse and buy Abby's machine? Dare he trust God to work out the rest?

Abby trusted God, but Cade wasn't ready to go that far. Not yet.

But if he took on the fund-raising wholeheartedly, maybe he could find someone else who'd contribute enough to buy Abby's machine.

He decided to wait and see how the building would work

for Abby. She had a relationship with God so maybe He would work things out. Maybe.

Cade smiled, almost hearing Abby's voice chiding him for his lack of faith.

Chapter Eight

Abby caught her breath at the beauty of the hoar-frosted morning at the ranch. She snuggled into the warmth of her coat, every sense on high alert as they glided toward the building, the sleigh runners making a hiss as they cut through the snow.

"It's so lovely." She glanced at Cade to see if he was as affected as she. But then why would he be? This was his normal, everyday world. "This is like something you'd see in one of those snow globes that you turn upside down and shake. Ivor is going to be mad that he missed this sleigh ride."

"We'll take him out another time." The horses whinnied as Cade drew on the reins to stop them in front of a massive red structure with a curved metal roof. "Here we are. I'm going to help Dad out first, so you stay put."

"Yes, sir." Abby saluted, then whispered to Mrs. Swanson. "As if I could get out on my own in this condition."

Cade ignored Mrs. Swanson's guffaw as he unfolded his father's traveling wheelchair and set it on the shoveled path. Then he basically lifted his father out of the sleigh and set him in it. "I shoveled the path but is it enough for you to make it to the door?"

"I'll help Ed. You help Abby." Mrs. Swanson nimbly stepped down from the sleigh, gripped the wheelchair handles and began moving to the door of the building.

Cade walked toward Abby, filling her gaze, strong and handsome, a part of this land as surely as the frost-flocked pines that surrounded the yard. A rush of pride suffused her. Cade was such a good man, a man worth loving. She wished she'd kept in touch with some of her single friends from work. She could have introduced him to them. Cade needed someone to love him for who he was, someone to share his life's work with.

"Ready?" At her nod he slid his hands around her waist and lifted her out of the sleigh.

As Cade set her down, her gaze melded with his and Abby lost her breath. Her fingers tightened around his arms as the world swooshed and dipped before her.

"Okay?" he asked when she didn't immediately release him.

"Yes, just a bit dizzy. I must have moved too quickly," she said and then thought how foolish that sounded. She hadn't really moved at all. Cade had moved her, both physically and emotionally.

She felt lighter since their visit to the graveyard, as if a burden had shifted off her. She was moving on with her life, but that didn't mean she intended to find someone to replace Max. Not that Cade would want that, either. She could hardly be considered desirable.

"Abby? Would you like to go back to the house? We can do this some other day if you're not feeling well." The blue gaze of his revealed his disappointment.

"I'm fine, just had another idea for a quilt," she said airily. And it was true; a quilt of multihued blues that she saw in his eyes would be amazing.

He helped her inside without saying a word, but she

could feel his gaze on her, waiting for her reaction. That made her stomach flip so Abby turned her attention to survey the room.

"It's perfect," she breathed, stunned by what she saw. She began to mentally organize the room into a workspace. "The church has those long folding tables. We could set them around the room. Cutting on that side," she said, pointing to the only window. "Sewing on this side."

Ed grunted and held out his pad. *Power?*

"We will need electrical outlets for the sewing machines." She nodded when Cade listed ways he could add more circuits.

As he spoke, Abby's mind drifted. He'd helped her in so many ways, even finding this wonderful room where people could gather, chat and work together. Saying thank-you hardly seemed enough. There had to be something she could do for him, or maybe give him.

"Abby?" His finger brushed her cheek. She realized she'd been caught daydreaming again. About him. "I'm sure your brain is whirling with all the things you plan to do," he said. "But if we're to make that meeting, we have to leave."

She glanced around. Mrs. Swanson and Ed waited by the door, watching her. Abby joined them as she pulled on her gloves.

"I think that if Cade can get the heating working and find a way to add more electrical outlets, this would be perfect for our quilting group. But we couldn't use it without your permission, Ed. After all, this is your ranch."

And I can come here and cut the pieces? Ed glanced up from his scribbled words, studying her, then Cade, his gaze revealing how desperately he wanted to be included.

"We couldn't do it without you," Abby assured him. "It will depend on what your son can do."

"I'll do my best. We'd better go now." Cade shepherded them outside and into the sleigh. When his hands circled her waist, Abby realized she'd been holding her breath. She exhaled, thrilled yet perplexed by her reaction. Why did Cade cause this unusual effect?

With a little flick of Cade's wrist, the horses moved toward the house. The motion unsettled Abby a bit so that her shoulder rubbed his. He turned his head and grinned at her.

"After the babies come you'll have to learn how to ride."

"I will?" Abby lifted an eyebrow in question. "Why?"

He listed reasons that left her bemused by the thought of his hands on hers. Images played through her mind of the two of them galloping across the pasture lands when the snow was gone and wild grasses swayed in the wind. She could almost smell the scent of sagebrush that she identified as Cade's smell.

"Does the thought of riding one of my horses terrify you into silence?" he teased. "I assure you they are all very well behaved."

"I'm sure." Abby inhaled the crisp air as she savored the view. "Now that the days are starting to get longer, I need to get out more." She glanced his way. "It's so lovely here. You must have missed it while you were away in Afghanistan."

"Yeah," he answered. She thought she saw his jaw clench and wondered if he, like Max, had bad dreams of that time, but Cade said nothing more.

At the house he helped everyone out of the sleigh, then returned it to the horse barn. Abby helped Ed remove his coat while Mrs. Swanson began setting the table.

"I started soup this morning," she said, lifting the lid of a big pot. A savory aroma filled the kitchen. "Won't take but a minute to be ready."

"You have a beautiful ranch, Ed." Abby hung up his

coat, stored his scarf and gloves and dried off his shoes. "It's so pretty with the creek running through it. I can imagine Cade skating on the creek with his friends."

As she said it the door opened. She turned to smile at Cade but the grim look on his face made her smile drain away.

"D-didn't you?" she stammered.

"I didn't have many friends," he said in a tight, quiet voice as he hung up his coat. "Most of them didn't want to come out here."

Tension crept across the room like ice fog. Cade's gaze meshed with his father's, both intense, hostility hidden just beneath the surface. Inside Abby a wave of guilt rose. It hurt to think she'd caused either man pain. New resolve filled her. Somehow she had to find a way to help them reach out to each other. But for now all she could do was change the subject.

"Mrs. Swanson's soup is ready so I suppose we'd better eat." She pretended a light tone but the obvious enmity between father and son left her with little appetite. She offered a short grace, then ate her soup.

"Will the meeting be long today?" Mrs. Swanson asked.

"We have a lot to go through." Abby grimaced. "If we can't raise some funds, I really question whether we'll be able to open in the spring."

"Is that the goal?" Cade looked surprised.

"If everything works out. But we need money because Wanda has used all her resources." She paused when Ed tapped her on the arm. He held out his pad. "Hilda Vermeer," she read. "Yes, Cade mentioned she had money, but he didn't think she'd be willing to help us."

She felt rather than heard Cade stiffen and wished she had kept silent. Beside her, Ed was frantically scrawling across his pad. When he held it out, Abby blinked her surprise.

"He wants to visit with Ms. Vermeer this afternoon while we're at the meeting," she told Cade. "Apparently it's coffee day at the seniors' center and she's a regular visitor there."

"*You* want to go to the seniors' center?" Cade asked his father, enunciating each word as if he needed the clarification. Ed nodded, his eyes narrow as he waited for some objection, but Cade simply shrugged. "Fine by me. I'll drop you off before the meeting and pick you up after. Okay?"

Ed nodded firmly, then looked at Abby. That's when she understood.

"You're going to ask Ms. Vermeer for a contribution to the adoption center, aren't you?" she whispered in Ed's ear. He jerked his head once, his grin flashing out. "I'm so glad you're helping us."

As Abby hugged him she met Cade's glance over his father's head and puzzled at the expression she saw. Wistfulness—no, longing filled his face. Her heart ached for the sadness he kept couched deep inside. As he drove them to the meeting, she brainstormed for a way to bring father and son together again. She so wanted Cade to make peace with his father.

The only thing, she prayed silently, *is that I need to help them without getting too fond of Cade. Okay, Lord?*

As Cade ushered her out of the truck and inside the building, Abby wondered if maybe she'd prayed that prayer too late, because in truth, she was already extremely fond of Cade Lebret.

"What's up?" Ivor asked, grabbing a juice box and two of the cupcakes left over from the coffee break of the adoption agency meeting at the seniors' hall.

"Talk," Cade muttered. "A lot of it. All afternoon. How come you're so late from school?"

"Tryouts for the school play. Why are you sitting here? Nothing to do?" Ivor asked in that snarky way of his.

"Lots, but nothing that can be done here." Cade resisted the urge to correct the boy's attitude. Instead he checked his watch for the tenth time, wondering if he should dare to phone Ms. Vermeer again. Last time she'd curtly informed him she'd let him know when Ed was ready to leave. But that had been ages ago.

"How was the visit with your relatives?" Cade asked, trying for the hundredth time to make a connection with the kid.

"Okay, I guess." Ivor shrugged. "But they don't want me to live with them. I'm glad. I like the ranch."

Cade blinked. Didn't Ivor know he couldn't stay on the ranch? Oh, boy.

"Abby looks tired." The boy glared at him, clearly placing blame. "She's not supposed to sit for a long time."

"How do you know that?" Cade asked, irritated but curious.

"I read about it online. It makes her blood pressure go up and that's not good for the babies." Ivor's superior tone said Cade should know that.

There'd been nothing about that in the pregnancy books Cade had borrowed from the library, but it made sense. He made a mental note to see if there were other pregnancy books he should read. He was about to question Ivor more when the door to the center opened and Ed came bursting through in his wheelchair with Hilda Vermeer mere steps behind him.

"Are you people still nattering?" she asked in her usual cranky tone.

Though everyone stared, no one said a word. Why was Cade not surprised when Abby rose and walked toward her?

"Hello. You must be Ms. Vermeer. I'm Abby—"

"I know who you are." Hilda glared at Abby's rounded stomach. "And I know what you're trying to do. You want to create a place for girls who've gotten themselves in trouble because they didn't follow Biblical rules." Hilda's voice echoed loud and harsh in the sudden silence.

"I wouldn't know about their pasts," Abby returned in a quiet voice. "But I'm not sure it matters."

"Of course it matters," Hilda huffed. She looked ready to launch into a diatribe but Abby continued before she could begin.

"We hope Family Ties will be a helping hand extended to those who are in trouble and have nowhere to turn." Cade marveled at the gentleness of Abby's voice. "We don't want to judge anyone. We want to be examples of Jesus's love. We want to make sure that children who are brought to Family Ties will be placed in homes where they'll be raised with love."

"What kind of example will it be to our own youth to have pregnant teens coming and staying in our town, living as if they've done nothing wrong?" Hilda sneered.

"I don't know that it will be pregnant teens that come here. But if they do, maybe we can teach them that God is all about forgiveness and that one mistake doesn't have to ruin your life." Abby's sweet voice didn't change though her green eyes darkened. "What good would it do to keep bashing them over the head with guilt? Don't we all have enough guilt already?"

Cade admired her restraint. In fact, he just plain admired Abby. He'd thought to protect her from Hilda but now he realized Abby didn't need protecting. She was like a tiger when it came to the babies and children she wanted to help.

"Well, I don't think it's right and I refuse to be a part of it," Ms. Vermeer said loudly. "So don't send anyone around to try to get my money." Having had the last word, she turned to stomp out the door.

But Abby didn't let her escape so easily.

"Please don't feel you have to rush off, Ms. Vermeer," she said in a friendly tone. "Won't you at least look at our plans, see what everyone's been working on? You might enjoy seeing the quilt patterns we have."

At the word *quilt*, Hilda stopped. She slowly turned to scan the room.

"I don't see any quilts," she said.

"There are a couple I'm working on over here." Abby walked to the left and drew her most recent quilt top from the big bag Cade had brought in earlier.

"What's she doing?" Ivor asked as the murmur of Abby's quiet voice wafted to them. "That old grump will never help."

"You might be surprised," Cade said, only then realizing how powerful Abby was because of her refusal to be refused. When his cell phone rang, he hurried outside to take the call so he wouldn't disturb the others.

But the call from the military left him irritated. More delays before they would release Abby's funds. At least they weren't still refusing her claim, but their excuses not to pay up immediately made Cade furious.

"You've been putting her off for seven months," he said in exasperation. "Can't you understand that your delay has caused her to lose her home? She's seven months pregnant with twins with no place to go!" Finally he played his trump card. "It would make a really good story for any investigative reporter. 'Military Leaves Vet's Widow

Homeless.' I don't imagine your bosses would like that coverage."

Having extracted a promise to expedite matters, Cade hung up and hurried back inside, almost running into Abby and Ms. Vermeer.

"You're welcome to stop by the ranch anytime and help us with the quilts," Abby offered. "Cade has found us a building where we can spread our work out, so we'll be setting up soon." She stopped, caught her breath and slid a hand over her stomach. "Sorry," she said a moment later. "False contraction."

"You should go home and rest until you have your children," Hilda scolded. "Let someone else worry about those quilts."

"Oh, I can't do that." Abby smiled at her, green eyes glowing. "This is the job God gave me and I intend to see it's finished."

Hilda huffed again, gave her one last assessing look, then left, shaking her head as she went. Cade touched Abby's shoulder.

"It's getting late," he said quietly. "You've had a long day. I think we should head home."

"The meeting's almost over," she agreed. A frown creased her forehead. "I've got a list of things I need to do around town though."

"Ivor and I could help. Just tell us what you need." He understood her mental struggle to delegate responsibilities but she was worn out. "Come on, Abby. Let us help," he urged, needing to shoulder some of her stress. And that wasn't just because of the babies. It came to Cade that Abby's burdens had become his. He who had always disliked responsibility.

"Thank you," she finally relented.

With Abby's list in hand, Cade dropped Ivor off downtown to hang the posters she'd made while he ran a couple of errands for her on the other side of town.

"I'll pick you up in twenty minutes," he promised.

Half an hour later they'd completed everything on Abby's list and were driving back to the seniors' center.

"She's really determined to get this adoption place going, huh?" Ivor pretended nonchalance but his tone told Cade he'd been thinking about it for a while.

"She is determined, but I don't think the funding is here," Cade admitted, feeling like a traitor. "As long as that's still outstanding she can't get the adoption agency up and running."

"But it has to open."

Surprised by Ivor's intensity, Cade parked but left the engine running.

"There is no guarantee here," he began but Ivor slapped his hand against the dashboard. "Calm down," Cade said sternly. The boy's obvious distress moved him. "What's wrong?"

Ivor's narrowed stare brimmed with suspicion.

"If you won't tell me why you're so bothered, I can't help you, Ivor," Cade said quietly.

"If the adoption agency doesn't open—" Ivor began speaking slowly. "Then Abby won't have a job. And if she doesn't have a job, she won't be able to stay in Buffalo Gap. I don't want to leave and I don't want her to, either."

Neither do I.

The knowledge hit Cade like a blow to the abdomen. The days before Abby's arrival seemed faded blobs of time. Since she'd come to the Double L he'd repeatedly caught himself looking forward to what his day would bring. He hurried through his work, anxious to be around her, to talk to her, to listen to the sound of her voice. She made his world enjoyable.

If she left, if he never saw her again—

"You're not saying anything." Ivor glared at him, then said in a sneering tone, "But then I guess it doesn't matter to you that Ed loves Abby. So do I."

"It matters." Cade scrambled for the words to explain his feelings, but as usual he struggled to find them. "I don't want her to go, either," he managed. "But if the agency doesn't happen, I don't see any way around it. She needs a job so she can raise her kids."

"She needs us." As soon as the words burst out of the boy he thrust open the door of the truck and jumped out, slamming the door behind him. He raced across the sidewalk and into the building.

Cade sat alone with his thoughts, wondering if he'd found a reason for Ivor's hostility. Confused, he went inside to collect Abby and Ivor, Mrs. Swanson and his dad. Abby handed him his cell phone.

"Thanks for lending me that," she said, then said thanks again when he held her coat so she could slip into it. "I managed to reach everyone who wasn't at the meeting. Unless they hear otherwise, they'll be at the ranch tomorrow morning at ten to help with the setup."

She looked so tired.

"Come on, you're getting in the truck first. It's running and should be warm." Cade held out his arm and she took it, too tired to argue her independence.

Once he had all his charges loaded, he drove to the ranch, very aware of the way Abby kept rubbing her stomach while Mrs. Swanson, Ivor and Ed chatted in the back.

"Is everything all right?" he asked finally, feeling guilty that he may have let her overdo. He was supposed to watch out for her; he'd promised Max. He'd better get on the ball lest something happened to Abby and her babies.

"They're Braxton Hicks contractions. It's this thing babies do, to practice for labor." She leaned her head back against the seat and closed her eyes. "They're not real labor but they sure feel like it. They start with no warning."

"You're sure it's not real?"

Abby shook her head but Cade surreptitiously watched her face anyway. He knew the exact moment she inhaled and how long she held her breath. When her eyes squeezed shut as she concentrated on what was happening, Cade's heart went into overdrive. Worry mushroomed. He had to get her safely home. He pressed the gas pedal with more force than necessary and heard a hiss of protest from the passengers in the back.

"Sorry," he muttered, sneaking steady glimpses at Abby. Finally, when he thought he'd go crazy with worry, she exhaled and opened her eyes.

"That was a long one," she said with a smile when she found him watching her.

Too long for Cade's comfort but he kept driving without a response. Finally they arrived. He placed a hand on her arm for her to wait as the others had entered the house. Then he voiced the words in his heart.

"Abby, I know you keep insisting God will take care of you, but I can't help seeing how much you're overdoing. I'm worried about you. You won't tell me anything the doctor says. I feel like I'd be helpless if something happened—" He cut off the words, refusing to reveal his deep-seated fear that Abby could die in childbirth. As his mother had.

"Oh, Cade." Abby's startled green gaze met his and held. "These contractions are normal—they're truly nothing. The doctor had no special advice or warnings. I told you he simply said I should get more exercise."

"I know you're confident about the births, Abby. You should be. And I don't want to worry you. But things hap-

pen." Cade hated that his words caused her face to lose
that blazing smile. But he couldn't go on with this nerve-
racking worry, afraid that if he left, he might not be there
if she needed him, might be too late to help. "I need to be
prepared. Can't you please let me accompany you to one
of your doctor visits?"

She smiled then, a slow smile that traveled from her
lips to her eyes, warming him with its intensity. "Don't
worry about me, Cade."

"I can't help it." The words slipped out in spite of his intent not to say them. "I brought you here and I'm responsible for you. I couldn't forgive myself if anything happened
to you or Max's kids." He cleared his throat and let the rest
spill out. "I'm also worried about what will happen to you
if the adoption center doesn't go through, if you don't get
the job. How will you live? How will you raise the twins?"

There was a whole lot more Cade could have said, but
just then the front door opened and Mrs. Swanson beckoned.

"We'd better go in," Abby murmured.

"Yeah." Cade sighed, then got out to help her from the
truck and walk with her toward the front door. As he did
he felt a rush of gladness that he hadn't said any more.

If he had, he might have revealed that he finally had a
buyer interested in the ranch. He might have told her that
the only reason he'd hesitated to take the offer was because
he knew she had nowhere to go. Besides, if the ranch sold,
the quilting group would lose their work space.

But mostly Cade was glad he hadn't said anything because he might have revealed his own longing for Abby
to stay in their lives, to keep enjoying her big, wide smile,
her happy laugh and her solid faith in God, a faith he now
craved for himself.

Chapter Nine

As a strategy, hiding out in her room when Cade was in the ranch house had left Abby frustrated. For two weeks she'd deliberately avoided spending time alone with him, certain that if he didn't see her, he wouldn't worry about her.

With the exception of meals, their trips into town to meetings about the adoption agency and the half hour he insisted on walking with her each morning, Abby made herself scarce around the tall, lean cowboy.

And the reason? Cade's insistence on knowing more about her pregnancy disconcerted her. She fought her desire to share every detail with him because doing so would lend a sense of intimacy to their relationship and she didn't want that. She already had these weird daydreams of sharing the twins' special moments with him, of standing beside him as they watched the babies grow. She had to keep reminding herself that Cade was Max's friend and that when she had the babies, he would no longer be in her life.

There were other reasons Abby avoided him. She tried to arrange times that would give Ed and Cade the opportunity to find a common bond. Mostly, though, she kept away because her time with this man she'd come to admire and depend on would soon be over. If the adoption agency job didn't happen and Cade didn't get the military to release her money, she'd be forced to leave Buffalo Gap and probably never see him again. Life here on the ranch was a balm to her soul. She yearned for more. But what was that more? Friendship? Sharing?

It had to be, because Abby was determined not to let herself fall in love again. She'd thought herself desperately in love with Max but that love hadn't been enough to help him. She couldn't let it happen again.

Abby knew all the reasons why she had to keep her distance from Cade. And yet—she felt something for Cade. Something that was growing into more than friendship. There were times she could read his thoughts, knew that his sideways glances at his father meant he was worried Ed would never regain his strength.

And the more she sat here in her room, the more the miasma of her feelings left her feeling uncertain.

"Put your money where your mouth is and have faith that God will work it out." She rose and left her room to head for Cade's study where shelves of books waited to be read. "Keep your mind busy."

She peeked around the corner to be sure he wasn't inside, then approached the shelves. There were all kinds of books she wanted to read, but one, a medieval tale, drew her. It was too high so she tugged Cade's chair away from his desk. As she did, the arm bumped a brown envelope that fluttered to the floor. And there, underneath, lay two books on pregnancy.

Oh, Cade. Abby smiled as she trailed her finger over one cover, then flicked it open. Inside there were margin notes and question marks all over the pages.

Things happen. I need to be prepared.

A sense of wonder filled her as she leafed through the books. She'd misjudged Cade. It hadn't been just a sense of duty or snooping that caused him to continually ask her questions about her health. He truly was worried about her. She noticed the red underlining of the chapter on pre-eclampsia. He'd scribbled, *How would I know?* on one side. And then in tiny letters—*Mom?*

Shame filled Abby. Cade wasn't just curious about her condition. He was worried about her because his mother had died in childbirth. He was trying to make sure the same thing didn't happen to her. And she'd shut him out, left him to deal with his misgivings because—why?

Because you can't pretend forever. Because he's getting too close and eventually he'll see you're not the confident Christian you pretend to be, that you failed Max when you didn't stop him from leaving.

All of these reasons raced through her mind. But the one Abby couldn't face was the one that asked if she let Cade get closer, could she control the burgeoning emotions inside that grew whenever she was with him?

She glanced down. *Mom?* The plaintive yearning in that single word decided her. She would ask Cade to come with her to her next prenatal visit. Let him pose his questions to the doctor.

He had a difficult enough job dealing with his father. She wouldn't add to his burden by keeping him away from the one person who could settle his mind about her condition. Anyway it would be nice to have someone to talk to about the strange things she was going through in preparation for motherhood.

Abby replaced the pregnancy books the way she'd found them and laid the envelope over them. When everything seemed as it had been, she left the study, walked to the kitchen and pulled on her coat and gloves. Then slowly, carefully, with the glow of the big yard light to guide her, she made her way to the workshop, inhaling the pungent odor of pine, hearing a hopeful neigh from the horse barn, feeling the soft brush of a melting February breeze caress her cheeks. She paused at the door, just to inhale the freshness, then walked inside.

She'd never been in this particular building before but Ed had tried to tell her many stories about the place, frustrated by having to write everything. She knew Cade was working on something, for the lights burned until late into the night. Perhaps the sleigh?

"Hello?" She closed the door behind her and stood in the dimness, waiting. Maybe she shouldn't have burst in. She heard a scuffle, then Cade appeared at the far end of the building.

"Abby?" He hurried toward her. "Is anything wrong?"

"Nothing. I just came to tell you that if you want to come to the doctor's with me next week, you're welcome." The words spilled out of her. She glanced at him once, then dropped her gaze.

Cade was silent for several moments before he said, "Thank you," in a very quiet voice.

Abby did look at him then, in spite of her thudding heart.

"I appreciate you allowing me this." His blue eyes glinted in the shadowy light.

Abby fought off the mesmerizing effect of his gaze and glanced around.

"You spend ages in here. What are you doing?" She caught the way he glanced quickly over one shoulder as if he didn't want her to see something. But when he waved her forward she thought she must be wrong.

"You're not the only one with a project," he told her as he led her back to what turned out to be a workroom complete with tools of all descriptions. "I'm making a table for the entry at Family Ties."

"It's beautiful." Abby slid one hand over the patina of the smooth ash wood, inhaling the sweet smell of oil he'd rubbed on it. The curves and bends of the legs proved he was very skilled. "Where did you learn to do this?"

"I've always built stuff." He shrugged. "I guess it's just a part of who I am."

"An amazing part." Astonished by the beauty of the work, she glanced at the shelves and caught her breath. A host of animals sat there. She carefully took them down one at a time, felt the life molded into them, saw the painstaking detail of each whorl and turn. At the end of the shelf sat several sculpted heads, her own included. "What's this?" She twisted to look at him.

"Just some whittling." Cade freed a stool from a box of wood pieces, wiped off the surface and motioned to it. "Want to sit down?"

"I want to look at these some more." Captivated by the sensitivity of the sculptures, she took her time, tracing her forefinger over the curves and indentations, noting the exaggeration of severe lines on his father's face, the wisp of hair he'd created to caress Mrs. Swanson's neck and the straight, firm line of her own chin. "You've made me look stubborn," she said with a chuckle.

"And your problem is?" He grinned but his face tightened when she pulled an old rag away from a piece almost hidden behind the others.

"What's this?" she asked. But then Abby knew exactly what it was from the tiny catch of his breath and its likeness to him. "Your mom," she breathed, staring at the face crafted with hints of his ancestry. She turned it round and round. "It's amazing." The piece was clearly a labor of love.

"I did it from an old photo so I don't know how accurate it is." He took the carving from her hand and set it back on the shelf, then covered it.

"Why do you keep such beauty covered?" she asked curiously. "It should be in the house where it can be appreciated."

"No." Cade motioned to the stool, waited until she was seated. "It would upset Dad. I don't want to do that."

"You're very careful of his feelings," she praised, admiring the way he fit in so comfortably wherever he was. "It's kind of you, but surely enough time has passed."

"I don't know about that." Cade began putting away his sander, his movements slow, organized. "He's never told me anything about her."

"Why don't you ask him, Cade? Maybe he's just waiting for you to show some interest," Abby suggested.

"I did show interest once. I paid for it dearly." The way he said the words left no doubt that he'd been punished.

"You're father and son," she exclaimed. "You must have done some things together."

"Not often. We don't like the same things." The calm steadiness of Cade's voice couldn't hide the barrenness of that statement. "He always wanted to make the animals obey him."

"And you didn't?" she pressed, needing to understand just how big a gulf spanned between them.

"I don't believe in punishing animals. I get better results with patience and persuasion." Cade hung his rubbing cloth on a hook, his back to her. "Mastery is important to my father. That's why he likes to hunt."

"Hunt?" She frowned until understanding dawned. "Hunt animals, you mean?" His head jerked once in a nod. "And you don't?"

Silence filled the room for several minutes, the only

sound the creak of the wooden floor as Cade shifted on it. When he spoke, Abby had to lean forward to hear his words.

"I tried once, to appease him. But I just couldn't pull the trigger. They were so beautiful, such wonderful creatures that took a risk in trusting us enough to come close. I'd fed the deer for years. They were my friends. I couldn't turn on them, kill them."

When Cade turned around and she saw the sheer pain in his eyes, something squeezed her heart so tight Abby could barely breathe. *They were my friends.* A second later his face changed and the tenderness she'd glimpsed was chased away by a self-mocking grin.

"I sound like a kid. It wasn't that bad."

But she knew it had been.

"Do you want to go for a sleigh ride?" he asked suddenly.

"Now?" Startled, Abby stared at him. "But it's late."

"And since you're still up and wandering out here, I'm assuming you're not tired." His coaxing grin sent a wiggle of delight right to her toes. "Come on, Abby. It's a beautiful world at night and since that chinook blew in today, it's not cold at all."

She shouldn't do it and she knew it. Hadn't she just spent two weeks trying to stay away from him, to ignore the feelings that being around him evoked? Nevertheless, Abby nodded.

"Great." His whole face brightened. "Stay here while I get the sleigh hooked up. I'll come and get you."

"Couldn't I go with you?" A picture of Cade with Liberty flashed through her mind, the way he caressed the horse, whispered in her ear. It couldn't hurt to watch him with his beloved horse, could it?

"Why not?" He slid on his jacket, then held out his arm,

waiting for her to link hers with it. When she hesitated, he arched an eyebrow. "Is something wrong?"

"No." Abby slipped her arm through his and tried to pretend that touching him had no effect.

But as they walked to the horse barn, she realized it wasn't true. She felt coddled, protected, safe when she was with Cade. *You feel a lot more than that*, a little voice in her head chided.

"I'm sorry you missed eating dinner with us tonight. Ed's made some progress with his speech. He kept us quite entertained." She tipped up her face to study the full, white moon. Its glow on the piles of snow lit up the night with a dreamy iridescence. "Was anything wrong?"

"No." Cade seemed to be thinking something over. Finally he said, "A man wanted to see me. He's from out of town and couldn't manage another time."

"Too bad. You should have brought him in for dinner." Watching his face, Abby felt as if there was something he wasn't saying. His next words confirmed her feeling.

"He couldn't stay."

"Maybe next time then," she said wondering what it was he was hiding. "Anyway, it's nice to see your dad not have to use his writing pad so much. He's only mastered words for now, but I don't think it will be long until he'll be speaking entire sentences."

"A lot of credit for that goes to your encouragement, Abby." Cade held open the door for her to enter. "You've been a great cheerleader for him."

"It's nice of you to say, but actually, I think being part of the quilt project for the adoption agency has made the most difference." She leaned against the wall, watching as he led Liberty out of the stall and began to harness the horse. "I think Ed now feels like he has something to do, something that makes a difference, something that matters."

"Also due to you," Cade murmured. His big, capable hands moved quickly and the horse was soon ready to hitch to the sleigh. "I guess I should have done more," he muttered as he led Liberty to the back of the barn and through big double doors where the sleigh waited outside. "Maybe I didn't pay enough attention to him but—"

"You can't blame yourself, Cade. You have your hands full with the ranch," Abby insisted, watching as he closed the door, then hooked Liberty's harness to the sleigh. "And anyway, you did try. You've been a great son, taking over despite all his grumbling. Helping with the quilts has been an answer to my prayer for something to grab his attention."

"It always comes back to God with you, doesn't it?" A teasing smile curved his lips as he spread his hands around her waist and lifted her into the sleigh.

When he climbed in beside her, Abby recited, "'The righteous man trusts in God and lives.' Habakkuk 2, verse 4." She grinned. "My mother taught me that when I was four years old. It's stuck with me."

"Habakkuk, huh?" Cade flicked the reins and Liberty began trotting down a path with which she was clearly familiar. "I had a friend, Anita, who used to quote from that book. She said the Minor Prophets had a lot of good advice about life."

"She was right." Somehow she'd never thought of Cade in love with someone from the past, yet she could tell from the way he'd said her name that Anita had been special to him. A flutter of something uncomfortable wiggled inside. How could she possibly envy this Anita? "Do you still see her?" Abby asked hesitantly.

"No. She wasn't from around here. I met her when I was in the military. We broke up after I brought her here to meet my dad." His lips tightened. "That was a mistake."

"He didn't like her?"

"He put her down, made rude remarks about her being a city girl who'd never make it on the ranch, things like that." Cade's voice hardened. "I was going to propose to her that weekend but she broke it off."

"I'm sorry." A new thought dawned. "So though you left the ranch to join the military, you intended to come back?" Abby asked.

"I wasn't sure. I had a dream of being the next generation of Lebrets to run the place but by then I was so fed up with our arguments…" He let the words trail away and pointed to the deer that stood bathed in moonlight in a meadow glade surrounded by massive pine trees.

Liberty stopped and for a few moments they simply sat together and watched the animals. Then the deer lifted their heads and dashed across the snow into the forest. Cade started them on their journey again, this time driving the sleigh under snow-laden boughs that felt like a secret passage, leading them into a more intimate world.

"I've always loved the Double L." Cade sounded amazed, as if he'd only recently realized how much the place meant to him. "It's not just that I'm my own boss. It's more that I can make my own goals and dreams come true. Or at least, I thought I could."

"What's changed?" she murmured, anxious to hear more of his innermost thoughts.

"Everything. Dad and I have never really agreed. He always focused on raising prize horses, but that's costly and you have to wait years, build up your reputation before it pays off. I insisted we start ranching cattle. He didn't like that but they provide our bread and butter. The horses are a sideline we can only continue if we sell our beef. Dad doesn't think that way."

"I see." It was clear to Abby that Cade didn't share his father's dream and imagined the tension that had caused over the years.

"The money that sustains this place really comes from the beef we raise. Our animals are always grass fed. We use no chemicals." He flicked the reins and Liberty turned right, picking a path toward what sounded like a bubbling creek. "Because we own so much land, we have the ability to let them graze freely and to bale our own hay. Our organic beef commands a high price because it's so clean. But lately the price isn't quite high enough to sustain all we need."

"Couldn't you sell some of the land?" she asked.

"Then we'd have to cut our herd. We need every acre to support the cattle and we need the cattle for our income." He smiled at her. "Anyway, the future of this ranch is really a moot point. Dad needs to be in some kind of care facility where he'll get the support and help that will help him regain full health. The only way I can think of to get the money to make that happen is to sell the ranch."

Abby stemmed the urge to blurt out "No!" Instead she sat silent, praying for help for this kind, hurting man.

"I'm glad he's improving, but his progress would be much quicker if he was where help was readily available and we don't have that availability in Buffalo Gap. The therapist's time is very limited." He made a face. "Maybe I'm hoping that when he finally gets well, he'll forgive me."

"For what?" she murmured.

"Being born." The gut-wrenching hurt in those words kept her silent as they rode deeper into the woods.

What can I say to help him, Lord?

"It will get better," she promised softly.

"Will it?" The dubious note in Cade's voice hurt to hear.

"Yes, if you'll trust God," she told him. "Even though you can't see how it will get better, even though you don't have an answer, trust God."

"I feel like He's angry at me," Cade admitted.

"He's not," Abby said. "When you hurt, God hurts because we're His children. Psalms says, 'Lord, You are kind and forgiving and have great love for those who call to You.' He's not angry, Cade. He's waiting for you to ask for help."

"Do I sound stupid if I say I'm afraid to do that?" Cade stared into the distance. "I trusted Him once and—"

"And you didn't get the answers you wanted," Abby finished. "But you see, where God's love is, there is no fear. You can let go and trust."

Cade didn't respond so she said nothing else, leaving it to God to work in the rancher's heart. Moments later they slid across a small bridge. Abby narrowed her gaze, peering to distinguish what she saw nestled into the trees.

"A log cabin," she exclaimed at last, amazed by the perfect location for the tiny building. She felt Cade go very still beside her. "Is it yours?"

"I built it when I was thirteen. At twenty I redid a lot of my original work." He directed Liberty near the front of the cabin, then stopped. "I guess you'd call it my sanctuary."

"Sanctuary from?" His childhood? Somehow Abby knew Cade hadn't visited this place in some time. Because it was painful?

"Life." He sighed. "I suppose you want to go inside."

"If you don't mind." Though she sensed his reluctance she couldn't suppress her longing to see his handiwork from the inside. Maybe then he'd open his heart to her even more.

"It's not locked. Wait, let me see if there's a flashlight here." He dug under the seat of the sleigh, produced a crank lantern. Once he'd wound it up, he lifted her down and helped her to the doorway where the snow had melted, leaving dry, bare earth. He flicked the latch and the door easily swung inward. Cade frowned. "I thought it would stick," he said.

"Maybe someone oiled the hinges," she said but Cade was shaking his head.

"My father hates this cabin. He once said it was inferior work and threatened to knock it over." He motioned Abby through the entrance.

"I don't think it's inferior. I think it's wonderful." She stepped inside and glanced around the tiny interior. After several minutes she sensed something was wrong and turned.

Cade stood in the doorway, staring at the back wall.

"That fireplace," he murmured in a dazed tone. "I never put that in."

Abby turned to survey a lovely river-rock fireplace. Someone had painstakingly chosen similar stones to frame a hearth. Kindling under logs waited to be lit.

"There are matches on this mantle," she said, pointing to the glass jar. "Shall we try it out?"

"I—I guess." He seemed utterly confused as he bent to light the kindling. "Who could have done this?"

"Your father?" she suggested as she sat down on a rough plank bench.

"I don't think so. This is where I came to hide from him when he wanted me to hunt with him." Cade's head twisted to the window. "I used to watch the animals through there. When I thought he was getting near, I'd make a noise to scare them away."

Abby ached to comfort Cade's tender heart.

"I can't figure out who would do this. Who would even

know it was here?" It was clear Cade wasn't talking to her. "He said it was ugly, a blotch on the landscape."

She waited until he blinked back to reality, his eyes widening as he noticed her sitting there.

"Cade, I think your father did it while you were overseas. I'm sure he must have been worried about you. Maybe this was his way of urging you home," she offered. "Maybe he didn't know how else to tell you he loved you, cared about you, wanted you back on the ranch."

Cade shook his head, obviously unable to accept that. But he said nothing more as he fell into thought. Abby sat in front of the flickering fire, content to leave him with his thoughts while she dealt with hers.

This was the kind of place she'd love to have for her children. A place to come and contemplate, to enjoy the nature God had provided. A secret place to talk to Him. She was growing to love the ranch with its wide-open spaces that offered a sense of freedom she'd never known before.

In this place she'd found people she cared about and promise for the future that could fulfill her dreams of helping children. If only the adoption agency could go ahead.

"It's late." Cade stood in front of her, watching her. "We should get back."

"Yes. You have to work in the morning." Abby rose. "But I'm glad we stopped here. I love your little hideaway." She tilted her head so she could smile at him and found her gaze locked with his. *If only*— Abby refused to let that thought grow.

"I'll throw some snow on the fire." He moved quickly to douse the flames. When it was out he waited for her at the door, casting one last glance around the room.

Neither of them said a word on the way back. Cade seemed impatient and let the horse move into a fast trot so they glided over the snow quickly. Abby mourned the loss of the gentle camaraderie they'd shared. Too soon Cade pulled up in front of the house.

"I'll let you out here so you don't have to walk," he said.

He lifted her out of the sleigh before Abby could step down, but when he swung her to the ground, she found herself light-headed. She reached out and grabbed Cade's shoulders, clinging until the world stopped spinning. Cade continued to hold her but there was a question in his voice when he murmured, "Abby?"

His face dipped close to hers, his eyes scanning hers, moving over her cheeks to her lips. She couldn't look away, couldn't stop staring into the blue vastness of his eyes. His hands tightened around her waist, drawing her infinitesimally closer. If he shifted just the tiniest bit, his lips would graze hers.

Longing rose in her, longing to be held, to be loved, to belong. But she couldn't have that. She wasn't any good at love. She'd failed Max. She could never forgive herself if she failed Cade, too. Sanity returned and Abby drew back, freeing herself from Cade's disturbing touch.

"I'm fine. Just a little dizzy from moving too quickly." She took another step away from him. "I'll be all right," she whispered. "You see to Liberty."

Then, turning, she escaped into the house without looking back.

Though Abby immediately prepared for bed and switched out her light it was a very long time before she closed her eyes. She couldn't stop puzzling over her reaction earlier. What was wrong with her? She couldn't have wanted Cade to kiss her or embrace her because she knew no good could come of it.

But no matter how much she repeated that to herself,

the image of Cade's blue eyes searching hers would not leave her mind.

Tomorrow she'd have to go back to hiding, maybe in the quilt room where she'd have something to keep her thoughts off Cade.

Chapter Ten

"So do you finally have all your questions answered?" Abby asked, trying to smother her smile.

"For now." Cade had never been more aware of the interest of the townsfolk as they left her doctor's office and walked down the streets of Buffalo Gap. The only thing that made it worthwhile was that it was Abby by his side. "Go ahead, make fun of me, but I like to be prepared."

"I am making fun of you," she chirped, her grin widening when he rolled his eyes. "As long as you feel better, that's the important thing. Now we'd better hightail it over to the seniors' center and get the finishing touches on that Valentine's party. We have a lot of money to raise."

"I know." He drew her to a stop, determined to say this. "Abby, you have to promise me you won't overdo today. You heard what the doctor said. This is an important growing time for the twins. It's not the time to overtax yourself."

"Okay, Uncle Cade. I hear you."

"Uncle Cade?" he said with a frown.

"That's what you'll be to the twins." Abby grinned. "Now let's focus on the party." She studied him for several moments until Cade got the feeling she needed to unload on someone. "Do you really think we can raise enough to-night to pay for what we need at Family Ties?"

Cade didn't, but he wasn't going to say that out loud. Anyway, Abby beat him to it.

"Forget I asked that," she said. "I'm trusting God and I'm not going to start doubting now, when we're nearing our goal. What we have to focus on next is getting those windows scraped and repainted."

"You're not doing any painting, Abby," he said, expecting an argument. "No way."

"I wasn't intending to." She shot him an arch look. "But I am hoping to persuade the local painter to do it for free. It'll be a detailed job and will take a long time. I'll keep praying he'll agree."

As if that settled it.

Cade said nothing more as they resumed their walk to the seniors' center. Frustration ate at him. Praying didn't seem to be helping with the adoption agency. Despite Abby's concentrated focus on the quilts, the group had only completed one quilt so far. There were several tops completed but the quilting itself seemed to be something few knew how to do and that added to the guilt Cade felt that he hadn't yet figured a way to get her quilting machine.

He'd also failed to drum up more funds to complete the mechanical room alterations at Family Ties required to meet government standards. But it wasn't only his failure to fund-raise and thereby help Abby help the town that bothered Cade. He'd run into a brick wall with the government about her funds. They'd stonewalled him for weeks and now the man he had been talking to was avoiding his calls.

Cade also felt he was failing to help Ivor adjust to a future that would mean leaving the ranch. Worst of all, Cade couldn't seem to connect with God.

Then there was the ranch. The buyer he'd hoped and prayed would take the Double L had backed out this morning, leaving Cade with yet another failure. Like the others, this potential buyer had pointed out the ranch's shortcomings, as if Cade wasn't fully aware of them.

He'd worked hard to rectify the disreputable state he'd found the ranch in when he came home, but apparently what he hadn't done was more noticeable than what he had. In Cade's mind, this was no different than when he'd been a kid and his efforts had never seemed to be enough for his dad.

"Hello in there?" Abby tapped his cheek. "Did you fall asleep?"

"Not yet." He noticed that they'd walked past the seniors' building. He followed her back, thinking how much he liked her cheeky grin and the soft touch of her fingers against his cheek. Maybe he was getting to like them too much, but lately it seemed impossible to control his affection for this spunky woman who'd married his best friend.

"What are you so deep in thought about?" Abby asked, pausing on the step above him.

"I got a phone call this morning. A space has opened at the nursing home. If I just had the money, Dad—"

"Cade, he doesn't want to go there," Abby said, a hint of steel lacing her voice.

"I know he says that, but I think once he got there—" He let it go. "Doesn't matter because we can't afford it."

"Here you are. I've been looking for you. Come inside. I need to talk to you both." Mayor Marsha ushered them up the stairs and into the building, dragging on Cade's arm so he'd follow her to the cloakroom. "Something's come up."

"Are you all right?" he asked, concerned by her pale cheeks.

"Yes and no." Marsha sat down and inhaled. "I've

been on a waiting list for knee surgery. Doc Treple said it wouldn't happen until June but he called today. I'm to be at the hospital tomorrow morning."

"How can I help?" Cade asked.

"I'm getting nowhere in drawing this community together and we all know it," Marsha said with a sigh. "I've lived here for almost ten years but people still see me as an outsider." She studied Cade. "But you're a local. You grew up here. You're part of them. You could unite them enough to make the agency happen."

"Me? But I don't know the first thing—I've been away—" Cade gulped and stared at her. "I can't."

"Yes, you can, Cade." Marsha bent forward and began listing ideas she had to bring the adoption agency more community support. "You just need to get out among them, be seen encouraging it. They'll listen to you and I believe more people will begin to pull together."

She kept on speaking, filling his mind with possibilities and the more she did, the more Cade began to imagine it happening. And yet...

"I have too many responsibilities now," he objected. "I haven't got time."

"I've found we always have time for what we want to do," Marsha said, her clear, straight gaze locking with his. "I believe God could really use you in this, Cade."

"I do, too." Abby spoke up and he realized she'd been standing there, listening the whole time. "Say you'll do it."

"It would be a great load off my mind if you would," Marsha said. "I believe that if we don't keep pushing ahead, Family Ties will never happen. And that would be a great loss to this community."

"But it's so much to take on." He glanced at Abby. It would mean working with her more closely than ever, but at least he'd be there to make sure she didn't overdo. He doubted he'd have much effect drawing people together but Abby was the one people flocked to. With her in his corner he might have a chance. "If I agree to do this, will you help me, Abby?"

"Of course." She grinned. "I was waiting for you to ask."

Cade glanced from her to Marsha. He'd failed at so many things. Maybe just once, if Abby kept praying and he pushed himself harder than he ever had, he could succeed. Maybe God would finally answer.

"Okay." He nodded. "I'll do it with Abby's help and you behind us."

"And God," Abby added with a grin.

"Thank you, Cade." Marsha rose and hugged him tightly. "You're such a kind, generous man. I know people will respond to your spirit of caring."

He desperately hoped so because he couldn't stomach another failure.

While Abby went to make sure the catering for tonight's Valentine's dinner and dance was in order, Cade sat with Marsha and went over the list and plans in her massive folder.

"These are just ideas," she said. "Change anything you want. Get Abby's opinion. She's got a great heart for others. You're lucky to have her working with you."

"I know."

"You care about her, don't you?" Marsha asked. Cade blinked in surprise.

"She was my best friend's wife. They loved each other deeply. She's still mourning Max," he added.

"From what she's said, I think Abby's dealing with some other things to do with Max's death." Marsha raised one eyebrow. "You should ask her about that. Just remember that Abby's a vital woman. One day she'll find love again."

Marsha leaned over and whispered, "I hope it's with you. You'd be perfect together."

"But I'm not staying in Buffalo Gap," Cade blurted.

"Oh?" Marsha frowned. "Your father didn't tell me you were leaving."

"Because he doesn't know and I'd appreciate it if you'd keep secret what I'm going to tell you." Cade waited for her nod, glanced around, then lowered his voice. "I'm trying to sell the ranch to raise enough funds so he can go into a nursing home. Then I'll do something else."

"Go back to the military?" Marsha shrieked. "But you can't. That would almost kill him. He was so worried while you were gone."

"Please." Cade winced. "I don't want this broadcast, especially with Abby approaching her due date. I don't want her to worry about a place to live."

"I'm sorry," she murmured. "It's just—I thought you were home to stay. We all did."

"I wish I could be," he admitted honestly.

"It can't be an easy decision," she said. "You've always loved the ranch."

Cade couldn't imagine how this woman knew so much about him. All he knew was that since he'd begun helping with the agency, Marsha had become as close to a mother as he'd ever known. Maybe that's why he felt comfortable talking with her so openly.

"But you will be here until June when the adoption agency opens?" she asked anxiously.

"There's no rush about leaving until we get a buyer. I'd like Dad to have one more spring on the ranch." He stopped speaking as Abby returned. "Everything okay?" he asked, seeing the way her green eyes had darkened.

"I'm not going into labor, if that's what you're asking. Not yet." Abby laughingly explained Cade's visit to the doctor's office to Marsha. "I'm only interrupting you because I need help to move a table. Apparently we've sold more tickets at the last minute."

"You're not moving anything." Cade turned to Marsha. "After the dinner, you go home and prepare for your surgery. Abby and I will be here if something's needed. And we'll carry on till you return."

"You make a good team," Marsha murmured when Abby had left the room. "Maybe you could make that a permanent thing."

Cade stopped and turned to look at her. He saw the flicker in her eyes and knew she was matchmaking. He also knew he had to stop it.

"Abby's a wonderful person," he said. "Any man would be happy to have her on his team. But there was only ever Max in her life and to me she'll always be his wife."

Abby heard Cade's words with a sinking heart, yet was confused by why that should be. She was determined that Max would be the only man in her life, yet she couldn't shake her growing fondness for Cade. Why was that?

Lord, what are these feelings? I failed Max. I wasn't the wife I should have been. Finally she admitted the worst. *I tried to love him, but it wasn't real love.* Again the black cloak of guilt almost smothered her.

"Are these feelings from You, God? What are You trying to tell me?"

Someone called her name. Abby hurried away from the cloakroom, confused and disappointed that the man she admired saw her only as Max's wife. But it was understandable. In this condition, who would find her desirable?

When Cade found her a few minutes later, Abby had pasted a smile on her lips. Since she couldn't dislodge the questions that plagued her, she made herself focus on the party. This was to be their major fund-raiser along with the silent auction to be held later. The success of both would bring them much closer to their goal of opening the adoption agency.

"Do you think we've covered everything?" Cade asked as people began to file into the hall.

"We've done all we can do. Now we might as well enjoy the party," she told him, not nearly as blasé as she pretended. She let him lead her to her seat and smiled when he held the chair for her. His hand grazed her shoulder as she sat and it wasn't just the babies who leaped for joy. Abby's heart thudded in reaction to even such a small touch.

"Abby, you look lovely." Karina Denver touched the velvet dress that Mrs. Swanson had presented to Abby just this morning. "This matches your eyes perfectly."

"Thank you, Karina."

"I'm so envious of you." Karina's gaze slid to her stomach. "As soon as the adoption agency is up and running, you can count on Jake and me to be your first customers. We want a child so badly."

"Then I'll pray that God will direct one to you," Abby promised. "I think you'll make a wonderful mom."

"So will you." Karina smiled and Abby returned it, glad for the wonderful friendship she'd found with this woman.

Mayor Marsha opened the evening by introducing Cade as the new lead on the project. After Pastor Don said grace, Creations, a local eatery, served a meal designed to enhance the romance of the evening. Abby relaxed in the flickering light of the candles. Caught up in a conversation to her left, she felt someone staring. She turned and found Cade watching her.

"Is anything wrong?" she leaned over to whisper in his ear. He shook his head, a faint smile curving his lips. "Is something funny?" She patted her hair.

"Everything is fine, Abby." Something glimmered in those expressive blue eyes but she couldn't decipher it in such dim lighting. "I suppose you're going to insist on dancing later?" he rumbled in a voice meant for her ears only.

"If someone asks me," she said coyly.

"I doubt you'll have a shortage of partners." The way he said it made Abby do a double take. It also gave her courage.

"Will you dance with me?" she asked bravely, holding his gaze with her own. Cade slowly nodded. "Thank you," she whispered.

"My pleasure." Through the rest of the meal his shoulder bumped hers as the servers picked up the dishes, brought coffee and distributed a chocolate dessert that had everyone groaning. "You're not having any?" Cade asked when she waved the server away.

"I shouldn't. The twins don't seem to like chocolate." She laid a hand on her stomach and smoothed it. "It looks delicious."

"Try a little and see how they react," he offered. He scooped a tiny bit onto his fork and held it out.

Abby hesitated. The gesture seemed so intimate. People would see them and probably gossip. She knew how Cade felt about that.

"What's wrong?" he asked in a low voice.

"Everyone's watching," she whispered.

"So?" He glanced around, shrugged, then returned his focus to her. "Taste it."

Since when didn't Cade care about the townsfolk watching him?

Abby forgot all about the others when he moved the fork closer to her lips. She tasted the chocolate confection, closing her eyes in delight as the flavors of chocolate, raspberry and caramel exploded on her tongue.

"Good?" Cade's voice was so close. She opened her eyes. Everything in her quavered when she realized his lips were mere centimeters away.

"Yes." Why couldn't she tear her gaze from his?

The rest of the evening passed in a blur for Abby. Mayor Marsha spoke of the importance of providing homes for children who could be the future of Buffalo Gap but Abby absorbed little of what was said.

Something was happening inside her. Something strange and wonderful. Something that depended on Cade. When he went to speak to his father, who'd come to the event with Hilda Vermeer, Abby felt a sense of loss. And when he returned she reveled in his presence at her side.

She cared for him. But was this affection right?

If You don't want this, please stop these feelings.

"Shall we dance?" Cade asked.

Soft, romantic music played. Red paper lanterns swayed overhead as if in time. The tables were pushed back to leave a cleared space where couples could dance together. Abby looked around but found no excuse not to slip into Cade's open arms. When she did it felt like she belonged there. That she was home.

His embrace fit her perfectly, and her hand felt comfortably right pressed against his shoulder. He led her into a waltz and she found that Cade was the perfect partner.

"Where did you learn to dance?" she asked, arching her back so she could see his face.

"You won't believe it but Dad insisted I take lessons." Cade's chuckle rumbled in his chest. "He said he didn't want me to be a total misfit. Turns out it was one thing I managed to do quite well. I won the gold award."

"You deserve it," Abby told him. "And a better partner than me. I'm so clumsy."

"I'm happy with the partner I have." In the moment that he held her gaze an arrow of electricity seemed to shoot between them until he said, "I hope we've made some money tonight."

At the moment Abby couldn't have cared less about the adoption agency or making money or anything else.

Because nestled there in his arms, in the sweet intimacy of the dim senior citizens' center, she realized that she'd fallen in love with Cade Lebret.

Chapter Eleven

"Ivor, I need your help." Cade drew the boy inside the horse barn.

"It's Saturday. I've got plans, man." Ivor, as usual, looked disgruntled by Cade's request.

"I know, but you might have to put off meeting your friends for a few hours." When Ivor opened his mouth to protest, Cade said, "It's for Abby. And it's a secret."

"So?" Ivor looked reluctant but Cade could see he was intrigued.

"I have to go to Calgary. I need to deliver a horse," he explained.

"Aw, man. How's that for Abby?"

"I have to pick up something for her, a surprise. But I don't want her to know in case something goes wrong. I also don't want to leave her alone," he added. "Yesterday the doctor said the babies could come anytime after March first."

"That's today." Ivor's eyes grew huge. "You mean she could have the twins today?"

"It's a possibility, but I don't think it's going to happen. Still, I need someone responsible to keep an eye on her." He had Ivor's attention now. The boy would do almost anything for Abby. "Today's Dad's physiotherapy day. The therapist will arrive about two and work with him for a couple of hours. Mrs. Swanson asked for today off. So I'm depending on you."

"To do what?" Ivor asked with a frown.

"To stay with Abby, keep an eye on her, make sure she takes a break, has something to eat. In short, I want you to be there for whatever she might need." He paused, then asked, "Can you do it?"

"What if something happens?" Ivor asked.

"You call 911. Can you do it?" When Ivor didn't immediately agree, Cade clasped the boy's shoulder. "I wouldn't ask if I didn't have to, but I'm concerned about her. She's doing too much to try and make the adoption agency a reality. What I'm going to get could make quilting a whole lot easier for her."

"That would be good." Ivor met his gaze seriously. "We can't let anything happen to the babies. Abby would blame herself."

"Exactly." Cade paused a moment, then added, "You're in charge, Ivor. Can you handle it?"

The boy's shoulders went back. A new maturity filled his face. He nodded once.

"You're sure?" Cade pressed.

"I'll be here for her. And for Ed. No matter what, I'll take care of them." Ivor zipped his jacket. "Go do your business. I've got this under control." He sauntered out of the building, his step sure, his confidence obviously restored.

As Cade watched him leave, he realized he'd been all wrong in his approach to working with Ivor. Apparently the way to connect was to give the boy some responsibility. At least Cade hoped that would be the start of building a relationship with him.

It took only a few minutes to load Liberty. Then Cade drove to Jake and Karina Denver's home. Jake was ready and climbed in the truck.

"Thanks for coming with me," Cade told him, and meant it.

"My pleasure but I have to ask, are you sure you want to sell Liberty? Seems to me you've had that horse since we were in grade school." Jake frowned. "Not easy to sell something you love so much."

"No." It took Cade a minute to regain control. "She's a great horse, but the time has come for her to move on." He wasn't going to mention that once he sold the ranch he'd have no place to keep his best friend.

"Long as you're sure." Jake leaned back in his seat. "I sure was glad you joined our Bible study group, by the way. Romans makes a great study."

"I just hope I don't embarrass myself with my questions," Cade muttered.

"Not possible," Jake assured him. "None of us know all we need to about faith. A Bible study is the place to ask your questions and it's the only way to grow and develop a relationship with God."

They chatted as they drove. Cade was surprised by how quickly they reached Liberty's new home. He made the sale quickly, pausing only long enough to give the horse a good, strong pat before he swung back into the truck, leaving the trailer to pick up later.

"Abby must mean a lot to you for you to give up something you love so much," Jake mused as they drove toward Calgary.

"She's getting desperate to finish those quilts before the twins come." Cade tried to sidestep the issue. But Jake wouldn't let it go.

"Abby's been a real boon to the community in helping

to make the agency become a reality. So have you." Jake smiled. "When folks know you sold your horse to buy her quilting machine back, you're going to be a hero. Again."

"I'd prefer if you kept that to yourself." Cade ignored the other man's surprised look. "Abby doesn't need to be worrying about what I spent."

"You're protective of her."

"She's my best friend's wife and I owed him my life. I figure I'll still come out owing." Cade punched the gas pedal to hurry them toward Calgary. Jake seemed inclined to talk.

"Karina's getting desperate to have kids," he confessed. "But the truth is it scares me spitless."

"Really?" Cade frowned. Jake did not look like a man who feared children. "Why?"

"Are you kidding?" Jake shook his head. "First of all, the responsibility for that tiny bit of life is overwhelming. It depends on you for everything. What if I fail? What if I mess up? What if I don't give that kid what it needs?"

"I doubt that'll happen. You have lots of family to depend on and you have a great relationship with your father. You have him to show you how to be a perfect father," Cade said, slightly envious of his friend.

"You think my dad was perfect?" Jake shook his head again. "Let me tell you, he wasn't. I was the oldest kid so I guess I was the one he experimented on. He did lots of things wrong. It took me some time and lots of prayer to forgive him."

His comments startled Cade, who'd always believed the Denvers' home to be the happiest in Buffalo Gap.

"That's partly why I signed up for the Bible study. Before we adopt anyone," Jake said in a firm tone, "I need to study God's word and find out more about the kind of father He is and wants me to be."

Intrigued, Cade asked questions and Jake answered, providing Cade with a deeper insight into what it meant to live out that faith you said you believed in. He decided it was time to do some digging on his own and see if he could learn more about God.

"Want to stop for lunch before we pick up the quilting machine?" he asked as they neared Calgary.

"Sure, but would you mind if we did it at a mall? It's Karina's birthday next week and I want to pick out a gift for her," Jake said. "I've never been able to surprise her and I'm determined to do it this year."

In a flash the date bloomed in Cade's mind. March first. Abby's birthday. He'd filled out the date repeatedly on government forms but hadn't given it a thought. Now he knew he could not let her day pass without celebrating.

"Jake, can you help me with something?" When his buddy nodded he explained his problem. "Max used to talk about how he always tried to make Abby's birthday exceptional. I'm thinking she'll really miss that this year so I'd like to do something special that will help her get past missing him."

"I think buying that quilting machine is pretty special but I guess a more personal gift wouldn't hurt, though I have no clue what that would be." Jake made a face. "I have enough trouble choosing something for Karina. You'd better pick up a birthday cake, too, because if Ivor doesn't know it's her birthday, I'm pretty sure Mrs. Swanson doesn't, either, right?"

Jake waited for his nod, then insisted on waiting while Cade deposited the check for Liberty at the bank. Then he pointed to a store. "Let's go in here. Maybe they can help us."

Cade entered the store with fear and trepidation, but

when they emerged an hour later he felt much more confident.

"If only I could get Abby's affairs straightened out this easily," he said to himself.

They picked up a fancy cake and stored it in the backseat along with their packages, then treated themselves to a steak dinner. Then it was time to visit Boris. The older man looked delighted to see them.

"God has answered my prayer," he said as he pulled a box from under the counter. "I wondered how I'd get this to her. This is for Mama Abby. Some baby things my wife made a long time ago."

"I'm sure Abby will love them," Cade told him, cradling the box. "I'm also here to buy back her quilting machine. You do still have it, don't you?"

"Of course." Boris looked grieved. "I have your deposit, don't I? I would never sell it with that. But I am glad you came so soon because I've decided to close the shop." He told how he'd been robbed, hit on the head, and still didn't feel recovered. "I want to spend more time with my grandchildren."

They chatted about his plans for a while longer but Cade was anxious to get home so he wrote the check to Boris, adding a bit extra.

"That's for your grandson's surgery," he said. "I hope it goes well. Will you phone and let us know? I'm sure Abby would appreciate that."

"Thank you so much." Boris tucked the check in his pocket. "She's still staying with you, then?"

"Yes. Her money hasn't come through yet." Cade endured Boris's speculative look.

"I see." Boris patted his shoulder. "You are a good man to look after your friend's wife so well. Perhaps you have feelings for Abby yourself?"

Did it show so much? Cade wasn't prepared to share his personal feelings about Abby so he pretended he hadn't heard Boris's remark and called Jake over to help him load the machine. When all the pieces were secure in the back of his truck, he said goodbye to the old man and wished him well. He was almost out the door when he stopped, fixated on an old cradle that sat by the wall.

"It needs some work," Jake said in the understatement of the year.

"Uh-huh." Cade bent and examined it thoroughly. "How much, Boris?" he asked.

"I'm having a clearing-out sale. It is yours for free, my friend. It will be the perfect first bed for the twins, no?"

Cade thanked him and carried the cradle to the truck. When they were once again on the road, Jake spoke.

"When are you going to have time to fix that thing?" he asked.

"I don't know." Cade twisted his head to grin at him. "I guess I'll have to ask God."

"Never a bad idea, my friend," Jake said with a chuckle. "I wonder how many problems we'd avoid if we stopped and asked God before we pushed away on our own path. You might want to ask Him how you should handle your feelings for Abby, too."

Another person who saw through his pretence. Cade said nothing. But while Jake snored all the way home, Cade tried to figure out exactly what it was he felt for Abby. In the end all he would admit was that when she left, it would be very hard to say goodbye.

Cade opened the door and led Abby inside the quilting workroom.

"Happy Birthday, Abby," he said quietly.

"But—but—" She looked from him to the quilting

machine and back again. "How—when—why…?" Tears spilled from her lovely eyes as she reached out and gripped his arm, her fingers curling around it as she leaned against him, her gaze on him. "Oh, you dear, sweet man."

Cade had never been called that before but now that he had, he kind of liked it. A rush of warmth spread through him.

"Check it out. Make sure I got the right one," he said as he fought to suppress a rush of emotion. Abby was the dear one.

"You got the right one," she said with a big smile and threw her arms around him. "Thank you, Cade. Thank you so much."

"You're welcome." He held her, thrilled to once more have her in his arms. Too soon he had to let go so she could hurry toward the quilting machine.

"Is it okay?" Cade asked anxiously.

"It's perfect. I can't believe you did this." Abby kept running her fingers over the quilting machine where Cade had set it up in the workroom according to Boris's explicit instructions. "It's too much, far too expensive." Her tear-filled eyes met his. "You shouldn't have done it, Cade."

"Too late. Boris said no refunds." He watched her smile burst to life and thought he'd never been so graciously thanked.

"He's a darling man, isn't he? I don't know how you found him but I'm so glad you did." Abby's fingers flew over the machine, tightening here, straightening there. "It won't be long until the quilts are ready now," she said. Then her forehead creased. "But we still have to get those windows fixed."

"Today's your birthday. It's not the time to be fussing about the adoption agency's windows. Let's go have dinner." Cade wrapped her arm in his and led her back to the house. He loved the trust she placed in him to guide her safely over the slushy path. "How was your day?"

"Fine. Except for Ivor hovering over me as if I was going into labor at any moment." She gave him an arch look as she stepped past him into the house. "You put him up to that, I suppose?"

"Sort of." Cade hung up her coat. "I'm relieved to know he took his responsibility to look after you so seriously."

"Cade," she said, exasperation obvious. "I do not need—"

"How are you feeling, Abby?" Ivor asked as he carried a bowl of potatoes to the table at Mrs. Swanson's behest. "Nothing wrong, is there? You can tell me if you need something."

"I'm fine, thank you, Ivor." She touched his cheek with her knuckles, then turned so her back was to him as she sent Cade a glower.

They sat down to eat Abby's birthday supper, teasing her about her age. Laughter filled the room and Cade soaked it in, wishing this could be his future—a home filled with joy. Ivor carried the cake to the table. Cade winced at the crooked letters the boy had dribbled across the top, but as they all sang "Happy Birthday" he realized that this was another part of making Abby's day special, another way to show love. It was the kind of thing family members did for one another, maybe not perfect but lovingly done. This was something Jake would learn when he adopted his own child.

But was it something Cade would ever know?

When the cake and ice cream were gone, after Abby had thanked them for her surprise birthday supper, Cade held out the package the saleswoman had wrapped for him.

"Happy Birthday, Abby."

"Oh, Cade." Her eyes welled with tears. "I can't take

it. You already bought my machine. That's above and beyond."

"I bought this for *you*," he insisted, embarrassed that the others were watching but determined she should know he'd wanted something specifically for her to enjoy, not something she'd use to make others happy. "Please open it."

"Thank you," she said finally, accepting the package. As if the foil paper was a sheet of gold, she eased the wrapping apart and peered inside the box. "Oh, Cade," she whispered as she drew the peacock-blue housecoat from the box. "It's lovely."

"I thought you should have something special for when the babies come," he explained, searching her face for a response. "Is it okay?"

"Okay? It's amazing." She jumped up, threw her arms around him and hugged his neck so tightly Cade thought he might expire. At least he'd die happy, he mused, lifting his own arms to embrace her.

What would it be like to be free to hug Abby whenever he wanted? But how could that be? Once the ranch was sold he'd have nothing to give her, no place where he could help her raise the twins, even if she'd let him. Even if he somehow learned what it took to love and care for her.

"I'm sorry," she said, pulling back, her face a bright pink. "I didn't mean to choke you. But I really do love it."

"Good." He leaned back in his chair and watched as Mrs. Swanson presented Abby with a white scarf-and-mitts set she'd made. His father handed Abby a check.

"B-babies," he said. Abby thanked him with a kiss on the cheek.

"You always like my stories so I wrote you one of your own," Ivor said, not to be outdone. He read it aloud then flushed at Abby's praise.

"It's been such a wonderful day," Abby said tearfully. "Thank you all."

Cade knew it had been the right decision to call ahead and tell his father about Abby's birthday. Each of them had helped make her day memorable. Now he handed Abby Boris's gift, accepted another cup of coffee, leaned back in his chair and savored the combination of family, joy, sharing.

A flicker of hope wavered inside him.

Maybe, somehow, God could give him that dream?

Dare he hope it would be with Abby?

Chapter Twelve

"Three more quilts finished." Two weeks later Abby almost danced down the pathway filled with puddles from the melting snow. "And you raised two more donations." She clutched Cade's arm, forcing him to stop. "We're actually going to reach our goal and get the adoption agency open. Aren't we?"

The last sentence came out uncertainly. Cade couldn't bear to hear the sound of desperation overtake the joy in her voice.

"We're doing it," he agreed, forcing certainty into his words when, truthfully, he wasn't certain at all. But he needed to protect Abby, to keep her outlook positive now, when she was in the hardest stage of her pregnancy and counting the days until her babies arrived. "You're going to get that job so you can care for your kids and for the ones who come to Family Ties."

"From your mouth to God's ear," she murmured.

"Getting that billboard made and selling space on it was genius. We'll have to find a way to thank Ms. Vermeer for suggesting it." He tugged on her hand and grinned. "Don't think you can sidestep me, Abby. We are going to finish this walk."

"Taskmaster," she chided but after a heavy sigh she began to walk again. "You think it's easy being this pregnant? I feel like a house."

"You look beautiful. Are you too warm?" Cade no longer felt strange asking about her personal needs. It was his job to protect her and he intended to do that job to the best of his ability.

"Yes. I love this spring sunshine." She paused to unbutton her coat and lifted her face to the sun. "Did I tell you Hilda has also designed a logo for the adoption agency and fashioned little labels to sew on our quilts?"

"Sounds like she's really taking an interest in Family Ties." Cade nudged her forward. "I thought she was against it."

"I believe God is working on her. She's getting less and less judgmental." Abby rubbed her back. "Could we sit down for a minute?"

"Sure." Cade checked her face for a sign that something was wrong as he led her to a wrought-iron bench. He waited a moment, then asked, "Okay?"

"Yes. I'm just tired."

"Not much wonder," he scoffed gently. "You go nonstop from dusk to dawn. You need to slow down."

"I will. Eventually." She closed her eyes and lifted her face into the sun's rays. Cade used the opportunity to admire her beauty until she opened her eyes and he got caught. "We've worked well together on the fund-raising, haven't we?"

"Amazingly well, given that you're so bossy," he teased.

This woman, this amazing woman. She never failed to fill him with confusion and wonder and joy. Somehow she'd crept into the secret parts of his heart and taken up residence there. Now Cade wondered how he'd bear it when she left the ranch.

"I'm quite proud of what we've accomplished," Abby said, her chin thrust upward.

"Are you?" He could look at her forever and never tire of her loveliness, inside and out.

"I am proud." Abby nodded emphatically. "Erecting that fund-raising thermometer in the town square keeps people engaged in our project. That was your best idea yet and it's reaping benefits for us."

"Your idea of holding that spring yard sale was fantastic, too. We had enough donations from that to fix up the kitchen." He smiled at her, savoring this togetherness they'd found, discovering true joy in partnering with her in Marsha's absence.

Cade had run across the word *helpmate* in his Bible reading. In his mind, Abby personified that. The more involved they got, the more their time together seemed precious, which was why he savored these special moments alone with her.

"Ed's doing really well, too." Abby chuckled. "I think he'll be throwing away his writing pad soon. And you and Ivor seem to have finally connected."

Because of you, Cade wanted to say.

"While we've got a moment alone, I wanted to say thank you to you, Cade, for being there for me, protecting me, caring for me. I don't know what I'd have done if God hadn't brought you into our lives." She touched her stomach to include the twins. Her green eyes shone, warming him. "I think you're beginning to realize God's place in your life, too," she added.

"The Bible studies have helped clarify a lot of misconceptions I had," Cade agreed.

"You are a beloved son of God," she said in quiet certainty. "Plus you've rebuilt some friendships. In fact the whole of Buffalo Gap sings your praises to me almost every time I'm in town. You're the local hero," Abby told him, a teasing grin lifting her lips.

"Yeah, some hero," he muttered, stifling the urge to lean forward and brush his mouth against hers. Would she push him away?

"At least you're not avoiding people anymore," she teased. "They're not as bad as you thought, are they?" She laughed out loud when he finally shook his head. Suddenly she sobered. "What about your dad, Cade? Any success there?"

The dream of embracing her evaporated, thrusting Cade back to reality.

"Not really. He's still carrying a grudge that I sold Liberty, even though she was mine to sell. Dad thinks I should ask permission every time I do something around here, but when I do, he berates me for not taking control."

"Did you ever ask him about the fireplace in your cabin?" She pulled off her gloves and stuffed them into her pockets as the morning spring sun grew warmer.

"He told me some story about having to camp there a couple of times and deciding that a fireplace would make it habitable in the event someone got caught in a blizzard. I don't believe that for a moment," he said.

"Then why did he do it?"

"Probably to make sure I didn't think it was mine, to show his power." He couldn't hide his bitterness. "It's always about control with Ed Lebret."

"He loves you, Cade," Abby said in that gentle, comforting voice of hers. "I'm sure of it."

"Are you?" *I wish I was.* His cell phone rang. Cade answered it, hope springing inside his heart as he heard the words he'd longed to hear. "I'd be happy to hear your offer," he said as he struggled to control his excitement. "Late this afternoon will be fine." He hung up, then stored his phone thoughtfully. Maybe God was finally answering one of his prayers.

"Offer?" Abby raised one arched eyebrow. "I couldn't help hearing," she apologized.

"Doesn't matter. I would have told you anyway. Someone is going to make an offer for the ranch." Cade watched the joy leech out of her lovely face as her fingers clutched the iron arm of the bench.

"You're going to sell the ranch?" she whispered.

"I have to. It's the only way to get the money Dad needs to stay in the nursing home. The timing is perfect because two men Dad knows well have just moved in there. He'll have someone to visit with."

"But Cade, he loves this place. So do you." Abby rose, her green gaze searching his. "This land, the cattle and horses—they're your heritage, your legacy. What will you do if you don't ranch?" Her eyes widened as horror filled them. "Don't tell me you plan to return to the military?"

Cade couldn't say anything. Abby had lost Max to the military and Cade hadn't yet been able to get her financial affairs with them settled. Going back? Well, that was something he couldn't countenance, not when his fear of dying in some far-off land was still so acute. And yet, his skill set didn't leave a lot of options.

"Selling is the only way I know to get Dad what he needs," he said with an unspoken plea for understanding.

"Or is it the simplest way to solve the differences between you?" she asked in a very quiet voice.

"Why would you say that?" he demanded, hurt by the accusation.

"I'm sorry, Cade, but I've spent a lot of time with your father and I know he has absolutely no desire to be in any kind of care facility." Abby fixed him with her most severe look. "Ed loves this ranch. It's where he's spent his life.

If you were honest with yourself, I think you'd admit that the Double L is your home. It's where you belong, too."

"You're right." Frustration erupted into anger. "This place is in my blood. I never felt this was where I belonged as a kid, but now—" He couldn't, wouldn't continue.

"It's where you fit," Abby said, her voice brimming with gentle compassion. "Because this is the work God gave you to do."

"Then why doesn't He do something about Dad?"

"Why do you think He isn't?" Her green eyes darkened to emerald, blazing at him in the bright sun. "Your father is recovering, Cade. He *is* getting better."

"Slowly, maybe. But his recovery isn't optimal. The doctor has repeatedly said he needs to receive better care so he'll regain his health more quickly. Dad should have been walking by now."

"And you think if he can walk that it will make up for losing his home?" Abby asked. "Does that make it okay for you to give up your heritage, Cade?"

She didn't understand. How could she? He was doing this for his father, denying himself. It was the only way he knew to make all the things that were wrong between them okay.

"Come on, let's get back to the house," he said dully. "I've got some fences to mend."

"Yes, you do," Abby said in her sternest voice, her hint obvious. She wouldn't take his arm and truthfully there wasn't really any need. Patches of green grass and dry dirt made walking easy. She marched toward the house without looking back.

Cade trailed into the kitchen behind Abby. She ignored him as she made herself a cup of tea, rubbing her midsection with one hand. He couldn't leave, couldn't let it go like this, with anger between them. He needed to make her understand. He needed her on his side, supporting him.

"Abby, please understand," Cade begged. "I'm doing what I think will be the best for my father. I know you're probably worried that you won't have a home but I'll make sure you—"

"I hope you're not basing your decision to sell the ranch on me." She glared at him. "This is about your unwillingness to trust God." She stopped suddenly, frowned, then returned her hand to her stomach.

"Sell?" Ivor stood in the doorway, his hands resting on Ed's shoulders. He glanced from Abby to Cade. "You're selling the ranch? But I thought it would be my home. I thought I'd be staying here forever."

"Ivor, I need to sell to get Dad into the nursing home so he'll get the therapy he needs." Cade watched anger and disappointment fill the boy's face. He knew he'd lost all the gains he'd made with Ivor.

"No!" Ed's voice thundered across the room, matching the thud of his cane against the floor. "W-won't g-go," he said, obviously mustering his strength to force out the words.

"But I'm doing this for you, Dad," Cade thundered. "Why do you always fight me on everything? You'd think—"

"Cade!" Ivor suddenly yelled. "Something's wrong with Abby."

Cade twisted, saw she was doubled over, her face closed up tight as she rhythmically hissed breath from between her lips.

"Abby?" Cade knelt at her side, grasping her fingers in his. "How can I help?"

She didn't answer immediately. He waited until she at

last drew a long, cleansing breath. Then she lifted her head and smiled the most beautiful smile.

"The babies are coming," she said in a calm tone. "Could you please take me to the hospital, Cade?"

He stared at her, totally discombobulated. He had a plan. He'd made a list. He knew exactly how to proceed. But in that moment everything left his brain. All he felt was pure terror. He couldn't mess this up.

"Ivor, could you get my bag, please? It's on the far side of my bed." How could she be so calm? "Ed, you and I will have a good discussion about everything later, okay?" When he nodded and wheeled near to take her hand, Abby touched his cheek. "I'd sure appreciate it if you'd pray for the babies and me."

Cade blinked. His dad—praying? When had that happened?

"Cade, could you bring the truck around. You'll have to help me into it. Cade?" She grasped his arm, squeezed it to draw him out of his funk.

"Truck. Right. Where's Mrs. Swanson?" he asked, suddenly unsure about transporting Abby to the hospital by himself.

"Gone for groceries," Ivor huffed as he burst into the room with the suitcase.

"We don't need her. We'll be fine," Abby said calmly.

Cade wasn't so sure but he yanked on his jacket and brought the truck as close to the door as he dared. When he entered the kitchen Abby was once more doubled over, huffing breaths and counting.

"Awfully close together, aren't they?" he murmured as he slid her coat over her shoulders.

"Maybe I'm not going to follow all those rules in your books," she teased between grimaces of pain. She waited a few minutes till the contraction had subsided, then turned her focus on Ivor and Ed. "You two come and visit the babies as soon as they get here, okay?"

They promised.

"Call Doc Treple and the hospital and tell them we're coming," Cade ordered as he escorted Abby out the door.

Before she could get inside she had another, stronger contraction. Cade didn't wait. He lifted her and set her inside the truck. Seconds later he was driving down the road, moving as fast as he could, trying to avoid potholes that would jar her.

"Don't even think about telling me to put on my seat belt," Abby told him, pushing her hair off her perspiring forehead.

"The contractions are too close together." He frowned, trying to recall what his library books had said. "Shouldn't your water have broken by now?"

"It did. This morning." She shrugged at his wide-eyed look. "When nothing happened I decided to wait. I'd hoped to finish the red quilt today."

"Oh, Abby." Cade struggled not to laugh, torn between hugging her and reprimanding her. He loved her.

The truth hit him so hard he nearly drove past the hospital, and in the flurry of activity that followed when they reached it, he had little time to think about it. Not until he was sitting on a chair in the hallway, waiting to help her through labor.

Loving Abby—what did that mean? Caring for her, protecting her, yes. He'd gladly do that. But what could he offer her? Not even a home if the sale went through. And yet, his every thought of Abby was inexplicably bound with the ranch.

Abby throwing a snowball, filling the house with fabrics, encouraging his dad, laughing with Ivor, teasing Mrs. Swanson. Abby sharing the colt's birth, taking his arm when the going was slippery, riding beside him late at night to his log sanctuary. Abby's laughter echoing up to the rafters of his home. It would never be home without her.

Was he wrong to sell it? To try to give his father a chance to be whole again?

"She's asking for you, Cade." Doc Treple frowned. "She's going to need you to help her through this. Can you handle that?"

"Yes," he said, rising. "With God's help I can handle anything for Abby."

Let me be strong for her, Cade prayed soundlessly. Then he pushed open the door and went to support the woman who filled his world. At least he could be by her side, where he belonged, for now. He yearned to tell Abby what was in his heart but held back. He could give her his total support, but for now that was all Cade had to offer.

The contractions were so close together she could hardly catch her breath. With the increasing pain, Abby felt she was losing control. Yet, each time, Cade coaxed her to push through it, to ride it out and move on because the babies needed her. He talked about the twins and how they would want to learn to ride his horses. He talked of his log house where he'd take them to play. He reminded her that they weren't yet finished the work they needed to do to get Family Ties operational.

And he spoke of Max. How much he'd loved her, how proud he'd be of her. How much he would have adored his children. How he was watching over her, willing her to complete this most difficult of all tasks.

Each time Cade's wonderful voice urged Abby to shake off her tiredness and tell him the truth about Max and her, how she'd caused his death. But all she could manage was to focus on bringing her children into the world.

In between contractions Cade would bathe her forehead and whisper encouragement. He'd tell her how much he admired her, how much he'd respected Max, what a great friend he'd been and how much he wanted to be there if Max's children needed him.

"Thank you," she murmured when he swabbed her dry, cracked lips with a lemon-tipped swab. "Thank you so much for being here, Cade."

"Where else would I go?" he asked, staring into her eyes. His fingers meshed with hers and held. "We're a team, remember? Besides, if I left, you'd probably have them move your quilting machine in here so you could stitch a few rows between contractions."

"Not likely," she gasped, feeling another one build.

"You're doing so well, Abby," Cade praised. He patted a cool, wet towel on her forehead. "Everything is fine."

Abby wanted to believe him. She wanted that desperately. Yet the longer labor went, the more she feared something wasn't right. Her fears were confirmed when Doc Treple checked her for the third time.

"What is it?" she whispered when he finished examining her.

"You're not progressing. We have to do surgery, Abby. We have to get the babies out before their heart rates are affected." He smiled gravely. "This is as hard on them as it is on you."

"Do it," she told him. "Do whatever you need to save them." When Doc Treple left to prepare for her C-section, Abby turned to Cade for support. "I feel like I've failed."

"I know you didn't want this," he empathized.

"I don't care what they do to me. I just want my children to be safe." She took his hand from her arm and wrapped her fingers around it. "I need to ask you something, Cade."

"Anything."

"Don't say that until you know what I want." She held his gaze. "If something happens to me—no." She put her fingers across his lips so he couldn't speak. "We don't have long. Please, just listen. If something happens to me, I want you to raise my children."

"Abby, I—"

"I want you to be their father," she interrupted. "You can do it," she assured him. "You're strong and dependable. Max trusted you and so do I. Promise me you'll be their father if they need you. Please?" she added when he hesitated.

Doc Treple pushed into the room just as another, stronger contraction grabbed Abby. She pushed through it by gazing into Cade's dear face, knowing there was no other person in the world she trusted as much as him.

"Please, Cade?" she gasped as the pain mounted.

"Of course. You don't even have to ask," he whispered in her ear. His lips brushed against her temple. "But I won't need to keep that promise, Abby, because you'll be there to love and guide them through their lives."

"Thank you." She clenched her teeth as they moved her onto a gurney. Cade stayed by her side, walking down the hall with her, coaxing her through the next contraction.

As they reached the doors to Surgery, the staff paused to give them a moment together.

Abby looked at Cade, startled when he bent down, brushed his lips against her knuckles.

"I'll be praying," he promised. He turned her palm and pressed a kiss inside it. "Don't let go of that," he said as he folded her fingers over the kiss. Then they pushed her gurney through the doors. Cade was Abby's last thought until a sedative blanked out everything.

Chapter Thirteen

Cade sat outside the surgery room doors and prayed as hard as he could. But he feared his prayers alone weren't enough. After all, why would God heed him? But Abby was God's child. Surely God wouldn't take her or her babies.

The inner tug-of-war continued. Cade felt completely alone. Jake had warned him he'd experience doubts. Cade was new to this battle of doubt. He needed help. Jake knew about praying. He led their Bible study prayer group. So Cade placed a call to his friend and explained.

"I'm in Calgary picking up feed," Jake told him. "I can't get to you right now. But you've memorized the verses about being a child of God, Cade. Nobody could care for you more. Repeat them over and over until they sink into your heart and your brain. I'll be praying for you, pal," he promised. "Call me when you know anything."

Cade agreed, then hung up. So he was alone again.

No, not alone.

In all things we have full victory through God who showed His love for us.

We have trouble all around us but we are not defeated.

One by one, verses circled in his head, promises of love, promises to answer.

Ask and you shall receive.

I'm asking, God. I'm asking You to keep Abby safe, to help the doctors to deliver the babies safely, to forgive me for the mistakes I've made.

A sense of calm slowly descended on Cade. Finally he opened his eyes. Two hours had passed and the doctor still hadn't appeared. Fear threatened to overwhelm him once more. To control his urge to push through the doors so he could be at Abby's side, he recited them again and again.

And that's when Cade truly understood why Abby mattered so much to him. She was everything good and right in his world. She made the future seem something wonderful instead of something he dreaded. He loved her so much he wanted the right to be with her always. He ached to tell her, to shower her with love so she'd never leave him.

The wonder of that love dazed him. How, when had it happened? Cade didn't know. He only understood that he loved her and that love was rooted deeply in his heart. He could no more stop loving Abby than he could stop loving his father, though Lord knew he'd tried.

It was Abby's presence that made the ranch home, Abby's smile he wallowed in, Abby's love he longed for. As soon as he saw her, he was going to tell her he loved her.

A hand touched his shoulder.

"Cade?" Doc Treple smiled at him. "Okay?"

"Abby?"

"She's the proud mommy of two healthy sons. We wanted to make sure they were breathing well so it took us a little longer than expected."

Cade started to rise. "But Abby?" he demanded. "How is Abby?" His heart pinched until the doctor's smile widened.

"She's coming out of the anesthetic but she's a little

loopy. We were in a hurry so we used a general anesthetic and she reacted more strongly than we expected." His eyes sparkled with humor. "Take anything she says with a grain of salt."

"I can see her?" Cade asked.

"Technically you're not next of kin but I don't know anyone that she respects more. You can see her in her room," Doc Treple explained. "But maybe you'd like to see the twins first?"

"Yeah, okay." Cade gulped and followed the doctor toward the nursery. He'd never been around little kids and certainly not newborn babies. What if they needed something he couldn't give? How could he protect them and Abby?

"There they are, the two side by side in front." Doc Treple beamed proudly. "Good looking kids, don't you think?"

Cade couldn't answer. He was transfixed by two infants clothed only in diapers in a plastic box. They snoozed under a warm-looking light, one with dark brown hair so like Abby's and one with the pale blond hair Max had sported.

"I'll see you later," Doc Treple said. Cade didn't respond, too busy soaking in the sight of the twins.

"There are your kids, Max, buddy," he whispered. "I hope you're watching over them. They're going to need that."

When the light-haired baby reached out a hand toward him, Cade froze. What was wrong? What did he need?

That's when he realized that despite his love for Abby, and now the same rush of love for her sons, he could never be a proper father to these tiny, helpless creatures. He wasn't wise like Max, didn't have the first idea of how a loving father raised a son.

His heart shrank, closing down on the glory of love that had lit it mere moments ago. He could never tell Abby what she meant to him. It would only cause her pain when he had to leave town. No, Cade would continue with his plan, get the ranch sold so his father would get the care he needed, pay off their debts and then get Abby's funding in place so she could make a home for her children.

It was then that Cade realized that not only did he not have it in him to be a father, he wasn't much use as a son, either, because the only way he knew to care for his dad was to find other people to do what Ed wouldn't allow him to do.

"Cade?" Ivor stood behind him, staring through the glass. Beside him, Ed also watched, a funny little smile tugging at his lips. Mrs. Swanson stood beside him. "Are those Abby's babies?"

"Yes." A rush of pride suffused him. At least he'd helped her by giving her a temporary home. At least he'd cared for her as well as he could. *I did that much, Max.*

"Can we see Abby?" Ivor asked.

"Yes, but just one at a time," Doc Treple said from behind them. "Come on, Cade. You go first."

The moment Cade entered the room, his eyes found Abby. He was pretty sure she was sleeping so he sat down by her bedside, content to wait. He scanned every detail of her face, love flowing through his body. How beautiful she was, even after grueling hours of labor and a major operation. He reached out and threaded his fingers with hers, anxious to feel the warmth of her skin on his. Her eyelids lifted slowly and she smiled.

"Cade," she breathed.

"Congratulations, Abby," he said as he squeezed her hand. "Two beautiful sons. Max would be so proud of you."

Her eyelids drooped and she seemed to drift back to sleep.

Conscious of the others waiting outside to see her, Cade rose and with regret began to release her hand. Abby clutched his fingers.

"Thank you, Cade," she said drowsily. "I love you."

Cade froze. He stared at her, trying to discern her awareness. But a second later her lashes drifted down again.

"Abby?" he whispered. *Do you mean it?* he wanted to ask.

It was highly unlikely that this wonderful woman who'd charmed the entire town felt anything like love for him, Cade decided. His mind danced with possibilities as he imagined the joy of days, weeks, years in her company, watching the twins grow, sharing each moment of their lives if such a love were possible.

He was jerked from his daydream by Doc Treple's tap on the door.

"I've got some very eager visitors out here," he said.

"Okay." Cade gently placed her hand on the blanket. Abby didn't stir. He left the room, his mind whirling. He decided to go to the chapel to pray but Doc Treple put a hand on his arm, stalling him. He drew Cade down the hall, his face serious.

"I need to talk to you about Ed," Doc Treple began. "As I'd already told you, he needs much more physiotherapy. If he was in the nursing home he'd get it because they have their own therapist."

"I've been trying to find a way to get Dad in there," Cade explained.

"Good." Doc Treple frowned. "The therapist the health region brings from Calgary doesn't come often enough for

Ed's needs. He needs more frequent, more intense sessions."

"I think I've got a buyer for the ranch," Cade told him. "When that goes through, I'll move Dad into the home."

"You think that's what he wants?" the doctor asked in a dubious tone.

"It's the only way I know to help him." And that was why there could never be anything between Abby and him, Cade realized. Because once he'd sold the ranch, he'd have nothing to offer her and the babies.

"If that's your choice, I believe the therapist in the home could certainly help him. In the meantime, I'll keep searching for other options." Doc Treple's voice softened. "Ed can't delay more intensive therapy much longer, Cade, or he'll lose all chance of fully regaining his mobility. He should be able to move with the walker by now but his muscles just aren't strong enough."

Cade thanked him, then sat in the waiting room. He'd prayed all he could right now and God hadn't sent another option. Abby's proclamation of love had been a spur-of-the-moment thing, caused by the anesthetics. Hadn't Doc Treple told him she was speaking wildly? If she mentioned it, he'd pretend he hadn't taken her seriously. Because he couldn't afford to do that.

Cade began planning. As soon as he got home, he'd phone the military one last time. If he didn't get a response he'd present the case to the news media. With newborn twins she'd have a perfect photo op. She'd get her money, build a home for the twins and leave the ranch. So would he.

That was good, because knowing how deep his love for Abby reached, there was no way Cade could be so near her, see her every day and not give himself away. Then Abby would feel sorry for him and the last thing Cade wanted from her was pity.

"We're ready to go home now, Cade." Ivor stood in front of him, his face quizzical. "Were you sleeping?"

"No." Cade rose, pulled on his jacket. "How did you get here?"

"Pastor Don stopped by to talk to Abby." Ivor patted Ed's shoulder. "Mrs. Swanson got home just in time to come with us. Pastor Don has a van, so the wheelchair was no problem for him."

He should be able to move with the walker by now but his muscles just aren't strong enough. The doctor's words haunted Cade as he looked at his dad hunched over in his wheelchair. He'd call the buyer back as soon as he got home.

There was no other way, or surely God would have shown it to him.

Abby had been back on the ranch for a week after spending that much time in hospital. She loved being back here, watching spring creep over the land, inhaling the vitality of new life all around. The twins were a delight but they still hadn't figured out day from night so, as usual, she paced the floor with Eric while Adam slept in the cradle she'd found in her room when she arrived home. Eric was named for her father, Adam for Max's father. She felt a little sad knowing neither would ever see their grandchild.

"Sleep now, honey," she murmured, patting Eric's tiny back as she paced her room, which was packed with baby-shower gifts.

She was tired and still in pain after the surgery. If only she could sleep for a few hours, regain her energy. Eric let out another mewling cry. Afraid he'd wake Adam, she left her room and went to the kitchen, which she hoped was far enough from the other rooms that they wouldn't disturb anyone. She set the baby monitor on the counter-top so she'd hear if Adam awoke.

Feeding Eric didn't work. Neither did cuddling him. In fact nothing seemed to help. Abby felt the sting of tears. What was she doing wrong?

"Problems?" Cade stood in the kitchen doorway, his red T-shirt bright in the moon's full glow through the patio door.

"He's restless." Abby jiggled Eric as love for this man filled her.

Feelings for Cade welled inside. She cared for him so much but she didn't know what to do with that. As days passed and those feelings didn't diminish, Abby had con-tinued to pray for guidance. Struggling to meet the twins' needs, she'd finally handed the problem to God, asking Him to show her what to do about her feelings.

Her feelings hadn't changed, but living in such close quarters with Cade, seeing him every day and trying to maintain the facade of mere friendship when her heart ached for so much more was difficult. Sometimes she felt she'd betrayed Max by falling in love with Cade, but she'd given that to God, too.

"Whatever you're doing isn't helping." Cade held out his arms. "You'd better let me try."

"No, you need your sleep. You have work to do. I'll handle him." Abby sat down carefully, trying to smother a huge yawn while wincing at the pain of her healing mid-section.

"You're dead on your feet and you haven't slept through the night since you've come home," Cade said, lifting the baby from her arms. "You've got to get some rest. Go to bed, Abby. Sleep. I'll watch Eric."

Abby was going to protest, until she noticed his face.

This was the first time she'd seen Cade hold her child. He'd always seemed to be busy with something else. But now as he cradled Eric, she saw his face soften, his blue eyes grow tender as they stared into the face of her son. Eric had stopped crying and was now returning Cade's look. A moment later a smile tipped the baby's pink lips.

"See," Cade crowed, grinning at her. "He likes me."

"It's probably gas," she told him, stupidly irritated that her baby had chosen to give his first smile to Cade and knowing that reaction was because of tiredness.

"Jealous, Abby?" Cade touched her cheek, flicking away the lone tear that dribbled down. "You're not usually this emotional." His fingers grazed her chin and held it so she had to look at him. "You're tired," he said, his voice low, compelling. "Go and rest. I'll call you if I need to."

His voice, those blue eyes—both coaxed her to give in. She wanted to sleep so badly. "Okay," she said at last. "Thank you, Cade."

"My pleasure," he said, ducking his head as he always did to deflect thanks.

Abby let her eyes feast on him for a moment, loving every line around his eyes, the hard jut of his cheekbones, the way his short, dark hair lay ruffled against his scalp. How she adored this man.

Finally, she turned and left the room.

Oh, Lord, please let Cade love me, she whispered as her head hit the pillow.

Cade sat through the night holding Eric, inhaling the delicate baby-powder scent, marveling at the perfection of two tiny hands and feet.

"Poor thing, you've got your father's nose," he murmured when Eric blinked awake to return his stare. But it wasn't Max that Cade was thinking of. It was Abby.

Beautiful Abby who'd suffered so much to give life to Eric and his brother.

"I love your mother," he said to the baby. The relief of saying it aloud made him say it again. "I can't stand the thought of letting her go, or you or your brother. You belong here. This is your home."

Eric didn't make a sound. He just kept watching Cade.

"This is a good place to live for a boy. You could learn to ride a horse. That's fun."

Eric cooed.

"There are hills and valleys to explore. There's the creek to swim in when it gets hot. There's even a little log cabin where you could have sleepovers when you're older, if your mom will allow it."

Eric sighed and closed his eyes. Cade did, too. He let himself dream of halcyon days with Abby at his side, watching the twins grow and change.

The Christian life is all about trust. Trusting God when it seems nothing's going right. Jake's words from their last Bible study filled his mind. *The Bible says that with faith all things are possible.*

"Is it possible that You want us to be together?" he asked hesitantly. "Is it possible that Abby and I could have a future?"

Trust.

How would he know until he opened his heart to Abby? She trusted God. She had faith. Together they could pray. After all, she'd said she loved him.

Trust.

Eric shifted in his arms, opened his mouth and let out a tiny sound that pierced straight to Cade's heart. How could he let this precious child go, never see him again, never be there if he was needed?

"I can't." He made up his mind. "I will trust You to work it out. I'm going to tell Abby I love her. Your will be done."

The decision brought Cade great peace. He wasn't the least tired as morning dawned and the sun peeked over the rims of the distant mountains. God had handled the adoption agency, bringing forward people to take over while Abby was busy with the babies. Things were progressing in spite of the fact that Cade had also been absent a lot as he prepared the ranch for sale.

God could handle the future. All Cade needed to do was trust.

Two hours later his cell phone rang, wakening him and Eric. The buyer wanted to proceed with purchasing the ranch.

Cade inhaled as the knowledge punched through to his heart. God didn't want a future for him with Abby. Or if He did, it was far different than Cade had hoped.

Very well. If God wanted him to sell, Cade would do that. And while he did, he'd try to trust and wait for God to show him the next step.

Chapter Fourteen

"Hasn't Ivor changed since he first arrived?" Abby said to Ed. "Look at him with his friends, running and laughing. I've never heard him so boisterous. It's good to see."

She rose from the bench next to his chair to ensure the twins were still sleeping in the stroller she'd purchased with Ed's birthday-money gift. Cade's nightly interventions had made a huge difference in her energy level.

"The Double L seems to have changed all of us," she said. "It's a beautiful place, especially in the spring."

"My home," Ed managed, his grin wide. After a moment it faded. "For now."

"Your speech is so improved. Good for you for working so hard on it." She patted his knee, then allowed her hand to envelop his when he grasped it.

"B-but my legs not good." Ed's troubled gaze moved to where Cade was unloading hay bales. "That's why he's selling."

"He loves you, Ed. He's trying to do his best for you." Abby ached to find a way to reunite father and son but so far all she'd been able to do was listen to both sides. "The doctor says you need more intense physio—"

"Doesn't matter," Ed interrupted, his face grim. "R-ranch more important."

"Cade thinks you're more important." She studied the old man's weathered face as he watched his son. Love, pride—they filled that blue-eyed gaze that was so like Cade's. "You love him, don't you, Ed?"

"Much," he said, his gray head nodding. "C-couldn't tell him."

"Why not? He needed to hear it so badly." *Still does*, Abby thought, but she didn't say it, too intent on finally learning what had created this awful barrier between father and son.

"Loved her but God took her," Ed blurted, his forehead perspiring with the effort of speaking so much. "If loved him too much," he said, inclining his head in Cade's direction, "God take, too."

"No! No way." Abby realized she'd spoken too loudly when both Cade and Ivor glanced at her. Cade started to come toward them but she shook her head. Frowning he returned to work. "God isn't like that," she insisted. "He doesn't steal the things or people we love. He loves me and He loves you. He wants you to love your son because God is love."

Tears trickled down Ed's sun-wrinkled cheeks. "Angry," he murmured.

"You were angry at God?" She squeezed his fingers. "I know. But God understood. He knows your pain, knows how much you missed your wife, how terrified you were to raise a child all by yourself," she guessed and knew she was right when he nodded. "God knew all that and He loved you anyway."

From the corner of her eye she saw Cade join in a game with Ivor and his friends, tossing a football that they raced over the fresh spring grass to catch. The ranch had changed

Ivor and Cade's relationship, too. If only they could all stay here.

"Apologize," Ed said. "Cade." His tears fell more freely now.

"Yes, and you need to tell him you love him because he doesn't know. He thinks you hate him because his mother died giving birth to him."

"No." Ed's eyes widened. He shook his head. "No, no."

"Then tell him that you love him. Make sure he knows that he's the most important person in your life."

"Can't." He stared at his hands. "Won't forgive."

"Of course he will. I told you, Cade loves you. That's why he's trying to do his best for you. God loves you, too, Ed. So much." Without asking permission, Abby bowed her head and prayed, asking God to reveal his forgiveness to Ed and to heal the breach with his son. When she was finished, she lifted her head and saw Ed's troubled gaze resting on Cade.

"Don't want the ranch sold," he said slowly and clearly.

"I know." She wrapped an arm around his shoulder and hugged him.

"It's home."

"Yes," she whispered, her gaze drawn again to the man she loved. "We have to keep praying." The babies began crying. Ed touched her arm.

"Hold?" he asked, his blue eyes hopeful.

"Of course." She lifted Eric from his blanket and laid him in Ed's arms. The old man's face filled with wonder as he gazed at the child.

"Looks good on you, Dad," Cade called, loping toward them. His face creased in a grin. "You look like a grandpa."

Ed lifted his head and stared at his son. "Home," he said. Cade shook his head.

"I know. I wish we could stay but selling the Double L

will provide the care you need. I'm doing it to make sure you can get back your health." Cade sighed. "I wish you could understand that if I could, I'd do anything else but sell this place. I know how much it means to you."

Ed studied him for a long time. Then he motioned for Abby to take the baby. With his hands free, he reached out and took Cade's hands. "Forgive," he said.

"What?" Cade glanced from him to Abby. "What do I need forgiveness for?"

"Cade, just listen, please." Abby smiled to encourage him, then glanced at Ed. "Go on."

"Forgive me. Treated you bad," Ed said slowly, obviously working hard to say the words he needed. "Bad father. Afraid."

"You were afraid?" Cade asked. He crouched in front of his father. "Why?"

In painstakingly slow speech, Ed explained his fear of God taking his son.

"Loved you," he finished. "Loved. Always. Built fireplace for you so you'd come back, come home."

Cade stayed immobile for a very long time. Then he leaned forward, and for what Abby was certain was probably the first time in his life, he hugged his father and Ed hugged him back. She felt like an intruder, in the way. She wanted to give them some privacy, but a moment later Cade enveloped her in an embrace from which she had no desire to be freed.

"You did this," he murmured in her ear. "I have no idea how, but I know you did it. Thank you."

"It's Ed, not me. He loves you. He doesn't want you to sell the ranch. You share this legacy." Abby did everything she could to make him see. "This is where you belong, Cade. If you could just trust a little longer—"

"Abby, I've only had one solid offer. There aren't a lot

of people who can raise the cash to buy a place like this." His forehead pleated as he let go of her and rose. "I don't have another choice."

"All I'm asking you to do is wait, don't rush into anything. It would mean so much to Ed," she added. "This ranch has been his home for a long time."

"I know. But the money is too good. Dad will have everything he needs." He glanced around, then his gaze returned to her. "It's my home, too, and you've helped me realize how much I love it. I hate giving up all the plans I had for the Double L but I don't see any other way."

"If you waited—" Abby stopped when Cade shook his head.

"I've given up on dreaming that some kind of intervention will happen. This is reality. I'm only sorry it hurts you so much." He said the last to his father, then turned and walked back to his bales.

"I'm sorry, Ed," Abby whispered, witnessing the devastation on his leathery face.

"No." Ed straightened. A new resolve filled his eyes so like Cade's. "Son back. God forgives. All good."

But it wasn't. Abby felt as though everything was falling apart around her and she could do nothing to stop it. Worst of all, when the ranch sold she'd have nowhere to go, no place to take her babies. If something went wrong with Cade's latest plan to raise funds for the adoption agency, she'd have no job, either.

Then how would she care for the twins?

Lord? she whispered when Ed returned to the house, leaving her to enjoy the spring afternoon. *What are You doing?*

"You did it." Two weeks later Abby gazed at Cade, her big emerald eyes wide, her voice hushed. "You got them to release my money."

"Some of it," he reminded. "At least you're no longer destitute and it represents a commitment on their part to follow through with what they owe."

"It's a lot of money, at least for me." She stared at the check, then held it out. "Use it for Ed's care. Keep the ranch."

"Your responsibility is to provide a home for the twins, Abby." Cade loved her for the gesture but he shook his head. "You have to use your money for that."

She looked so lovely sitting on the garden bench, the climbing rose vines leafing out behind her. The soft spring air played with the few tendrils of hair she hadn't caught up in a green-checkered bow.

"There's a place in town that might be suitable to rent until your plans firm up," he said.

"I could stay here," she whispered, watching him.

"There's nothing to stay for," he said, and clenched his jaw against the pain. "The new owners will take over in a month. We'll all have to leave then."

Abby being Abby frowned at him but he knew she hadn't given up. His spirit sighed with relief when she changed the subject.

"What's happening with the adoption agency? You haven't said much." She tilted her head to one side. "Is there a reason for that?"

"Things have come to a halt while I've been sorting out terms on the ranch sale," he told her. "I'll get back on it soon."

"I'd like to help," she said, her smile lighting up her eyes. "But as you say, for now I have to focus on the twins." She giggled. "And getting some sleep. You've been so helpful. I don't know how I'll manage on my own."

"The kids are settling down." Cade hated that the twins would no longer be there for him to check on, protect and watch over. He hated it even more that he would no longer be able to help out Abby.

The thought that she might need him and he wouldn't be there plagued him.

"Maybe I could come over some afternoons and take them out while you rest," he offered.

Despite his determination to remain objective, the twins had nestled into a special spot in his heart. Right next to Abby.

"Come anytime." She smiled, then sobered. "I guess I should go look at this rental house."

From then on, things moved way too fast for Cade. Abby rented the house, he moved in her few belongings and added others from the ranch house, including a crib his father had mentioned storing in an outbuilding.

"He said it was once mine." Cade showed her the teeth marks on one side. "I restored it as best I could but I couldn't completely erase those."

"It's perfect," she told him.

Her hand reached for his and Cade automatically enfolded it as they stood staring at the twins, one nestled in the cradle from Boris, the other in the crib. At least he'd been able to provide a bed for them.

"I wish I didn't have to leave the ranch," Abby said in a soft voice. "I love it here, Cade."

He slid his hand free.

"Do you want me to leave?" she asked. If she only knew how much he wanted her to stay.

"Staying wouldn't work." How he hated saying that.

"Because you won't trust God," she murmured. "But I do. I trust Him with my life. You need to, too, because God is going to work things out, Cade. You'll see."

After filling her pantry, Cade returned to the ranch. But nothing was the same. Her lilting voice wasn't there to tease him about being late for dinner, the babies didn't call out for him in the night and Abby didn't share the early sunrises as she had for the past weeks.

Why don't You do something? Cade prayed as he rode the ranch, checking on his stock and the new arrivals that filled his pastures. *Why can't You work this out?*

But he found no response.

Life on the ranch no longer brought Cade the joy it once had. Watching the place burst with new life, working with the animals—it was a bittersweet time. At least every five minutes he questioned whether he was doing the right thing or not. But when he came home one afternoon and found his father sprawled on the floor, too weak to get back in his chair, Cade knew selling was the only option.

Oddly enough, Ed didn't seem fazed by his fall. In fact, he told Cade to bring him ropes and had him rig up a workout station outside in which he could cling to the ropes while walking around them. The first day he barely made it three steps. But Ed persisted, humming songs Cade vaguely remembered from his Sunday school days, songs of faith and promise. Cade didn't see any progress but that didn't seem to bother Ed.

Was Cade the only one who didn't trust God?

And then the worst possible thing happened. The painter they'd finally been able to hire to redo the windows at Family Ties found asbestos in the paint on the sills. The building could not be entered, let alone used for anything, until remediation was complete. Wanda phoned to tell him she could not afford to pay for that. Everything was on hold.

Cade could hardly bear to tell Abby the news.

"You're saying I won't be able to work there." Devastation washed over her face. "So I don't have a job and I don't have enough of my money to cover the cost for repairs. I'm some partner."

"Nobody can go in," he told her. "It's too dangerous. The dream of an adoption agency opening in this town is dead."

"Don't say that!" She glared at him, both hands on her hips. "You may be finished but God isn't. He still has a plan and His will is going to be done. I know you won't believe that and because you don't you'll miss out on the best God has in store for you. You won't even believe in me."

"Abby, I can't wait around hoping—"

"Faith is believing God will do what is right," she said, dashing away the tears that spilled down her cheeks. "It's a choice you have to make, Cade. Either you'll trust and believe God's doing His best for you, or you push along your own path, trying to manage everything by yourself."

"It's not that easy," he protested.

"Yes, Cade, it is." She held his gaze. "He's forgiven me for my failures. I should have phoned Max's commanding officer and told him my suspicions that my husband was suffering from PTSD, but I didn't and Max died. Maybe that was my fault. I certainly wasn't the loving wife he deserved."

"Max thought you were," Cade murmured. "He loved you. He'd have done anything for you."

"Anything but share the horror he kept locked inside. He always kept me at arm's distance from that." Abby wept, releasing it all into God's hands. "I was determined never to let myself trust in love again. And then I met you and you showed me what true love is. It's total sharing. It's believing, hoping, trusting in the other person with nothing between you. That's what I want from my love for you, Cade. I love you. If God is with us, no one and nothing can defeat us."

He was the most unlovable man in town. Everyone knew that. And yet—how he wanted to be the man she thought he was. But he wasn't and never would be.

"I can't be that person, Abby. I'm sorry." There was nothing more to say. Cade turned and left, wishing with all his heart that he didn't have to but knowing there was no other way.

To drag Abby and the twins into his uncertain future was a betrayal of everything he'd promised Max, of everything he wanted for her. She'd received enough money to tide her over for a few months. Eventually the rest would come. She would find a job. Abby's friends would gather around her and help her through whatever she encountered.

She didn't need Cade messing up her life.

I love you.

Abby's words to him the afternoon of the babies' births wouldn't be silenced. Cade drove himself relentlessly to finish up the things on the ranch that needed doing, but no matter how long he worked, the image of her face and her profession of trust never left his brain. He longed to hold her and the babies, to assure them that he would always be there.

But when God didn't answer his plea for help, Cade knew that even though Abby was the woman of his dreams, some things just weren't meant to be.

Chapter Fifteen

Abby opened her front door two weeks later and blinked in surprise.

"I've brought you a baby gift." Hilda Vermeer pointed behind to an old-fashioned red car sitting in Abby's drive-way. "I know it's not the usual gift, but I thought you needed transportation more than another fancy outfit or stack of diapers for those babies."

"Hilda, that's—"

"Don't argue with me," Hilda said sternly. "It's been sitting in my garage doing nothing for years. It might as well be used. Oh."

Abby cut off the rest of her words by the simple expedient of reaching out and folding the older woman into her arms, hugging her and ignoring Hilda's stiffening body.

"You are a darling," she said and kissed the woman's perfumed cheek. "What a lovely, thoughtful gift. Thank you so much."

Hilda huffed and grumped, withdrawing, then blurting, "Well, are you going to show them to me?"

"The twins? Of course. I'm a very proud mama." Abby ushered Hilda into her tiny home. "Have a seat," she said, moving a stack of fresh laundry. She lifted Adam and set him in Hilda's arms. "Meet Adam Maxwell McDonald. This is his brother, Eric."

"Oh." Hilda seemed frozen, her arms rigid as she stared at Adam. "He's—small."

"Well, yes." Abby laughed. "He's only a baby but he'll grow."

"Maybe the car seats I had installed are too big," Hilda worried. "I don't know anything about babies. I never had one." She lifted her head and looked straight at Abby. "I always secretly wished I'd been a mother."

"I'd love for you to be godmother to my twins. I'm going to ask Ed to be their godfather." She saw Hilda's frown and hurried to explain. "It's not that I'd expect anything from you. It could be an honorary title only."

"That's too bad." Hilda finally moved, cradling Adam against her. "I think I'd have to object to a mere honorary title."

"Oh." Abby sighed. What mistake had she made now?

"I'd need more of a relationship than a title." Hilda grinned at Abby. "Much closer. Like maybe godmother and honorary grandmother. And not so honorary that I can't stop by to spoil them. Okay?"

"Absolutely." Abby hugged her again. Then Hilda asked her a hundred questions about the babies and Abby answered them all. After a while she put the twins down for their nap and served tea. "Peppermint because caffeine keeps those two up," she explained.

"I like peppermint tea. My mother used to make it." Hilda accepted a cup and leaned back in her chair, eyes narrowed. "Now tell me about the adoption agency. I haven't seen anyone working there for days."

Abby explained about the asbestos.

"We worked so hard," she said sadly. "And the community was so gracious in their donations. But Wanda can't afford the remedial work that needs to be done to get rid of the asbestos and I haven't got enough money to help her." She named the figure she'd been given. "That's way beyond our means."

"So you've had to abandon the project. Which means you're out of a job," Hilda added.

"I'm afraid so." Abby sighed. "I think I can manage six months of what I'm calling maternity leave. Then I'll have to start looking for work."

"Here in Buffalo Gap?" Hilda asked.

"I'm a social worker. If the agency doesn't go ahead, there's really nowhere else for me to work in town. I'll have to move, make a new home for my children." Abby told her sadly. "But at least, thanks to Cade's persistence, I won't have to give them up."

"I hear Cade will also be leaving." Hilda leaned forward, peering into her face. "I thought the two of you had something going."

"I love him," Abby told her honestly. "And he loves me though he won't admit it. He feels compelled to get his father additional therapy and since the only place that offers that is the nursing home, Cade intends to sell the ranch to pay for it."

"Ed Lebret will hate a nursing home," Hilda said with an inelegant snort of disgust. "He's always lived for that ranch."

Abby nodded but said nothing more, unwilling to speak lest she reveal to Hilda that her faith in God's leading wasn't as solid as she made it out to be.

"I've never met anyone like you before, Abby." Hilda frowned, her gaze scrutinizing Abby.

"Like me?" Abby stared at Hilda. "What's so different about me?"

"You're someone who stands on her faith no matter

what. Someone who isn't afraid to say what they believe and match your actions to it." Hilda smiled. "Of course, that's what we're all supposed to do, but I'm afraid most of us fail. Including me." She rose suddenly and walked toward the door. "I think I've failed God more than anyone," she murmured, almost in a whisper.

"God always forgives," Abby reminded, confused by her sudden departure. "Do you have to leave?"

"Yes. It's time I took a stand, too." Hilda smiled and fluttered a hand. "Enjoy the car," she said. "Maybe you should take your babies to see Ed. I'm sure he misses them. Cade, too." Then with a wink, she left, pulling the door closed behind her and leaving Abby staring after her in confusion.

Just then Eric wailed.

Maybe taking the twins for a drive was just the thing, Abby mused. She would visit Ed. And Cade. Her heart leaped at the thought of seeing him again.

Ten minutes later she was on the road to the ranch.

Drawn to the house by the sight of a strange vehicle, Cade wondered who had arrived. He found Abby and the twins in the garden with his father. He drank in the sight of her, his heart turning to mush.

"Hi, Cade." Abby had only to smile at him and his world turned rosy. "Hilda Vermeer gave me the car as a baby gift so we came for a drive to try it out." Her emerald gaze held his. "How are you?"

"Good." His gaze slid from her to the twin in his father's arms and the other in Abby's. "They've grown." As if drawn by a magnet his eyes moved back to her. "You look well."

Her smile lit the embers that lay deep in his heart. He

knew now that he would never get over Abby. She was part of him. Like breathing.

She watched Ed hand him the baby, then roll his wheelchair inside, giving them privacy.

"I'm feeling much better now that Eric has figured out a sleeping schedule," she said, struggling to fill in the silence that stretched between them.

"Good." He couldn't stop staring at her lovely face.

"Ed tells me that the sale is going ahead," Abby said with no hint of reproach, though Cade knew she still disagreed with his decision.

"Yes." It was painfully difficult to watch his dad mourn the loss of his life's work but even Ed finally agreed that he needed help to achieve the next stage of health. The past was over. Now they'd begun to build a real father-son relationship. And it was Abby who had made that possible.

"I don't suppose you've learned anything more about the adoption agency?" She shook her head almost as soon as she said it. "No, of course not."

"No." Cade didn't know what to say to her now. A thousand things flew through his brain but all of them had to do with his feelings for her. He could hardly tell her he loved her now. What good could come of that?

"If you don't mind, I'd like us to finish the quilts, though I don't know what we'll do with them," she said, her face downcast. "I guess we'll have to remove the tags Hilda made, too. I'm so sorry you sold Liberty for nothing, Cade."

She sounded so sad. It pierced his heart but he couldn't let her think he wished for his horse back.

"It was worth it. I'd sell her again in order to get your machine back," he murmured.

"Thank you," she whispered, tears welling in her emerald eyes. "Oh, Cade—"

"Don't," he pleaded. "Please don't." Suddenly he couldn't stand there any longer and not embrace her, hold her, tell her he would make everything all right somehow. But it would only hurt more when he had to let her go. "Sorry," he apologized as he set Adam in his car seat. "I have to go."

Abby nodded, but said nothing.

Cade left as quickly as he could, needing to escape the look of love that glowed in her eyes. He saddled a horse and rode away from the house and Abby, out into the open space of the foothills, where he'd always run when he needed to get away. He had no idea how long he rode. It didn't matter. All that did matter was that he was giving up the one thing he cared about more than his own life and the pain of it was excruciating.

When the horse tired, Cade slowed him to a walk, turning his thoughts upward.

God, please help me.

Trust in the Lord with all your heart. The verse he'd memorized kept echoing through his head. He couldn't ignore it. It was the only way to deal with sense of loss that threatened to drown him. He could not go on like this and he knew it.

I'll trust You, he finally conceded. *Your will be done. Just tell me what to do.*

There was no response, no answer that rushed into his mind. All Cade felt was a sense of peace, a calm that said God would take over, that He was in control. He dismounted in a flowery glade near the creek and found a sun-warmed stone to sit on. And there he prayed, allowing the biblical promises he'd memorized to soothe his soul.

The first spatter of rain surprised Cade. He lifted his face, letting the droplets trickle down as he scanned the sky. This was no spring storm. The air was heavy with humidity, the wind dead. Black clouds loomed overhead, blotting the sun that had warmed him such a short time before. Lightning arced across the sky, stabbing the land with its electrical darts. It was as if nature held its breath, waiting.

It was dangerous out here. Cade had to get home.

He grabbed the reins and mounted the horse, wheeling around to head for the ranch. Above him the skies opened and rain fell so heavily he could barely see the path in front of him. Not twenty yards away, lightning ripped through the late afternoon sky and sliced open the ground. He prayed Garnet had finished branding the newborn foals and left them in the barn where their mothers would comfort them through the storm. Those foals were going to be the bonus to the sale of the Double L.

But as he mounted the last hill before home, Cade watched a spear of lightning hit the horse barn.

"Oh, no," he whispered, urging his horse to move faster as the old wood ignited into a blaze, aided by the mounting wind. He kept riding, praising God when the lightning storm moved on. He spurred his horse on. Maybe he could put out the fire. Maybe…

Suddenly his heart stopped. In the distance he could see Abby standing in front of the barn. She was obviously calling someone. That's when he saw the empty wheelchair in front of the barn door. His father knew the value of the foals. He would spend his last breath trying to rescue them. If Abby went in after him and they both died—

Dread sucked at Cade. He kicked his spurs in the horse's sides.

"I can't lose them, God," he yelled. "I love them. Both of them. Please help us."

As he raced through the valley toward the barn, he could see nothing but the billows of smoke soaring upward. Cade fought back terror.

Then the words filled his mouth and spilled out, verse after verse, promises reminding him of God's great love for His children. And that Cade was one of those He loved.

"'God is our protection and our strength. He always helps in times of trouble,'" he recited in a loud voice. His words were immediately ripped away by the wind but Cade recited another verse. "'The Lord hears good people who call out to Him.'"

He repeated them over and over until finally he arrived near the barn. He slid off the horse and screamed for Abby and his father. When there was no answer, he prepared to enter, another promise filling his head.

When I am afraid, I will trust You.

"I trust You, God." He put his neck scarf over his mouth and reached for the barn door handle.

"Cade!" Abby's voice. Behind him. He turned and saw her, Mrs. Swanson and Ed sitting in the gazebo, well away from the fire, the foals and their mothers in the paddock behind.

Cade could think of nothing but that his loved ones were safe. He hugged his father who sat grinning, the babies in his arms. Then Cade tugged Abby near, certain he could never let her go again.

"I love you," he said right before he kissed her, intending to show her without words how much he cared.

Sometime later Abby drew back in his arms, her face rosy, her eyes glowing with joy.

"I've never been so afraid in my life. I thought you'd gone inside the barn," he told her, unable to release her from his embrace.

"I did. I left the babies with Mrs. Swanson because I thought you were in there," she said, smoothing a finger over his frown line. "No way was I going to let you die. Instead I found your dad. He got the back door open so the horses could get out. We went that way and came over here." Abby grinned at Ed. "He walked, Cade. Your father walked."

Cade shared a grin with his father. *Thank You, God.* Two prayers answered.

"Not for long and not very far, but I did walk," Ed confirmed. "I'm kinda looking forward to that therapy now."

"Finally." Cade threw his head back and let out a roar of laughter. Then he dropped to his knees in front of Abby. "Sweetheart, I don't have a future to offer you. It's too late to cancel the sale on this place so we'll have nowhere to live. I don't even have a job."

"Neither do I," Abby murmured.

"So we're both going to have to trust God with our future." Cade took her hands and kissed her palms. "All I have to give you is my love and I offer you that freely, forever. Abby, will you marry me?"

"Cade, you're my life, my world and my heart," Abby whispered. "I never understood about true love until I met you. These months here on the ranch, waiting for the babies, God helped me realize that love can be many different things. Sometimes it's being there for someone, helping them through the night. Sometimes it's only for a short while. Sometimes it lasts the rest of our lives. But the important thing is that love is from God. It's a gift He bestows on us and wants us to enjoy."

"So?" he said, impatient to hear her response.

"Yes, I will marry you. I love you. As long as we trust God, nothing else matters to me." She stood on her tiptoes and kissed him, offering her commitment.

The sound of sirens drew their attention. They stood arm in arm and watched as seconds later the Buffalo Gap fire department pulled up in front of the barn. Though the men turned their hoses on the blaze, Cade knew the barn was a write-off. And he couldn't have cared less. His loved ones were safe. That was all that mattered.

"I don't think Mrs. Swanson would mind watching the babies a little longer. Could you help me make some coffee and lunch for these guys?" Cade asked Abby when the last ember had been doused.

"I'm still the cook," Mrs. Swanson sputtered.

"Of course you are." Abby handed Cade Eric and took Adam in her own arms. Two of the firemen helped Ed rise. "But we're your helpers." She winked at Cade. "After all, we should celebrate our engagement here on the Double L, don't you think?

"Sounds like the perfect place," he agreed.

Half an hour later, Cade's heart overflowed with thanksgiving. There were tables and chairs scattered all over the patio as the fire department, made up of friends and neighbors in Buffalo Gap, used their lemonade to toast his and Abby's happiness.

"How great are You, Lord," he whispered as he manned the barbeque. "I trust in You."

When his cell phone rang, Cade handed his burger flipper to Jake to take over cooking before answering the call. Several moments later he hung up in disbelief.

"What is it, honey?" Abby murmured. "What's wrong?"

"Nothing," he said and lifted her in his arms to whirl her around. "Everything is absolutely perfect."

"How?"

"The sale of the ranch is off. The buyer said he specifically chose this ranch because the barn was operational and he could begin his business immediately. He was in town and heard that the barn was totaled. He doesn't want the ranch now. I agreed he could back out."

Abby and Ed shared a whoop of delight.

"That's God for you," Abby said.

Then Ed asked, "What about my therapy?"

"You know what, Dad," Cade said to him, his arm around Abby's waist. "I think we're going to have to trust God on that one, too."

"I'm good with that," Ed said, his grin huge.

"So am I, Dad," Cade said, hugging Abby. "So am I."

Chapter Sixteen

Abby held up her August 20 wedding to Cade by insisting on talking to him privately before the ceremony.

"Are you sure, Cade? I'm not sure you know enough about me to marry me," she said, fiddling with her wildflower bouquet. "I mean, I failed Max—"

Cade cut off her words with a kiss.

"Abby, I know everything about you that I need to. You're kind and generous and determined to serve God no matter what, and you help me do the same. You always put people first. You use your words to bring comfort and joy and blessing. And with you I'm no longer 'poor Cade.' I love you."

She frowned, uncertainty still lingering. "But you don't know all the bad stuff about me."

"Lady, I was there when you were in labor." Cade chuckled. "I think we can agree that I've seen you at your very best and your very worst." He cupped her chin in his palms. "And I love you more than ever. You and Eric and Adam and me and Dad and Mrs. Swanson. We belong together."

Abby studied the man she loved more than life. She saw the blue sheen of happiness in his eyes, loved they way they lit up when they landed on the twins in their tiny tuxes. Joy shone there along with peace and satisfaction. Cade looked more contented than she'd ever seen him.

She caught her breath when he kissed her. Yes, this was the man for her.

"By the way, your wedding gift is over there," she said, wondering if she'd ever get used to being in his arms. "I hope you like it."

Cade turned and stared at the hanging quilt. She'd made it a picture of a cowboy, of Cade, with a newborn foal. Abby had used the photos she'd taken the night Recitation gave birth as a guide. But for the horse she'd used a photo of Liberty.

"It's amazing," he said a long while later. He embraced her again. "So beautiful, just like you."

"Thank you, darling," she said sweetly and stood on her tiptoes to kiss him back.

"Since I'm here, I might as well ask you something," Cade murmured, still holding her.

"Anything," Abby assured him.

"Would it be okay with you if we talk about adopting Ivor when we come back from our honeymoon?" Cade asked. "I mean, he kind of belongs here now, doesn't he?"

"Yes," she whispered, hugging him close. How she loved this bighearted man. "You really want to marry us, the twins and me, I mean?" she asked just to reassure herself.

Cade gazed into her eyes, certainty in the depths of his. "Abby, I insist on it."

"Okay then. What are we waiting for?" she asked, deliriously happy.

Two minutes later, using his walker, Ed escorted Abby down the aisle of the new barn built by the folks of Buffalo Gap as thanks to her and Cade for their work in the community with Family Ties, even though the agency had never opened. Ivor stood at the front, Cade's best man. Mayor Marsha, clinging to her cane, said the words that united the couple as husband and wife.

"I don't know how we can thank you enough," Abby said to Marsha when the reception started to wind down. The party lights had flickered on and the townsfolk were enjoying the summer twilight, good friends and Mrs. Swanson's delicious treats.

"Ed has made so much progress. Finding government funding to provide a van to take patients to the outpatient therapist in Calgary three times a week was genius," Abby told her.

"A gift from God," Mayor Marsha agreed, tapping her cane for emphasis. Abby was pretty sure that's why she'd hung onto it. "If I hadn't gone in for knee surgery and rehabilitation, I'd never have found out about it."

"Timing is everything." Hilda Vermeer stood behind Abby. "I once said I'd never met anyone like you and I was right." She held Eric in one arm, balanced on her hip just as Abby had taught her.

"I still don't know what that means," Abby said with a chuckle. "I'm just like everyone else."

"No. You really live out your faith." Hilda smiled. "I've never known anyone like that before. I hope you won't mind that I'm using you as my example in faith matters."

"Well, I don't mind," Abby murmured as Cade's arm slid around her waist. She smiled at him, then turned back to Hilda. "But just how are you doing that?"

"I've hired an asbestos removal company to begin working on the Family Ties building first thing Monday morning. At my cost as my gift to your business," she added before Cade could interrupt. "You and Wanda will be partners."

"That's—wonderful," Abby gasped.

"It's about time I joined this community instead of judging it. You taught me that." She smiled when Abby hugged her and Cade followed. "I could get used to that," she said, a smile twitching at the corners of her mouth. "Now go enjoy your honeymoon, because when you come back, there will be a lot to do to get Family Ties up and running."

"You are an answer to prayer, Hilda Vermeer. And the best godmother-grandmother the twins could have. Thank you." Abby rescued Eric while Cade announced the news to their guests.

Soon everyone was hugging Hilda. And she didn't seem to mind.

Abby and Cade gathered the twins, said goodbye to Ed and Mrs. Swanson and quietly left for their honeymoon in Calgary. But first they drove to the graveyard where Max was buried.

"These are your sons, Max," Abby whispered, the sleeping babies cradled in her and Cade's arms. "I won't fail them."

"We're going to fill their lives with love, just as you would have," Cade added.

Abby and Cade said their goodbyes, then left arm in arm, knowing there would be challenges in the years ahead, but confident that if they trusted God, He would be with them every step of the way.

* * * * *

WE HOPE YOU ENJOYED THIS

LOVE INSPIRED®

BOOK.

If you were **inspired** by this

uplifting, **heartwarming** romance,

be sure to look for all six Love

Inspired® books every month.

www.LoveInspired.com

SPECIAL EXCERPT FROM

HQN™

*Read on for a sneak peek at
the first heartwarming book in Lee Tobin McClain's
Safe Haven series,* Low Country Hero*!*

They'd both just turned back to their work when a familiar loud, croaking sound cut the silence.

The twins shrieked and ran from where they'd been playing into the little cabin's yard and slammed into Anna, their faces frightened.

"What was that?" Anna sounded alarmed, too, kneeling to hold and comfort both girls.

"Nothing to be afraid of," Sean said, trying to hold back laughter. "It's just egrets. Type of water bird." He located the source of the sound, then went over to the trio, knelt beside them, and pointed through the trees and growth.

When the girls saw the stately white birds, they gasped.

"They're so pretty!" Anna said.

"Pretty?" Sean chuckled. "Nobody from around here would get excited about an egret, nor think it's especially pretty." But as he watched another one land beside the first, white wings spread wide as it skidded into the shallow water, he realized that there was beauty there. He just hadn't noticed it before.

That was what kids did for you: made you see the world through their fresh, innocent eyes. A fist of longing clutched inside his chest.

The twins were tugging at Anna's shirt now, trying to get her to take them over toward the birds. "You may go look as long as you can see me," she said, "but take careful steps by the water." She took the bolder twin's face in her hands. "The water's not deep, but I still don't want you to wade in. Do you understand?"

Both little girls nodded vigorously.

They ran off and she watched for a few seconds, then turned back to her work with a barely audible sigh.

"Go take a look with them," he urged her. "It's not every day kids see an egret for the first time."

"You're sure?"

"Go on." He watched her run like a kid over to her girls. And then he couldn't resist walking a few steps closer and watching them, shielded by the trees and brush.

The twins were so excited that they weren't remembering to be quiet. "It caught a *fish*!" the one was crowing, pointing at the bird, which, indeed, held a squirming fish in its mouth.

"That one's neck is like an S!" The quieter twin squatted down, rapt.

Anna eased down onto the sandy beach, obviously unworried about her or the girls getting wet or dirty, laughing and talking to them and sharing their excitement.

The sight of it gave him a melancholy twinge. His own mom had been a nature lover. She'd taken him and his brothers fishing, visited a nature reserve a few times, back in Alabama where they'd lived before coming here.

Oh, if things were different, he'd run with this, see where it led…

*Don't miss
Lee Tobin McClain's Low Country Hero,
available March 2019 from HQN Books!*

www.Harlequin.com

Looking for inspiration in tales
of hope, faith and heartfelt romance?

Check out **Love Inspired**® and
Love Inspired® **Suspense** books!

New books available every month!

CONNECT WITH US AT:

Facebook.com/groups/HarlequinConnection

Facebook.com/HarlequinBooks

Twitter.com/HarlequinBooks

Instagram.com/HarlequinBooks

Pinterest.com/HarlequinBooks

ReaderService.com

Inspirational Romance to Warm Your Heart and Soul

Join our social communities to connect with other readers who share your love!

Sign up for the Love Inspired newsletter at **www.LoveInspired.com** to be the first to find out about upcoming titles, special promotions and exclusive content.

CONNECT WITH US AT:

Facebook.com/groups/HarlequinConnection

 Facebook.com/LoveInspiredBooks

 Twitter.com/LoveInspiredBks

LISOCIAL2018

Reward the book lover in you!

Earn points on your purchase of new Harlequin books from participating retailers.

Turn your points into **FREE BOOKS** of your choice!

Join for FREE today at
www.HarlequinMyRewards.com.

Harlequin My Rewards is a free program (no fees) without any commitments or obligations.

MYR18